THE CHRONICLES OF CHRIS
BOOK 1

ORION

BEARER OF LIGHT

JASON KOCH

Orion: Bearer of Light
The Chronicles of Chris: Book One
Published in the United States of America
By Aharonite Publishing, LLC

Copyright ©2020 by Jason Koch

ISBN: 979-8-9889290-0-0

Printed in the United States of America
First printing 2023
Aharonite Publishing
www.AharonitePublishing.com

Book cover Illustrations by Streetlight Graphics
www.streetlightgraphics.com

To my son Jared,

Who with five simple words,
'*You should write a book*,'
sparked a ten-year endeavor.

TABLE OF CONTENTS

WARNING!

This will be a life-changing journey —

You will see the world as you have never seen it before!

No longer will you see the world through a glass darkly!

You will see reality face-to-face!
Read if you dare, but be forewarned:

Reality is not what you have been taught. And there
is no going back once you know the truth...

FRESH JUICED

GROCERY SHOPPING WAS A LIVING hell that day—the day *it* happened. I know what you're thinking: prices that empty your wallet, zombie-like cashiers, food-damaging baggers, and crazed shoppers that almost run you over with their carts. Hardly. Something *crazy* happened. Like, "This defies the laws of sanity, and this can't be happening" type of crazy, something that changed my mundane teenage existence into a fight for survival.

My day of destiny happened on a typical sunny day, and like most days in our small town, the sun was blazing hot, and the air was hotter still. It felt like stepping into a blast furnace. My clothes, hair, and skin just shriveled up as the moisture was immediately sucked out of them. Now I know why those desert lizards... what are they called? Oh yeah, iguanas. Anyway, that's why they look like a dried-up, weather-beaten old shoe. The intense heat and sun in New Mexico will do that to you. That's why every living thing out here eventually looks like an iguana, even the people. They all look a hundred and twenty when they get past their fortieth birthday.

"Chris! Hey, Chris!"

That's my mom calling, and like with any parent, the longer it takes for you to respond, the louder your name is called. Then it steps up to your full first name, and it keeps ramping up from there, to full first name plus middle name, then first, middle, and last name, then... well... you know how it goes.

"Christopher! Christopher Thomas! Oh, there you are," she huffed as she walked past me. "Time to go shopping for eats. We need to catch the city bus. It should be out front anytime now."

When the food cache is low, moms, especially my mom, tend to go on shopping crusades. Since my mom and I are really close, when our shelves are low, we crusade-shop *together*.

My mom is very athletic. She has short blond hair, cut sporty style, brilliant green eyes, the body of a gymnast, and a voice that can put most football coaches to shame. She dresses like a teenager and looks it too. Well, she had me when she was fourteen, and now she's twenty-eight. Most people think she's my older sister, and she lets them.

For the most part, Mom, or Jennifer, treats me like a kid brother, teasing, hassling, and roughhousing. I like it that way. She's my best friend, and it's really important to have a best friend, especially one of the opposite sex. I can talk to her about girls—what they think about, daydream about, how to talk to them, why they do what they do—all the things we guys don't understand about girls.

Well, let me tell you, they are from another planet or something. Jennifer is my girl-to-boy translator. If someone could only make an app, it would be the most popular app of all time! Well... maybe not the most popular. That might be the boy-to-girl translator.

"Chris, let's go! Bus is here!"

"Okay, sis! I'll be right out!"

She likes me to call her sis or Jennifer instead of Mom, especially when other people are around. I think it makes her feel better not having people know she was a teenage mom.

I zipped up my worn navy-blue backpack and headed outside. I looked down the street. About a block down, Jennifer was in front of the bus. She had flagged it down and was standing with both hands firmly planted on the hood, keeping it stopped till I got there. Talk about a super-mom!

These people, especially for a small town in New Mexico, are always in a rush. I don't know why. What do they need to get to? There's nothing around here but sand and lizards! All we have are a few diners, one school, a couple of gas stations, six bars, a strip mall, and two manufacturing plants. One plant makes leather products, probably from the lizards, and the other makes tortillas. So, what's all the rush about?

Oh yeah, there's another thing. This is a small town, but we have a mayor, or at least that's what he likes to think he is. He's really just the town clerk. We call him Pancho, because his last name is Villa like the infamous Mexican general that raided the United States in 1916. The great Pancho Villa, notorious bandit turned general. He ransacked and burned the city of Columbus, New Mexico, to the ground... the very city I now call home. Many call our self-proclaimed mayor "Paunchy Villa." Well, he does have a rather large beer belly. No one remembers his real first name, and he has resigned himself to going by Pancho. He should be grateful that Pancho has stuck more than Paunchy.

Despite what one might assume, he's very big on being eco-friendly, so our one and only city bus is bright yellow and smells like popcorn and fries. That's because he has it run on used cooking oil, probably from our tortilla plant, Old New Mexico Tortillas. That smell just makes me constantly hungry for popcorn and fries, my two favorite health foods. No wonder most people here are paunchy, just like Pancho.

I finally made it onto the bus with Jennifer right behind. She sat beside me on the bus and elbowed me in the side.

"Oof!" I let out under my breath. "Why'd you do that?" I complained as she ruffled my hair.

"Because I had to block the bus with my body for you, slowpoke!" Jennifer smiled and gave me another elbow in the ribs.

"*Ouch!*" At this rate, my ribs wouldn't last the trip.

The grocery store is part of a small strip mall in the northwest part of town. The store is salmon-pink, modern adobe-style architecture with rounded corners and arches everywhere.

Inside, we split up.

I wandered over to the health food section… potato chips, pretzels, corn puffs, and soda. That was where I saw this guy. He had long, scraggly, stringy hair, like that of an English sheepdog. I couldn't see his eyes or face even; just his hawkish nose poked out. He had on a tattered, blotchy gray shirt that once was white, with 'Anarchy Rules!' across the front in bold red-and-black cursive lettering.

Everything about this guy stank, especially his body odor. He walked slouched over, carrying a folded newspaper in his left hand. His skin was darkened and leathery from the intense sun. He had a nervous twitch and walked with a shuffled gate.

I kept my distance, and as I backed away to the side of the aisle, I bumped into something or someone.

I heard, in a deep, mellow voice, "I hope that's not how you introduce yourself, especially not to the ladies!"

I quickly turned around and faced the stranger. He had a grin on his face and a head of gray hair as thick as a lion's mane.

"You can call me Barry," the man said.

He stood with dignity and a sense of inner strength. Something about this man said very old, ancient, yet he didn't look a day over forty. He had a mass of two-inch-thick, dense gray hair that was spiked up on his head and smooth wrinkle-free skin. This man moved with an air of confidence and authority, yet I was completely comfortable in his presence. Barry felt like family, even though he was a complete stranger. He could have been the grandfather I never had.

"Hi, I'm Chris." I extended my hand.

Barry grasped it with a firm grip that would have put any gorilla to shame.

"Ouch!" I winced. "Are you a gorilla in disguise?"

He chuckled warmly and shook my hand vigorously with a sincere smile on his face. It made me feel all warm and fuzzy—but I didn't need to feel any warmer. It was a hundred and five outside, and it wasn't even noon. Whatever happened to ice-cold air conditioning in most stores? It must have to do with saving money or being eco-friendly. Yeah, save a buck or two, or a few trees, but let your customers sweat to death! Now don't get me wrong, I'm all for being ecologically mindful and good stewards of the earth's resources, but it must be in moderation and meet the needs of society. Oh, sorry for the lecture...

"We'll meet again, son... soon!" With that, Barry strode off down the snack aisle.

I trudged through the store and over to the refrigerated section that housed the milk, cheese, meat, vegetables, fruit... basically everything not canned or boxed.

"Aaah," I said, sighing with relief, feeling the chilly air from the refrigerated goods. Let me tell you, the refrigerated section is the best place to be in a hot store with little or no air conditioning.

I was near the checkout by the fruit and veggies. I picked up an orange and tossed it up. Picking up a few more, I maintained a slow, high-arc juggle.

I'm pretty good at juggling. I can juggle just about anything. Well, probably not running chain saws! Now Jennifer doesn't like me juggling our food, either, even if it's only a half pint of milk, an orange, and a couple of cans of mixed fruit while I decide on what snack I am going to eat. I don't know what she has against juggling. I haven't made a mess since I was seven, and that was her fault. She startled me by coming up from behind and touching my shoulder when I was just juggling two half pints of milk, a juice box, three single-serving cans of mixed fruit, and two limes. What a mess. It took half a day to clean up the kitchen. Milk and orange juice were splattered from floor to ceiling. She did laugh and said my Picasso artwork would have been better on canvas.

I was watching the cashier check people out. She was kind of cute, a little lanky, and definitely too old for me, probably around seventeen. When I have time, I like to watch people. I can tell their likes and dislikes in food, music, clothes, people, what they dream about, what hobbies they have, and whether they have ambitions of taking over the world.

Now, I don't know whether I am right or not. I've never tried to find out; it's just fun to do. This was what I was doing while watching the cashier and absentmindedly juggling.

Jennifer had checked out and pushed her cart through the doors. I looked over to my left and saw Barry a few aisles down, looking at the Anarchy Rules guy, who was checking out. The guy was carrying only the folded paper he came in with. I now noticed Barry had on a loud short-sleeve shirt, one of those Hawaiian flower prints with pink, red, yellow, and white flowers on a black background. He wore knee-length khaki shorts with a dozen-plus pockets and had top-of-the-line running shoes. A glint in his eyes shone as he turned toward me, then he gave me a wink as if to say, "Heads up. Something is about to happen."

Just then, I heard it in my mind, or I thought it was in my mind. It was coming from Mr. Anarchy Rules. I believed I was hearing his thoughts. It was just scary and downright creepy.

A low, menacing voice spoke in a very airy and throaty fashion, emphasizing with an alligator's predatory hiss, *"Make a statement"* [hiss] *"that"* [hiss] *"the community won't"* [hiss] *"soon forget!"* [hissss]

A weaker, higher-pitched voice pleaded with the lower one, *"I d-don't w-want to."*

"Shoot her" [hiss] *"six times"* [hiss] *"at close range."* [hiss] *"Make it … messy,"* the menacing voice compelled, emphasizing the word *messy.*

The weaker voice tried to fight. *"No, no…"*

Mr. Anarchy Rules started raising the newspaper toward the cashier's upper body.

"May I help you?" the cashier asked.

6

He just kept raising the paper. It was now nearly at her face. His movements were robotic, with nervous erratic twitches, as if he was exerting tremendous effort against something.

Just when the rolled-up newspaper reached face level of the cashier, I heard a still, small voice in the back of my mind say, "*Take aim, and take him out!*"

I answered myself—or whatever the voice was—with "*You've got to be kidding. All I have are the three large navel oranges I'm juggling, and he must have a gun in that rolled-up paper! Oranges against bullets? You've got to be crazy!*"

But deep down, I knew I had to do something, otherwise there was going to be a bloodbath.

It all happened in a fraction of a second, but it seemed like an eternity. As my hand caught an orange at the bottom of the juggling arc, I whipped it up and around as hard as I could at the back of Mr. Anarchy Rules's head. *Wapp!* The orange splattered with such force against the back of his head that juice and bits of orange sprayed everywhere.

The man fell forward against the counter as a gunshot rang forth. He immediately dropped the newspaper. A gun clattered to the floor, spinning to a halt at the cashier's feet. He stumbled to regain his balance, still partially bent over. I threw the second orange when it came to the bottom of the juggling arc. The orange flew true to its target, right between Mr. Anarchy Rules's butt cheeks. The impact was enough to send him stumbling toward the exit doors, totally out of control. The third orange came down, and I winged that one hard and fast too. It hit him between the shoulder blades, and he went flying out the doors, landing spread-eagle on the pavement.

The cashier was in shock. Her eyes had a blank stare. She emitted no scream, and her whole body trembled uncontrollably. Barry came up to the cashier out of nowhere, literally. He was aisles away when this whole incident started to happen.

He touched the girl on the shoulder and said in a gentle, soothing tone, "Everything is going to be okay. This will all be like a bad dream."

She sobbed, and tears came rolling down her cheeks.

Barry patted her lightly on the shoulder as he waved me over.

We both walked out into the blazing afternoon sun, leaving the girl standing there, still frozen in disbelief. She knew she had come close to death, but she didn't how grisly a death it was meant to be... only I knew or thought I knew.

Mr. Anarchy Rules was gone by the time we got outside. People in the parking lot were looking around in confusion. Many thought they had heard what sounded like a gunshot. Some saw a man falling out the exit doors and hitting the pavement. Others saw someone stumbling and fumbling through the parking lot. I could tell he had landed face first. There was a bloody outline of part of a face imprinted onto the pavement. You wouldn't be able to identify the man from the bloody print, but you could tell it was made by someone's face. He most likely had a broken nose and some very major facial abrasions from the asphalt hitting his face.

Barry touched my shoulder and looked me in the eyes. "You did good, son," he said in a warm, fatherly tone. A quick smile came to his face as he said, "It would be best to go now."

I watched in a trancelike state as he walked away, nearly jumping out of my skin when I was touched from behind. Where was that still, small voice to alert me now?

I heard laughter and turned. Jennifer had a big grin on her face. I couldn't do anything but laugh.

"Why so shocked?" she asked.

I gave her an incredulous stare. "Didn't you notice what just happened?"

"No. I was deep in thought sitting on a bench over there, waiting for the bus."

Just then, we heard sirens coming our way. Jennifer rather urgently said, "Let's go. Now!"

We quickly finished packing the remaining groceries that didn't fit into Jennifer's backpack into mine.

We walked through an alley and over a few blocks to another bus stop. Jennifer looked at me with question and concern in her eyes. The bus came, and we sat down at the back of the bus, where we could talk without being overheard. I told her I had juiced a guy with some oranges because he was going to shoot the cashier.

She touched my lips with her finger and said, "We'll talk later. Let's get home before we get involved any further."

Puzzled at her anxiousness, I asked, "Why? Are you wanted by the police? Did you kidnap me from my real parents?" I shook my finger at her. "Is that why we keep moving all the time?" We had moved eight times, according to my mom, but that's a whole 'nother story.

She looked at me sternly then broke into laughter and elbowed me in the gut. "I just don't want to get caught up in something we don't have to. By the way," she said, "who was that dressed in a Hawaiian shirt and neon-blue running shoes?"

"Oh, that's Barry."

"Who's Barr—aiee!" she shrieked as I started tickling her sides.

She squirmed, and I laughed.

"We'll talk later," I promised.

I had to have time to think through the events that had happened, before I could explain them, and how much I should tell her. Like, should I tell her about smelling a stench as Mr. Anarchy Rules passed by me in the aisle at the grocery store? I couldn't really explain it. The stench wasn't in the normal sense; it was a mental smell, like I was getting a warning that this man was foul, that he was going to do something evil. What about hearing Mr. Anarchy Rules's thoughts as he pleaded with that other voice in his head? Or how about the feeling that Barry was at the grocery store because he knew what was going to happen? How he gave me a heads-up, with a wink and a nod toward Mr. Anarchy Rules, as if I was to be aware of this man and prepare myself for what was going to unfold.

Then there was the feeling that Barry could have stopped the whole incident. Was it some kind of test? My brain started to hurt, so I decided to stop thinking about what happened and just enjoy the ride home.

It's surprising how the sense of smell can influence one's thoughts, especially when it comes to food. I was getting hungry smelling the aroma of buttered popcorn and fries. Now my mind was focused and relishing, on thoughts of fries smothered with cheddar cheese. We were both silent the rest of the ride home. She was probably thinking about food too. Believe it or not, our trip back home was uneventful. Nothing out of the ordinary happened... yet. Well, maybe I shouldn't have said that.

We got off the bus at our apartment complex. It has five buildings with thirty units in each one. We walked up a flight of stairs and down the hallway to our apartment door.

"Oh! Oh! My turn!" I shouted excitedly, snatching the key from Jennifer's hand.

She smiled at my childlike eagerness. While I struggled with getting the key into the lock, three oranges fell out of my overstuffed backpack. The three oranges rolled three doors down the hallway. The door opened. What happened next creeped me out. I mean, out of a town of fifty-five hundred-plus people and an apartment complex of a hundred and fifty tenants, what were the chances? Zero. Absolutely zero!

CHRONICLE 2
DEATH'S GRASP

J ENNIFER AND I STOOD STARING at the man in the doorway. He wore khaki shorts with enough pockets to hold the contents of an entire hardware store, a black short-sleeve shirt with pink, red, yellow, and white orchids plastered all over it, and bright-blue running shoes with neon-yellow soles.

I stood there with my mouth wide open. *This is not a coincidence,* I thought.

Barry picked up the three oranges, did a quick juggle, and tossed them back to me. He had a big smile and said with a laugh, "Hi, neighbors!"

Jennifer spoke up. "Weren't you at the grocery store this afternoon?"

"Why yes," Barry said with a slight English accent. "Why don't you put your groceries away and come back for a visit."

Back at our place, we unpacked our groceries while discussing the events of the day. I was doing my usual juggling of the groceries while I unpacked them, with a quick toss here and there to Jennifer. I laughed as she tried to catch and shelve the items. The ketchup and a box of Crispy Crisp cereal fell to the floor. That was no big deal, but the pineapple angel food cake was. It landed upside down.

I laughed. "Now we have my favorite—pineapple upside down cake!"

Jennifer wasn't pleased; I saw it in her eyes. She was not amused. Her eyes had that intense look like they might vaporize me at any moment, but then she shrugged and with a slight smile said, "Go get the spatula and scrape our dessert off the floor."

We were at Barry's apartment within the hour. Jennifer was just about to knock when the door opened. Barry was there with a smile, and he gestured for us to enter with a wave of his hand.

The apartments were small, with the kitchen, dining, and living areas making up one room and two bedrooms down a hallway ending with a bathroom.

Barry's walls were covered with tapestries and paintings. Each of these seemed to be of a different place and time, and many depicted places from around the world. They were so fascinating, so vivid, and so surreal. It was as if you could walk right into them.

In one of the paintings, you could almost feel the intense heat of a noonday sun, the air moist and thick with heavy droplets of water vapor. The wind rustled through the dense trees while a rushing river pounded its way over the rocks. In another, you could imagine smelling the sweet fragrance of flowers in bloom, hearing the birds singing and seeing the horses frolicking on a plateau. They were beautiful, mesmerizing; they seemed alive.

Barry motioned for us to sit down on an overstuffed couch. We both sank into its softness as it conformed to our bodies. All stress just seemed to flow out of us. I was so relaxed, and I could see Jennifer was also. Then I looked at the coffee table in front of us. There was a sports drink, lemon-lime, which was my favorite, and raspberry iced tea on the rocks, which was Jennifer's. It was even her favorite brand too. If I hadn't been so relaxed, I would have high-tailed it out of there. I mean, how did he know our favorite drinks? How did he know we were at his door? Who was this guy?

Barry looked at us, his eyes friendly and inviting. You could almost get lost in the large black pools of his pupils. I bet you would lose all reasoning and forget who you were if you stared into them too long.

Barry broke the silence. "I told you we would meet again soon. Do you two believe in destiny?"

He continued without waiting for a response, talking about what he did for a living. It just felt so natural being with this stranger, like he was a close old friend. He said he was an independent energy consultant. He traveled all over the United States and even to other countries. His job was to meet with companies, local officials, and even residents, to discuss the impact a particular energy project would have on the environment and the people in the area.

"I am in the process of explaining the impact a 200-megawatt wind turbine farm would have on the area southeast of Albuquerque. This little town is my home base. I've been living here six months... I am always where I need to be."

You would think that a statement like that would raise a red flag and we would question why he was here, but Jennifer and I felt so relaxed and comfortable, like we didn't have a care in the world. We were like three old friends enjoying being together. That was the aura that Barry gave off, or I thought it was Barry. All through my childhood, it seemed I could sense if there was danger or if something just wasn't as it seemed to be, but that was not so tonight with Barry.

Earlier this afternoon, my internal radar did go off when I saw the gunman at the grocery store. What did I call him? Oh yeah, Mr. Anarchy Rules. I knew something was up, but this was like nothing I had experienced before. I had never heard anyone's thoughts. That was just freaky!

Barry came over to the table, carrying a snack tray with Old New Mexico tortilla chips and some Hot N' Zesty salsa. That is an oxymoron—Old New Mexico. Is it old, or is it new?

Barry brushed my shoulder as he set the tray down, and everything went dark, and I mean dark. Have you ever been way out in the country, away from any city, on a moonless and starless night? That's the kind of dark I mean—pitch black and what's more, no external sounds. All I could hear was my blood rushing through my ears like when you put a seashell to your ear. You hear the waves of the ocean—at least you think you do—but it's really just the amplifying of the sound of your blood flowing inside your head.

Then I felt a jolt like my feet hit the earth, hard, hard enough for tears to well up in my eyes, and my stomach rose into my throat. I was nauseated and lightheaded to the max. It was like when I had gotten off the Sky Master at the state fair last year. It is a ride that has a cage at each end of a long arm, and the arm rotates three hundred sixty degrees in a vertical circle going faster and faster, and then to top it off, the cages rotate and spin too. When the ride was over, my head was spinning, my stomach was in my throat, and I was puking my guts out like a dragon spewing flame.

This time I wasn't going to let it get that far. I gave it to God, shook that feeling off, wiped the tears from my eyes, and just like that, I was back in the norm. Well, everything wasn't back to normal. I felt good again, but I wasn't back on Barry's couch!

I heard the bustling sounds of life…cars honking their horns, braking, screeching to a standstill, then speeding up again—you know, the flow of traffic going to work and school.

Where was I?

It was early morning, and the sun was partially up. People were busy getting into their normal daily routines. I saw a group of teenage girls walking on the sidewalk adjacent to the traffic whizzing by on the street. Four girls were slightly ahead of the fifth girl, who was lagging behind. She was wearing a short skirt, leather boots, a body-hugging sleeveless shirt and had a gray-and-white backpack hanging from one shoulder. Her choice of tight-fitting clothes embraced her extended belly. She stopped and looked my way as if she'd heard something.

My heart stopped. This girl was the spitting image of my mom, Jennifer.

She looked at me and smiled. It was definitely my mom when she was my age. She turned and continued walking behind the group of four girls, who were now twenty feet ahead of her. Cars were still streaming past, and a semi driver behind them was blowing his horn. He was trying to make it through the stoplight before it turned red.

Just then, I saw her lunge forward into the street. It was as if she had been pushed, but nobody was near her. All I saw was a greenish shadowy silhouette on the sidewalk, extending up the wall behind her. It looked like shadows of people, but there was no one nearby to cast the shadows. She screamed as she fell in front of the semitruck's front tire. Bump, bump, bump, as eight tires rolled over the top of my mom. I saw her lifeless body spread out on the road. All traffic behind the semi came to a screeching halt, horns blaring and brakes screeching. The group of girls ahead turned and screamed when they saw what had happened.

Everything just seemed to move in slow motion. A group of shopkeepers on the opposite side of the street came over to keep the traffic stopped. One stayed on the other side in the shadow of an awning. He looked like he was talking on a cell phone. His body style and gestures looked familiar, but he was too far away for me to place who he was.

It seemed like just moments had passed when an ambulance showed up. I don't know how it got there that fast. It must have been in the immediate area. I ran over, trying to push through the crowd, tears welling up in my eyes, my heart pounding, and my body shaking. It couldn't be, but it was like I was really there. I heard and felt the people pushing around me. I knelt down and lifted my mom up to a sitting position. Her body was limp and lifeless, but her eyes were wide open.

I looked into her unfocused eyes and spoke in a loud but shaky voice, "Mom, come back to me. You can't die. I'm here. It's your son—Christopher."

Just then, the ambulance came. Two EMTs stepped out, opened the back and hurriedly came over with their equipment. The EMT that drove the ambulance spoke up, "Son, you shouldn't move her." They gently laid her on a stretcher.

The truck driver came near, his hands in front of his chest, palms facing outward. "I couldn't stop! Honest! She just leaped out in front of my truck!"

The other EMT, a slightly younger man, took him off to the side.

I noticed then that my mom didn't look like an eighteen-wheeler had just road over her. My mom's body was limp and lifeless but not crushed. They gave her an IV and oxygen then put her in the ambulance. I moved forward to get in, but the younger EMT blocked me with an outstretched arm.

"Who are you?"

"I'm her son."

He looked at me with a quizzical expression. "Son? You look the same age as she does, around fourteen."

"I'm Son... nny, her younger brother."

"I thought you..."

"Let's go!" shouted the EMT that drove.

The younger EMT lowered his arm and hastily guided me inside the vehicle. We drove off to the hospital, sirens blaring.

We came to a halt at the emergency entrance of the hospital. I walked alongside my mom as they took her to the ER. One of the attendants there asked who I was. I informed him that I was Jennifer's younger brother.

"You must remain in the waiting room over there," he instructed, pointing at an open area with couches, chairs, and a few tables. While I waited, I heard bits and pieces of what was going on as the nurses were coming and going out of the ER.

"She has a slight pulse, but the baby..." was all I heard before the door shut as one nurse went in and another came out. The nurse that just exited went over to the nurses' station and started excitedly talking. "The young girl went into labor from the trauma of the accident and... the baby was stillborn." She paused for a moment and then continued, "The doctor said the baby was brain dead for

16

months. He could tell by the way the muscles were atrophied that there was no nerve action from the brain stem."

The nurses kept going in and out of the room, each taking turns trying to calm Jennifer. Even through the closed door, I heard her scream, "No! No! My baby is alive! He is not dead! He told me he was my son! My baby boy lives…"

When I looked at the clock, it was nearly two hours past the time of the first screaming episode from Jennifer.

The doctor came out and went over to the nurse's station, shaking his head. "That young girl won't give up her dead baby boy. She's still cradling him in her arms. I don't understand. At her age, probably fourteen, this should be a godsend. It's no fault of her own, and she can get on with her life as a normal teenager."

A nurse spoke up. "She would be condemning herself if she had to give the baby up for adoption. Or she would be condemning herself to being a teenage mom and missing out on all the normal stuff teenage girls do. This is truly the best for her, not having to make a choice and regret it later."

As they were talking, I quietly slipped into Jennifer's room, or I thought I had. It was actually one of those observation rooms where you could view an operation without being seen or heard.

A man walked past the viewing window and stood at the foot of Jennifer's bed. I couldn't make him out since his back was turned towards me. I stepped closer to the glass and placed my ear within inches of it. I could just make out what they were saying; their voices were muted and somewhat distorted.

"My dear child, you are persistent and unwavering…"

The manner in which he spoke was eerily familiar, but I just couldn't place where I had heard it before. The man was calm and reassuring. Jennifer was still crying and sobbing. Tears were still rolling down her cheeks. I doubted she could even see the stranger, not clearly for sure.

I leaned closer, with my ear just grazing the glass. The man had a slight English… a British accent.

"He has heard your prayers, and because you still have no doubt in your heart that it still can be as you desire, your prayer has been answered. The power of death will release its grasp on your son."

Then I saw the infant in her arms move. It actually *moved*. Color came back into that little body, and he cried. Jennifer squeezed him so tenderly and gave the baby boy a kiss on the forehead.

The man walked to the door. He turned back towards Jennifer. "We will meet again when it is time."

I still could not make him out; he was too far past the viewing window. But the man's gestures, the way he walked and spoke... Could it be...? No, it couldn't be! This...this... man was Barry?

It all made sense, or at least a little sense. The man under the awning probably had been Barry, calling for the ambulance.

Had Barry been stalking us? Was he our guardian angel? What did Barry say earlier tonight? *I am always where I need to be.*

Jennifer was laughing with joy and doting over the baby boy.

Two nurses came into the room. They stopped suddenly; their faces held looks of astonishment. Both started yelling for the doctor. I thought one of the nurses was going to faint. She just plunked herself down on the floor. The other nurse was taking deep breaths.

It seemed like an eternity had passed before the doctor finally strode in. When his eyes fell upon Jennifer, he dropped his clipboard.

"It can't—it can't be," he marveled, reaching out toward the now life-filled child. "It's impossible... impossible. That baby has been dead for months!"

Jennifer wore a wide, beaming smile and responded, "My baby boy is just fine. He's healthy and strong."

The two nurses were taken out of the room. They were visibly shaken. Another nurse came and talked gently with Jennifer.

"Let the doctor take the child and tie off the umbilical cord. We will then clean him up, and you can have him right back."

In a short while, he was back in Jennifer's arms, being nursed. She looked around the room and stared right at the glass partition

I was standing behind as if she could see me, and just smiled. She looked at the nurse that was cleaning and rearranging the room.

"I will call my baby boy Christopher. Or maybe just Chris."

The nurse smiled warmly at her. "That is a fine name. This hospital is named after the great explorer Christopher Columbus."

Just then, everything started fading to black. My head and stomach started spinning, and the nausea returned with a vengeance, but both faded quickly after I was back on Barry's soft sofa. Jennifer was talking to Barry as he set the tray of snacks on the table. How could what I had experienced, which seemed like hours, happen within only a fraction of a second?

I caught a whiff of diesel fumes. I sniffed my shirt. Yep, it was diesel, all right, and it didn't come from our city bus. When you get done riding that bus, you smell like fries and popcorn.

I then felt something underneath my left foot. It was a blue wristband. I discreetly picked it up and looked at it before slipping it into my pocket.

I couldn't believe it! The band had Columbus Memorial engraved on the inside. On the outside, in white stenciling, was my name, Christopher Gahrlan. This must have been the band Jennifer had in the hospital that was a match to the band on her baby boy. What I had just experienced was real, and someone or something wanted to make sure I didn't think it was just a freaky daydream.

The three of us talked for some time. It was easy talking with Barry. Topics just came naturally. But I couldn't help wondering about what had happened to me and why. My mom had never told me about the events surrounding my birth or how she came up with my name! Then it hit me... perhaps I was sent back to bolster my mom's believing, that her baby would be okay and was not dead, at least not permanently. And... was that how she had gotten my name—from me telling her that I was her son, Chris? Oh... this was getting deep.

Jennifer and I were in death's grasp, but something or someone brought us back. But why? Were we under God's protection or that of some other spiritual force?

We ended the evening, and Barry let us out. He smiled, gave me a slight nod, and said, "Remember this evening. You will need it in the days ahead. Good night, you two."

I didn't think Barry meant remembering our evening of socializing. It was what I had just experienced and learned from my trip into the past.

Jennifer looked at me and then at Barry but just shrugged and said, "Good night."

I had a foreboding feeling deep within that my life was no longer going to be mundane, like that of most teenagers... well, okay, at least semi-mundane!

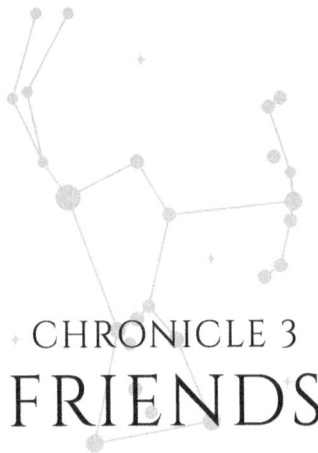

CHRONICLE 3
FRIENDS

I AWOKE EARLY THE NEXT MORNING. It was a bright, sunny Sunday. Jennifer came into my room, gave me a good-morning smile, and said, "Ready for a run, sleepyhead?"

I looked at my clock. It was five a.m. Sleepyhead? She must be kidding. Not that I normally sleep in late, but five a.m. is not sleeping in late! Here in New Mexico, this is the best time to begin your day. If you wait till midmorning, the temperature climbs to nearly ninety degrees.

I quickly got dressed, ate an energy bar, and stuffed my running pack with the usual long-distance-running necessities, like my Nintendo DS.

Jennifer was waiting for me outside our apartment complex. She was occupying her time by doing some freakish yoga stretching, like where she puts both of her legs behind her neck while sitting. It makes her look like a human pretzel.

When she was finished with her contortionist stretching, we started jogging at a nice, easy warm-up pace. It only took ten minutes till we were outside the town limits. The dry, foreboding desert lay ahead of us.

The deserts in New Mexico are semiarid with scraggly shrubs, Joshua trees, cacti, and lots and lots of dry, semisoft sand. The air was crisp and clear, probably around fifty or sixty degrees. That's what I like about semidesert regions: cool mornings and evenings. There is very little moisture, making for little cloud cover, and without a cloud layer to trap the heat of the day—you got it—chilly mornings and evenings.

We headed toward a mountain range that lay about a hundred miles northwest of our town. Its peak looms prominently ten thousand feet above the arid floor. The contrast was striking, even at our distance, with shades of brown giving way to shades of green and white. There was sparse green vegetation near the bottom, with tall conifers starting about midway up. It is surprising how a quarter mile up a mountain range can change the flora and fauna from a sparse arid desert to a lush dense forest with lakes and rivers where abundant animal life thrived. In the winter months, there is even snow for skiing, while down on the desert floor, it's still forty to fifty degrees.

Jennifer and I were enjoying the crisp, clean air filling our lungs along with the semisoft sand cushioning the impact of our steps with a slight *koosh*. Yes, I said *koosh*. I like my made-up word. It's fun to say, it annoys my mom, and it has a myriad of definitions. Its meaning is whatever fits the context it is used in. For instance, "It was nice just to get out together for a run and feel the koosh," or "That guy over there has koosh." You get the idea.

I can run forever. It is nearly effortless for me. My legs don't get fatigued, and I never run out of breath. It's always been that way for me. I was born to run. Why? I don't know. Jennifer gets tired, but she can do ten miles fairly easily. We had gone about six miles when she decided to head back. I continued toward Mount McKnight. My run had only just begun.

I had on my favorite pair of running shorts, bright red with two white vertical stripes on the sides and a silver stylized wolf on the right front leg. They were shorts from my favorite college basketball team, the New Mexico Lobos. *Lobos* is the Spanish word for wolves. The wolf is my favorite animal; it is fierce yet loyal to its family, the pack. Plus, they are just pure, majestic creatures... that sometimes chew your face off.

Indigenous to New Mexico is the Mexican gray wolf found in the mountainous regions. If you happen to be in their territory, they will likely track you without you ever knowing about it. Although, if they make their presence known, you are going to be in a world of hurt! I wouldn't see any of them today; they very rarely come down to the desert floor.

The sun was just beginning to come up, a beautiful, fiery red ball on the far horizon. I saw a few jackrabbits scampering about, and the desert lizards were just coming to life as the sun's rays heated up the sand and rocks.

We have desert iguanas, but the whiptail lizards are the most common, with dozens of varieties. The desert seems lifeless to most people, but if you are quiet and observant, it's teeming with life. Much of it can be dangerous. I always carry flint to be able to start a fire, a canvas tarp for a makeshift tent, a knife just to be cool, and water because Mom says so.

When I say a knife, I mean a *knife* like the one Mick Dundee has in the movie *Crocodile Dundee*. One of my favorite parts in the movie is while he is visiting in New York, two young muggers pull a five-inch switchblade to rob Mick. He looks at them and then back at the knife, then just smiles and says, "That's not a knife, mates." He pulls out his ten-inch hunter's blade and brandishes it toward their faces. "Now *this* is a knife." The two would-be robbers turn and hightail it out of there. That would be so fun to do, put a little fear into some lowlife dirtbags.

I have a ten-inch survival knife, and when I say ten inches, that's just the length of the blade. It's even got wicked teeth on the top edge of the blade for sawing through whatever.

Jennifer never worried about me when I took my all-day runs by myself in the desert. I always thought it was because of the survival skills I picked up by watching survival TV shows. I really love those shows and also read anything I can find on the topic. Most kids my age have comics and fantasy fiction books galore. I, on the other hand, have a selection of survival books that would put most public libraries to shame.

Now, I understand—from what I experienced last night at Barry's place—it was not my survival skills, but that death's grasp had no lasting power to hold me! Every now and then, my mom would say to me that she believed I was born to do something earthshaking. I always thought she was just teasing or building me up, but now I know it was much more than that! Just thinking about what that might be sent a sudden chill rippling through my entire body.

A few minutes later, I started feeling nauseated and disoriented, but I just kept on running. Eventually, the feelings dissipated, and I felt great again, but something just wasn't right—it felt all wrong. You have probably had moments like this too. You just can't put your finger on it, but you know something is just not right.

Then my eyes opened wide. I blinked and shook my head in disbelief. I had been running in the desert, but now, when I looked around me, I wasn't in the desert! I was now running in a dense forest with trees towering overhead. No way. It was not possible! How long had I been running in this terrain with a feeling something was wrong? Oh no, I had been hijacked again, teleported or whatever to who knows where. This was becoming downright unsettling.

Those words I had heard Barry say a couple of times came popping into my head: "I am always where I need to be." That was what I believe was starting to happen to me. Now not knowing where or when or, for that matter, why you are someplace is downright irritating to say the least. This traveling through space and time could really get on one's nerves. The million-dollar question: Why me?

All of a sudden, I heard a still, small voice saying, "*Get back to reality. Pay attention, or you are going to be in deep guano.*" I started focusing all my senses and mental energy on my surroundings. I began attentively, listening, looking around, and thinking what is out of place, what is not normal.

The vegetation and trees were becoming even denser, and moisture was thick in the air. Insects, birds, and animals were... we'll stop right there. Something with this picture was not right. *Think, Chris, think*. It dawned on me. There were insects, yes, plenty of them, buzzing around and being annoying, but there was... an eerie quietness otherwise, no animals or birds making any sounds.

There was a snap. A few more snaps. A series of louder crunches. Then, peering out of the dense brush around me, yellow eyes.

I slowly spun around. There I was, surrounded by a dozen pairs of fierce-looking yellow eyes! Now what should I do? I didn't know whether my survival skills kicked in or that still small voice in my head, but whatever it was, I suddenly knew exactly what I was going to do.

I slowly took off my backpack and reached in for my knife. It made a very soft shushing sound as I drew it out of its sheath. The blade glittered in the dim light as the early-morning sun's rays penetrated the forest canopy.

I heard some low, menacing growls and snarls. Then the brush parted as a dozen-plus wolves pushed through into the small clearing I was in. Their lips drew back in unison, and saliva flowed as they snarled, showing their deadly canines. The hair down the center of their backs stood straight up, as if they weren't intimidating enough already!

Even in their aggressive stances, they were beautiful, majestic-looking animals: long, lean, and powerfully built. Their lower legs were white as snow, turning gently to gray, speckled with black and yellow. This coloring gradually grew darker along their backs, where black guard hairs proliferated. They all had that stunning facial mask common to wolves and to wolf-type breeds of dogs, like huskies and malamutes.

I raised my right hand, brandishing my knife in front of me, while my left hand swung my backpack in small, slow circles. I crouched slightly on the balls of my feet and spun slowly around. Suddenly I lunged forward and gave a blood-curdling battle cry. To my surprise, this did startle the wolves. Well, at least for a few seconds, but my triumph was short-lived.

They attacked, lunging forward. The alpha male came first. He launched himself high in the air. It probably blew his mind that I had leaped at the same instant to meet him in the air. I threw my right shoulder into his chest while shoving the backpack into his deadly snapping jaws.

As we fell, I rotated my body to be on top, forcing him to fall with his back toward the ground. We hit the ground hard, with my knee driving into his stomach just below his rib cage. I could feel the jolt of the impact vibrate through his body. He was down for the count.

I took no chances and quickly went in for the kill. I brought my knife across his throat, slashing deeply through his neck. Bright-red blood spurted into a high arc, spattering me and the other wolves that were closing in on me. I could feel the life go out of the alpha male as his body went limp.

His eyes remained open, radiating a malevolent intelligence. The wolf was dead, but... I could feel a life force that still lingered there. It was trapped, imprisoned in a lifeless body. How did I know this? When I looked into its eyes, feelings of rage, hatred, vileness rose within my being. It was supernatural—intense—and nearly overpowering. I had to look away.

The commotion around me brought me back to the life-and-death struggle I was still in. I was coming out of my own little world of fighting just one crazed wolf, mano a mano. I learned early on, from my mom, to focus on the most urgent or pressing matter. Take care of that first and let nothing distract you from it. She drilled me intensely on this, the ability to focus my energy and effort on the immediate, most pressing threat—in this case, a deranged, lunging wolf. *Thank you, Mom.* I would have been dead meat if I had tried to keep tabs on everything else going on around me, like the other attacking wolves.

Speaking of the other wolves, why wasn't I being torn to shreds at this very moment?

I rolled myself off the dead wolf and came to a low fighting crouch, teeth bared and a low growl emanating from my throat. I held that menacing knife, dripping with blood, out in front of me. What a pretty sight I must have been, all disheveled and spattered with blood. Adrenaline was rushing through my coiled muscles, and my senses were on high alert. I could even hear and feel the blood coursing through my body, that warm life-giving fluid pulsing and thrumming through my arteries.

Every muscle fiber and tactile nerve stood up in attention, ready for action. It was an amazing feeling that I'd never had before. It seemed as if I could control every function of my body even down to the cellular level. If I hadn't been in a life-and-death struggle, it would have been koosh, oh, so very koosh.

The other attacking wolves were busy; four of their own were keeping them from attacking me. Go figure! One of the wolves looked over at their dead leader, then it howled. The others stopped attacking, perked up their ears, and looked toward the wolf that had howled. It looked back at the others, howled again and then ran off into the woods. The other wolves watched it go, and before it completely disappeared, they too fled into the woods.

Now, you'd think I would have relaxed, but four wolves had stayed behind. I tensed as they started walking slowly toward me. The four fanned out in a circle around me. They stopped. There was dead silence. And then they lunged.

I was totally overpowered. The first wolf knocked me over on my back, and the knife I held clattered to the ground. She was blindingly fast. Her front two paws held my chest as she brought her head down. We were nose to nose, her eyes looking keenly into mine. I didn't even try to fight back. Her mouth opened, showing her deadly canines. I felt her hot breath on my throat. I waited for her to rip out my jugular.

Instead, I felt a hot, moist tongue licking my face. I squirmed. It tickled. The other three wolves were on me, licking me all over my body. I could sense that the four wolves were female. Don't ask me how I knew this. I just knew it.

When they stopped licking me, I stood up. Still feeling a little queasy, I took a few deep breaths to calm myself and regain my composure.

I looked myself over. I had no major wounds, just a few scratches. They had cleaned me of blood from the alpha male. That was why they were licking me. I could still see some slight discoloration on my clothes where the blood had spattered. They did a pretty good job for just using their tongues. The four wolves now concentrated on cleaning each other.

I picked up my knife and walked over to the dead wolf. His eyes looked like they were tracking me, holding a glimmer of life and still radiating a malevolent intelligence. That was just freaky and very disconcerting.

Now maybe I was being paranoid, but I still felt as if someone or something was watching me... and it wasn't coming from the dead wolf. I looked over my shoulder and saw the alpha female watching me. At least that was a relief. Now the others were lying down, not paying any attention to me, just swatting flies, and grooming themselves.

I turned and walked over to the sitting female. I knelt and looked her directly in the eyes. "Thank you for coming to my rescue."

She looked at me and gave me a big lick on the face.

"I hope you're not tasting me," I said.

Then I laughed and gave her a big hug; she just relaxed and allowed my embrace. Gee, we had a full sharing moment there. I knew then and there I had a friend—actually, four ... and we were going to be close.

I didn't have many close friends, and those that I considered close were my long-distance friends—internet gaming friends—which I had never met face-to-face. They were with whom I had built truly long-lasting and close friendships. I have school friends, but it wasn't often we chummed around outside of school. The internet is a godsend for those of us that never stay in one place very long.

Back to my wolf friend. When I stood up, the name Tassi came to my mind.

I looked at her. "Do you like the name Tassi?"

She tilted her head, like a nod.

"Tassi, my name is Chris."

She stood up and came over to me.

She was a beautiful wolf, different from the others. She did not have that classic Mexican gray wolf coloring or size. She was larger—well, more like taller—at least six inches taller with fur that was a striking platinum silver, interspersed by a speckling of yellow and tan flecks. Her eyes—I didn't know how I missed that—were bright blue like sapphire gemstones in brilliant sunlight. They were captivating and intimidating at the same time.

She was a very imposing creature, to say the least! I was glad she was my friend, and I knew then and there from looking into those imposing eyes that she and her companions were always going to be there for me—even death would not part us.

I walked over and grabbed the dead wolf and started dragging it through the woods. My new friends just followed me.

I dragged it about three hundred yards or so, till I came to the river I'd first heard when I realized I was no longer in the desert.

I proceeded to skin the carcass. It was an easy job; my knife is razor-sharp, and it separated the pelt from the flesh as easily as if I was filleting a fish. I pushed that dead carcass into the rushing river, where it quickly disappeared. I thought about those intense, malevolent eyes from that dead alpha wolf; it was supernatural... just downright spooky, even creepy. There was a living lifeforce trapped in that dead carcass... just waiting to rip out my throat! Well, that was the feeling I got—at least it was now far downriver.

I washed the pelt in the cool mountain water. It was a beautiful pelt. It was my first battle trophy but not a smart one to keep. The

Mexican gray wolf is an endangered species; it is illegal to kill one. I shrugged at that thought; after all, it had been a matter of life and death. It's also illegal to have a wolf, and I had four, but I wouldn't call them pets. They were here with me totally by their own choice. I was immediately inundated with thoughts of: how would I keep them, where would I get the money to feed four wolves, would Jennifer accept my furry friends. I would be concerned about that later. I had more pressing matters, like what was for supper?

I decided to take my bloodstained shirt and shorts off and lay them in the sun. The enzymes in the wolves' saliva plus the sunlight would do the job on those stains. I stretched out in the sun, feeling totally secure with my new entourage around me.

The wolves took turns scouting the perimeter. Tassi stayed close by my side, my personal bodyguard. Once in a while, I caught her looking intently upon me. Was she checking me out? If she had been a girl, I would have blushed; I was down to my skivvies.

I took a quick bath in the icy river. Talk about refreshing... well, I wouldn't say that. It was downright freezing. I stretched out on a boulder and enjoyed the warmth of the bright sunny day. Tassi came over and nudged me. I guess it was time to get dressed and set up camp. The bloodstains on my clothes had totally disappeared. That was Mother Nature's spot treatment: saliva and a good dose of sunlight.

I decided to set up camp on a very large boulder by the river. It was the size of a small house. I laid the tarp out on the flattest part of the boulder, placing rocks along the edges to hold it down. It was not more than ten feet from the rushing river, with its constant gurgling, sloshing, and slapping sounds; how soothing and relaxing... Oh, I am just pulling your leg. Those sounds would keep most people awake, but not me; I can sleep through just about anything.

I threw the wolf pelt down on the tarp. The pelt felt warm, soft, and very inviting; there was no evil presence there.

Camp was set up.

Downriver from camp, along the riverbanks, I spotted piles of dry deadwood from the spring runoff. I made ten trips or so. I lost count. I now had plenty of wood to keep a fire going through the night.

I used my flint and started the pile of wood shavings and bark I had placed underneath some wood I had arranged in the shape of a cone. The small spark blazed to life as the flames licked up the wood shavings and bark. Soon I had a roaring fire to keep me warm and to cook food, if I had any.

I looked over to my makeshift sleeping arrangements. There on the pelt, looking very majestic, was Tassi. She was watching my every movement with keen interest. There was sentient intelligence, possibly even supernatural, behind those piercing bright-blue eyes. My wolf friends weren't just your normal everyday wolves; that was already quite evident to me.

SNAP! CRUNCH! SNAP! SNAP!

I turned and looked toward the woods; the sounds were coming from the breaking of branches. The other three wolves were gone. Boy, they were uncannily quiet creatures; I wouldn't want them stalking me.

I looked over at Tassi. She was not even curious or concerned. It must have been her fellow wolves. Then I saw them, dragging what looked like a mule deer. I heard a low growl and a gurgle. Oh, just my stomach, saying, "I'm hungry."

"We will eat well tonight. You are going to taste Chris's specialty, mule deer with wild onions," I said out loud.

Tassi's ears twitched, and she tilted her head toward me.

"After tonight, you will never want to eat raw meat again."

I dressed the deer and proceeded to roast it on a spit with wild onions I found at the edge of the woods. Tassi stayed close, never far from my side.

The wolves and I ate well. I saved about twenty pounds of meat in a garbage bag and sank it in the river. It would be our breakfast in the morning.

Calling it a night, I curled up on my wolf pelt with my furry bodyguards stationed around me.

It was a beautiful cloudless night, with a nice breeze that kept the bugs away. I prayed, thanking God for my new friends and a safe night. I looked up at the star-filled sky and wondered what tomorrow would bring.

CHRONICLE 4
DREAM SWEET

Y OU'D THINK WOLVES WOULD BE quiet sleepers, but no such luck for me. I must have the noisiest ones around. No wonder their pack deserted them.

Well, that was not exactly true. *They* deserted their pack to rescue me.

These wolves really did snore, yelp, and fidget in their sleep, even whining and growling. They must have some action-packed dreams, not the boring ones I usually have. But that was going to change for me tonight.

I looked up at the clear, starry sky. There was no light pollution out here. When you get away from populated areas, the true darkness of the night reveals stars that you could not see before.

I started looking for constellations I knew. Two jumped out right in front of me— Orion and Lucas, both bright and easily recognizable.

Now that was not possible! I shouldn't be able see these two constellations till closer to wintertime in this part of the country.

Yes, I was dreaming. Okay, that was cool, knowing that I was dreaming. I would not have been aware I was dreaming if not for the fact that this was the wrong time of year for these constellations to be seen… or was I dreaming that I was dreaming that I was conscious of myself dreaming?

Oh, enough of that. I was just confusing myself.

I went back to enjoying my stargazing.

I thought of Orion, the Mighty Hunter. The constellations didn't really look like what their names implied. It wasn't like a connect-the-dots puzzle, drawing straight lines from dot to dot forming a picture of something. In this case it was star to star.

The ancient peoples of the world gave names and associated pictures to groups of stars, what we call constellations, representing and declaring a story given by the Creator of the Universe.

Wow, this was truly impossible. Now I truly knew I was dreaming.

The Orion constellation had become like connecting dots, or in my case, stars. It was like looking at an artist's outline sketch of a person. A hunter with his weapon, a spear held high in his right hand. He even had boots on.

A mist started forming around me. I stood up. The mist became heavier and thicker around my feet and lower legs. I no longer could see anything below my knees. All of a sudden, I felt like I was floating. I started to rise into the air. Faster and faster, I shot into the evening sky with the swirling, mist-like cloud below me.

I was thankful for it, because otherwise, it would have really, really creeped me out if I could have seen how far below me the ground was.

I continued to accelerate. It became impossible to keep my eyes open. How many G's was I pulling? Was I going faster than a speeding bullet... faster than Mach 3?

I was beginning to feel very hot. I was glad I couldn't open my eyes; it was bad enough that I envisioned my clothes, smoldering. I didn't want to see if they actually were.

The extreme pressure and heat dissipated almost as fast as it came, and I could now open my eyes. I was still going very, very fast, but it didn't take long, and I began feeling downright cold. The air seemed thin, and straight up, I could see the stars like never before—they were brilliant, and Orion was immense.

I looked around me. All I could see was the blackness of space, dotted with stars.

My cloud was gone. I looked below me and saw nothing but stars. Where was the Earth? I began to freak out. I started hyperventilating.

This dream felt all too real, and it was just too much for me to handle. I kept saying to myself, *It's just a dream, JUST a dream, nothing but a dream.*

I was starting to lose consciousness and, just as bad, started spinning out of control. *Jeez, I'm going to wet myself, get sick, black out, and spin off into oblivion.* I said to myself, *no, this is not a dream—it's a nightmare.*

Then I heard a voice call out, "Chris, Christopher. I am here."

"*Who* is here?"

"Chris, open your eyes. Look straight ahead."

"I'm not sure I want to. I might not like what I see."

The voice became firm. "Open your eyes, look straight ahead. It is I."

"Who is 'I'?"

Well, I did something stupid. I listened to the voice.

I opened my eyes and focused them straight ahead. My body slowly stopped its out-of-control spinning. *Holy koosh!*

All I could see ahead were two immense black areas, black as black could be, with swirling debris being sucked into them.

My God... I was looking at tandem black holes. Fortunately, they were extremely far away. That was good. I didn't think it would be fun being sucked into them. I could just envision being stretched until my body snapped in two, with my torso going into one black hole and my lower body into the other.

This was not helping!

The voice came booming into my head. "I am behind you."

How do you turn around in space? More important, why was I able to breathe? Why wasn't I exploding? My body's internal pressure was much greater than the vacuum of space; I should have puffed up like a big balloon and popped—Chris confetti all over the place.

"Just turn your head, and the rest of your body will follow where your eyes focus." The voice had an edge to it. It was starting to get a little irritated, a mite touchy.

"Look upon me," the voice said rather sternly. It was a command but still carried a tone of gentleness to it.

I did what the voice said and turned my head. My body actually followed suit. I couldn't believe what I was looking at. I shook my head in disbelief. It was Orion, the constellation—in the form of a man. My God, he was huge, humongous.

He inclined his head toward me and gave a slight smile. "That wasn't so bad, was it?"

"Well, I guess not, if talking to an immense figure made out of stars that are a zillion light-years from Earth is okay."

"I am only 1,342 light-years from Earth," Orion corrected.

"Oh, that makes me feel sooo much better. By the way, how far am I from Earth?"

"Oh, about 1,300 light-years," Orion said.

"That means I'm forty-two light-years away from you... and even at this distance away, you look to be at least a mile high!"

I continued to study him. He was spectacular, composed of yellow, red, white, and blue stars with dazzling white comets interspersed among them. Even black holes and white holes were present.

His body was buffed, I mean *really* buffed. Don't ask me how he could have a buffed body made up of millions of planets, meteorites, and stars. It looked like a pointillist painting—you know, those paintings where the artist just uses dots of paint to make up the picture. At a far enough distance, the painting looks real, but close up, it's just a hodgepodge of colored dots. In this case, it was with stars, and it was in 3D!

Orion looked like someone who had worked out for hours in the gym every day. He had a perfectly proportioned, muscular body like that of the statues depicting the Greek and Roman gods. What he wore was totally off the wall. It looked like he had on a rugged, short-sleeve chain-mail tunic, a heavy leather kilt arrayed with metal studs, and what looked like hi-tech commando boots. That clothing combination was totally bizarro and out of the wrong time period. But it was a dream—wasn't it?

Orion continued, "Now, let's get to the point of why you are here. There are forces coming together, being marshaled against mankind, that we anticipated would occur around this time. That's where you come in."

"What?"

"You are our intervention, which we set into motion over fourteen years ago, to counter this possibility."

"You... brought life back to a dead child fourteen years ago... me!"

Orion just smiled.

My trip into the past the other night was proving helpful. I gestured for him to continue.

"There are events unfolding now, right now, in New Mexico."

"Please don't say it," I said.

"Yes, you are where you need to be." Orion chuckled.

"I told you not to say that." I huffed.

Orion continued, "Evil spirit beings called Daimonia—the fallen or evil angels from the spirit world—are becoming more and more active. There seems to be a massing of the imprisoned Daimonia in the Great Abyss, and two of the free Daimonia Lords, Anarkos and Kakos, are causing unusual turmoil in your world... the physical."

I looked at Orion. "I gather you are the good angels, the angels working with God?"

Orion nodded.

"Why don't you and your friends fight them? Why send a fourteen-year-old kid against these evil creatures?"

"We cannot fight mankind's battles directly; it is mankind's fight here on Earth. We fight in another realm—the spirit realm; but when the Forces of Darkness overstep the boundaries of the realms, we will intervene."

He paused. "You, my son, are the Orion of this day and time—the Mighty Hunter, Bearer of Light—that will dispel and subdue the Forces of Darkness."

"You've got to be kidding. Do I look like a hunter? Much less a hunter of spiritual beings, spiritual creatures... what did you call them? Oh yeah, Daimonia." I shook my head in disbelief. "You've got to be nuts."

His torso twisted toward me, or it seemed that way. There was no way a constellation could change direction that quickly; but then again, this couldn't be real.

He looked at me directly with eyes made from two brilliant blue dwarf stars. They radiated immense power and projected intelligence I was not even capable of comprehending.

He continued, "My son, you were born from the dead. This gives you a distinct advantage. They are not of the living; you will be seen as one of them. They will not be able to detect your presence as easily as any regular person."

I interjected, "Are you telling me I am not a regular human just because I was dead for a couple of months in my mother's womb?"

"Chris, you are human and yet so much more."

"Hey, you mean I'm like Superman? What's that in the sky? It's a bird! No, it's a plane! No, it's Superman!"

Suddenly, I felt the heavens quake in a low, immense vibration that rumbled through space. Planets and stars just quivered in their trajectories.

Oh, it was just Orion laughing! I thought he was going to take out that entire quadrant of space.

There was silence for what seemed like an eternity. Then he said with a chuckle, "No, you're not Superman. You are not a fictitious character. You are real, and you will be immensely powerful. You will be capable of defeating whatever lies ahead."

"Does that mean I cannot die?"

"No!" He seemed taken aback. "Why does every Orion always think that?"

Yeesh. Testy constellation.

Then he continued, "Remember, Chris, great heroes, even the superheroes of fiction, relied on others."

"I have no one but my mom."

"No...?" His voice trailed off in a questioning tone.

"Oh, yes, I have Tassi, Nila, Cami, and Kora."

That was weird. How did I know the names of my other three wolf friends? Was it just my imagination? *No*, something deep inside me, that still, small voice, assured me, *these are their names indeed.*

Orion nodded as if he had heard my thoughts. That would leave a mark on anyone's psyche, a cluster of galaxies, comets, meteors, and planets forming a mighty giant that moved and had facial expressions, carrying on a discussion with you! This dream—or whatever it was—I would not forget. I would remember every subtle detail; it was seared into my conscious mind, branded into my very essence.

Orion's voice boomed into my mind. "Know your enemies yet know your friends even better. Your friends will make you far greater than you could ever be on your own. Keep them close, get to know their strengths and weaknesses, work them to your advantage. You will build that trust, that confidence, that faith, knowing beyond a shadow of a doubt that you can rely on them in the difficult and even grave situations."

Orion paused then continued, "In the days ahead, you will face many challenges. Take these challenges as your personal schooling and training sessions."

"Are you saying I should want challenges to arise?"

"No. But what was meant for your harm, turn it into good. Whatever the enemy throws at you, overcome; become greater. Your enemies will make you into their most formidable foe.

"Have faith and face your challenges head-on. Only then will you develop your true potential. Do not run from these challenges. Embrace them."

"So, it's like the comic book superheroes... The heroes only become greater in the face of the villain's attacks, finding their true powers."

"Yes. Their talents, abilities, and powers would have remained dormant, never developing into their true potential without the confrontation from their adversaries. These attacks from their adversaries made them into the direct antithesis, a perfect opposite, a counterpart to their adversaries' abilities and strengths—if they survived, of course."

Yes, that would be key... surviving their attacks while growing into my full potential. How ironic was that; them bringing about their own downfall.

"In the same regard, you, Chris, must keep some of your talents, abilities, and powers hidden, unused till the day you really need them. Your enemy will not then have time to develop a potent counterattack or defense."

"Now let's cover a little background information on the Daimonia."

I looked directly into Orion's eyes. "Go on."

His brilliant-blue eyes riveted upon mine. "The Daimonia are very, very old. They have been in your world since near the beginning—feeding off and possessing... living souls!"

"Do you mean they are vampires?" I jokingly asked.

"Yes, they are."

I was taken aback. "You are kidding me, aren't you?"

I could feel a low rumble emanating from him that resonated through my body.

Orion smirked. "They do not feed off blood nor are they repelled by garlic nor destroyed by sunlight. Oh, the folklore, myths, and movie embellishments that surround vampires... so much fun."

He let that sink in before continuing, "The Daimonia live in and among you, feeding off the living, residing in the shadows. They are beings of the Dark, but unlike vampires, they are real... and they need Light to exist."

Oh, I just loved it when his answer to a question raised more questions. "Are you talking about light as in visible, ultraviolet, or infrared?"

"No," said Orion. "This is how Light is manifested or brought into concretion in your world, the physical world. We will talk more about what Light truly is—and the Daimonia—after you have experienced more of your journey."

That did not sound good. He'd used the word "journey." A journey usually took a considerable amount of time and effort. I'd already been pushed almost beyond my mental and physical limits. What more could Orion or whomever expect?

Orion must have picked up my train of thought. "Chris, the key to continuing and overcoming is to just keep battling through. Take it as it comes, break it down in manageable-sized pieces, and focus only on the now, the immediate, the present.

"If you do not, it will become too big, and it will weigh you down. Your fear will then consume you. Your thoughts will become your end.

"Chris, don't become your own worst enemy. Control your thoughts; take them captive, which will control your actions, which will then determine your destiny."

Orion's voice suddenly took on a tone of urgency. "You must leave soon. The enemy is becoming aware that something of importance is taking place in the heavens."

"I thought this was a dream... If not, why haven't I puffed up and exploded?"

Orion decided to humor me. "Chris, the human body is very resilient. You may puff up a bit, but you wouldn't explode. Your internal body pressure is not enough over that of the near zero pressure of space."

"Oh, then I would immediately freeze to death, one giant Chris popsicle."

"No, you would not quickly freeze to death either. Your body produces enough heat... as long as it is alive. Chris, there is essentially no heat loss due to the near-perfect vacuum of space."

"Hold it... hold it... I caught that... the words, *as long as it is alive.*"

"Chris, in space one would suffocate within 15 seconds. The oxygen in the body would immediately boil off into the emptiness of space. Then the dead body would eventually succumb to the absolute cold."

"I haven't experienced any of this... did you put some kind of forcefield around me... or is this really a dream?"

He ignored me. "Enough of the science lesson. It's time to go, Chris."

Orion started to become smaller. I was accelerating very fast away from him, in light-years per second, I imagine.

He broke the silence. "Look, Chris, this is your destiny foretold in the stars."

Now I could see the other constellations around Orion. I saw one showing Orion standing over a snakelike serpent. From below his left foot, a fiery river stretched downward as far as I could see. To the left of this another showed a large hawk going in for the attack on a serpent, its immense talons closing in on the serpent's body. Above the attacking hawk constellation, the stars depicted a man with the head of a hawk.

Orion's voice came again. "You are not the last or the mightiest Orion the heavens declare, but you are the Orion of this time, immensely powerful... Bearer of Light."

I interrupted, "So I am going to turn into a hawk, or even worse, have the head of a hawk!"

He chuckled. "Chris, you will understand more of what these constellations foretell as the days unfold."

He continued, without really answering my concern of becoming a bird or a bird man. "The Constellation Orion is also called Hagat in Egyptian, meaning 'This is he who triumphs.'

Keep these truths deep in your heart, for these truths will become that hope that will sustain you, that will encourage you, that will allow you to overcome those challenging circumstances you will face.

We will meet again, Chris. Goodbye and sweet dreams. *Live the moment. Enjoy the moment. Be the moment.*"

Those were his final words.

I continued to accelerate at an unimaginable speed. I just closed my eyes and hoped I didn't run into an asteroid belt, hit a planet, or get vaporized by a star. I still wasn't sure if what I was going through was real or not. These were my last thoughts until...

CHRONICLE 5
METEORIC DESCENT

I FELT INTENSE PAIN AND HEAT over my entire body. It felt like I was on a spit, being roasted over an open fire, slowly spinning with flames licking my skin.

I did something I should not have. I opened my eyes.

That was a big mistake! All I could see were flames. I still didn't know if this was a dream or real. It was vivid in every detail. I could feel my body hair being singed, and even that putrid smell of singed hair came to my nostrils.

The roaring of the flames was like that of a jet engine. All I could see were swirling flames of bluish white, red, orange, and yellow. The bluish white was in front, and all around me were the red and orange, with the yellow behind. I was like a meteor going through the Earth's atmosphere.

The sensations were all too real. I started screaming. I could not even hear my own screams, for the roar of the flames. Then I thought, *What's going to happen when I hit the Earth?* I screamed even louder.

Just then, I rocketed into an icy-cold fluid. I felt a series of sudden jolts upon entry that sent shivers of pain running from my head to my toes. Had I just splashed down in the ocean? It was a body of water at any rate, and now I couldn't breathe! That was just dumb. I hadn't needed to breathe earlier, when I was in space, so why now?

My lungs felt like they were on fire for lack of air. I tried thrashing my arms and legs, but they didn't respond. All I felt was an intense, throbbing pain over my entire body. I had no idea which way was up, but then I felt a slight tug or buoyancy pulling me, presumably upward to the surface.

I wriggled my body like a worm, trying to move in that direction. I was losing consciousness fast because of the pain and lack of air. My last thought before I succumbed to unconsciousness was *Oh, what a relief; this is the end. Death will soon embrace me. It is over.*

The comfort of blackness enveloped me...

But it wasn't over! I awoke! I didn't know how long I had been out. I could feel myself breathing. I was alive! Yet it was a struggle to breathe. It felt like there was a heavy weight upon my chest. No longer did I feel any real pain, though I was pretty sore. I could flex my arms, fingers, and toes, but something bulky and smelly was on top of me!

Dare I open my eyes? What kind of nightmare was I awakening to? I couldn't get that smell out of my mind. It was familiar, but I just couldn't place it. The smell was like that of wet, decaying grass from a compost pile. Then it came to me: it was that stale, musky smell of a wet dog.

I opened my eyes. Two brilliant-blue orbs loomed within inches of my face. Then something warm and wet but rather rough rasped my cheek. My eyes were not focusing; everything was in a blur.

"Is that you, Tassi?" I hesitantly spoke.

I felt it again. It was a lick from a tongue, and the weight dissipated off my chest and arms. Normality came back; my eyes were now able to focus. I could clearly make out that it was Tassi getting off me.

Nila, Cami, and Kora were there too. The four wolves backed away as I sat up. I brought both of my hands to my face and examined them, twisting and flexing my fingers. They looked and felt unscathed.

I stood up and took a quick look over of my body. Nothing had been damaged except my psyche. Even my clothes and my hair were intact, though I was totally soaking wet. I was a little shaky, swaying back and forth, but was able to keep my balance. I took a few steps and breathed a sigh of relief. I was alive and back on Earth, or at least to where I was when I went to sleep. Had I actually gone into space? Had it only been a dream? If it had been a dream, why was I wet? Whatever happened, I didn't want to go through it again. Everything I knew or thought I knew was now in question. It had taken me to the very limits of my being. It had torn the very fabric of my sanity.

Mankind is living in a world with other beings or creatures that our five senses cannot pick up: spiritual beings, some good, some evil. They are of another realm, the spiritual, encompassing both beings of the light: the good ones, and the dark: the evil ones. Whether I like it or not, I have a very strong feeling I am going to experience firsthand the spirit realm... if I haven't already!

The morning light was just starting to filter in through the forest. Life was starting to wake up for another day of survival.

The birds were the first boisterous creatures to start the morning serenade. I looked across the river. The brilliant reds and oranges of the sunrise overcoming the darkness of night emerged as a new dawn awakened.

I heard a twig snap. My mind raced to thoughts of being attacked, but no way could intruders have gotten this close without us being aware of them. My friends would surely have noticed. Had they snuck away to hunt, leaving me alone?

Turning around toward the sound, I saw three of them encircling me. They looked at each other, nodded their heads, then bounded with uncanny speed toward me.

I sprinted right past the first one into the knee-high grass and came to a screeching halt in front of another one. That was a mistake. Before I could make another move, the three pounced.

There was not even time to make a sound before I was taken to the ground by three snarling, growling, playful wolves. Yes, I said *playful* wolves; Nila, Cami, and Kora were all over me. Just when I got my head out from between them, Tassi launched herself right at us.

What a pileup! It was just like in football when the ball was loose, and everyone piled on top of it. In this case, I was the football.

We rolled and tussled in the semisoft grass, each wolf trying to get a part of me.

I was glad they were playing. I never thought wolves were this playful, but then, I was already getting the sense they were more than just wolves.

We must have romped, tussled, and wrestled for half an hour or more. I was breathless and totally exhausted; I didn't even get that way from running. I crawled and heaved myself on top of Tassi, who was on her back with her legs up, wriggling around in the grass.

She turned over on her side and curled around. Now we were nose to nose. She was soft and cuddly like a dog. The other three came over and plopped themselves on us. I was bundled up in warm fur. It was damp, musky-smelling fur, but never mind; I just enjoyed it anyway. I contemplated what Orion had said: "Live the moment. Enjoy the moment. Be the moment." That was what I was doing, with no cares or concerns for what lay ahead.

I must have dozed off. The next thing I felt was a warm tongue licking my face.

"All right, all right! Stop... stop!"

I thrust my arms upward to hinder Tassi from licking my face. She just nuzzled through and kept on licking.

"Okay, okay, I'll get up."

With that said, she stopped. I crawled out from under my fur comforters.

Standing up, I stretched my arms toward the sky and yawned. Each of the wolves did the dog stretch in which they reached out their front two paws and swayed their backs toward the ground with their butts up in the air.

When I saw them, they reminded me of man's best friend: cuddly, cute, friendly, playful, and above all, loyal. Anyone else… just dangerous wild predators that could turn on them at any time. I knew deep down—that inner, small voice told me—that there was nothing that could turn them against me, nothing!

That was very consoling, that loyalty I could rely on, count on. As the old saying goes, I could "put that in the bank." When everything else was against me, their loyalty would not wane or retreat. It would be steady, reliable, just like the sun rising in the east every day.

I thought back to yesterday, which seemed like weeks ago… to my battle with the alpha male. When I singlehandedly slew him and my sheer ferocity scared the rest of the pack into full retreat and turned four into loyal protectors. Well, so it hadn't happened like that, but when I write my memoirs, I'm sure that's the way I will remember it.

Now, what was I getting to? Oh yeah, after the whooping of the pack leader, I had acted tough, but when the four renegade wolves attacked me, I hadn't even felt the need to defend myself.

How about this morning, with that playful attack from my four new friends? I hadn't known it was just wolf play. I didn't put up any real defense, although I did run and scream. Oh, didn't I mention earlier that I was screaming like a little kid as I ran? My bad.

Anyway, it seemed I was getting good at listening to that still, small voice, or the absence of it. I believed Tassi was building my trust and confidence in listening to it. Showing me that I could depend on it to warn me. If there wasn't imminent harm or a need for guidance, then I would not hear from that still, small voice.

Now, you may say I was giving these wolves, especially Tassi, too much credit, like attributing human intelligence to them. Well, the more I was around them, the more I began to realize that their intelligence was not that of a wolf, and not that of a human either but of an intelligence not of this world.

These wolves were different or special, outwardly too. Have you ever heard of wolves with green eyes? Nila, Cami, and Kora had the brightest green eyes I had ever seen. How about Tassi's build? She dwarfed any wolf I'd ever heard of. Her color was a metallic platinum silver not like any color I had seen on any Earth animal. Her eyes were an intense, brilliant blue—a supernatural blue. Have you ever seen the movie, *Dune*? The people called the Fremen had blue eyes...no whites. That was what Tassi had, blue-within-blue, but hers was a far more brilliant blue.

Most people would be freaked out at having four wild wolves just taking a liking to them but to have ones that were much more than normal wolves would blow their minds! I knew they were here to be not only my loyal friends but my compatriots and my teachers.

I took it all in stride, trusting that still, small voice. Now that I thought about it, that still, small voice had guided me many times in the past.

One of the most memorable times was when Jennifer was walking me home from kindergarten. She was holding my hand when we had come to a crosswalk. "Look both ways to make sure it's clear," my mom said. We both looked. "Okay, Chris... it's clear. We can walk."

She then began to step into the street. Something told me not to go; I didn't hear words but got the impression it wasn't safe. I threw my arms around my mom's legs and hugged her tight... she stopped.

Before she could say anything, a car whizzed by, tires screeching. Right where we would've been. It saved both our lives that day, I am sure of it. She knelt and gave me a big hug.

"You are my shining knight, saving the maiden in peril." She laughed, and a few tears came down her cheeks, but she was happy, and so was I. We walked home without further incident.

I felt fur brush against my leg. I looked down. Kora was looking at me.

"What do you want, girl?"

She did some playful bounces and twirled around in circles, then bounded off, toward the river. I ran after her, calling her name. The others followed at a slower pace.

Kora was all bubbling and giddy. She moved and acted like a first- or second-grade kid. She was slighter of build than the rest, somewhat lanky, with feet a little too big for her body. Her face was full and puppyish with white below the snout and down the front of her neck and chest. She had a light rust color on the sides of her snout that curved up just below her brilliant green eyes. When we had direct eye to eye contact, it seemed as if she was able to peer into my very soul. It didn't feel like being trespassed upon or invaded. I felt feelings of warmth, comfort… togetherness.

She had rust-colored spots above her eyes. When she was asleep, the spots made it look like her eyes were open. I didn't believe anyone or anything could sneak up on these wolves, even when they were sleeping.

Kora had a faint cross on her forehead. A line of lighter fur at the base of her snout ran up her forehead, and a perpendicular line of the same color fur curved above her left eyebrow over to her right eyebrow. The other three wolves had the same cross markings. I'd seen these cross markings on pictures of Mexican gray wolves. It was not uncommon among these wolves, but these markings were much more prominent with Tassi and the others.

Kora did not stop when she reached the river; she bounded in and thrust her head into the water. After several seconds she came up with the garbage bag that held part of the kill from the night before. She pranced over to me in a very proud, playful gait and dropped it at my feet. She then sat on her haunches and looked up at me.

I smiled. "You're hungry. You really want breakfast, don't you?"

She wagged her tail.

I'd never seen wolves wag their tails like dogs. Again, not your normal wolves. Now that I thought about it, their faces were gentler looking, having softer facial features than a wild wolf. Don't get me wrong, though; they were still very ferocious looking when they snarled or glowered at you.

The other two, with Tassi in the lead, hauled branches and dropped them by the firepit I had made the night before. These wolves were all on the same page. It was remarkable, as if they could silently communicate with one another.

Eating was foremost on their minds at the time. Then I thought, *don't wolves gorge themselves on a kill and then not eat for days*? Were they already looking toward three square meals a day?

"What a bunch of softies," I muttered under my breath.

In unison, each of them gave me an icy cold stare and a low throaty growl.

"Okay, okay!" I waved my hands in surrender. "I was just kidding. Jeez,

you guys... scratch that, *gals*, have no sense of humor."

I should have stopped while I was ahead...

Just then, Tassi nudged her head into my stomach and knocked me over. I fell butt first into the firepit. I got up and tried brushing the black soot from my butt to no avail.

"Come on! Now I have a black butt!"

They almost looked like they were smirking.

"You gals do have a sense of humor... a very base one."

I knelt and started making the fire. Tassi came over and gave me a nuzzle on the neck.

"I know. I'm glad we are friends, but... there will be payback." I grinned broadly.

We had a satisfying breakfast; everything seems to taste so good in the great outdoors. Why is that? Probably because you're out of the humdrum of your normal daily activities... like school and the bombardment of modern civilization with all its technology and people, struggling for the attention of your thoughts and senses. In the outdoors, there are only four things to think about: eating, sleeping, relaxing, and eliminating. Ahh! The elimination. That's where it's best; out in the great outdoors, it's simple—every tree, every bush is your toilet. Oh, back to the food. You can give complete attention to the task at hand, your taste buds on high alert, your smell heightened, all your senses completely absorbed in enjoying the food. You are living the moment, enjoying the moment, being the moment.

Hey, if you don't believe me, go to the internet and google it. You won't find a better explanation than what I gave. My thinking, my understanding, had become much clearer after meeting the Orion of the stars, or whatever he was called. What he discussed and taught me was engrained in my memory. That was incredible. I'd never had a dream like that before, so vivid, so real... so painful.

Biblically, you would call it a vision. A vision it was, because it was accurate, precise, and gave me knowledge, understanding, and wisdom that I could not get by my five senses. It was real, as real could be. I experienced it truly, lived it, yet I didn't—what a paradox.

When we awaken from a dream, things become hazy and more incoherent as time goes by. Visions are just the opposite. They become clearer and more coherent with time, and most importantly, the events come to pass. Visions come from another realm, the spirit realm.

I looked around. My four companions were just watching me intently. You'd think that would've bothered me. Now if they were listening in on my thoughts...

It's time we break camp, I thought to myself.

They all jerked to attention in unison.

I looked at them. "You gals weren't actually eavesdropping on my thoughts, now, were you?" That would be freaky and a touch unsettling, but for the most part it would be pretty koosh.

I shook my head, shaking away that thought, and went down to the river.

There was a quiet pool a few yards down. The sun was past noon now and behind me. I could see my reflection in the smooth, ripple-free water. It was as clear as looking in a mirror. I was good-looking—handsome, even. My hair was blond with brown streaks and was blowing gently in the wind. It was rather long in front, and every now and then, I would give a sudden jerk of my head to the right to keep it out of my eyes.

Speaking of eyes, mine were emerald-green and shone brilliantly in the water. Where had I seen that color green like my eyes? Oh, how could I not have noticed that before! Nila, Cami, and Kora had the same emerald-green eyes. That was strange, especially since wolves didn't have green eyes. It was another conundrum I would have to await an answer for.

I brushed the hair from my right ear and tilted my head toward the serene water. Yes, my ears are a perfect size, not too big, not too small, but they are slightly pointed. Oh, how my friends used to razz me in fun. "Hey, how's Mr. Spock?" "You bleed green?" I would glare back at them, and in a low, menacing, but joking tone, I would say, "Keep that up and I will do the Vulcan death grip on you." We would all laugh and start pushing one another around. I wear my hair slightly over my ears because I like the look. My friends were the only ones who had ever mentioned my slightly pointy ears.

I was still kneeling, gazing at my reflection in the quiet pool, when I felt a familiar presence. There, looking over my right shoulder, was Tassi; what a stunning creature, with those brilliant-blue eyes and platinum silver fur. She could capture anyone's attention.

Boy, these wolves were quiet—too quiet. It was disconcerting how they could walk right up to me without making a sound.

She was intently gazing at my reflection in the pool, like I was. Did she see what I saw? I had a nice, chiseled jawline, not too square, though. My nose was proportionally sized, but the tip had a slight indentation, not that it made me look bad. It just gave me character, a ruggedly handsome look. Yeah, people never seemed to forget my face. I could never become a bad guy; I would be picked out of the lineup every single time.

I heard a slight whine from Tassi. I gently grabbed her neck with my left arm and pulled her head to rest on my shoulder. "No, Tassi, I'm very pleased with my looks. I was just reflecting and taking note of them." Tassi and the other three definitely could hear what I was thinking! Yeah, pretty koosh, but it would take a little time to get comfortable with.

She gave me a slight nuzzle on the cheek.

"Yes, I'm glad to have you too."

Then I thought of my mom. What was she doing? Had I been gone long? Was she looking for me? Did they have search-and-rescue teams combing the desert?

MISSION IMPOSSIBLE

I AM NOT A NATURAL LIKE my son Chris. I enjoy jogging, but Chris can jog all day. It is as effortless and natural as walking for him. Jogging is something we both enjoy, and it's a good excuse to appreciate the great outdoors.

The desert is a beautiful place to jog, especially early in the morning. It is so serene, so peaceful. My cares and concerns just melting away. The air crisp and clean, and the sand cushioning my strides with a slight crunch. It was not jarring like jogging on a hard, uncaring surface, like asphalt or concrete.

The daytime animal life was just beginning to awake. The stars and moon were still visible as the sun's appearance approached, with the red and orange hues advancing in the eastern horizon.

Chris and I had just split up. He continued toward the mountains. I was returning home; we had gone roughly six miles. Twelve miles round-trip was enough for me. If Chris continued, by mid-morning, he would reach the mountains, then I wouldn't see him till the following day.

I looked back for Chris; I could barely see him but for the shadows of the Joshua trees. We were very close, a strange but satisfying relationship. I was his mother, and yet I was like a sister and best friend to him. We were only fourteen years apart, so we shared many things in common. We enjoyed jogging and a lot of the same music, books, and TV shows. We both preferred watching the classics: *Bewitched*, *I Dream of Jeannie*, *Mission Impossible*, *Star Trek*, and... of course *Scooby-Doo*.

Thinking back on it, the harm that was done to me, God turned into good. He blessed me with Chris.

Now I was a pretty good kid for the most part. My foster-care parents were never around much; I was usually fending for myself. My parents both died in a car accident when I was eleven, and I had no other family. It wasn't a very close or loving home life, but it wasn't all that bad either. I had plenty of "me" time... which wasn't a good thing.

I hung around with three or four girls. We always had fun, stretching the boundaries between being good and almost getting into trouble. Now and then, we hung around some boys that were trying to get in with the in-crowd. I ended up in a bad situation. I was now going to be a young mother at the age of fourteen. Peer pressure, home life, and counselors just made it that much worse. I even started condemning myself, believing it was my fault. The only fault was the choice I had made of who to hang around with. It had been a bad choice.

The guilt and condemnation became stronger day by day. I even contemplated suicide; that was how far I had slid down into the depths of despair. Our church pastor and the congregation didn't help. They gave off an air of disdain, a condescending attitude toward me. I could tell it in their faces and in their voices when they talked to me. I had no choice but to leave that bad situation before it became worse.

I left my foster parents a note, and instead of going to school, I went to the bus terminal. I don't know what I was thinking; all I had was my backpack, a few changes of clothes, and twenty bucks. If you want to change something, the first step is to take action, and that was what I was doing. What was going to happen next would be life changing. It was God smiling down on me, blessing me, and not condemning me like everyone else. I would see His great love in action.

I left it in His hands and proceeded to the bus station. I now felt a glimmer of hope that life would change for the better.

The day was hot and sunny, a beautiful day to run away. The station was a dilapidated old building, although in its day, it must have been impressive. It had been an old train station. I could still see the remnants of the train tracks in the pavement going through the center of the building. The roof was that orange Spanish clay tile with multiple peaks and valleys. Out from the center of the roof arose a cupola, with a large clock face on all four sides, the analog type with a short, wide hour hand and a long, narrow minute hand.

It was of a bygone era when architecture was a form of art. Now builders just slap-up buildings in short order. They are functional but sterile and fake for the most part.

I walked in through the two large arched doors that were swung open. They reminded me of the doors in a medieval castle, massive black hammered hinges holding together oak planks a foot and a half wide and half a foot thick, all of ten feet tall. Now that was impressive architecture.

I found an open wooden bench; the bus station was filled with them. They looked like old church pews. I looked around the station. It had enough people coming and going that a person, a young person, might be able to blend in and be lost in the crowd. That was what I hoped to do.

The more I thought about my situation of getting out of town, the more depressed I became. How could a fourteen-year-old girl purchase a ticket? Even if I had enough money for the fare, the ticket agent would never sell to an underage girl. I crouched over, resting my head on my knees, and began to cry. I had not thought this through; the authorities would be searching for me eventually. My picture would be plastered on every TV screen, mobile phone, and tablet....

I was still sobbing when I felt a light touch on my shoulder. A gentle, kind voice said, "Young lady, may my wife and I be of assistance?"

I didn't even raise my head. I retorted, "Only if you can buy me a bus ticket to the West Coast."

I felt someone kneel and gently reach out and lift my chin off my knees. I was looking at a kind, fatherly man. He probably was in his early forties, wearing bright-red suspenders to hold up overly large trousers and a wide-brimmed hat pushed down to his eyebrows. The sleeves on his pale-green shirt were rolled up to his elbows. He reminded me of a farmer, maybe Amish; that was just the impression I got.

I looked up at his wife, who was looking at me with motherly concern. She had on a cream-colored dress with pale-violet flowers and a white bonnet draped over her head.

Around them were two boys and three girls dressed similarly to their parents.

The man's wife spoke softly to me. "For a young mother to be, you should be beaming."

"How do you know I'm expecting? I'm not even showing yet."

"It's simple my dear. You don't look like a young lady running away to find her fame and fortune, and neither do you look like one on drugs or one in trouble with the law. What else could it be?"

I straightened up and wiped the tears from my reddened eyes. "I don't want them to abort my child or take it away from me, even if it was begotten under bad circumstances."

The man stood up and looked directly at me. "God will open doors for you. Just look for them. He is smiling down on you, young lady. Always remember that."

The mother called her children together and looked at me. "What is your name, dear?"

"Jennifer, ma'am."

"Well, Jennifer, things usually have a way of working out, so don't ever give up. If you don't give up, neither will God."

With that said, they walked away. I was deeply absorbed in my thoughts of what to do next for quite some time. When I looked beside me on the bench, there was a rolled-up bundle where my backpack used to be.

Now this was just dandy. What had happened to my backpack? I picked up the bundle, and a ticket fluttered to the ground. I bent over and picked it up.

This was like being in a *Mission Impossible* episode, a clandestine operation starting with the change of identity. I got into character and played along with the cloak-and-dagger mission. I mingled with the crowd and weaved my way to the restrooms.

I unrolled the bundle; it was a summer dress and a bonnet. I put the dress on over my clothes; it went down all the way to the floor. Hey, nobody would see my running shoes, even. I put the bonnet on and positioned it to obscure my face, like the mother had. I walked out of the restroom and made my way over to the family.

The bus would be boarding shortly, so I pressed in close with the family as the bus driver called for our tickets. I took a seat three rows behind the couple. One of their girls, the oldest, scooted in beside me.

We sat in silence; I dozed off and on, just aware of the many stops and the coming and going of passengers.

We had probably gone five or more states before the Amber Alert would have gone out. I was sure my dad—well, my foster dad and mom—would not have called the authorities until seven or eight p.m. They would have tried calling my friends around suppertime to find out where I was. Then, out of their parental responsibility, they would have notified the authorities. That was twelve hours of travel time. It was nearly sixteen hours after my departure when we reached our last stop.

Still being cautious, I followed the family off the bus. I did not want them to get into any trouble for aiding and abetting a minor, or worse, kidnapping.

I went to the vending machines in the bus terminal and used some of the twenty I had for a nutritious meal—a stale club sandwich, Fritos, and a Pepsi. I had to start eating better, I told myself... for the sake of my baby.

I sat down behind the family on an adjacent bench. *Now what?* I thought. *This is my stop, the end of the line.* I didn't even know what state I was in, let alone the city.

My family started getting up. We were sitting back-to-back, so I turned around to see what they were going to do. They turned and walked past me, the older daughter brushing up against me. I felt something hit my knees and bounce off the floor. I looked down and picked up a wad of paper. It was another ticket, and money wrapped together with a rubber band.

They proceeded to board another bus; I followed closely. The man talked with the driver then stepped off the bus, shaking his head and muttering to himself. His family settled themselves in, and I showed the driver my ticket. He looked at it and waved me to my seat.

The man came back after a short while, showing the driver his newly purchased ticket. This family was playing this to the hilt. They could disavow helping me if anyone questioned them. The first time, they lost a ticket, and the second time, it was stolen, or something to that effect. I didn't think their story would hold up under tight scrutiny, but there wouldn't be enough evidence to charge them with anything either.

As I sat directly behind the couple, one of the boys sat beside me. I heard the couple talking; it was deliberately loud enough for me to hear.

"Charles, I saw them loading up our belongings, and they threw a gray-and-white backpack in with our stuff."

"Dear, it's probably another passenger's. We will leave it and take our belongings when we transfer to the bus going to Salt Lake City."

That's my backpack! I thought. They were letting me know to take it.

The boy sitting near me knew I had overheard the conversation.

Wow, this family had everything thought through. It was eerie how well they had things planned out. Had they done this many times before? Were they part of an underground railroad for runaway teenage moms?

If you remember your history, back in the 1800s, there was a network of people called the Underground Railroad that covertly helped slaves escape from the Southern states to the freer Northern states.

Had I just met a Harriet Tubman and a Levi Coffin of the present day for teenage runaways?

I settled in, dozing off and on again throughout the night in a semi-restful sleep, that type of sleep in which it seems you are awake for a few seconds here and there throughout the whole night, but in the morning, you feel like you had a decent night's sleep.

The bus pulled into the Oklahoma City bus terminal early the next morning. I would have to board another bus for the final leg of my journey.

I started feeling alone, as I knew my *Mission Impossible* family was going on to Salt Lake City, Utah. It seemed weird to have that feeling, since we had barely talked to or looked at one another, but they had been there for me, watching out and supporting me from afar.

We got off the bus and waited for the driver to open the luggage compartments. I picked up my backpack and headed toward the women's restroom. I looked back over my shoulder and saw them watching me discreetly. There was genuine, sincere concern and compassion in their eyes and faces.

I would miss them, even though I had only really met them for a few minutes. This must be the quality of kindness—the spiritual kindness—that the Bible talked about. I vowed I would learn this kind of kindness and bestow it upon my son and others, like this family had for me.

Now I did say "son." Call it a mother's intuition or God working in me... I knew I was going to have a baby boy!

With a smile, I said farewell.

I decided to change back into one of the outfits I had packed and stuffed the sundress and bonnet into my backpack. I put my hair up in a bun and brushed it to form bangs and a few longer strands that dangled in front of my ears. *There.* Now, I could easily pass for eighteen.

For the first time, I truly felt in control of my life, and I knew what I was doing was right. I had support from others—my rescue family and God. They had given me confidence to continue without anxiety or doubt.

It was drifting into midmorning now, so I decided to find out where I was going to be traveling to. I unwrapped the wad of paper with excitement. A business card fell to the floor, and I picked it up; it said Heavenly Farms, Salt Lake City, Utah. Strange. No phone number, no address, no name. I looked at the bus ticket; where was my new life going to begin? It said San Diego, California, and with it was $200.

I knew very little of California or San Diego. I guessed I would be able to make a fresh start without any preconceived biases. It would be a clean new beginning; I would make my life what I wanted it to be.

Walking out of the restroom with my head held high, I took long, determined steps. My rescue family was still over at the far end of the terminal, all looking my way. They each gave me a nod of approval then turned and walked toward their bus.

I was truly on my own now.

There came a call for boarding the bus for Albuquerque, Las Vegas, and San Diego. It was a long, lonely ride; the mountainous terrain gave way to the rolling flatlands and then back to the mountains.

I tried not to think of what I would do when I arrived at my destination. But those thoughts kept popping up. How would a fourteen-year-old find work? Should I try going back to high school? Who would watch my child while I was at work or school? I was becoming more frazzled by the mile, fraught with uncertainty and doubt. I decided to give it to God. He got me this far; He would get me the rest of the way. No sooner had I made this decision than I was filled with comfort and peace.

My stomach interrupted by gurgling, telling me I needed to feed it. Back at the bus terminal, I had purchased some vending-machine sandwiches and snacks along with my favorite beverage, raspberry iced tea. It wasn't a stupendous meal, but it appeased my stomach, at least for the time being.

Soon, I dozed off to dream world. Well, I assumed so, but usually I never remembered much of anything.

I felt myself being shaken. I woke to the haggard face of the bus driver.

"Miss, it is time for you to get off. We have arrived in Reno, Nevada."

"I was supposed to get off at San Diego!" I said, almost in hysterics.

The bus driver looked at me and, with a broad smile, began to laugh. He laughed so hard he started coughing and wheezing. He kneeled and put his hand on the upper seat back to steady himself until he got his breath. It took several seconds till the spasms of laughter subsided.

"Miss, you should have seen the look on your face; it was priceless! This bus doesn't even go to Reno."

I gave him a poke in the chest and a stern look. "You nearly gave me a heart attack!"

"I'm sorry, miss. I just couldn't resist. You didn't pass your destination; we're only at Albuquerque." He stood up. "You'll need to board another bus to continue on from here."

Whew! I sighed with relief. I wasn't sure why I got so frazzled. Did it really matter where I got off? I thought to myself, *I think I'll stay here in Albuquerque. It is as good a place as any.*

The driver helped me off the bus and pulled out my backpack from the cargo compartment. "Here is your backpack, miss. Have a good rest of the trip." He gave me a wave and strode off into the bus terminal.

When I entered the terminal, a woman in her late thirties or early forties immediately came over and gave me a great big hug. She whispered quietly in my ear, "Just follow along with me, Jennifer."

Whoa, I said to myself, *how did she know my name?*

"Come, come, the family is waiting," she said aloud. She grabbed my backpack, and off we went.

Well, I know what you're thinking: nobody in their right mind would go off with a complete stranger. That would be more than just plain stupid; that would be dangerous. She must've felt me tense up.

"Jennifer, you do need some looking after."

She said it in such a motherly tone, and her face shone with sincerity. How could I not trust her? I had trusted two strangers earlier in my journey. How could I stop now?

She put her arm gently around my waist, and we walked through the terminal and over to her car. She was chatting away like we were family. I felt comfortable talking with her. It just came naturally.

I thought, *Did Charles and his wife notify her I was coming?* How could they have known I would decide not to go to San Diego but get off here at Albuquerque instead?

"This is our ride," she announced as she touched a pink convertible. It looked like an oversized bug. "This is an antique, a Volkswagen Beetle convertible. Cute, isn't it?" she said proudly with a twinkle in her eye. She threw my backpack in the back and said, "Get in."

As we were driving away, she asked, "Do you like my car?" It was pink with white upholstery, and on the hood was painted a big white daisy.

I said, "It's very cool. Even boss."

She laughed. "You know some hip words from the 1960s. This car is a 1963 classic; it's worth quite a bit nowadays. I just like driving it because it reminds me of a time when people were trying to find out who they were and making bold stands on their ideals. They also wore groovy clothes!" She pointed to her outfit and then changed the subject. "Do you know why I have a daisy on my hood?"

I shook my head.

"It's the same as my name. You can call me Daisy."

She continued, "The Volkswagen Beetle was made in Germany, and what's interesting is the hood—that's the trunk. The engine is in the back where the trunk should be. If you drove a Beetle back then, it was making a statement. It was saying you thought of the environment. The car got thirty-plus miles to a gallon. That was when gas was only thirty-two cents per gallon. Most cars back then were big and heavy, built like tanks, and were gas guzzlers, getting maybe ten miles per gallon." Daisy gave me a quick glance and then got serious. "Jennifer, you know that what you are doing is quite risky."

I looked at her. I was thinking along the same lines. Nobody in their right mind, let alone a fourteen-year-old girl, should go with a stranger, even if they didn't have any options. But with me, everything felt right. I was calm and at peace. I just knew this was right deep down in my heart. I believed God was directing my path, because otherwise, how could Daisy have known my name? And... nobody knew I was getting off in Albuquerque, not even me! It was a spur-of-the-moment decision.

Now, you can call me crazy, even naïve, but I had to take drastic measures and get away. I said out loud, "This is right. This is okay."

Daisy looked at me and laughed again. "You're right. In this case, I am here to help you. To answer the question, you are about to ask, I was sent here by Pastor Dan, from Deming, New Mexico. That's where we're heading. He told me he received a vision from God when he was doing his early-morning prayers for the congregation. He asked me to drive up to Albuquerque in three days' time and pick up a pregnant teenage girl named Jennifer with a white-and-gray backpack at eight a.m. today."

Did I hear her say "a pregnant teenage girl"? This was obviously supernatural! God was watching out for me!

"Jennifer, he gave me a description of you and what you would be wearing! If I didn't believe before that God was working with Pastor Dan, I certainly do now! He described you to a T, even where you would be standing! God is guiding your path, Jennifer. I am sure he tried to give you a vision, but your mind wasn't willing to receive it. So he impressed upon your heart the feelings of comfort and peace and of everything feeling right. That is why you are here with me right now."

Didn't Daisy say Pastor Dan had received a vision of me three days ago? I thought to myself. That was before I had even decided to run away.

God was on top of things, but I sure wasn't.

My reminiscing was cut short, and I was back in the desert jogging, or should I say falling. My left foot had come out from under me. It had twisted and slipped on something that shifted underneath it. I came down hard on my backside with arms and legs splayed like I was making a snow angel.

Let me set you straight: the desert floor is not soft and cushy like snow. In fact, it felt as if the sand had come alive; it was moving and seething underneath me. I tried rolling over to get away. That was not the right thing to do. Once I started rolling, I couldn't stop.

I found myself rolling down a steep embankment with the ground still moving, wriggling, and squirming beneath me. I came to an abrupt stop in a deep hollow. If that wasn't bad enough, what happened next was! I found myself being covered alive by hundreds upon hundreds of squirming and thrashing creatures that had slid down the same embankment!

What was a girl to do but scream and scream and scream hysterically?

CHRONICLE 6
SWIM PARTY

W E BROKE CAMP, MAKING SURE we left no trace of our presence. Tassi took the lead and went upriver, which from my best estimate was due north.

We were heading up the mountain. Why she was going that way I didn't know, and she didn't say. I would've headed downriver, which would eventually lead us to civilization. I had a foreboding feeling that this was not just a fun camping trip.

A daymare came upon me... of being on a safari expedition into deepest, darkest Africa. Any moment, headhunters would surround me and take me down with a poison dart from one of their blowguns. They would then have me for supper and keep my shrunken head as a souvenir of an unfortunate trespasser in their territory.

I wasn't in deepest, darkest Africa, and we didn't have any headhunters here, but this was a dense forest with very rugged terrain. We kept the river within hearing distance. It was much easier making our way through the forest interior. Little light penetrated the tree canopy, and this made it less dense with foliage. We still had to contend with trees galore. The proliferation of vines and man-sized ferns hindered traveling within 50 yards of the tree edge, and following close to the river was not an option either. It would be like climbing a mountain but horizontally. Rock strewn wouldn't even begin to describe the terrain along the river. Besides, the insects, especially the river flies, would make a meal out of a person in minutes. I try to keep my blood where it was supposed to be—inside me.

Tassi knew what she was doing, travelling within the forest interior was the best, but it did come with many a downside. It was hot, muggy, and stuffy. The air was so heavy with moisture that if I breathed in to deeply, I started sputtering and coughing up water. The moisture-laden air with the intense heat also produced profuse sweating, drenching me as if I was in a light rain. When a stiff wind came up, we would fight our way to the river for a quick cooldown in the icy-cold water and to get a little sun.

For the most part, the only wolf I could see or hear was Tassi. She stayed ahead of me, ten or so yards. Every now and then, she would allow me to catch up and walk alongside her. Once, I put both hands on her shoulders and made as if I was going to mount and ride her. What a reaction! She immediately lowered her butt to the ground and swiveled in a quick, circular fashion, sending me sprawling to the forest floor. Immediately I scrambled to a squatting position. I found myself nose to nose with her. Darn, that wolf was fast.

"You do like making me feel like a fool, don't you?"

Her ears went down and then back up, she nudged me with her nose, and then she sat on her haunches.

"You know I was just teasing about riding you, though you are as big as a Shetland pony."

She gave me a quizzical look and shook her head.

We just kept following the river up the mountainside with Tassi in the lead. The other three wolves remained unseen and unheard. They were probably scouting; what for, I had no idea. I was along for the ride wherever it took me.

Now, you might be thinking, "What an idiot to just follow along." Let me stop you right there. I had been transported to another place and maybe even another time. I didn't even know if I was still on Earth. Just because the terrain looked like that of the

Devil's Mountain range in New Mexico, I still wasn't a hundred percent sure we were on Earth.

I decided it was better being with four wolves as companions than being alone. I would let them lead for now. We would do this together, whatever *this* was.

It was probably late morning, and I was starting to get hungry again. Where were my energy bars? It's the pits when the only time you can have a snack is when you go out and forage or kill something.

I grumbled to myself, *The next time we get a nice kill like a deer or something, I'm going to make lots and lots of jerky.*

Tassi must've sensed my pang of hunger; she tilted her head and gave me a quizzical look as if to say, "How can you be hungry already?"

I looked at her and said, "I didn't gorge myself this morning like you gals did. Besides, wolves can go for days without feeling the need to eat."

It's crazy, having a conversation with a wolf, but it just felt better being able to talk to someone, even if that someone was a wolf and didn't talk back.

Tassi and the others were great listeners, just like man's best friend, the dog. I could talk to them and share all my cares and concerns without being lectured or judged. Well, maybe they did judge. These wolves did understand what I said to them.

While I was deep in thought, Cami, Kora, and Nila showed up, silent as usual, all ninja-like.

"Geez! You gals are going to give me a heart attack. Next time I have a chance, I'm going to get each of you collars with little bells on them." I laughed.

They gave me icy-cold stares. They didn't think it was funny.

"Hey, I was just teasing!"

They each looked at me and lowered their heads. I knelt and gave each of them a big hug. Tassi brushed past me and swatted me in the face with her tail, letting me know how she felt about my idea.

She headed toward the river, and we all followed.

It was a picturesque place: a thirty-foot-plus waterfall with a quiet pool backed by a rocky bluff. The area was spotted with ponderosa pines on one side and a meadow where wildflowers proliferated on the other. We were no longer in deepest, darkest Africa.

Downriver from the serene pool, the water became extremely turbulent from the large boulders that gave the river something to dash and spray upon. This would give even the best whitewater rafters a chill down their spines.

The wolves waded into the water just a few feet from the pounding waterfall. It was here the water slowed as it circled around a big boulder. They started thrusting their heads into the water. Nila jerked her head out of the water. Her jaws were closed around a large salmon.

These wolves were fishing. They waited with their heads down, staring intently into the still water, for an unlucky salmon to appear. It was fun watching them thrust their heads into the water and come up shaking them vigorously to get the water out of their mouths and noses. When they caught one, they pranced out of the water with their prizes wriggling to get free.

They dropped the salmon by my feet. What were they expecting? Was I supposed to clean the fish and cook them over an open fire? Yep! That was what they were waiting for, because after they caught five salmon, they went and hauled branches for a fire. I had to have civilized wolves looking for gourmet meals. They probably even expected me to serve them on plates with a garnish of watercress or something.

After we ate, my friends buried themselves in the tall grass while I stretched out on a boulder for some much-needed rays.

Kora and Cami didn't nap for long. They had their heads down, sniffing through the grass along the river. Every once in a while, they hopped into the air above the grass and pounced down on something. These two were like little kids who couldn't stay still for long. I was sure they were always getting into something.

Cami was of medium build, with darker and more reddish-brown fur on her body than the others. She had silver-gray fur lower down on her sides, legs, and up the front of her chest. There was a small patch of white on her chest that went up under her chin. She had the reddish-brown spots above her eyes like the rest, but they were not as prominent because of the prevalence of the same color on the sides of her face and snout.

She had a carefree look from the tufts of long black fur shooting out of her cheeks. It made me smile and feel…. yeah, carefree when I looked at her. If Cami had been a human, I could imagine her as having light reddish-brown skin and chestnut colored straight hair, long thick eyelashes, high cheekbones, a prominent nose, and eyes… brilliant green of course.

Now back to the two wolves with their comical playful antics.

They were sniffing, jumping, pouncing, and pawing the marsh grass along the river's edge. Cami pounced then lowered her head and, with a quick jerk of her neck, sent something flying into the air. Before it even hit the ground, Cami was ready for it. She sniffed and butted the little creature just like a little kitten would with a ball of yarn. I moved in closer to see what she was playing with. It was a large toad.

"Cami, you got yourself a toad, girl."

She picked it up in her mouth gingerly. After just a few seconds, she dropped it like a hot potato.

"Cami, what's wrong?"

She looked at me, and her eyes glazed over. Then she started opening and closing her jaws quickly. It wasn't long before she started drooling and gagging then foaming at the mouth.

I started laughing. "You must have been playing with a skunk toad."

This kind of toad excretes a foul, skunk-like substance through its pores. It's extremely noxious. Have you ever been near where a skunk sprayed? It's horrendous. Your eyes and nose burn from the smell, and you start gagging and salivating uncontrollably, and this is even if you aren't sprayed directly.

This toad must have really given it to Cami. She was still foaming at the mouth and now rolling on the ground. It even looked like she was trying to rip her nose off using her front paws. Initially it was comical, but now I was becoming concerned. Was she having an allergic reaction? Or was that toad as bad as being sprayed by a skunk?

She needed to get to the river and plunge her head in the icy water and swirl it through her mouth. No sooner had I completed that thought than the other three wolves herded her into the river.

Cami must've had it really bad. She was thrashing uncontrollably in the water and got too close to the waterfall. The force of the falling water pummeled her under.

I called out. The other wolves stopped and looked. I couldn't see her anywhere.

I ran down to the river, where the water started getting turbulent. Did I see a reddish-gray lump being thrown against the rocks?

I jumped from rock to rock, scrambling to catch up, and then plunged into the icy cold river. I swam and kicked, trying to follow the hairy lump that was being carried downriver. Finally, I was in reach and grabbed for it. I barely caught hold, but I had something. Unfortunately, I was taking quite a beating, being slapped into rock after rock.

I continued to pull and grab. I must have caught a tail. I hauled whatever it was closer to my body, hoping it was Cami.

Now we were one big lump being carried downriver. Adjusting our bodies, I cradled the deadweight between my legs, with my feet out in front. I was now able to keep my head out of the water with the weight being distributed toward my legs and feet. My body was no longer being pummeled into the riverbed or the boulders we sped past anymore; my feet now took the brunt of it.

I could see I had Cami's head on my chest. Great. At least I wasn't holding onto some wild animal caught in this turbulent river. My adrenaline must have kicked in, for I felt strong. Even the icy water hadn't numbed my body, but I probably didn't have much more than twenty or thirty minutes before I would succumb to the cold. Hopefully we would get to a calm stretch, and I could get us to shore before this happened.

The river was getting more turbulent, not a good sign. Our bodies were being buffeted by the waves. It was like being in a speedboat, with the hull hitting the crests and troughs of the waves. Scratch that; it was much worse. I didn't have a boat hull absorbing the grueling shocks and jolts. If something didn't change soon, my body was going to be battered into a myriad of pieces.

I shouldn't have thought about change, because the change coming up soon was worse than being battered to the extreme.

The current now became less choppy but extremely fast and turbulent. We were… being drawn over a waterfall!

"Father, I need a little help."

That was all I could think of to pray, and with that, we plummeted over the falls.

WE GO SPELUNKING

THE END. NO, BUT I almost wished it was. Do you know the sheer terror of shooting over a waterfall in free fall? People say free fall is exhilarating, a rush! That's a bunch of hooey if you are a sane person. Let me retract that statement. Maybe it's exhilarating and a rush if you're in control of the free fall, but I didn't have a bungee cord or a parachute.

All I could do was wait and listen to the roaring of the pounding water and watch as we plunged into oblivion. Well, actually, into a thick white mist of water droplets.

I focused my mind upon holding Cami and counting...

One thousand one... one thousand two... one thousand three...

Impact.

The turbulent waters below the waterfall cushioned our entry into the river. We were propelled deep into the frothing water. I felt a powerful downward pull. We were drawn underneath by a strong riptide.

It felt like we were submerged for an eternity. My lungs were ready to explode for lack of air. Then we started rising to the surface with almost as much velocity as we had descended into the waters. Our heads popped up above the smooth surface. We bobbed up and down as if we were on a lazy river in a water park. We were carried along in the pitch-dark quietness of an underground river!

I could not see the ceiling or the sides of the cavern we were in; I didn't know whether we were behind the waterfall or deep underneath the river. Speaking of the river, now that I thought of it, the water was no longer icy cold. This was getting stranger by the minute.

I hoped Tassi, Nila, and Kora were all right. I didn't know if Cami was still alive; she hadn't moved a muscle. I couldn't even tell if she was breathing. If she was, it was extremely shallow. A thought popped up: maybe her lungs were filled with water. If so, I had to act quickly. I couldn't wait till we found dry ground to resuscitate Cami.

In fact, how do you resuscitate a wolf? Would you do the Heimlich maneuver? How do you do that on a wolf? While floating in the water? Is the Heimlich even the right thing to do? Then, out of nowhere, a thought came into my mind: *Blow into her nose.*

Her head was on my chest, so I used my left hand and brought her snout toward my face. I tilted my neck down and placed my mouth over my cupped hand on her nose. I forcibly breathed into her nose, and her chest expanded. I took my mouth off, and a foul mixture of air and water sprayed out of her nose and into my mouth and face. Yuck, yuck, yuck!

I took another breath and breathed through my cupped hand into her nose forcibly again. This time, I quickly turned my head to the side and felt her warm exhale on my neck. I kept on doing this for what seemed like a very long time. Finally, she started breathing on her own. She took shallow breaths, but at least she was breathing.

She suddenly tensed up then started thrashing and heaving her whole body against my grasp. I held her tightly and yelled, "Cami, Cami, it's okay!"

She emitted a low, menacing growl from deep down in her throat. I said to myself, *Not good, so not good, she's going to rip my throat out!*

I yelled in a deep, commanding, throaty voice, "Camiiii... Cami, stand down. It's Chris!"

Her body relaxed, and she relinquished herself to me.

"Good Cami. You are safe now," I said in a calm and reassuring tone.

We were both okay, trapped in an underground river going to who knew where, but we were alive—for the time being.

Cami shifted her weight a few times but very gently, as she must've known it took all my effort to keep our heads above water. It's not easy trying to float with a hundred-plus-pound, wet—very wet—wolf and being fully clothed with shoes on. Oh, all right! So, I was wearing running shorts and a T-shirt. They were still heavy when wet.

I didn't know if my eyes were deceiving me. It had been pitch dark, but now it was like twilight. Being trapped underground whether in complete utter blackness or not can be quite unsettling. I am glad I'm not claustrophobic. Cami was taking it very calmly. In the now-dim light I could see her face. I stared at her; she was looking directly at me, but I couldn't see her eyes. Well, what a cop-out! She had her eyes closed.

"Cami, you're such a wimp!"

She just breathed out a relaxed sigh and snuggled her snout under my chin. Well, she was being in the moment, relaxed, carefree—being Cami.

This cavern must have been immense; when I yelled, my voice just disappeared in the vastness—no echo. I felt a sharp tug, and we were pulled to the side, away from the main current of the river. My butt hit bottom. We were beached.

I rolled to my side. Cami slid off. She stood up from her crouched position and shook vigorously, spraying water all over. I decided to return the favor for the wetness she threw my way. I stood up, casually wrung out my shirt and shorts then bent down and shook my head briskly, flinging the water from my hair in her direction. She didn't even react. Well, that was a bust.

I put my hand on Cami's shoulder and nonchalantly said, "Lead the way, girl."

We walked out of the shallows onto dry, packed sand. She stopped, started sniffing strongly and sweeping her head from side to side. She was using her sense of smell to determine what direction to start walking.

She must've caught a scent; her body tensed, and off we went into the twilight. I hoped we wouldn't walk off a cliff, stumble into a pit, or slam into a wall.

We continued to move in a zigzag pattern, sometimes going backward and sometimes going side to side. It was confusing. I had no idea whether we were making headway or not. But I trusted Cami. It was up to her to lead us out. At least the ground was rock free. It was hard-packed sand, presenting no threat of tripping or stumbling. We kept going like that for quite some time.

Suddenly what little light we had winked out. We were now in complete utter darkness and...completely enveloped in some kind of viscous fluid.

It reminded me of sea walking. If you have never done sea walking, you've got to try it. You are submerged under water, with a helmet connected to an air hose, and wearing weighted boots or a belt. You then walk on the bottom of the ocean or lake, exploring your surroundings. It is a neat experience; you move like in slow motion due to the weight of the water hugging your body.

Now that was where the similarity ended. This wasn't wet, cold, or hot ... and I heard nothing, not even the sounds of our steps or our breathing. We continued like this for maybe twenty or thirty steps, and then it winked back to being twilight, as it was before. This was very strange.

We took a ninety–degree turn to my left, and then I saw light! It was dim, but it was light, a beacon calling us.

I put my hand out and extended my arm; my fingertips touched what felt like a rock wall. I leaned over to the other side, touching again. We had entered a passageway.

Cami pushed on. It was getting lighter and lighter, with every step.

Finally, we came out into a mighty chamber.

"My God!"

It was immense. The air was clean and crisp with a sweet pungent smell that I could almost taste.

I knelt down and gave Cami a hug. "Thanks, girl."

She gave me a big nuzzle just below my ear.

"Oh, you're welcome too. You would have done the same for me."

When I looked around, what I saw was no random act of nature. But who had conceived and constructed this place? I was in complete awe. It was breathtaking.

Then I looked up at the ceiling and nearly fell over in shock!

HOUSE OF ORION

WHAT I SAW AS I looked up nearly floored me. It was beyond anything I had ever seen, and I mean anything! Even my video games did not compete with this. If I had not already accepted my role as Orion, the Mighty Hunter, I did now.

The ceiling was hundreds of feet up and was made of a pitch-black translucent material that formed a gentle sloped dome. It looked like I was staring up into a cloudless night sky with brilliant stars, planets, comets, and even meteor showers.

But this was not a picture or painting of the heavens on the dome's surface; I was viewing actual stars at a distance of 42 light-years. Yes, that's right, not from 1,342 light-years as on earth. It was the same quadrant of space where the constellation Orion was, and others: the wolf, the river flowing beneath Orion, the serpent being attacked by a hawk, and the hawk man.

I expected Orion's voice at any time to come booming out of the depicted heavens on the ceiling.

I called out, "Hey, Orion, where are you?"

Nothing.

"Come out, come out, wherever you are."

My mocking got no results. I heard no booming voice. Well, I guess I was to learn about this underground expanse on my own.

Now I should give it a name. How about I call it my Fortress of Solitude? You know, from *Superman*—his secluded place in the far Arctic. At least mine was not in the frigid cold.

Maybe it could be the Bat Cave—well, there were no bats. Or maybe Merlin's Crystal Cave. No, the more I thought about it, the more fitting it seemed to call it the House of Orion. Yeah, that sounded koosh. House of Orion. That kept it very vague and somewhat mysterious, and nobody, I mean nobody, would ever guess or imagine it to be something out of this world.

I didn't know how it was built, but I did know our technology was not advanced enough; we were light-years behind. It was probably built by spiritual beings like this Orion constellation dude.

I called him Orion, even though I was the Orion. He never told me his name. He showed himself as the Orion constellation, but I was sure he was not really a constellation. That had been just to teach me who I was—and to mess with me.

Now back to the House of Orion.

We had just crossed the center of the chamber when we came upon a path. It brought back to remembrance the one in *The Wizard of Oz*, the yellow brick road, but this path was not yellow and not made with brick. I knelt and touched a smooth crystalline surface. It reminded me of rose quartz; it was very hard and had a pink, translucent look. This walkway was seamless as far as my eye could see. The rose-colored path on both sides was fused to what looked like polished granite.

I was intrigued and wanted to look around more, but Cami proceeded on our trek along the path. She used her nose, following the scent trail left behind by someone or something. She didn't veer off the path. We came to a blunt dead end at the chamber wall. Cami scratched and tried to dig. This rock chamber was hard and seamless, like it was poured or fused together. Cami started whining and jumping at the wall. I knelt and tried to calm her down, but she just paced and walked in circles, every now and then clawing at the side of the chamber.

"There is no door here. It's totally solid. See?" I said as I placed my hand on the wall. I gave it a big shove and yelled, "Open sesame!" to no avail.

She glared at me with her big, brilliant green eyes, as if saying, "Try harder. Try something different."

"Okay, okay."

I put both hands on the wall and said, "I am Orion. This is *my* house. I command you to open."

Before I could finish, "I told you..." my hands started sinking into the rock wall. It caught me by total surprise. I had just been kidding around when I commanded the wall to open. I never in my wildest thoughts expected anything would happen. Who or what would listen to a teenager ordering them to do something?

I lost my balance as the wall unsolidified and tumbled right into total darkness. I was able to stand and move but was hindered by something that conformed to my body. It was that same viscous fluid-like sensation as when we first entered the House of Orion. I thought, *This is like being nowhere... just pure nothingness around me... in limbo. I wouldn't want to be stuck in here!*

I felt something brush my leg. I reached down and touched fur. It was Cami.

"Lead the way out, girl."

I could only hear the words in my head; no sound came out of my mouth. She must've sensed what I said, or she just wanted to get out of wherever we were. She did not head back the way we came but proceeded forward. I kept my hand on her back and counted the number of steps. As I said twenty-two, we were out of what I'll call limbo land and... into a forest!

Before I could even look around, we were gang tackled by... none other than Tassi, Nila, and Kora.

"I can't believe it's really you gals." I laughed and yelled, "We're out, Cami!"

The four of us tussled and rolled around, enjoying being reunited. After I had my fill of wolf camaraderie, I rose from my knees and looked over the area. All I saw was dense forest and... heard the sounds of a rushing river. I bet any money this is where Tassi was taking us... to the entrance of the House of Orion... this portal!

I don't think Cami and I were meant to go in the way we did. Dad made a back door when I asked him for help as we plummeted over the falls. Now what Tassi and the gals knew about the House of Orion I didn't know. Cami just seemed to follow a scent that took us to the far side of the chamber where the doorway, or should I say portal to this forest, was. It wasn't like she knew where she was going. I had a lot of questions; they would just have to wait.

I turned toward where we had just come out in the forest. At least to my best estimate after all that tussling and rolling around, we did. There was no sign of the portal in any direction! "Oh, come on now, somebody is playing with us!" I said, quite annoyed.

Cami sniffed around and proceeded to walk in a direction just slightly to the left of where I was looking. Then her head vanished, and finally the rest of her body. I wasn't too sure I wanted to follow her back in, but I knew eventually I would have to. Besides, the House of Orion is a koosh place.

I motioned for the others to enter where Cami had... nothing happened. They didn't vanish.

"Come on, gals. Cami and I will personally escort you in. That should work."

We walked in together. I felt one wolf but not the others. I walked back out with Cami.

Tassi, Nila, and Kora were waiting for us with confused expressions on their faces.

I looked at them. "I guess you gals are not on the guest list."

Tassi lowered her ears and gave a low growl and then a little whine.

"There must be some reason you gals can't enter. I see you know where the entrance is. You were waiting for us when we came out. Can you gals see it or smell it? Or do you just sense it?"

They stared at me and shook their heads. Then it hit me, I had asked them three questions at once. I would have to ask my questions one at a time and look for a yes, or no, head response. Well, it really didn't matter how they knew, so I just dropped the questioning.

My friends were able to detect where the entrance was but could not enter. They could be standing right in the entrance, but they would still be in the forest. It was as if the entrance didn't exist in the normal physical world, yet all four of the wolves could find it.

I would never have any unwanted solicitors.

Now I could enter, but I didn't know where the entrance was without Cami. This was not koosh. Why don't I know where it is? I took a long shot and spoke to the entrance. "I am Orion, entrance. Show yourself!"

I was flabbergasted. Once again, I didn't expect anything to happen, but the entrance, the doorway, appeared. It shimmered off to my right... a Roman-style stone archway. I would describe it as seeing a mirage, like on a very hot day where you see water shimmering off in the distance, almost life like but not quite real or substantial.

Then it hit me. *I can command the doorway to allow the other three to enter.*

I boldly declared, "I am Orion. Allow Tassi, Nila, and Kora to enter." I gave them the all clear. "Okay, girls, go ahead."

Tassi walked right up and passed through the doorway like it wasn't there. She was still in the forest.

I looked at Tassi, Nila, and Kora. "Well, you three are just going to have to go over the falls like Cami and I did!"

The three gave me some brutal stares.

"Oh, I am just kidding."

"Wait, wait. I was holding onto Cami the whole time, so I probably need to carry each one of you through."

"Tassi, you are first."

I decided to have a little fun with her. I scavenged around, finally finding a suitable tree branch. I broke off a three-foot section about the diameter of a baseball bat and took a few good swings with it. I then walked over to Tassi, holding the stick high. She backed away from me.

"Tassi," I chided, "Cami was unconscious. I must knock you out to carry you through."

She growled and backed up some more.

"Don't you want to enter?"

After a long moment, she sat down grudgingly. I walked right up to her, raised the stick, and swung it toward her jaw swiftly.

I veered off just before I would have hit her. Dropping the stick, I slouched to my knees and began laughing hysterically. I laughed so hard I fell to the ground, coughing and wheezing.

Finally, I regained control and looked at Tassi. "I just couldn't resist giving it back to you, girl. You do know, it's not like in the movies. A swift hard blow to the head isn't necessarily going to cause unconsciousness. If it does, only for a few seconds. What it will do most often than not is cause permanent brain damage… especially if hit by a large stick!

You should have seen your expression. Even for a wolf, it was priceless." I started laughing uncontrollably again and almost doubled up. In between my bursts of laughter, I coughed out, "Cami wasn't even unconscious when we entered." I was almost scared to look up at Tassi. There was going to be some major payback.

I got my composure, came to a kneeling position, and looked her square in the eyes. She looked directly back with those brilliant-blue eyes and gave me a long lick on the face.

"Thanks, girl." I gave her a great big hug then stood up and said, "I wasn't kidding about the part of carrying you through."

She sprang straight at me without any warning. I allowed myself to stagger backward as I caught her. She was quite a load.

"Tassi, you need to lose a little weight; I feel like I'm carrying a tank."

She gave me a low growl.

Stumbling over to the entrance with Tassi in my arms, I walked us through. We were in complete darkness... limbo land.

"We made it," I said out loud, but my words of exuberance didn't come to my ears.

I lowered Tassi and gave her a pat on the head then pushed her butt down. I didn't know if she could hear me. I couldn't even hear me, but I said it anyway, "Tassi, sit."

I hoped she understood that I meant for her to stay. I turned around and went out for Nila and Kora. When I thought about it, I hadn't actually carried Cami when we'd first entered limbo land in the cave passageway. I just had my hand on her. I decided to try that for the two of them and walk them through.

It worked.

Cami followed me back in on the last trip. Now we were all inside limbo land. She proceeded ahead with all of us touching the one in front of us. I didn't know if we could get lost but if we did, we all would be together. Could we starve in limbo land? Could we get tired here? Could we even die in limbo land? Those questions would just have to wait to be answered.

I counted twenty steps, and we were out. In a dignified yet dramatic tone, I said, "Welcome to our lair. The House of Orion." That sounded so koosh.

Now I think someone was playing around with me... making it difficult to get my other three friends into the House of Orion.

It was now time for us to do our own playing around. "Let's go do a little spelunking, girls."

This cavern, or whatever you want to call it, was immense, and it had many passageways extending to who knows where. I bet that even after a year of wandering around, I still wouldn't have seen it all. Hey, I needed a guide, a mentor, or at least an owner's manual. But then again, if it followed what was happening lately in my life, I probably would have to learn it by trial and error, by me stumbling and fumbling around.

We wandered back to the center of the chamber. I shouldn't say "wander," really, because the wolves were following their noses.

I hadn't realized this earlier with Cami, but we had crossed this center area too. How could I not have noticed a fifty-foot, iridescent-blue circle on the floor with twelve rose-colored paths radiating out from it?

This was weird. Now, I'm not going to say I am the most observant person in the world, but to miss this just wasn't possible. Somebody was truly playing around with me.

Now, the pearl-white dots within the circle... yes, those I could have missed.

I started counting the white dots... twelve in total.

It dawned on me that was the number of stars depicting the Orion constellation! I shook my head in amazement.

I took a quick scan of the cave. Something gnawed at the back of my mind; something was missing. I took another look around, then it came to me...I didn't see the entrance where Cami and I had entered. It was missing; no longer was it there.

The way we first came into the House of Orion was not a normal entrance to this place... it was provided by Dad.

I turned back toward the cave wall where the rose pathway to the forest wall abruptly ended. I couldn't believe my eyes. That wasn't like that before!

I took a deep breath and slowly exhaled to get my composure back. It was just a sheer, immense rock wall moments ago.

Now... I was looking at a forest teeming with wildlife. As we got closer, I could hear the wind rustling through the tree branches and smell the dampness mingled with the pine scent of the trees. Birds were chirping and swooping down, catching insects. I could even hear a river with what sounded like a waterfall. It was like I was standing in the forest!

Looking more closely, this was the same section of forest that Cami and I came into after falling through the cave wall when it unsolidified. Now, get this...where the wall had unsolidified, there was now a magnificent Roman-style doorway! It was light grey and built out of stone with elaborate ornate double columns on each side topped with an arched lintel that was even more grandiose than the columns. The forest scene was around and within the doorway. This was a portal to the forest. A thought came to me that sent a shiver down my spine. My House of Orion might not even be on Earth, or for that matter, it might be in another time or even another dimension.

I reined in my thoughts and came back to the now. I needed to find out if my other friends could come and go as they pleased, like Cami was able to.

I called out, "Tassi, Nila, Kora, why don't you three go out the doorway."

They turned and trotted down the rose path and disappeared through the arched doorway.

Immediately, they appeared in the forest. Kora started chasing a rabbit, the other two just watched.

I went over to the wall. I could not touch a leaf or a tree branch that was right at the surface of the wall; my hand was met by an invisible barrier. I walked back and forth along the wall. I could view the forest but not enter. Neither were the three aware of my presence.

This was so koosh!

Walking over to the doorway, I stepped through into the forest. Well, not *directly* into it; first, I had to go through limbo land.

I called to the three, "Let's go home. It's starting to get dark." I gestured toward the shimmering doorway. It was beautiful with just a touch of lichen and moss that accentuated the ornate motifs that adorned the side pillars and lintel.

I followed them back inside.

Cami was waiting for us.

"Did you feel left out? I'm sorry. I was just making sure the others were able to come and go on their own, like the two of us."

I looked over to the forest scene wall. It was three hundred to four hundred yards long and about a hundred yards high. Making a slow three-sixty, what I saw was eleven other walls, all of the same size. These were solid rock and made up a dodecagon, a twelve-sided figure. I wondered, would the other eleven walls become active like my forest one? Oh, this House of Orion was bodacious. "I could just spend the rest of my life exploring it." Did I just say that out loud?

"Now, Chris, that's not your destiny."

I nearly jumped out of my skin when I heard that booming voice, one which sounded like many deep voices harmonizing together. It was a familiar voice. I looked up at the ceiling.

There looking down at me was Orion, the constellation dude. He gave me a wink. Was that a meteor that passed one of the two blue stars that made up his eyes? It made it look like he winked.

I waved and said, "Hello, big guy. You nearly scared ten years off my life... again."

He chuckled. The whole place shook.

"Please don't laugh. I wouldn't want this place destroyed... being shaken apart and all."

"Chris, this place cannot be destroyed by the physical." He laughed again, sending out more shockwaves. The effects from his first outburst hadn't even subsided.

"This place, what you call *House of Orion*, binds the realms together. Without it, everything would cease to exist."

What he just said sent internal shockwaves through my body. How, who, or what, could...

"Chris, Christopher. Keep this for another day." He must have known where my thoughts had gone.

"Okay, okay, I will try..."

Orion continued. "Tonight, just explore your house and enjoy each other's company."

"Now, wait just a minute! Orion!"

"Chris, all things will answer themselves in time. Just continue advancing forward." His voice started fading away as he ended with "Live the moment. Enjoy the moment. Be the moment."

That was just ducky. I just hated that. Orion would just show up, explain a few things then leave me hanging with more questions than I started with.

"Well, girls, let's explore. It will keep our minds and stomachs from thinking about our next meal."

This place would have been really koosh if it had a grocery store or a few restaurants, even.

Just then, Nila's head went up, her nose twitching, smelling the air...

RECORD II

SAND, SAND, AND SAND

I FINALLY STOPPED THRASHING. IT WAS of no use; the creatures just kept piling on. My hysteria was mounting, and then I heard Chris's voice in my head. *Mom, take a few deep breaths then grab hold of your mind; focus it on God by bringing to remembrance verses on trust and peace.*

I laughed to myself. That was what I used to say to Chris when he became overwhelmed with something big. I learned it from Pastor Dan, who was instrumental in me being able to apply God's word in my life and Chris's.

Aaah, going to God and giving the situation to him; trust and peace go together, you know.

Now I thought, *Jennifer, think, think. What is going on?*

I tried to move but was pinned down by the little creatures, probably hundreds if not thousands. Oh, the thought of thousands, that just gave me the chills.

I could move my fingers. I touched what seemed to be a tail. Little tongues flicked my skin. Then I felt legs. Thank God for them having legs. They were not snakes! I couldn't handle being buried by snakes.

The creatures felt leathery and somewhat rough. Their tiny claws clutched my clothes and skin. They were not biting or taking any interest in me. It was as if they were hiding from something. They moved and squirmed slightly over my body, giving room for others.

The sand started shifting down around me. I was being buried alive with these lizards! Yes, that was what the little creatures were: lizards.

Wasn't that just crazy? I was in a precarious predicament, and my mind was just analyzing the situation rationally and calmly as if I were in my living room, sitting on the couch, just watching it happening on a TV show. That's the power of godly peace and trust; handling and then overcoming any situation. No matter how dire.

Hey, I bet these were whiptail lizards; well, their tails were long and thin. Chris would know for sure. He knows a lot about desert creatures. I decided they were whiptails. I was thankful. They could have been snakes, tarantulas, or even scorpions.

Ew! That last thought made my flesh crawl.

I kept my eyes shut; it was probably too dark to make out anything. Besides, I didn't want to get clawed in the eyes or get sand in them either. So, I focused on listening intently.

I could hear breathing and panting from my little whiptail friends, but what was that other sound? It was like a torrential howling, getting louder, like the roar of a jet engine. Then came the pummeling of the ground, like hail. Oh my gosh, this was not hail—this was sand. I was in a haboob!

The ground trembled with wavelike impacts as tons of sand and debris pummeled it. This one felt like the granddaddy of all haboobs. Haboobs are sandstorms, with sand flowing down in waves. They can reach a half mile in the air and more than fifty miles across. Just imagine a half-mile-high tsunami, only in sand. If I had been out in the open desert, I don't think I would be alive now. I would've been sandblasted or crushed by the sheer magnitude of the sand coming down from this storm. I just hoped I was not being covered by tons of sand. Then I truly would be buried alive. What a way to go!

As fast as haboobs can come is as fast as they can go, but some can last for days.

This storm seemed to be lessening already; it was going to be fast and furious. Good! I didn't know if I could make it for hours upon hours, let alone days, being covered by lizards. Ew, they would probably have to urinate.

I no longer heard the roar of the storm. I decided to wait and let the dust settle, ha, ha, ha!

It was only a few minutes later that I felt or heard what seemed like footsteps. They were quick and jarring—left, right, pause, left, right, pause. There was definitely more than one body moving around above me. What were they searching for? After a few minutes, I heard voices.

I squirmed to position an ear upward, and more sand shifted down on me. The slight movement opened some small passages around my lizard friends to the surface. I could now make out what the voices were saying. They were throaty and machine-like... monotone and expressionless. Their words ever so often interspersed with clicks, grinding noises, and hesitations, not unlike that of a parrot. I didn't think they were human.

Did these monstrosities have beaks? Or, freakier yet, mandibles? And what were they looking for?

One of them started to talk again. "Regent (click), we (grind) have (click click) found no presence of them (click). The boy vanished just before the storm hit. The woman was heading back toward town."

The one called Regent spoke. "Find her. We need her alive to control the boy."

The first voice replied, "She screamed, and then we lost her. We have scoured this entire area where she was last observed."

Then I heard a third voice. "Regent, we can sense no human here."

"That cannot be. She is just covered by the sand."

The third continued, "No sir, the sand would not interfere with us sensing her spiritually. It only might impede us smelling her physical scent if she was too deeply covered by it."

The second voice spoke up. "The boy is different from the woman. We can sense nothing of him from a distance. It is as if he is... of the dead."

"Nonsense," the Regent coldly stated. "He is just human... unless... Melchizedek. He's a cunning and crafty one... that angel of light. He continues to be a thorn in my side."

"Maybe he brought forth an Orion," the second voice said.

"Naw." The Regent scoffed. "That would not explain why we are not able to sense the boy as... one of the living. No matter. Find the remains of the woman."

The third voice responded, "Regent, we have combed this entire area. She must have taken the full onslaught of the first wave of the storm... sandblasted into minute particles. There is nothing left of her to find."

The first voice added, "The boy is gone. Whether he is alive or dead we do not know."

"So, you are telling me the sandstorm that Anarkos summoned killed the woman and lost the boy."

The third voice interjected, "It annihilated twelve of our own."

"The storm should not have been of this magnitude nor in the direction of the boy and his mother. It was summoned to release us (click grind), his minions, into this physical world from our entombment beneath this desert (click)," the Regent stated.

They started moving away, and the last of the conversation I heard was "We were to capture the boy and his mother. Somehow (grind), something went (click click) very wrong (grind click)."

I started shaking and hyperventilating. They are after Chris and me! Then a deep, provocative thought came to me: *Why are these creatures, these things, speaking English? It's quite fortunate... as if someone wants me to know what's going on. Did these creatures really speak my language, or did I just hear it that way, somehow?*

I had to calm down. I needed to think of my happy place and forget that I was buried alive with hundreds of lizards under I didn't know how much sand... and monstrous creatures looking for me.

I thought of some verses of peace and trust, and then when I was at peace, I thought of my happy place, which was in North Carolina. Chris and I would go to the ocean before daybreak to play in the surf and watch the sunrise. It was just the two of us, mom-and-son time. We found a beautiful little secluded cove. When the tide was low, we had our own little beach. We could smell and taste the salt in the air as the waves pounded the surrounding cliffs, spraying the air with water droplets that gently caressed our bodies as they found their way to the ground and back to the ocean where they were born.

It was peaceful and secluded, just the two of us. Chris would play with some of the sea creatures that got trapped in small pools where the rock had been carved by the never-ending waves crashing onto it. One of the pools, which we called the aquarium, was big enough that we could swim in the warm water. It was heated by the surrounding rock that soaked up the sun's rays and was refreshed with new seawater at high tide. It held peculiar saltwater fish, not the small, colorful tropical fish you see in home aquariums. These were fish adapted to extreme microenvironments. One of the cutest and craziest-looking fish was the hogfish. It had a pig-like snout that it used to suck up minute food particles trapped among the sand and rocks at the sea bottom, like a vacuum cleaner.

Oh, and how about the puffer fish? It is mottled in color, decked out with spikes, and can puff up to nearly three times its original size. You might ask why. Well, it's not called chicken of the sea for nothing. The meat of the puffer fish is a delicacy, a very white meat that tastes like sweet chicken. Now, being homely, having needle-like spines, and becoming three times larger is usually enough of a deterrent for not being eaten. But some varieties of puffer fish have gone extreme and adapted to produce a deadly toxin that saturates their skin and internal organs. This toxin is up to twelve hundred times more lethal than cyanide. While cyanide can paralyze and kill you in a couple of minutes, with a puffer fish, you don't even have time to pray.

Chris played with the hogfish and even the puffer fish. Now, you ask, what mother would allow her son to play with such a deadly creature? I'm a good mother, I'll have you know! Along the coast of North Carolina, we have the Atlantic puffer. It's nontoxic. The predator fish around here won't eat them; they must think all puffer fish are poisonous. Their bad.

I suddenly felt my little lizard friends start to move; they were working their way to the surface. The sand started shifting around me. This was my chance. I needed to move with them, or the sand would pour down and entomb me. As they squirmed to the surface, I pushed my way upward. It was working. The more I wiggled and moved, the freer my legs and arms became. I felt sorry for those lizards that got pushed beneath me, but I was in self-preservation mode. They would have to fend for themselves.

It took me only a matter of minutes to reach the surface. My head popped out of the sand first. I continued to claw my way out and upward toward freedom. My lower body followed suit, with my feet last. I sat up, the sand falling in waves off my upper torso.

The lizards kept pouring out of the sand and scampering for cover. I didn't open my eyes; I just sat there for a few minutes. I didn't want an actual image in my mind of those lizards I had been buried with...my imagination was enough.

I finally heard no more movement. I opened my eyes. There was still a dust haze in the sky. I could hardly make out the sun. Slowly, I pulled myself to a kneeling position then stood up and looked around. I gasped at what I saw.

It looked like an atomic bomb had exploded. There wasn't a trace of vegetation or life except for my lizard friends. Just sand, sand... and sand. It now looked like the Sahara Desert, wave upon wave of sand dunes stretching out as far as the eye could see. If not for the total destruction of this desert ecosystem, I would have enjoyed the serene and beautiful new landscape.

I crawled up till I was at the top of the dune. In just the few quick glimpses I took, I saw nothing. I didn't want to be found by those creatures that had been released by this destruction. Where had they gone? What to do next?

My mind was racing at a hundred miles an hour, with thoughts, images, and emotions popping in and out. I finally took a few deep breaths and stopped my mind. I wasn't going to allow the storm from the outside to continue—on the inside. You have probably heard the saying "Still waters run deep." Well, that was where I took my mind. Deep, deep down inside me. I grabbed the peace of God, my deep still waters. He was my refuge and safety. I was safe. Chris was probably safe... No, check that. Chris *was* safe!

Whatever was hunting us believed I was dead. Great. I intended to leave it that way. God surely had protected me. Now, you're right, I didn't like being buried in sand with lizards all over me. Even just thinking about it gave me the shivers. But their tough, leathery bodies had protected me from being sandblasted by the storm and formed pockets of air for me to breathe during my interment in the sand.

Hey, what about the lizards masking my presence and smell? Hold it right there! I don't smell. I took a shower this morning. If anything, I smell of my perfume.

Anyhow, these lizards had masked my human presence and my human smell. To put icing on the cake, the creatures that were released by the storm believed I was dead. Now they couldn't use me against Chris. If that was not God working in the situation, I didn't know what was.

I waited a few hours then began my trek back home.

I wondered if the town was still standing. Was my apartment complex still there? Wait, I couldn't go back to my apartment. Chris and I had to remain dead or at least missing and presumed dead.

I kept the mountain range north and west of me, which should point me in the right direction for home. I wasn't going to jog; that would be a killer. The terrain was all sand dunes now, soft shifting sand under my feet rather than the firmly packed sand of before. Even walking in this soft sand was just plain drudgery.

My mind kept going to the times in my past when God was there for me. I grasped and focused on the time of my first encounter with Pastor Dan and his family. This truly had been a godsend. They had healed my heart and brought peace to my life.

At that initial meeting when Daisy had dropped me off at Pastor Dan's house, his whole family had come out to greet me. His kids had even been there, and it was a school day. Pastor Dan was a big man, and when I say big, I mean *big*. He stood six foot five and weighed two hundred eighty-plus pounds. He wasn't fat, just large, big boned, with a full, kindly face, curly brown hair, and large eyes that were kind and inviting. When he spoke, it was with a soft, soothing baritone voice.

He gave Daisy a big hug, lifting her off the ground. Then he grabbed me and gave me a great big bear hug while twirling me in a circle. This man was light on his feet too. He was just a big, lovable teddy bear.

That was the beginning of a sweet family relationship. He told everyone I was his niece from out east and that my parents had died tragically. Only his wife, his two kids, and Daisy knew otherwise.

A week later, while we were sitting around the kitchen table, having breakfast, he asked his kids to go outside and play.

His wife, Sandy, looked at me and kindly spoke. "Jennifer, it seems you are more withdrawn and quieter as of late. Do you want to talk about it?"

Before I could even speak, Pastor Dan placed his hand on top of mine and said softly, "Jennifer, we love you, and God loves you. The decision you make about your child is yours and yours alone to make. We know some doubt and anxiety has crept in about keeping your child. Throw those thoughts out. Don't be concerned about the future. Just live in the present, the here and now, day by day. God is with you, and Sandy and I are with you."

Sandy shared. "The Bible is God's word when you allow it to interpret itself. Allow it to guide you. It will bring stability to your life, with truths that do not change."

Then Pastor Dan expounded, "For instance, if you've chosen to abort your baby, it would not be murder." Then he and Sandy opened a Bible and shared God's truth on the topic. They read about how lovingly God had set up everything about birth, and there was no condemnation from God on a mother's choice. It was hers to make. Even Jesus Christ was considered a "holy thing" when he was in Mary's womb. There might be consequences to work through, but God would not condemn.

This put my heart at peace that day. Today was no different; I became more peaceful as I focused my thoughts on God, the truth of his word, and what he had done in the past.

I came back to the here and now as the haze waned. The sun was just starting to set when the town came into view. It was still there! Untouched by the storm. I should have known the town was okay miles ago, when the soft sand had given way to the normal semi-hard-packed sand and vegetation.

I moved through the town, trying not to make my presence known. It was weird that I saw no one. How fortunate! Was it a matter of coincidence that no one was around? I didn't think so. What should I do?

I came to the apartment complex, but I couldn't go to my apartment. Where should I go? As I walked down the hallway, I saw the door to Barry's apartment, three doors down from ours. I would go there. I put my hand on the doorknob and turned it slowly. The door opened! He had left it unlocked. How convenient.

I walked in and closed the door behind me.

"Anyone home?" I hesitantly breathed out. No one answered.

I made myself at home on Barry's cushy couch and waited. I didn't wait too long, however. There was something I really needed to do. It was ages since I had last gone pee. I followed the hallway to the bathroom. Upon leaving the bathroom I noticed that Barry's bedroom door was slightly ajar. I figured I'd just peek in to make sure he wasn't sleeping.

As I suspected, he wasn't home. This man kept even his bedroom clean and organized. No clothes laid helter-skelter. The place was clean and tidy. It was modestly furnished. There were a few tapestries and paintings on the walls, but the painting above his bed caught my eye. I was riveted to it. The painting left me breathless. I couldn't believe what I saw. It just couldn't be... but it was!

CHRONICLE 9
SURF-N-TURF

NILA SUDDENLY DASHED OFF TOWARD who knew where or what, with Tassi, Cami, Kora and me in hot pursuit. Nila was the tank, the most powerfully built of the four. She was shorter and stockier than the rest. That didn't mean she was slow. Nila was subtly fast and agile but definitely a tank. When she ran through a forest, she didn't go around the brush. She just plowed right through it, making her presence known.

Blood-red guard hairs profusely erupted through the soft light-brown underfur over the majority of her body, giving her a reddish appearance. White fur dominated her belly and the insides of her legs, her face, and the underside of her neck. Her eyes were brilliant green, shrouded by bushy reddish eyebrows.

Now, I know what you are thinking: with those holiday colors, red and green, she could be Mother Christmas. Let me set you straight. She did not look motherly or comical, just the opposite. She looked fierce—menacing, even—and in the twilight, Nila's white face gave her a ghostly appearance. The brilliant green eyes cutting through the darkness added to the ethereal effect.

Suddenly, she stopped, her head went upward, and her nose started some serious twitching. Then off she went again, head down, following a trail of some sort, zigzagging her way across the chamber, until finally, she stopped at a wall. Nila was pacing and clawing at a section of the wall. This was not the forest wall but another wall.

"Now what?" I complained. "You want me to lay my hands on it and open another portal?"

She gave me a serious look that said, "Duh."

"You think it works just by me putting my hands to a wall? That's ridiculous," I chided as I touched the wall.

Before I could finish saying, "See nothing happen..." the wall started to dissolve, and I tumbled into limbo land, with the four wolves bounding over the top of me.

I would never get used to this. What I called limbo land was some sort of transitional state that transcended all physical rules. It was pitch dark, absolutely devoid of all light; there was no sound transmitted either. And get this, there was nothing physical to touch or walk on. Yes, you heard me right. No ground, not anything substantial underneath my feet, really no, up or down, left or right. Yes, definitely the definition of being in limbo. When I moved, it was as if I was moving in something viscous, like being submerged completely in water. Yet I couldn't touch or feel anything, and I wasn't wet!

When I tried to touch what I was seemingly walking on, there was nothing there. Yet I didn't fall.

The ancient Greeks believed in a fifth element they called aether. The other four elements were earth, water, air, and fire. The Greek gods lived and breathed aether, yet it had no substance, no qualities like being hot or cold, wet or dry. Direction in aether was not static either; it could change at any time. What was up could change to being down, and what was east could change to north.

That is kind of creepily similar to my limbo land. I was able to breathe all right, and no matter what direction I walked in, so far I had always ended up where I was supposed to be. I think aether does exist and it is what I call limbo land.

I have a hypothesis to check out someday, which is that in limbo land, time does not exist. Neither does life or death, meaning I would never get hungry, thirsty, tired, or sleepy or change in any way. I'm going to have to do an extended campout in limbo land someday to test my hypothesis.

After being pounced upon, I did not have any idea which direction Tassi and the three headed after they entered limbo land. Well, here in limbo land, it didn't seem to matter... so far.

I shrugged and set off walking. I counted five steps. Ten steps. Twenty steps. I still wasn't out. Was it time to start freaking out yet? My wolf companions were going to get an earful if I ever found my way out.

Just then, I felt something brush my legs. I instinctively reached down. Feeling fur, I took a gentle hold and was led out into a vast grass prairie edged by deep forest. It was a temperate temperature, probably around fifty to fifty-five degrees. The air was moist, and the subdued light looked like early morning. Hadn't we just left the setting of the sun?

I looked down. Tassi was glaring at me.

"Oh." I released my hold on her fur. She nuzzled my hand in response. I looked directly into her eyes. "Thanks, girl."

I did a complete three-sixty. This place did not remind me of anything on Earth—at least not in my time. The landscape looked like something out of the prehistoric era.

I turned and gazed directly into Tassi's brilliant-blue eyes and stated, "Let's go bail out Nila—she's probably in trouble."

Tassi tilted her head slightly to one side and perked up one ear, giving her a questioning look. I did not need the spoken language between us; her body language was easy to pick up on. I turned around and placed my hand on her head and gently ran my fingers through her soft fur.

"Tassi, to answer your question, it's quite obvious even from just the little time we've been together that Nila's actions show impulsiveness... a brashness.

With these characteristics, trouble wouldn't follow her. Trouble would call her."

Tassi gave a little whine.

"The more I'm around you gals, the more feelings, thoughts, and memories awaken in my mind of all of you."

And with that just said, a kaleidoscope of thoughts came popping into my consciousness:

Nila was courageous and impetuous but loyal to a fault. She would unquestionably have your back covered under any circumstance, no matter how dangerous. She had Viking warrior traits: powerfully stoic, courageous, honorable, loyal, and yes, bloodthirsty. When I say bloodthirsty, I mean she craved a good fight. She loved nothing more than to do battle. She was headstrong and lacked any fear of the consequences of her brash actions.

I now knew and felt so much about Nila. It was as if we'd been together for years, more years than I'd been alive. These traits were what I loved about Nila. Through her, I could see myself being bold, daring, brash, thirsting and hungering for any challenge.

For the most part, I was quiet and reserved. I thought through all my actions before I did them, making me somewhat dull, methodical, and predictable, but not so for Nila. She was just the opposite. She made imaginative, unexpected, split-second decisions.

A baying came to my ears, like when a pack of wolves caught a fresh scent of their prey. I had the distinct feeling that here, where-or whenever this was, one's prey might well become one's predator.

We were on top of a grassy knoll. To the back of us was a vast grass prairie, and in front of us, the prairie gave way to a dense forest miles away. This was no ordinary forest. Even from this distance, the trees still looked massive, the foliage vast and dense. I bet the trees were more than thirty feet in diameter and easily five hundred feet tall. Everything looked so vibrant and larger than life. I just hoped the animal life that lived here wasn't huge too!

The sun was just rising above the grassy plain, draping it in beautiful orange and red hues. I was brought back to the here and now by the excited baying from the direction of the forest.

I looked at Tassi and said, "Lead the way, girl."

She bounded down the grassy hill with me in hot pursuit. I just love to run; it is exhilarating and energizing for me. I can truly run with the pack. We ran through the knee-high prairie grass, following what looked like an animal trail.

Tassi's nose was to the ground, following the scent of the other three. We ran at a comfortable gait, stopping every now and then as Tassi decided which path to follow. The grass became higher the farther we went, and soon, it was over my head.

The trails were well traveled, but now it was like running through a maze. We took so many twists and turns that I became lost. I made sure I kept close to Tassi. If I lost her, it would really put my tracking skills to the test.

The baying was getting louder and didn't seem to be moving. Whatever the wolves were chasing, it must have stopped.

Shortly, we broke through the tall grass. I couldn't believe my eyes. What was that animal that Nila, Cami, and Kora had trapped? It couldn't be! It looked like a possum, but it was the size of a small elephant, around six feet tall and possibly two thousand pounds. What did they feed these animals here?

The three had the possum cornered at the edge of a tall cliff that dropped off steeply. There was nowhere for the possum to go except through the three wolves or over the cliff into a ravine.

This was a steep and deep ravine. The cliffs must have been nearly a thousand feet tall and ran as far as the eye could see in either direction. Below, down at the bottom, was a river that meandered, following the ridgeline of the cliffs.

I looked up and down the river. The sculpting and erosion of this deep ravine was very recent. There was no vegetation along the river or up the sides of the ravine. There must've been an immense amount of water over a short period of time, like what happens in the Amazon rain forest basin. During the rainy season, the Amazon River can rise thirty to forty feet and extend more than six miles from its normal banks. In this case, the water was channeled through a narrow region, carving this very deep ravine.

I was brought back to the here and now by the snarling and gnashing of teeth. The possum looked fierce as it lunged toward the wolves, showing its long, needle-sharp teeth. They were pearly white and four inches long. It snarled, lunged, and bared its menacing teeth while raking the air with its six-inch-long, curved front claws. This possum was putting on a truly vicious show. The wolves were backing away as it continued to aggressively advance toward them.

Didn't these wolves know that possums were all show and no bite? They never attack, but they do put on quite an act, trying to intimidate and scare off their attackers. Possums would never actually fight for their lives.

The three wolves looked at me then proceeded to challenge the possum. It was if they listened in on my thoughts. That would totally be an invasion of my privacy!

"Whoa, now, gals, I could be wrong! Possums might be entirely different here... they could be vicious carnivores! Look at the size of that thing!" I wildly gestured.

I tried backing away, but my feet wouldn't budge. What was going on? I looked down. I couldn't even see my ankles. I had sunk into the soft, grassy earth. This was not good. The ground was fully saturated with water. I had stayed too long in one spot. The wolves and the possum had not suffered the same fate yet... they were not standing still.

The three wolves lunged. The possum whirled in circles and rolled over and over, attempting to save itself without fighting. The wolves were all over it. The snarling and growling were deafening. The possum made one last attempt to free itself then stumbled theatrically, headfirst into the ground, lying motionless. If I hadn't known any better, I would have thought that possum just had a heart attack and died. I'm telling you, some of our modern-day actors could learn a thing or two from that oversized, prehistoric possum.

I could still hear snarling and thrashing, but the battle was over. I looked closely at the fallen possum and couldn't believe my eyes. Nila was pinned down by the weight of the possum. It was hilarious watching her trying to extricate herself. She was like a turtle on its back. She was not going anywhere. Her back must have sunk into the soft ground under the weight of the fallen possum. Only her upper torso was free, her front legs pushing against the possum as she tried to wriggle free.

Kora, Cami, and Tassi were just sitting there, watching her. If they could have laughed, I was sure they would have.

Nila finally gave up struggling and laid her head back with a big sigh.

I couldn't contain myself. I slumped to my knees, bursting out with a round of laughter. I finally got it under control and looked at Nila, choking out the words, "The great—warrior wolf—laid out—by a mere possum!" My body started trembling with another wave of laughter. I stopped laughing when I saw the shocked look in Kora and Cami's eyes and the alarmed expression on Tassi's face.

The trembling of my body was not stopping. Suddenly, I heard a big sucking sound followed by a low, powerful rumble.

Then the earth gave way.

I gave a high-pitched heroic scream and grabbed Tassi as I saw huge sections of the bluff start collapsing into the ravine. It was like watching dominoes falling in succession. It wasn't even a matter of seconds before our section of the bluff was sliding down into the ravine a thousand feet below. We were all trapped in a massive section of soft mud hurtling down the steep embankment.

I clung to Tassi with my left hand as my right hand reached out, searching for anything to grab onto and stabilize us. My right hand found a large root. I hung on for dear life as we slid down, sliding from left to right and even twisting around. Our section seemed to be floating on top of another section as it was cascading down. I gave a quick glance around and saw we were all together, even the possum.

I started yelling, "Mudslide! Mudslide! Yeah! Mudslide!" at the top of my lungs.

Letting all caution go, I relinquished my grasp of Tassi and the tree root. I raised my arms high into the air and screamed at the top of my lungs just like when I am on a roller coaster as it nose dives. It makes me feel so much better. This was as exhilarating and adrenalin pumping as being on a ride at Six Flags! True, it didn't have any safety features, but hey, this ride was free!

My wolf friends didn't seem to be enjoying it as much as I was. Hey, if you're going to die, you might as well try to enjoy the last few seconds. I even put my arms out like I was surfing, moving my upper torso back and forth. I wasn't going to be thrown from this surfboard! My feet were firmly stuck to the ground from the suction of the saturated soil.

I continued to yell and scream as we plunged toward the bottom. Our section of the mudslide rocked, pivoted, and twisted. It was the coolest ride I had ever been on and probably my last. It looked as if we were going to hit the bottom with an abrupt stop, but the sections of mud just piled up on one another, gradually slowing us down. I grabbed Tassi and the tree root again just in case. We did have some jolts and jostling but nothing earthshaking.

The mud piled up into the river and became a mud flow. We were all trapped in it. Now the question was, how could we get out of this mud flow?

I decided to treat it like getting out of a fast-moving river—by swimming at a slight angle upstream. We were not going to swim in the mud, but the concept of angling upstream was our best shot at getting out. The problem was that we were all still stuck in the mud section. I started pulling on the tree root to try to free my feet.

It suddenly began to coil up and away, pulling me out of the muck. I was holding onto the possum's tail! He wasn't dead, just playing possum.

I hung onto his tail as he clawed his way through the mud. He was built for moving through this muck, low to the ground, light for his size, and with sharp, long claws for traction. I grabbed and held onto Tassi, pulling her out of the muck as the possum passed by. He then passed by Kora and Cami, and I heaved them out. This possum was helping us to extricate ourselves from being mud pies... go figure. I let go of the possum's tail when we came back to where Nila was stuck. Now the three of us commenced digging around Nila with paws and hands.

I looked over my shoulder to see what the big guy was doing. He was watching us with keen interest. This possum seemed quite bright, and on the off chance he was, I beckoned him with my hand to come over. He tilted his head as if considering my request, then got up and came over to us. He started digging next to us. He was smarter than the average possum! He tunneled right underneath Nila, lifting her up as he passed underneath. She was now sprawled out on his back. It looked very comical—a wolf carried by a possum.

I grabbed hold of the tail again. The possum moved through the mud with ease. We finally made it out of the mud flow, crawling out onto a large boulder. The possum shook its body, flinging off the mud and Nila along with it.

The possum didn't run away. He stayed, staring at us with his small, beady black eyes. He was kind of cute, with a long snout, a tiny pink nose, pink feet, and a long bare pink tail. His body was covered in brown fur with dark rings like that of a raccoon's tail. Oh, and did I mention his small, very small, pink ears? He would have made a cute plush toy if he hadn't been so large and weighed two thousand-plus pounds.

The wolves shook their own mud coats off then turned toward the possum.

I dashed in between the possum and the wolves, raising my hand. "Whoa! You gals aren't going to kill and eat our rescuer! If it wasn't for him, we would all still be stuck in that mud flow."

They each tilted their heads in a quizzical fashion.

"Yeah, you heard me. I think I will call him Rescue. Well, maybe that's not a great name. How about... Rascal? No, no, I know! I'll call him Roscoe! Yes. Roscoe the Rescuer! That's a fitting name."

I turned to the possum, my hands outstretched to the heavens, proudly declaring, "I'm naming you Roscoe."

The wolves all lowered their heads and gently shook them from side to side, expressing their disapproval.

"Well, even if you gals don't like the name, I do," I said, hands on my hips, elbows bowed outward. "Roscoe the possum. It has a nice ring to it."

I moved closer to Roscoe, extending my hand with the palm down. Roscoe stretched out his neck, his pink little nose sniffing the back of my hand. I laughed. His nose tickled. When I raised my hand to the top of his head, he did not back away. I lowered my hand and scratched his head behind the ears. He seemed to like it and moved closer to me, lowering his head so I could reach better. His hair was silky and thick to the touch.

I turned toward my wolf friends. "Come on, we're going to have to find something else to eat. Roscoe is off the menu."

RECORD III

LONG-DISTANCE CALL

W HAT I WAS LOOKING AT couldn't be, but it was—a painting of Chris. An older Chris, probably eighteen to twenty years old, but it was Chris. His hair was brown with streaks of blond and was partially covering his eyes. It had that blown, windswept look. His eyes were unsettling. They were brilliant blue, like blue sapphires... but my Chris had green eyes.

This Chris had a stature that exuded power. He presented a very daunting figure, especially with those piercing eyes. I could feel them now, as if they were searching out my true essence. They were mesmerizing.

It took all I had to break away from them before I lost control. I quickly closed my eyes and turned my head away for a moment to regain my composure. I turned again to the painting and gazed upon it. His eyes were still piercing, riveting, but no longer seemed to be searching my very being.

I walked up closer and knelt on the bed so I could reach the painting. I had to touch it. The painting seemed three-dimensional, like I was viewing through a window. I could almost believe Chris was standing on the other side. That was why I felt compelled to touch it... it was so real.

Now that I was kneeling in front of the painting, I could see more. It truly was like looking through a window. I could now see behind Chris if I moved slightly to the side. What I was able to see changed depending on my viewing angle.

I got up my nerve and raised my hand to the height of Chris's face. I cautiously extended my index finger out to his cheek. I gasped; my finger went right into the painting! I extended my other fingers and caressed his face, feeling his nose, lips, chin and even down his neck. His skin felt warm and responded to the pressure of my fingers. Chris needed to shave. He had three-day stubble! I could feel the contour of his body, but I could not reach my whole hand in, just my fingers up to the knuckles. There was some force stopping me from going any further.

What really was peculiar was the fact that I could touch a tree and feel the coolness and texture of its bark. Yet the tree was far in the background, maybe miles behind Chris. I reached up and felt his hair, which was moving with the breeze that was present. I continued up over his head and touched the clouds. My fingers met a slight resistance as they penetrated the cloud and droplets of water even started clinging to them! This was in 3D, but somehow a morphed version. This was no... painting!

Next to Chris was a majestic wolf. It was metallic silver in color with rust-colored highlights. What a beautiful creature. I had never seen an animal with that coloring; it was out of this world. This wolf was an imposing creature standing more than four feet high from head to ground with long, lean, muscular legs and slightly oversized paws. It gave off a majestic aura. Chris's hand was gently caressing its head. I studied its face, which was beautiful, even exquisite.

I touched its nose with my fingers; it was warm and slightly moist. I ran my fingertips up the bridge of its snout, following a light line of fur that formed a hint of a cross above the eyebrows and down the snout. What a strange marking. Did it mean anything?

The fur was soft and inviting. I continued up its head and touched Chris's hand. I could feel the blood flowing in his hand. His flesh responded to the pressure of my touch. It even turned white as I pushed hard and then turned normal again as I released the pressure.

This was real, as if they were suspended in time. I looked directly at the wolf's face. This was a female. She had feminine features: high cheekbones, slender nose, long, thick eyelashes. Yes, for sure a female. She had an air of royalty but not in a pampered or prissy way. She seemed more like a warrior princess. Our eyes met. What vivid, striking blue eyes she had... the same powerful eyes as Chris.

Suddenly, I felt a consciousness invading my mind, as if someone was sifting through my thoughts, my memories... searching for something.

I was totally helpless! I couldn't even move a muscle! It was as if someone or something had commandeered my body.

I heard a voice.

"*Who?*"

It was a strong, very authoritative voice; it was feminine.

Then I heard a masculine voice responding firmly but respectfully.

"*Mom.*"

The presence withdrew immediately. I started falling backward, my body totally limp. I had no control whatsoever.

Two forcible but gentle hands caught my shoulders and gently lowered me the rest of the way to the bed. I was staring rather closely into an upside-down face. The face pulled away, allowing my eyes to focus clearly. I breathed a sigh of relief. Even upside down I recognized that face... it was Barry.

He said rather jokingly, "Hi, Jennifer. I don't usually get any company in my bedroom."

I stammered, totally flustered. "I-I- I'm... sorry."

Before I could say another word, he swung my legs over the side of the bed and had me sitting up. He sat down next to me and looked at me with concern.

I blurted, "I didn't know where to go. I can't go back to my place."

He tilted his head slightly, and I continued to explain.

"Someone or something is after Chris and me; they want to use me against Chris. They think I'm dead, and I want to leave it that way, so I can't go back to my apartment."

"Go on, Jennifer," Barry gently bade me.

"When I knocked on your door, nobody answered. I tried the knob, and it was unlocked, so I entered. I called out then looked around to see if you were home. When I came to your bedroom, the door was ajar, so I peeked in to see if you were there. That was when I saw that!" I pointed behind me.

Barry stood up and said, "Oh, you saw my painting."

"Painting!" I said, "That's no painting! And what's more, why is it of Chris?"

He started to say something about Chris, and I cut him off, rather tersely, I might add. "Don't tell me that's not Chris! And we just met only a day ago! Have you been stalking us?"

Barry gave a big sigh. "Yes, that is of Chris... and no, I wouldn't call it stalking."

"What would you call it?"

He raised his hands. "If keeping an eye out for you two is stalking, then guilty as charged."

My gaze shifted to the so-called painting on the wall. He followed my gaze.

"That is called a Facsmere. I acquired it just over six years ago. It is like, well, a living picture, a window into the events of the past, present, or future." He eyed me with concern, not sure how I was going to react.

I stood up. My mind was reeling, trying to make sense of it.

Barry remained silent, waiting for me to say something.

I continued thinking out loud. "This is portraying Chris being older. He looks to be eighteen or twenty years old and in fine physical condition. Therefore, I know he is alive now and will continue to be so into the future... at least up until six years from now. Isn't that right?"

Barry looked at me.

I looked back and said again, "Right? Isn't that right?"

Then it hit me. I blurted, "Is this just a possible event that might not happen, just one of many possible ones?"

Barry gently replied, "For now, this is the most likely outcome, but present and future actions may change this. Only God knows if the Facsmere will remain this way."

That just burst my joyful hope.

Barry patted me on the shoulder. "Jennifer, Chris is safe and well for the time being. That is what's important—now."

"I know that. I just... I heard him say, 'Mom.'"

Barry looked at me as if he had lost his best friend and said, "What do you mean you heard Chris?"

"Just before I fell backward, and you caught me... something or someone sent a surge of power. It was like being hit by lightning. It took control of my body and was searching or probing my mind! I think it was... that... wolf." I pointed toward the picture. "I instantly tried to think of nothing, or nothing in particular, just random meaningless thoughts."

Barry looked at me incredulously.

"Then I heard the word 'who' very forcefully in my head. I couldn't even respond. I was in shock."

Looking down, I spoke quietly at first. "Have you ever had something trying to sift through your mind? Picking through thoughts and memories, discarding some, then moving on and just leaving behind a jumbled-up mind. Then I heard Chris's voice respond unequivocally, 'Mom.' With that word..." I pointed at the painting. "That... that wolf withdrew its searching of my mind, and my body immediately started collapsing backward, with no one in control. That was when you caught me." I looked up directly into Barry's eyes and said assertively, "It was Chris's voice."

Barry turned and sat down on the edge of the bed. He was quiet for a few moments with his eyes shut. Then I heard him take a deep breath, and his eyes opened.

"I never ever thought that would be possible, being able to communicate in real time with the spiritual constructs of a Facsmere!"

I said, "What's the big deal if Chris spoke and I heard it?"

Barry hesitated before he spoke again. "Facsmeres are what might be, what have been, or what are, but they are not the actual or real counterparts. Besides that, communicating through space and time, where past, present, and future coexist—the ramifications are immense. Think about it. An enemy could use them to coordinate their attacks... prepare the past, coordinate the present, and inform the future."

My mind started to reel... wait till Barry finds out what else could be done with them! I walked around Barry's bed to the painting, to the Facsmere, and leaned over. I touched it, and my fingers went right through to Chris's face.

I gently caressed his cheek and said, "Mom is here." I didn't know why I was so calm about something so bizarre, so impossible.

Barry rushed over and pulled me aside. He then reached out and touched the Facsmere. His fingers just remained on the surface. He looked at me with a rather puzzled expression on his face. He inclined his head to the side, deep in thought.

Then he asked, "Can you enter into the Facsmere?"

"No. Only my fingers enter, but only an inch or two."

Barry breathed a sigh of relief. "That's a good sign. It means that they are not easily opened."

"Why?" I asked.

Barry looked at me, astonished. "Our enemies could use you or whoever had the ability to enter a Facsmere. They could then attack us anywhere the Facsmere depicted!" Barry cringed at that thought.

"Maybe it's just this Facsmere... or Chris," I said hesitantly.

He raised his hand to quiet me. "That's enough on this right now; we will talk more on this later. By the way, Jennifer, do not talk to anyone about this, even to Chris... until you are taught more about our enemies and how to determine if they are present."

I thought to myself, *This is getting rather deep—scary, even—like a waking nightmare.*

Barry gently grabbed my hand and said, with a big grin on his face, "Let's adjourn to the living room. We've been in the bedroom long enough."

I was once again sitting on his overstuffed couch, all comfy. It was just yesterday evening that Chris and I were sitting on this same couch. It seemed so much longer ago than that.

"Jennifer, stay in the now," Barry said. His facial expression and tone of his voice then turned serious. "We need to get you out of town before people start coming back. They and the creatures must believe that you and Chris were lost in the sandstorm."

I looked at him, rather perplexed. "I never told you that creatures were looking for me."

"Not now, Jennifer. We have more pressing matters to attend to. I'll go over to your apartment and get some of your clothes."

"Just bring my gray-and-white backpack. It's in my bedroom closet, on the top shelf."

He was back in a few minutes with the backpack. I went into the bathroom and changed into what I had in it. I came out wearing a pale-yellow summer dress with pink flowers and a white bonnet. The dress went down to the floor, covering my running shoes.

Barry looked at me and nodded with approval. "No one will recognize you," he said with a chuckle.

I gave him a reproving stare.

He just shook his head. "You are not the stereotypical Amish young lady. I'm just saying, I can't see you being in the patriarchal family system; you are too self-reliant, independent, and assertive."

I smiled and nodded then performed a quick curtsy.

He laughed.

Barry made me feel at ease. I had only known this man for a few hours, yet I would have trusted my life to him. That was not typical of me. There was just something about this man that allowed me to disregard my usual cautiousness.

A strange thought, off topic, popped into my head. I have these kinds of thoughts pop into my head every now and then. It seems my brain is always analyzing things around me, what's happening or will happen. It's a trait I passed on to Chris. I am not even consciously aware, but my mind is always attentive, working to protect me. Sometimes it just takes a few moments, maybe minutes, while other times, it may be hours or even days before my mind pops up with an answer or thought about something that might affect me.

The thought that popped up was *Why was Barry here?* A good question! Everyone else in the town had evacuated, but Barry had showed up at just the right time.

I saw Barry looking at me, reading me. "Jennifer, like I told you and Chris earlier, I'm always where I need to be. And right now, that's here!"

Eerie, very eerie. Had this man just read my thoughts, or just read my body language in the context of our conversation then just made a good, educated guess about what I was going to ask?

Before I could say anything more, Barry announced, "Your ride is here."

"My ride! Who's giving me a ride?"

He just shuffled me out of his apartment and outside to the parking lot. Guess who was out front, or should I correctly say, out back since we were at the back of the apartment complex. None other than my good friend Daisy!

"Hi, girl, I hear you need a ride to a new place to live."

Barry guided me with his hand lightly on my lower back. "Your chauffeur is waiting."

"Hi, Barry."

Barry waved. "Take good care of her."

Daisy had already grabbed my backpack and thrown it into the back seat of her pink Volkswagen convertible.

"Get in, Jenny. It's a beautiful day for a ride."

We made it out of town without anyone and, I hoped, anything noticing us. Daisy was her perky self, all bubbly, yakking away at ninety miles an hour. I don't think that gal ever ran out of something to talk about. That was my Daisy. How could you not love her?

"Daisy, how did you know I needed to get out of town in a hurry? Did Barry call you?"

"No, I've never met Barry till just now."

Have you ever got the feeling that everyone else around you knew something you didn't? Well, recently, it seemed that way for me. I knew God was working in my situation, but boy, he seemed to have people showing up at the most opportune times. Maybe there was an organization that was watching over Chris and me.

RECORD IV

WE PICK UP SOME BAGGAGE

D AISY LOOKED OVER AT ME. "Girl, why don't you get normal?"

I knew what she meant; I took off the bonnet and struggled with pulling off the sundress. Do you know how difficult that is when you have on a seatbelt?

Finally, with a little squirming and twisting, I was able to pull the dress up over my shoulders and head, extracting one arm at a time. I rolled the dress and bonnet into a tight ball and leaned between the seats, looking for my backpack to stuff them in. Wouldn't you know, my backpack had fallen behind my seat. Not thinking, I undid my seat belt and leaned over between the front seats to reach for it.

Daisy decided on having a little fun with me. She accelerated quickly and then suddenly stomped on the brakes, hurling me into the backseat. Then she swerved from side to side while continuing to speed up and slow down quickly. I was rolling around back there like a ball in a pinball machine, making all the lights and bells go off.

She just laughed. "Haven't I told you numerous times, young lady, never to take off your seatbelt in a moving vehicle?"

"Okay, okay," I said. "I give."

She slowed down as if she was going to let me get back into my seat, then she lurched the car forward, almost sending my face toward the dashboard, but then instantly braked, making me fall back into my seat.

I quickly belted up.

Daisy was notorious in teaching people not to break one of her rules in a memorable way. You never forgot her lesson.

I looked at her as I swept a few strands of hair out of my face. "There's going to be payback," I said in a rather husky and raucous tone.

Daisy laughed, blew off my playful threat, and said, "Now you look Jennifered."

"What do you mean by that?"

Daisy smiled. "You dress comfortable, so practical, so laid back."

I said, "Anything wrong with that?"

"No, if you don't ever want to find a man and get married." She added, "You'll never get noticed dressing like that all the time."

Hey, I am a practical person. Jeans, running shoes, and a pastel T-shirt—that is my norm.

"Give me a break. I just came back from running through a sandstorm, no less."

She chuckled. "Just trying to get you to raise the bar, get a little wild, get a little crazy, in a Jennifer way."

I supposed I could learn from Daisy on having a little flair, going a little wild with what I wore. Daisy was a master at this; whatever mood she wanted to express that day, you knew. It was right in front of you, staring you in the face.

Today, she was a mid-1960s, carefree, spirited, single, accomplished woman. She had on form-fitting capris in canary yellow with a brown-and-pink plaid pattern. Her blouse was loose fitting in a cream tone with subdued pink stripes. Dangly purple hoop earrings and bright-yellow open-toed loafers finished off the look.

Back in the mid-1960s, you were in fashion if you wore brightly colored plaids and stripes together and accessorized with colorful eye-catching earrings, shoes, belts, and scarves. She fit in with today's fashion or should I say no-fashion... anything goes... wear whatever you want. You wouldn't or couldn't miss Daisy.

"Daisy, with what you are wearing, no one would or could miss you. Aren't we trying to go incognito?"

She threw her head back and laughed. "Girl, they will notice me... they won't even remember seeing you!"

"Daisy, you are your usual subtle self. By the way, where are we going?"

You would think that would have been the first thing I asked when we started our trip, not twenty minutes into it.

"We're going to Salt Lake City." She announced it as if I already knew.

I gave her a questioning look. "If we are going to Salt Lake City, then we should be on Highway 65 going to Albuquerque."

"Oh, we're taking the scenic route through the mountains; it's actually more direct and quicker." Then she gave me a mischievous smile.

I looked at her. "Isn't this the way to the City of Rocks State Park?"

"Yes, it is, girl."

Pastor Dan and Sandy used to take us, my siblings and me, camping there three to four times a year. "Are we meeting them there?"

Daisy just gave me a quick impish smile, and I knew that meant yes. I was ecstatic. How I loved those two. Mom and Dad; that was who they were to me. They had not given birth to me, but I considered them my real parents.

Time couldn't go quickly enough now that the anticipation of seeing them again was high, even if it had only been three months ago that we were last together. It now seemed like an eternity.

We pulled into the City of Rocks State Park. It was almost like being on another world, like Mars. The terrain looked so strange, with weird-shaped, tan-to-brownish-red rocks up to fifty feet tall jutting up out of the ground in patches as if someone had planted rock seeds all over the park. Some of the rock pillars had other large oblong-to-round rocks on top. It was just plain out of this world.

Dan and Sandy always liked camping near the rock formation we called the God Rock. It looked like a hand with just the index finger pointing up toward heaven.

Daisy was weaving around the rock patches, following the dusty gravel road till she came to the God Rock. There they were, the entire family: Dan, Sandy, Tad, and Sarah. I was out of my seatbelt even before Daisy stopped the car.

I gave her a quick look as if to say, "I'm sorry."

She smiled. "I'll let you go this time without any repercussions."

I ran out to meet my family with kisses and hugs. My dad always gave me the biggest hugs. His powerful arms completely enveloped me, smothering me with his caring embrace. Then he would twirl while lifting and swinging me about. Light on his feet he was.

Tad and Sarah were laughing. They thought my hug from Dad was the most theatrical and comical of all. He had a unique hug for each of us kids. Even though now we were all grown adults, he still hugged and played around with us.

Mom came over, and he hugged both of us together, lifting us off the ground in one big, loving embrace.

We talked and reminisced around a bonfire that Dad and Tad had started. It was fun like the good old days; we even toasted marshmallows and made s'mores.

I watched as the smoke rose into the sky, its various tendrils spiraling upward and uniting, eventually forming one large column of smoke. This column would then continue united for a span then break apart into individual puffs of smoke that drifted upward into the sky, each on its own unique path into the heavens. It was beautiful to watch and reminded me of a person's life.

Each of us are like embers in a fire that then produce tendrils of smoke. That's our individuality, our personality making up our lives. Then we unite and grow together, and that's family. We mature and separate, living our unique lives, influencing those around us, making our stamp on life; that's the tendrils of smoke that break away into puffs, floating away on the separate currents of the wind, the paths of life.

That brought a few tears to my eyes, as it brought thoughts of Chris to my mind. He was breaking away, spiraling into his own journey of life. I was hoping that this was just a short excursion from each other, and we had many years yet as mom and son. He wasn't even eighteen yet! I hoped that after we had each gone our separate ways fulfilling our own journey of life, we would reunite many times. And each time we came back together, we would grow even closer.

I closed my eyes and gave a tender prayer to God for this.

Dad broke the silence. "Jennifer, you and Chris will have many more close times together—we all will."

That comforted my heart. Dad didn't know what I had prayed for, but God did, and God let me know through my dad that He had heard it and confirmed it.

Back to being less solemn, I smiled and saw the tenderness in the faces of my family.

Dad continued, "Chris is very resourceful, adaptive, and reliant. You, Jennifer—well, all of us—have nurtured and grown these strengths of Chris's. It will bode very well for him.

"He is not alone in this. God has given him some great friends and companions that he will grow with and rely heavily on. They will become very formidable together.

"Jennifer, God has directed us to send you north, to Salt Lake City. I don't know what awaits you there, but you will be safe and continue along a journey of your own."

Dad was great at pastoring: comforting and nurturing people, God's people, and especially his own family.

Daisy spoke up. "We better get going."

"Not till after we eat," Sandy interjected.

"Eat? We just had dessert. Now we're going to eat?"

We grilled out over the open bonfire. Food tastes so great when you're camping. Why is that?

We broke camp, each giving hugs and saying our goodbyes. I got into the car. Daisy didn't come right away; she was talking with Dad and Mom.

She walked over to my side of the car and flung the keys at me. "It's your turn to chauffeur me."

Her little car looked to be fun to drive because of its smallness. Even though it didn't have power steering, power brakes, or automatic transmission. How did Daisy know I could drive stick?

"Hey, Daisy, how did you know..."

"Your dad and mom told me. That was what we were talking about just now... and how I was to look after your heart."

It wasn't till much later that I found out there had been much more to that conversation. My dad was concerned about Chris and me but didn't want to let me know.

He told Mom and Daisy that he felt something really big was brewing spiritually. Something was spawning an evil that hadn't been seen for thousands of years. My mom spoke up, telling him that he had taught Chris the Word of God and kindled Chris's deep love for God. It was this love that would carry Chris through whatever dangers he might face.

She also reminded my dad of what God had revealed to him more than fourteen years ago, before I had even come into their lives: that I would have a son, and he would be a man after God's own heart.

My mom continued, "He will be able to rise to this threat, whatever it is. God will enable him, empower him, and protect him."

That put Dad at peace.

I would never have guessed he had any concerns that day. He was taking care of my heart, and Mom was taking care of his.

We drove on through Silver Lake City to St. John's. It took us a little short of four hours. We needed to feed the car, and I needed a pit stop. We pulled in at the first gas station in town.

Daisy filled up the car while I decided to check out the restrooms. I was nearly crossing my legs; I'd had to go really, really bad for the last half hour. The restroom at the back of the gas station was surprisingly clean. These outside restrooms are usually scuzzy; you almost need a hazmat suit to safely enter one.

I found a stall and parked myself on the white porcelain throne. My hair was a mess. I started running my fingers through, fluffing it up, trying to get the sand out. It was everywhere on my body. No matter how well I brushed myself off, I still had traces of sand. What I needed was a nice hot bath or shower, but I didn't think that was going to happen anytime soon. I took off my shoes and pants and shook each vigorously; even my socks had sand in them.

Suddenly the restroom door opened rather abruptly. Someone flung it hard.

Loud, heavy steps entered, with labored breathing cutting the peacefulness of the room. It was not Daisy coming in.

I became seriously still and quiet, intently listening. Then I heard the faucet turn on and the vigorous washing of hands.

I breathed a sigh of relief and told myself, *See? Nothing to be concerned about.*

The water shut off, and I could hear hand towels, one after another, being torn from the dispenser, then rather roughly used before being tossed indiscriminately to the floor. I was still not making any unnecessary noise.

The room became deathly silent, and then loud labored footsteps started shuffling back and forth in the room. There was a sound like hyperventilating. No... it was sniffing, like that of a dog following a scent. It was crazy. The shuffling about of loud, heavy steps, along with the sniffing, became frenzied... even frantic.

Then I heard and felt banging on one of the sides of my stall. When I looked down, there was a person trying to look underneath the stall. It was sniffing like a dog. The person must have been immense, because it looked like it was having trouble peering underneath my stall.

The wall started shaking violently. I snatched up my shoes and socks in one hand and my pants in the other, ready to make a wild dash out of there.

I happened to look up, and to my astonishment, a face was peering over the top.

I screamed.

Hey, it startled me. Boy, it was a homely face. It was that of a woman who had a ruddy complexion, with long, stringy black hair that looked like it hadn't been washed for weeks. The face was rather round and very pudgy, with a large, flat, pushed-in nose and eyes that were bulging out. To top it off, she had a triple chin. You know, three folds of loose, fatty skin hanging under the chin.

She kept sniffing while she was trying to look at me. She even started to drool. Ew! I didn't believe she could even see me. Her head just rested on top of the stall. She was too short to tilt her head down at an angle to get a clear view of me, thank God!

I tried unlocking my stall door, but it was jammed.

The wall started shaking again, and then there was pounding on the door. This thing was trying to get in! If it threw its whole weight against the door, the latch wouldn't hold.

I scurried underneath into the adjacent stall with my clothes and shoes in hand. Just in time! I hadn't even fully stood up when the door of my original stall exploded inward with her tumbling in. I came out of the other stall in a mad rush.

She was struggling to turn herself around. Boy, that woman was large. I ran at her and threw all my weight at her backside. My momentum and her weight caused her to hit the back wall with such force that I could hear the tile wall crack, and then water started spraying all over.

The woman's head had dislodged the toilet valve. She was thrashing and gurgling as water sprayed into her face.

I kept throwing my body into her, slamming her head into the wall, hoping to knock her unconscious. This just made her more furious. She tried even harder to turn around in the stall but just wedged herself in even tighter.

Just then, Daisy rushed in. "My gosh, girl, what is going on?"

I was so shaken that I couldn't even blurt out a response.

Daisy pulled me back and grabbed the only thing she could find to protect us: a plunger.

The woman finally extricated herself by deciding just to back out of the stall. She had worked herself into such a frenzy that she backed into the washroom sinks on the far wall. The impact broke one of them off the wall and sent her and the sink to the floor with more water spraying forth.

It was like we were in a water park. Water was spraying everywhere.

Daisy ran up and started hitting her with the plunger. She even used it like a plunger and plunged her face. If it hadn't been such a scary situation, it would have been comical.

Finally, Daisy picked up the small porcelain sink that had broken off the wall, wound up, and gave a big swing to the side of the woman's head. The sink connected for a knockout punch. The woman crumpled to the floor.

Daisy was breathing hard. She had used all her might to take that woman down.

"I hope you didn't kill her!"

Daisy looked at me. "It would take more than that to kill her! Come on. Help me drag this lady out."

"What? Are you kidding me?"

"I'll explain later."

It took both of us to drag her out of the now-flooded restroom.

Daisy brought the Volkswagen around back. She opened the trunk, or more correctly the hood, and pulled out a roll of duct tape.

I asked, "Do you always carry duct tape with you?"

Daisy laughed. "Girl, duct tape has over a thousand uses, and this makes a thousand and one! I always have a couple of rolls with me. You just don't know when a girl's going to need it."

She taped the woman's mouth, her eyes, and even around her ears. Then she rolled the woman over, taping her wrists together behind her back. She went four or five times around her wrists and then did her ankles likewise. Daisy was puffing from all the exertion.

She threw the tape into the trunk then said, "Get her legs. I'll take her arms."

"You can't seriously be thinking of throwing her in the trunk," I said. "She must weigh at least four hundred pounds!"

It took all we had to roll her into the trunk. Daisy slammed it shut, looked at me, then said in a motherly but concerned tone, "Go get your clothes on."

I had been so caught up in the struggle that I'd forgotten I had only my shirt and underwear on. I went back into the restroom and grabbed my pants, shoes, and socks off the wet cement floor. I quickly slipped the pants on using my one free hand. I didn't bother putting my socks and shoes on. I just threw them in the car.

Daisy was already in the driver's seat. "Get in. I'll drive."

Daisy drove back around to the front of the station. She went inside and got two sodas. She told the clerk that the restroom had been vandalized. It was trashed, with water spewing out from under the door. She waved goodbye to the clerk, and off we drove into the sunset.

"I can't believe you went inside and told them about the restroom, especially since we kidnapped a person."

"We didn't kidnap. We woman napped."

"Oh, like that's any better!"

Daisy patted my knee. "Relax. They won't think we did the trashing of their restroom. We just reported the incident."

"Well, how about the woman?"

"Hopefully nobody will know she's missing, at least not until we are far, far away." Daisy looked at me. "Tell me the whole story of what happened in there."

It took nearly half an hour going over it because Daisy was asking me so many questions. Then she was quiet for a spell.

Daisy finally looked at me and said, "You somehow got the attention of a scout; we endearingly call this type a doggie. They act kind of like dogs, relying on smell and hearing. They're excellent at tracking, and they are very tough to seriously injure."

I said, "What do you mean, a doggie? That was a big, homely woman."

"You'll learn more later. For now, suffice it to say that this doggie picked up your scent, and we can't let it report that it found you. What or who was trying to get you and Chris today must not find out you're still alive!"

Just then, we heard a wailing sound. It was rather distant but was becoming louder and more distinct. I started getting sick to my stomach. It was a police siren.

I dared a look behind us. Yes, I could see the flashing lights.

"Now what do we do?" I asked in a high-pitched, nervous tone.

Daisy put a hand on my shoulder. "Just calm yourself. He may not be after us."

"Oh, yeah," I said rather sarcastically, "there's nobody else around for miles. Do you see any other cars?"

"Just relax and follow my lead."

It took only a matter of seconds before an Arizona state trooper came up right behind us. Daisy pulled over. The trooper got out of his car and soberly walked over to us.

Daisy spoke up. "Hi, Officer. Anything wrong?"

He kind of sized us up. I hoped we didn't look threatening.

The trooper tilted his head toward us and, in a low Southern drawl, "Where you girls heading to?"

"We're going to see relatives in Salt Lake City," chimed Daisy in a nonchalant tone.

He walked around to the front of the car. He was making me downright nervous. "It looks like you must have a lot of baggage; your front end is almost scraping the road."

Daisy peered at him through the windshield. "Did we do something wrong, Officer?"

The trooper put his hands on his hips. "Well, you seemed to be swerving, and you even crossed the centerline a few times. I thought maybe you'd had too much to drink."

I spoke up. "We just got too deeply into our conversation."

He started walking back toward us. Before I could breathe a sigh of relief, the front of the car started rocking from side to side. I got sicker to my stomach.

The trooper got very serious. "Do you have something *alive* in your trunk?"

Daisy retorted, "We just have baggage in the trunk."

"Pop the trunk. I mean the hood," he ordered.

Daisy reluctantly pulled the hood release. The trooper lifted the hood. He was deathly silent for a few seconds then said in a very cool but authoritative voice, "What are you two doing with a woman gagged and bound in your trunk?"

The woman started thrashing again. The whole car swayed from side to side.

"Do you know what the penalty is in Arizona for forcibly abducting a person, possibly with the intent to do bodily harm?"

Daisy spoke up quickly. "We had no intent to do harm; we just didn't want her to make a scene."

For a while there, I thought Daisy was going to start the car and run the trooper over. Then she seemed to think better of it.

The trooper walked back over to us, started shaking his head, and got a big grin on his face. He looked behind us and motioned with his arm. A large black SUV pulled up in front of us. The trooper smiled even more then said, "They are here to pick up that baggage you have."

I looked at him dumbfounded. "What?" I exclaimed.

He just laughed. "I'm sorry, girls, but I just had to have some fun with you."

I looked at him with a motherly glare. "You almost got run over by Daisy here. And fun? You call giving us such a fright fun?" I was rather hysterical. "You scared twenty years off of my life!"

While we were talking, three men from the SUV put the woman in their vehicle and drove off without a word.

I looked at the trooper. "How did you know?"

"I just received a call from the organization, alerting me that my help was needed. A scout had possibly identified one of our people." He straightened his shirt a bit then hooked his thumbs in his belt. "The three men that did the pickup I don't know anything about. I was just told they would be here. My role in this is to make out a police report saying that a pink Volkswagen had a flat tire and that I assisted. The report will specify that I reached into the trunk to get the spare. If it ever comes to suspecting you two in abducting that woman, there will be a trooper's field incident report containing no evidence of any involvement concerning this woman. Besides, we already have people doing a containment story for the station incident."

He must have noticed the look of bewilderment on my face, because he added, "Your friend here might be able to fill you in. Now let me get what I need for my report, and you two can be on your way."

After taking our information, he tucked his notebook into his shirt pocket. "When you get to your destination, seek out Shark and tell him Trooper Donaldson says hello."

"What's a shark? Who's a shark?"

He just smiled. "He's a great guy. Don't let the nickname and his demeanor scare you off."

He then said goodbye and left.

Don't you just hate that? You ask questions to understand something, and you're left with more questions and less understanding than you had initially. Oooh! I think he did that on purpose.

Daisy chuckled and, noticing my annoyed look, tossed me the keys. "It's your turn to drive."

We drove in silence for a while, just chilling out. I breathed a sigh of relief.

Daisy broke the silence. "The organization was formed a long time ago and is called the Aharonites after Aaron—Moses's brother. The name means 'light bringer.' They are to bring light and protection to God's people."

Her eyes never left the road.

"From Aaron's descendants, three organizations developed: the Aharonites, the Templars, and the Freemasons. The Aharonites and the Templars are the military side of bringing light, or in other words, dispelling and fighting the darkness, the evil, and protecting God's people."

I quickly interjected, "Barry spoke of enemies... are they this darkness, this evil?"

"Yes!" Daisy answered then briefly made eye contact. "We call them the Daimonia."

"Daimonia?"

"It is the Greek word that has been translated 'demons.'"

"Demons!" I blurted, inadvertently jerking the wheel a bit. "Demons are after Chris and me!"

"Jennifer, we refer to them as Daimonia. The word 'demon' has been so corrupted by man over the centuries that it no longer connotes the truth. They are not the hideous, malformed creatures portrayed by myths, books, and movies. The Daimonia have no physical form. They must inhabit a person, animal, or object to function in our world."

"What about the monstrous creatures that were after me in the desert? They had a physical form."

Daisy shook her head. "I do not know about them, though I am sure there are others who do. Jennifer, you will be taught more about this at camp. I am just giving you the basics. Now back to the Templars.

"They allowed themselves to be led by men instead of God, leading to their eventual infiltration by the Daimonia in the guise of godly men. They now are promoting darkness in the appearance of light. The Aharonites chose to be directed by God. We are organized as a network of people with God in charge. The organization is made up of many people, each doing their own part, using their own talents and abilities as needed."

"What is your function, Daisy?"

"I am a helper."

"What's a helper?"

"It is a person that does various duties in assisting others in the organization. When we get to Salt Lake City, you will be assessed to see where you fit into the organization."

"You have to be kidding... assessed? What? Are they going to have me take placement tests? What if I don't pass? How do they know I even want to join?"

Daisy shook her head. "They already know your answer. Remember, we are directed by God. Besides, Barry gave them a pretty good heads-up that you would do anything to help your son, Chris. What better people could you have to help you?"

I thought to myself, *Barry must be held in high regard by the Aharonites.*

We drove on through the night, taking turns driving and napping. Daisy was just fun to be with; she was so carefree and spontaneous.

We decided to stop at a little all-night roadside diner. It looked like a mom-and-pop place out of the 1960s. The décor was oversized chrome ceiling fans, a chrome-accented counter and barstools, and a black-and-white tile floor. The walls even had photos and prints of popular 1960s music groups plastered all over.

Daisy and I took a booth in a quiet corner. It had big, high-backed black leather seats. The table's top was made of 1960s vinyl phonograph records overlapping one another and covered with a thick sheet of glass. This diner was so nostalgic that it gave me a yearning for days gone by.

We each had the diner's specialty: a hamburger called the Haystack. It was made with a large homemade pretzel bun that nurtured a half-pound burger with sautéed mushrooms, all topped off with haystack fried onions drizzled in a special horseradish-and-mustard sauce. The haystack onions on top of the burger made it deliciously outstanding.

Just as we finished our meal, several truckers came into the diner. They seated themselves at the far end of the counter from us. One of them started acting peculiar, moving his head, side to side and slightly upward, in a stop-and-go fashion. It seemed like he was sniffing the air. Daisy put out money for our bill and tip, got up, and grabbed me.

"Let's go, girl… now!" she said quietly under her breath.

She herded me to the doorway as she said good night to the waitress. Out the door we went. It was rather fast but not noticeably in a rush.

Daisy headed straight for the car, and no sooner was I buckled in than she pulled out of the parking lot.

After a few minutes on the highway, Daisy finally stopped glancing in the rearview mirror. She breathed a sigh of relief and looked at me. "Girl, do you have a sign on your back saying, 'Here I am. I'm the person you're looking for. Hey, come get me'?"

I turned toward her. "Was that another scout? Another doggie?"

"I think so. I wasn't going to take any chances. You must be on their most-wanted list. I don't think they're actively looking for you, though—they do believe you're dead."

"How do you know that?"

"They are not out in force," Daisy replied.

"Maybe I should change my perfume."

Daisy laughed. "They are not smelling your physical scent. It may look like that, but the scout is actually picking up your spiritual scent, your essence. We need to get your spirit de-scented!"

"Can that be done?"

Daisy shook her head. "I don't know, but if you're around more of us, we will somewhat mask your presence. You'll be a lot safer with people of the organization around you."

We arrived at the outskirts of Salt Lake City about four hours after meeting Donaldson, the state trooper.

"Where are we actually going?" I asked.

Daisy was having fun with me, being all aloof and secretive. "You'll know when we get there."

"Have you been there before?"

"No, this is the first time."

"How come you seem to know where you're going?"

Daisy shook her head side to side and laughed. "Nothing supernatural. No revelation guiding me, just good old Google."

"What?" I blurted.

"I was given the location by your dad, then I just googled it. It's just that simple, just that normal. God expects us to do what we can do, and He'll do the rest."

"Wait, wait... my dad told you when we were at the park? That can't be... we were already sent on our way by Barry."

"Jennifer, your dad gave me the location of where to take you, when to pick you up and where you would be... days ago."

I thought, *This is definitely God working.* He had it all arranged even before the sandstorm... my getting out of town, my family being at the park, and my new place to live. I had many more questions flood my mind, but one prevailed. "Daisy, how long are we going to stay at wherever we're going to be?"

"Oh, I'm not staying, girl. I need to get back to work." She glanced at me. "Most of us live normal lives. Just now and then, we are needed." She paused for a moment. "Except for the Hunters."

My eyes lit up. "Hunters! Who or what are the Hunters?"

Daisy continued, "There are some groups within the Aharonites, like the Hunters, that work full-time for the organization. It is their life to help others and protect God's people from the Daimonia. What I know about them I have gathered from others in the organization that I've come in contact with.

"The Hunters do battle with the Daimonia. They hunt them down, cast them out, and just cause havoc with them subjugating humans."

Just then, Daisy slowed down then backed up a few hundred feet and took a road that veered off the highway. This was very desolate country and getting even more so the farther we distanced ourselves from the lights and noise of Salt Lake City below. We seemed to be winding through the foothills and canyons of the mountains that surrounded the city. It was beautiful yet disconcerting. The darkness was pierced only by starlight; the moon was in hiding.

It became unnaturally quiet. We heard no sounds from any animal or insect life, no sounds from the city below us. It was as if we were the only two beings left on Earth. The only sound that broke the stillness was the constant hum of the car engine.

We seemed to be passing through a cavern with sheer vertical walls that were too smooth and too straight to have been naturally made. We followed the twisted curves of the passageway. It seemed to get narrower as we progressed farther in.

It was very dark, then suddenly, it went completely dark. There was no more starlight. Even the light from the headlights of our car vanished! It was very eerie. I couldn't even hear the sound of the engine. Actually, there wasn't any sound at all. Had I become deaf and blind? Small shivers commenced through my body.

I turned to Daisy. She'd better still be here! Panic was starting to rise in me. I called out to Daisy, but no sound proceeded from my mouth. I was starting to tremble, losing what little sanity I had left. I reached out for Daisy. She was there but didn't respond. Suddenly, I heard my voice yelling, "Daisy!" over the hum of the engine.

I felt a touch on my arm then heard, "You don't have to yell, Jenny. I can hear you just fine."

I looked around. It was still very dark, but I could start to make things out again... the stars were back. Everything was returning to normal; the close, sheer vertical cavern walls were even gone. Now we were in a large open area, surrounded by canyon walls in the far distance. Our surroundings and senses had returned to the norm.

Up ahead, I could just barely make out two large figures standing on either side of the road. They were very tall and very massive, standing fifty feet or more. I could make out a faint glow coming from the center of the foreheads of the two figures. I inhaled quickly, and Daisy patted my leg gently.

I nervously croaked, "Are those... are those... cyclops?" Maybe we hadn't returned from the Twilight Zone!

Daisy didn't say anything right away. She just continued to motor on toward them, but her hand was now grasping my leg rather firmly.

As we came closer, we could finally make out that they were just statues. We both relaxed and breathed a sigh of relief. It was just light from a star reflecting off the foreheads of the statues.

Daisy drove between the two immense statues. Up ahead, spanning the road, was a large sign that read Welcome to Camp Aharonite.

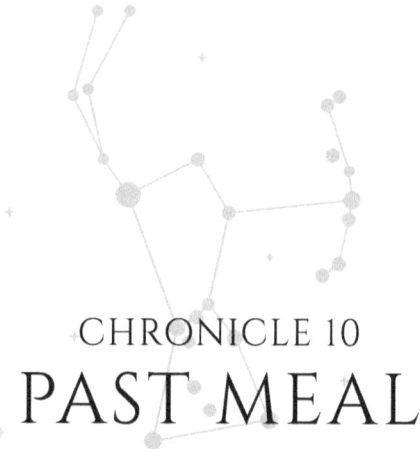

CHRONICLE 10
PAST MEAL

T HE SMELL CAME TO MY nostrils... Jennifer's homemade
fettuccini alfredo. My nose smelling food that wasn't there
and a growling stomach, that was not a good sign. We
needed to find some food. That meant either foraging or hunting.
I'm not much of a vegetarian. I'm a carnivore, a meat eater; you
know, a boy. That meant we were going hunting. Technically, I am
really an omnivore because I do regularly eat fruits and veggies.

It would've been nice if our doorway had opened up to a place
that was civilized, a place that had grocery stores, restaurants, even
fast-food chains like... a McDonald's. But no, we had ended up in
the Land That Time Forgot. If possums grew this big here—and
Roscoe, I believed, was just a young one—I didn't want to see the
carnivores here. There were probably saber-toothed tigers that
would tip the scales at four thousand-plus pounds and maybe even
dinosaurs. Hopefully no raptors!

I turned toward my companions. "Let's be a little more careful
about what we track. We were fortunate this time."

My mom would have been proud of me for saying we had been
fortunate and not lucky. From a young age, Jennifer had instructed
and corrected me that there was no luck, whether bad or good.
God was all sovereign, and nothing happened without Him. Yes,
He could play an active or a passive role. In the passive, He just let

the natural laws He'd set up determine the outcome. But she would never forget to remind me that God was still always in control, and nothing was left to chance.

We walked along the mud flow with the wolves in the lead, Roscoe next, and then me. Roscoe seemed to have adopted us as his new packmates. Did possums run in packs? I thought they were solitary creatures. I shrugged. I had four wolves that seemed to understand me, even read my thoughts. Why not a two thousand-pound-plus friendly possum? That was easy enough to accept, wasn't it?

The mud flow started to diminish. It was becoming waterier, finally giving way to a naturally flowing river. I did not know what kind of fish or creatures lived in the water here. I had a feeling it would be best to be very careful by the river's edge. I was not being irrational in my concern, because no sooner had I finished this thought than a big bird fluttered down gently in the middle of the river. This was a large, and I mean a *large* bird with probably a nine-foot wingspan. It was beautiful, mainly all gray with white tips on its feathers and a long yellow beak. It reminded me of a crane or heron, a fish eater.

The slight ripples on the river's surface from its graceful landing hadn't even ebbed when the water around the bird started to collapse into a rapidly swirling vortex. A very large set of jaws with immense, needlelike teeth appeared at the edge of the vortex and engulfed the bird in one large bite.

I was *not* going in the water here! I backed away even farther from the river's edge, a good hundred feet.

We continued moving upriver, where we came to a large rock-strewn area spanning it. This was the remnants of sections of mud flows that had released their contents as the river slowed from broadening out. It did not look easy to cross, but I was in no way going to swim across this river.

Tassi had the same idea. We picked our way through the rocks, gravel, silt, and entire trees that had been torn out of the earth.

Roscoe meandered through it at a slow but steady pace. He was low to the ground, had broad feet and his long claws gave him great traction. The wolves were not faring as well with their narrower paws and longer legs sinking into the muck and silt between the rocks. Many times, they sank up to their bellies. Over a few of the nasty stretches, they resorted to crawling.

I, being a two-legged creature, had it the worst. The best way for me to cross was to walk on top of the uprooted tree trunks or jump from rock to rock, which made my traveling very slow. This was not fun, but we needed to get back to the other side of the river... that was where our doorway, our portal to home, was.

We had come to a long stretch that was all mud. There was no way of traversing this without getting mud caked. Then I had an idea. It was a wild one, but I had to give it a shot.

I whistled then yelled, "Roscoe, Roscoe... come here, boy."

He actually stopped and turned his head toward me. I crouched down and patted both knees with my hands in a quick, emphatic rhythm while saying, "Come here, boy. Come. Come here, Roscoe."

He turned and came lumbering over to me. I patted his head and said, "Good boy. That's a good Roscoe."

Stroking his neck, I leaned over and grabbed his fur then slowly pulled myself up enough to swing my left leg over his back. I straddled his back facedown and waited. He didn't move. He didn't panic. Gently sitting upright, I stroked his neck with both hands and said, "Giddy up!"

Roscoe started slowly making his way to the other side. I was elated and couldn't hold back my smugness. I was grinning from ear to ear. Tassi and the other three wolves were looking at me with expressions of shock, amazement, even disbelief. It was priceless. Yes, it was probably a very comical picture: a boy riding a colossal possum.

I could not hold back my exuberance, waving my hands in the air and yelling, "I'll see you gals on the other side!"

Hey, no longer did I have the muddy chore of picking my way through the rocks and debris or sinking up to my knees in mud.

This river was immense. It was miles across and I bet, in stretches, six to eight hundred feet deep, not unlike the Amazon River. I was glad we had a shallow stretch, where a temporary rock-strewn bridge had spanned the river. I could already see the muck and debris being replaced with pockets of water. The constant river currents underneath the surface were making passageways through the submerged rocks and debris. Some of these larger pockets of water formed pools that we had to walk around. This was evidence of what was being done under the surface. Soon, the river would be flowing full bore, and then this bridge would be gone, scattered over miles and miles of river bottom.

The wolves and even Roscoe stopped and sniffed at some of these pools. A few of the larger pools of water had trapped fish and other creatures. They were looking for supper... hopefully something that would not have us for supper! Kora and Cami, the playful and care-free members of the pack, were romping in and out of one of these large pools that we had come to. They were jumping and splashing in the water. It seemed as if they found something, because every now and then, they backed away quickly from the rippling circles that broke the surface.

I thought I saw something splash through the surface. Was that a fin? If it was a fin, this would be a mighty big fish. It had better be a fish and not some sort of prehistoric creature. Kora and Cami quickly backed out of the pool.

Roscoe noticed their sudden departure. He came sauntering over and entered where they had exited... with me still on top of him.

Roscoe pawed the water where there was just a faint ripple left from a recent disturbance underneath. He pawed again, going a little deeper. This time he connected with something, because suddenly, he got excited. I could feel his body tense up, then his tail stiffened upright into the air. He began using both paws. The water began to boil. Roscoe reeled backward onto his back two legs, lifting a gigantic fish partly out of the water. I clung to his fur with both hands, holding on tightly so as not to be thrown off.

The fish struggled, slapping the water with its tail and trying to wriggle free. Kora and Cami were in and out of the water, trying to get in on the action. Roscoe paid no attention to them or to me dangling precariously on his back. What a commotion! Tassi just sat and watched the five of us with amusement and interest.

Roscoe grabbed the fish behind its head with his razor-sharp teeth. The fish thrashed and wriggled even more, pulling him down on all fours. Roscoe vigorously shook his head from side to side, trying to break the neck of his prey. This fish was not going to give up; it fought hard, pulling Roscoe's head under the water. Roscoe then started backing up toward the edge of the pool. There was a back-and-forth tussle between fur and scales. Fur was winning.

Kora and Cami stayed in the action but didn't venture further into the water than the shallows. Now and then, one of them would get smacked in the face with the fish's massive tail, and it would send them floundering in the water. They would get back on their feet, shake the water off and regain their composure before entering the fray again. It was quite comical even though it was a death struggle for the fish.

Tassi seemed to be enjoying herself just watching everything unfold... like me trying to stay on a broncin' buck—or should I say broncin' possum. For those of you who have not watched old TV westerns, the saying "broncin' buck" comes from the words "bucking bronco."

The tussle became more frantic, and I was thrown into the water. I quickly scrambled out of the water by swimming and wading. I needed to get out of harm's way.

Finally, Roscoe dragged the eight-foot-long, two hundred plus-pound fish onshore. It was a mudfish, more properly known as a bowfin. This fish was not unlike the bowfin we have today, just a lot larger.

The bowfin is an ancient relic descended from prehistoric times. This fish breathes air, unlike a normal fish. It also has scales that look like armor, formidable jaws lined with rows of razor-sharp teeth, and a dorsal fin that starts a short way behind its head and goes the length of its body. The tail is not like a regular fish's either; it's oval shaped, like the head of a badminton racket.

The fish continued to flip and toss itself around on the rocks, trying to get back to the water. Tassi came over and grabbed it behind the head and gave one mighty flick of her neck, using her entire body weight. There was a loud snapping sound, then the fish lay motionless.

Tassi released it, backed away, and sat down. I sure wouldn't want to be her enemy. She dispatched that fish with a quick, military-style execution, with no last rites. To Tassi and the others, it was just our meal. I like to hunt and fish, but I still felt bad taking an animal's life. In our modern-day societies, food is for the most part packaged and ready to cook and eat. If I had to kill for my food all the time, I guess it would become easy and just the natural order of things.

In no time, I had our fish dressed and on a spit. Roscoe ate all the innards. Yuck! The wolves did not partake of the inner delicacies of the fish. I guessed they had now acquired the taste for meat, cooked meat. My bad. Well, they really weren't your normal wolves.

We ate our meal. The mud fish tasted very good over an open fire. Now, I didn't know whether I was eating breakfast or supper, because here, it was early morning, but when we'd left the cave, it was early evening. This popping in and out of time couldn't be good for one's digestion, let alone one's sleep.

I decided to try to take a nap while drying my clothes in the sun. We were far enough from the water's edge that we didn't have to worry about being someone's meal. I felt safe with my companions. They could fend off anything that came our way, maybe even a *T. rex*. I smiled to myself. Nila would probably enjoy an encounter with a *T. rex*.

We still had a long day ahead of us, and a nap would reinvigorate our minds and bodies. We needed to ascend nearly a thousand feet and then trek a couple of miles inland to get back to the portal. I found a large flat rock and sprawled out on it as if it was my comfortable bed at home. I dozed off almost immediately.

I woke with the wolves curled around me. Tassi had her head on my chest, Nila was curled up around my head, and Kora and Cami each had a leg. Roscoe was at the foot of the boulder; he was too big to fit on my rock bed. I was surprised I had fallen asleep so quickly and remained sleeping. This place was forever with noise. If it wasn't the rushing river pounding and gurgling over the rocks, or the numerous waterfalls, it was a myriad of eerie animal noises. None of these noises did I recognize. They were loud, incessant, and daunting, to say the least. This was no place for an insomniac to visit.

I didn't know exactly how long our nap had lasted, but the sun hadn't moved perceptibly in the sky. I would have guessed less than a half hour. I felt reinvigorated, ready to continue our trek; this truly had been a power nap. We had a mile to go before we would be on the other side of the river to start our climb. This river was immense, and we were very fortunate to have this temporary rock-strewn bridge. In no way would I attempt to swim across this river. Just thinking about what had happened to that bird earlier brought shivers that ran the whole length of my body.

We made it to the other side, not too muddy or fatigued. Now we needed to rise up in life, about a thousand-plus feet. This seemed like a daunting task, but like my mom taught me, if the problem is too big or appears insurmountable, then just start. Don't look at the end. Break it into smaller parts that are easier to complete. Where to start? Well, we were at the bottom, so that seemed as good a place as any.

We had found a section that was not so cliff-like, but it was still a steep bluff. We started walking at a gentle incline up the bluff. When it became too difficult or became a dead end, we reversed and walked upward at an incline in the opposite direction. We were zigzagging our way up the bluff in what is called a switchback. If you have ever traveled through the Rocky Mountains, then you have experienced switchbacks. Those mountains and this bluff were too steep to go straight up.

The wolves were making a steep switchback. Now at times we met a dead end and had to backtrack, and sometimes we even had to climb straight up for a small stretch then start another switchback. Numerous times, I grabbed onto Roscoe's tail to help with the climb. He didn't seem to mind it. The first time I tried it with one of the wolves, it was quite different. Nila stopped, turned her head, and gave me a contemptuous glare.

I looked her directly in the eyes and said, "You gals have four-legged traction and are built lower to the ground. I'm just a mere two-legged creature!" With that said, Nila proceeded forward. It seemed from then on, the wolves would rotate position so that they would each get a chance to tail me up the climb. I could count them in for a helping hand—well, scratch that, a helping tail—when needed.

We made excellent time even with some setbacks. At times, the section of the bluff we were on would start sliding downward. We would then quickly scramble to one side or the other. Many a time, we went down twenty to fifty feet before we could get off the sliding section. Thank God for not sliding all the way down to the bottom then having to start over, or worse yet, being entombed beneath tens of feet of rock and mud.

We finally made it to the top of the bluff; all I could see up ahead... grass. It was well over my head, allowing us no visual markers of our position. The portal had to be in front of us, due east, since that was the direction the sun rose. I decided to call it east since I needed some reference for determining direction... even though this might not be Earth. Now depending on how far we had walked upriver from where the mud flow had taken us, we could be south or north of the portal.

I called Tassi over. "Now let's see how good at tracking you gals are!"

Without another word, the wolves set out in different directions, trying to pick up our original trail. Well, no one went west since that would have been over the bluff.

I looked around, even though I could not see anything but grass. I chose a direction on a whim—no, scratch that, a gut feeling. It was strange and hard to describe, but when I thought about the portal or pictured it in my mind, I felt a slight tug in my gut, drawing me to take a certain direction.

I already had a soft voice that I heard that helped me from time to time, so why not my stomach? That soft, still voice only whispered when there was a need for guidance or information that I could not obtain through my five senses... like imminent death approaching. Just kidding! It was not something that I was meant to rely on. I was supposed to rely on myself to the best of my capabilities, and when that was not enough, then a whisper would come—or in this case, a twinge from my stomach.

You may think it was unwise for me to proceed on my own, but my stomach said, "That way." I wasn't going to let the wolves have all the fun, and the wind was coming toward me. Therefore, no animal would get my scent except downwind, over the bluff. Nothing would follow us up that bluff... if it did, we would be in big, big trouble.

I heard a lot of noise and commotion in the tall grass. Was it my wolf friends? Like I said before, this place was constantly noisy. I bet even when nighttime came, there was no relief from the din.

The grass started to rustle in four different directions. *It better be my wolf friends.* No sooner had I finished that thought than I was immediately hit in the chest by something big and hairy! I started backpedaling, trying to keep my balance, and then I was hit on the left side and then instantly on the right side, the two blows canceling each other's effect. I was being gang tackled. I struggled to stay upright, but their weight was taking me down. The final blow was another frontal assault, and the momentum from that impact sent us all flying backward. The tall, dense grass cushioned our fall. I was at the bottom of the heap, totally laid out by four big, furry bodies. I lay there for a moment, stunned by what had just happened. I was learning that wolf play was rather rough and could come at any time.

I bellowed, "It's bad enough that you've covered me in bruises from head to toe. But one of these times, you gals are going to give me a heart attack!"

To someone watching, it was probably hilarious, all the stumbling, thrashing, and crashing through the grass with four wolves smothering me.

"You know that you gals have broadcast our whereabouts to every hungry predator in the area!"

I rolled out from under them but was immediately besieged with nudges to my sides and licks to my face. I couldn't help laughing. I squirmed, trying to get away from the extreme tickling sensation. That just intensified their efforts.

"Okay, okay! I give up! I surrender!"

They finally relented amid my pleas to stop.

"Whew!" I wiped my face with my forearm, drying off the tears of laughter. That was intense.

A thought came to my mind: Where was Roscoe? In all the commotion, I had forgotten about Roscoe! I called out his name a few times, to no avail. I guess he must have taken off. I'd miss the big guy. I hoped we would see each other again, but for now I had to focus on our immediate concern, finding the portal.

I looked at Tassi and the others. "You couldn't pick up our previous scent, could you?"

They lowered their heads to the ground, affirming my suspicions. I had a feeling that here, things were accelerated, like growth and decay. The soil was probably teeming with microbes and bacteria, making quick work of any matter on the ground like our sloughed-off skin cells, hair, and body oils. Those are what make up a scent trail that can be tracked. I bet our scent had been gone in less than a half hour.

It made sense, since the mammals were so big here, that for them to have a fighting chance against the predators, scent tracking played a minor role in catching prey. The predators would have had to stumble upon a very recent site of their prey in order to track it. That was both good news and bad news for us. The good news was that predators had a very short period of time to come across our trail to track us, but the bad news was that we wouldn't be able to sniff our way back to the portal either.

The wolves followed my lead for a change. That was new. Now I had no idea where I was going; I was following my gut. If I felt a twist or tightening on the left side of my stomach, I went left. If it came on the right side, I went right. If we came across a trail, I took that and then veered off when my stomach said to. The trails made it a lot easier than fighting the dense, man-high grass.

Being guided by one's stomach is weird and not logical. Someone or something was drawing me toward it. I was hoping the portal was doing the beckoning, not some weird creature craving us for its supper.

The man-high grass became boy high and then child high rather quickly. I gazed across the beautiful panoramic view. All the eye could see was prairie and three large grassy knolls. Yes, you heard me right: three grassy knolls. But only one was beckoning me. It was to the far left of us, about two miles away. It wasn't my stomach that told me this was the one. It was the two yellow arches that formed a very large, stylized M. I shook my head in amusement. My Orion constellation buddy sure had a sense of humor. There in front of us stood the golden arches of McDonald's! You know, the iconic golden arches of the McDonald's fast-food restaurant.

My four friends looked up at me with smirks or grins on their faces.

"Now what are you girls up to?"

I didn't know how wolves could grin, except Kora. She always looked like she was grinning because of the whitish fur that curved up at the ends of her jaws. Suddenly Nila, Kora, and Cami bolted off toward the golden arches.

I yelled, "Wait for me!"

I sprinted after them with Tassi by my side. Into mile two, we were all together, and then I poured it on. Only Tassi kept up. We waited for what seemed like an eternity—well, perhaps just a minute—till the three slowpokes showed up.

I laughed and mocked, "You let a mere human beat you! You gals are getting old."

They each gave me a deep, throaty growl and bolted past me, disappearing through the golden arches.

I looked at Tassi and said, "Here we go again!"

Before entering the arches, I looked up... and to my amazement, there was a large red sign spanning the first arch. It had the words *Over Six Billion Served Here* in bright yellow.

I shook my head and yelled, "Very funny, Orion, very funny. What a droll sense of humor you have."

We walked through the first arch into absolute nothingness. Ahh! Limbo land.

Tassi stayed by my side as I counted twenty-five steps and stumbled back into our lair, the House of Orion. It was good to be back home. I already missed the place, and I hadn't even spent a night.

Tassi stopped, turned, and looked at me with a surprised expression.

"Are you trying to tell me something?"

Before I could say anything more, the word *surprise* formed in my mind. I looked at Tassi and asked, "Are you doing that? Are you talking to me in my mind?"

She stared intently at me, then I definitely heard the words *surprises coming!* in a strong feminine voice.

Just then, the wolf trio came bounding out of the far side of the chamber toward us.

HAWAIIAN DELIGHT

WOLVES ARE FAMILY-ORIENTED CREATURES. WHEN you are accepted as one of the pack, you are in for life. They are very caring, nurturing, and protective, but their sense of play is another thing. They are robust and rough in play. Wolves bring roughhousing to an entirely new level... at least these wolves. Now I refer to them as wolves, but even very early on I knew that they were not wolves. Tassi speaking to my mind definitely confirmed this.

I could see the three wolves running full steam toward Tassi and me. I wished I had a football helmet and shoulder pads. I could already anticipate the hurt. Oh yeah, the "wolf love"—the more pain, the greater the love!

They were excited, totally full of it, whatever "it" was. They were cutting one another off, launching quick sneak attacks from the back, grabbing and pulling one another's tails, and ramming into one another. Each was trying to remain in front. It was comical. They even ended up entangling one another into a large fur ball that rolled and spun out of control. The spinning force was strong enough to fling each wolf outward to the hard, smooth cave floor. They skidded spread eagle on their stomachs, twisting and turning till their momentum finally subsided.

Each dazed wolf got up slowly, shook it off, then got back into the race. They were now within twenty yards, all still jockeying for lead position. I moved behind Tassi, hoping she would end up with the brunt of the attack. Fifteen feet away, Cami and Kora launched themselves at us. I waited for their midair impact, then just before they would've reached me, I dove under Tassi.

"Hah!"

They creamed Tassi.

But I laughed a little too soon. Where was Nila?

WAPPPP!

I was blindsided by Nila. We both tumbled to the floor.

Even though these wolves were very independent and competitive, they always relinquished those traits for the common goal of the pack. In this case, creaming Chris.

We rolled and tussled on the ground, and the other wolves decided to join in on the fun. I had four wolves each trying to get a piece of me. Finally, they were exhausted. Well, scratch that. They were up and romping around eagerly, trying to get my attention. All three were either twirling in circles, chasing their tails, or yapping and barking. It was playful bantering, but they all seemed to be trying to get my attention.

"What do you gals want?"

The three stopped, looked toward the opposite side of the cave, then at me, then back at the opposite side of the cave.

"You want Tassi and me to follow? Okay, I guess I'm curious at what the surprise is too." I looked at Tassi. "Aren't you going to say anything, girl?"

Tassi motioned with her head toward the opposite side of the cave.

The wolves started at a trot then picked it up to a full run. They made a near-instantaneous full stop just before we reached the cave wall. Not me. I couldn't stop that fast. I tumbled uncontrollably to the cave floor, taking Nila with me.

I enjoyed giving her payback, even though it wasn't intentional. Wolves can stop on a dime. Well, I guess most four-legged creatures can, thanks to their lower center of gravity, forepaws for better braking, and a tail to transfer some of the momentum in the opposite direction. Humans? We just fall. Usually ungracefully.

Kora was hopping up and down as if she was standing on hot coals. She truly was a kid at heart. The other wolves were animated too. I looked up at the cave wall. There in front of us was an arched doorway. Above the doorway was a sign that read—Home Sweet Home.

"Is this my surprise?"

It was painted in purple, red, and yellow with very stylized and flowing lettering. It had been done by someone young, carefree, and artistic.

Hey, don't look at me—I always analyze things and determine the kind of people that are behind them. This had been done by a boy, even though it had a girl's flair. It had neat, graceful lettering and beautiful pastel colors. In fact, a large boy, one who liked to eat, a laid-back surfer dude. I didn't know if I had been right about the cashier at the grocery store, but today, I had a feeling I was going to find out whether this character analysis was accurate or bogus.

The wolves encircled me and literally shoved me through the doorway. We entered a large open chamber with a floor of sand, spanning out to a beautiful mountain range in the distance with mesquite and Joshua trees and loads of cacti.

This House of Orion was immense... to have a chamber within with a desert and a mountain range! So very koosh.

The wolves turned toward me. They looked like they were staring behind me.

"What...?"

I turned around. There, built into the cavern wall, was a dwelling, like that of the Gila Cliff Dwellings in New Mexico, but this was much more modern. It was made with smooth, evenly sized adobe bricks with all the doorways and windows having rounded edges and corners. It even had skylights. All these openings were just holes—cutouts in the walls and roof. Hopefully it never rains here!

Just then, out from around a rock formation near the dwelling came… I couldn't believe my eyes—out sauntered a *very* large possum.

"Roscoe? Roscoe!" I couldn't believe it.

He came moseying over to me and the wolves.

"Is *this* the surprise, girls?"

He nudged my hip with his head. I scratched him around the ears.

"What a surprise! I thought you just took off, and we wouldn't see each other ever again." I gave him a big hug around the neck. Then I looked at him, somewhat peeved, and shook my head in disapproval. "You could have taken us to the portal. But we probably wouldn't have followed you anyway." I laughed.

A thought then occurred to me. Yes! Roscoe had been here before—maybe he even lived here.

I turned toward Nila. "You must have picked up Roscoe's scent as he headed out of the cave… leading to our little jaunt to the Land That Time Forgot."

Just then, I caught a whiff of smoke. It smelled like someone was grilling out—another surprise? Well, Tassi did change it to "surprises." I allowed my nose to follow the delicious smell.

Still underneath the rock overhang, we came around a large outcropping of rocks at the edge of the house. I stared in disbelief. There I saw a very large boy roasting a pig over an open fire.

He must've heard our approach. He looked up with a big smile on his face and said, "Aloha!"

I played it very cool and waved all friendly-like. I walked over, extended my right hand, and introduced myself.

He grasped it firmly with both hands and gave a big up-and-downward handshake while saying, "I am Momi, and I have supper for us." He pronounced his name like "Mommy."

He had natural golden-brown skin with thick, straight jet-black hair. His face was round, somewhat larger than normal, with a body to match. Momi looked like a small sumo wrestler—very well-fed. His clothes... now where had I seen that fashion statement before? Oh yes, Barry. Momi had on an overly large Hawaiian flower-print shirt, khaki shorts, and neon-green running shoes. Unlike Barry, this dude was Hawaiian, and the attire actually seemed to fit with him.

I couldn't help but ask if he knew Barry. Momi didn't know a Barry, but when I asked him where he had gotten the clothes, he said Pahli brought them to him. I asked him to describe this Pahli. It was an exact description of Barry. I knew it! Barry was tied to much of what had recently happened to me.

I walked over to what Momi was roasting. It most assuredly wasn't a pig. Momi said it was a ground squirrel. This was one big ground squirrel, enough to feed all of us and still have plenty of leftovers. I hadn't noticed till then that the wolves were lying down around the fire. Roscoe, on the other hand, was sneaking a closer look at the ground squirrel being roasted. They all were waiting for supper to be served.

Momi moved toward Roscoe and shooed him away.

"Have you met Roscoe before?" I asked.

"He keeps distance from me, but cleans up, eats scraps."

"So, he's your garbage disposal."

Momi tilted his head as in not understanding. He didn't know what a garbage disposal was. Momi spoke slightly broken English. It reminded me of the English from the King James Bible, English spoken in the 1600s.

"Momi, how long have you been here?"

"Almost a full moon," he said.

"You mean a month."

"Yes. That's the word for it."

There was something peculiar about Momi. He just seemed out of place... out of time. That was it. Out of time!

Before I could say anything more, Momi announced, "Time eat." The wolves and even Roscoe perked up at the mention of supper. You've heard the expression, "Food soothes the savage beast." Well, no, that's wrong. It's "Food is the way to a man's heart." I think this works just as well for wolves and possums.

Momi was an excellent cook. Now I knew why he was big. I'd thought I was full from the mudfish we had eaten earlier, but I couldn't pass up the roasted ground squirrel. It smelled so good! Roscoe even ate all the remnants. That possum was a walking disposal unit. I think he was the surprise referred to when Tassi had said "surprise" the first time. Then when she said "surprises," I think that was for *Momi* and my new *home sweet home.*

Momi was a happy-go-lucky guy, carefree, just fun to be around. If you had elevated stress levels, they would just dissolve with Momi there. My prediction of the person that did the sign, *Home Sweet Home,* was spot on.

Maybe I had revelation?

I had so many questions to ask Momi, but before I could, he grabbed me. "I show you *home sweet home.*"

He led me inside. I couldn't believe it. What a cool pad. It had three floors. There was even running water and electricity. I didn't know where the water or electricity came from. Did the cave have its own water and electric utility plants? I didn't even see any water pipes, electrical outlets, or power cords. It had a bathroom with a shower and a toilet, and they all mysteriously worked. All the comforts of a modern home in a cave. What was next?

The place had a high-definition TV, high-speed Internet, and two large laptop computers. The kitchen was fully functional with a fridge, a stove, a microwave, a coffee maker, a blender, and even a food processor. The fridge was stocked with food, and even the cupboards were chock full. Where did they have a grocery store around here? Well, I was not going to be concerned about the how and why. I decided to just enjoy it.

Momi was excited about showing me all the cool stuff. He was like a five-year-old, touching this, lifting that, emitting "oohs" and "aahs." Finally, he calmed down, and we sat on an overstuffed couch. We were on the second floor, overlooking the open area in the center, from which we could view the downstairs and the third floor. This was a pretty koosh open-concept pad. We chatted and kidded around for a while before I asked the question that was gnawing at me.

He was from the past like I had presumed. Actually, about the 1850s. Hawaii was his home, and get this: his father was King Kamehameha I. Yes, this would make Momi a prince. But being a king's son or daughter during that time period in Hawaii was not necessarily a good thing. The possibility of him ever becoming the king was remote. This was the time when every ruling family was trying to position itself to rule all of Hawaii and the surrounding islands. And... he had twenty-six other siblings. Now he was moving up in the family line of succession. Over half of his brothers and sisters were killed or went missing, never to be seen again. Assassination was a common method of succession within and among ruling families during that period.

One night, the children's quarters were raided. The next thing Momi knew was being here. He was okay with this. He loved having all the amenities, especially all the creature comforts of our time. Pahli, or Barry, seemed to show up from time to time to acclimate Momi to his new life in the twenty-first century. Momi was adapting very well. He was all for adventure, and that was what Barry had told him he would have with me. I wondered if Barry had told him what we were up against.

Momi started asking me questions, like when we were going to start our big adventure. I sidestepped the question by introducing him to Tassi, Nila, Cami, and Kora. The wolves took to him. Momi gave them all ear rubs. He seemed great with them and Roscoe. Momi was one of those people that others just immediately took to.

I looked over at him and said, "Hey, you're going to be my Tonto."

Momi gave me a quizzical look. "What Tonto?"

I laughed, patting him on the back. "Well, my friend, we're going to have to bring you up to speed."

He looked at me again and said, "Speed? You make me fast? Do I look like I go fast?"

I laughed again. "I'm sorry. I'll have to be careful how I say things."

I needed to get Momi more current in the twenty-first-century vernacular. How to do that? Then it came to me. Hah! I would have him watch educational programs for kids. I wondered if we got the public channel with all the educational shows.

"Hey, Momi, want to watch some TV?" I pointed at the large flat-screen TV on the adjacent wall.

"Oh, like watching talking box."

"Good. You can watch all the kids' educational programs. It will allow you to learn as a child learns about our world."

I turned on the TV and surfed the channels till I came to *Martha*. Momi spoke excitedly. "I like talking dog. Fun watch."

I quickly flipped the channel. *George* came on.

"Oh, I like fun monkey too."

"Now, Momi, you do know these are cartoons."

"What cartoon?"

Oh, this was going to take a lot of work!

"Just watch and learn, Momi. If anything seems out of the ordinary, like talking animals, or animals acting like people, then it's not real. You can ask me, and I will explain."

I left Momi watching *Tiger's Place*. I hoped he didn't believe that stuffed animals and toys were alive.

This pad was cool, and I was okay with having a roommate. Yes, I know what you're thinking: I have four wolves, but they weren't exactly roommates. They didn't talk, at least not to the point of having a conversation—yet! I shook my head and started rubbing somebody's furry head.

I looked down. It was Tassi by my leg. "Hello, girl."

I didn't know what had happened earlier. I wondered if I really did hear the words from Tassi, "Surprise—surprises coming," in my head. It was probably just my imagination, my mind playing tricks on me.

I continued to walk through the place, haphazardly surveying it. I came to the fridge and was starting to open it when my eyes were drawn to the brand name of the fridge: Manna Elite. I opened it and found water bottles from Spirit Springs, cheese from Heavenly Farms, and Moses's Extreme Barbecue Sauce.

I closed the fridge door. Manna Elite? I shook my head. Manna was the food from heaven that God supplied to the Israelites for the forty years they wandered in the wilderness after their escape from Egypt. Now it was a brand of refrigerator?

I walked over to one of the laptops. It said Mark V with Genesis 3 Operating System. The flat-screen TV was made by a company called Prophecy. My Orion constellation dude was playing around with me—again.

I put my head out the nearest window—well, it really was just a hole in the wall—and yelled, "Very funny, Orion."

Momi was looking at me. I shrugged and said, "I was just talking to my angel friend."

We continued watching educational shows. Momi had questions galore. Tassi was curled up with her head on my lap. Kora snuggled near Momi, and Cami and Nila rested by our feet.

Momi looked over at me. "I'll make drink."

The next thing I knew, he was up and in the kitchen. I heard slicing and dicing then the sound of a very powerful blender. It sounded like the revving up of multiple race cars waiting for the start flag to drop.

I went to see what Momi was doing. "Hey, what are you making?"

"Doing smoothie," he proudly answered.

I found out Barry had shown him how to make a smoothie. It became his favorite drink.

He had just crushed the ice and was adding the fruit—I believed it was fruit. The only thing I was familiar with was the coconut. "This dragon fruit, rambutan, and jackfruit. I put in."

I said, "Ram's butt? What's ram's butt?"

"No, no. Rambutan."

"Oh, that's a big help."

He smiled. "Google it." He laughed.

I learned that Barry was teaching him to use computers and other tech stuff. Well, I did google it, and I found out that this fruit was not native to Hawaii. Nothing that we're familiar with is... pineapple, coconut, sugarcane, and bananas are not indigenous to Hawaii either. Basically, the only edible things indigenous to Hawaii are tubers and roots—yuck.

He turned on the blender again to blend the fruit in, but he forgot one very important step: the blender top! We had smoothie thrown all over us and the kitchen. All four wolves had been with us in the kitchen when we started, but when I looked now, they were all at the doorway. And they were all clean. I had some very perceptive and observing wolves. If they could giggle, they would have.

Momi made some more smoothies while the wolves and I cleaned up.

I raised my smoothie and made a toast to Momi. "You truly are a Hawaiian delight, and so is this smoothie."

We both laughed and gave each other a high-five. He was already becoming modernized; he knew the high-five. That was not real current, but it was a start.

We watched some more TV. Momi fell asleep, and I channel surfed. Boy, did we get a lot of channels and networks. Most of them I didn't think existed on normal cable or satellite.

Then I came to a network that jolted me out of reality. It was called—get this—the Christopher Gahrlan Network.

CHRONICLE 12
MY TV TALKS TO ME

HAVING YOUR OWN TV NETWORK might seem to be really koosh. In my case, I didn't think this would be so. I was probably going to find out more things—scary things. The shows on this network I don't believe were going to be comedies, musicals, or lighthearted dramas.

Orion—oh! I needed to find out his real name, because calling him Orion was confusing. Anyway, he had already given me a glimpse into the unfathomable, the unimaginable, something right out of a pure horror flick.

Mark my words, there would be a show giving me glimpses into my future. It would most likely be scary glimpses. Have you ever read a book or seen a movie that had prophecy about the characters? Isn't it always, yes always, very twisted and convoluted? Their totally obscure meaning continuously changes as the story unfolds. Yeah, you know what I mean. It does bring suspense, but did I really need suspense?

I hesitated a moment before I clicked the remote to see what programming was available on the Chris Gahrlan Network. It was inevitable that I would have to take a look. I knew it was going to be like opening Pandora's box, but I had to know. A stupid thing to do, but like I said, inevitable!

The first show was titled *Angels*. I watched a few minutes. "...
and he, Amemnon, was not selected by God to be one of the three
archangels but became Lucifer's second-in-command."

I thought to myself, *What a bummer, so close to being one of the
top three! Well, that show was not so bad. Let's see what else is available
for my viewing pleasure.*

Click. Next up: *Anarkons: Fact versus Fiction*. Hey, I was feeling
lucky. Click: *Spiritual Warfare*. Click: *History of Orion*, a documen-
tary. Click: *Prophecies of Chris Gahrlan*. Yeah, I knew something like
that was going to happen. I clicked on it: *Momi and Chris take a
road trip*. Oooh, that was helpful. I didn't think I wanted to know
any more. Click, click, click. The channel would not change, and
neither would the TV turn off. The remote had stopped working!

I went up to the TV and flicked off the power button. The TV
stayed on! I shook my head and mumbled to myself, "This is not a
good sign."

The screen flashed, then the message continued. "...Momi and
Chris take a road trip to Camp Aharonite near Salt Lake City, Utah."
Well, that didn't sound so bad. It didn't say anything about battling
menacing creatures or fleeing for our lives.

I clicked the remote. To my relief, the channel went to a show on
the Spiritual Shopping Network. Items up for sale: pieces of cloth
from the Apostle Paul's tunic. The host was an older-looking man
with long white hair and a beard to match. Now get this—he was
wearing a Hawaiian flower-print shirt with chartreuse flowers on it,
gray khaki shorts, and neon-yellow running shoes. The man started
describing the cloth remnants and how they had healing qualities.
They even came with a one hundred percent money-back guarantee.

The channel suddenly went all blue, then a message flashed
across the screen, saying, "This show is preempted by a special message from our sponsor, Melchizedek."

I felt something brush my side. It was Tassi. She was looking
intently at the TV.

"Have you been watching?"

She inclined her head and perked up her ears. I gave her an ear rub, and she nuzzled my hand.

"Yeah, you were probably watching the whole time."

Then a booming voice came over the TV, a voice I was all too familiar with—my Orion pal.

"Hi, Chris. Do you like your new pad?"

"Hey, it's pretty boss, and Momi is, too… thanks. By the way, is your name Melchizedek?"

"Yes, it is. You didn't really think my name was Orion?"

"Nah, I just wanted to see how long you would put up with me calling you that." I laughed.

An image came into my mind of a large stylized golden 'M.'

"Hey, Melchizedek, the portal to the Land that Time Forgot, it is a large 'M', is that referring to you?"

He smiled, then grinned and whispered, "That refers to the name of the place you went to… though I do like your name, *The Land that Time Forgot*."

He just left me hanging. He wasn't going to give me the name. Just let me wonder. It wasn't a need to know at this time apparently. Now I wasn't going to let on that I even cared and just dropped the subject.

Orion—no, Melchizedek—was easy to be with. I could be myself around him. I didn't think I could be anything else anyway; he had that kind of presence. Now that name of his was just too long, too formal, and too ancient. I will call him Mel, that sounded much more koosh.

"Mel, how come you're talking through the TV?"

There was a slight pause before he responded.

"Mel… I like the sound of that… *Mel*." He said it slowly, pausing slightly on each letter. He continued, "I just thought it would get your attention. Besides, it's fun spicing things up. Don't you agree?"

I hesitated. I didn't want to give him a yes or no. He didn't need any encouragement either way. I thought I would give him a dose of his own medicine and not answer him, but in turn ask a question of my own.

"Why are you here?"

"Chris, I thought we could have a little one-on-one time and bring you up to speed. Let's continue our discussion of Daimonia.

"The Daimonia are organized in a hierarchy. There are the Daimones, which are the generals, and the daimonions, which are the troops, the grunts.

"The Daimones will stay hidden, unperceived in the person they are inhabiting. They remain very discreet. It is difficult to find where the Daimones, the generals, are operating from. They orchestrate from behind the scenes by controlling hundreds, even thousands of daimonions, which in turn possess and control the individual person. There may be more than one daimonion inhabiting a person. They like to be in groups. They're very communal. But they never really get along with each other. Totally doesn't make any sense... but that's daimonions." He snickered.

"Now, your mission, should you take it"—Big Mel laughed but then became serious— "is to hunt down and take out Anarkos's Daimones, for without them, there is no coordinated effort among the daimonions."

"At least you don't have me going up against the big gun right away—Anarkos.

Mel, how am I to hunt these Daimones of Anarkos's?" Before he could respond, I blurted out, "They will seek... hunt me!"

Mel gave a slight downward nod, for a silent yes. "Chris, just keep moving forward, taking it in small manageable pieces."

"More like chunks," I quipped.

I decided to lighten things up by getting off topic. "Big Mel, what are you wearing?"

He didn't even get perturbed at me calling him Big Mel or that I interrupted my training session. He just chuckled. I felt tremors, like a small earthquake precipitating throughout the pad and, most likely, the entire cave.

There on the TV screen was Big Mel, with a brightly colored Hawaiian shirt partially open, blowing slightly in the breeze, revealing a muscular, very tanned chest. He had on white casual shorts and—get this—to complete the ensemble, bright-neon-pink running shoes. He was standing on a pristine black-sand beach, palm trees swaying with the breeze as waves of the ocean were gently caressing the beach.

"Hawaii! Hawaii!"

I looked over my shoulder; there Momi, and the girls were looking on.

Momi spoke up again. "That Hawaii!"

Mel laughed. "Hawaii, Heaven on Earth—that's their tourism motto."

I shook my head and declared, "We have eavesdroppers."

"They can hear this too, Chris." The scene switched to a glowing, pure white being with a shimmering white robe. "Is this what you envisioned, Chris?" The screen then went back to Mel in his casual wear. What completed the outfit was the baseball cap; he wore it with the bill to the back. The cap had large, stylized lettering that said Angels.

"Hey, I'm a fan of the Angels." He smiled.

I thought to myself, *A fan of which Angels—the spirit beings or the baseball team? And what's up with the Hawaiian shirts and loud athletic shoes? Is this the spirit fashion style this season? What gives?*

Mel continued from where he left off, where I interrupted him. "The Daimonia are subject to the physical laws God has set up for the natural world, just like everyone and everything in this world. They can inhabit anything physical: people, animals, and even objects. It's very important to remember though... their abilities are limited to the natural laws pertaining to the things they inhabit."

I raised my hand and started waving it. I had questions galore.

"Chris, you will get more training. I'm just covering the main points so you're not totally in the dark."

"Mel, just wait, hold it... I get the feeling this training is going to be like on-the-job training."

"Chris, what better way to learn... than *on the go?*"

Mel continued back on topic before I could complain. "Knowing the type of Daimonia you are working against is another important concept to remember. This will determine your tactics, techniques, tools, and weapons that will be most beneficial in controlling and defeating it. Think of it in the natural sense, as if you were hunting an animal. Knowing the food it eats; its habitat; whether it's aggressive, fast, slow; how well it sees, hears, and smells; these are all important if you're going to be safe and successful."

I smiled as I thought to myself, *That's why I only hunt shy vegetarian animals like rabbits, deer, and quail.* I understood full well what Mel was trying to get across. The better I knew my prey... the Daimonia, the safer and more successful I would be.

"Chris, another important key: knowing the name of the Daimonia gives you the power and the ability to influence, to even control it. You may think this is nonsense, but it is true. Using its name is acting on your authority over it."

"Now, let me cover a few things about Anarkos. He has many Daimones under his rule as well as daimonions and Anarkons. He specializes in spreading lawlessness, or anarchy, as his name implies. The Daimonia that are under his rule are called Anarkai; they are lawless, riotous, insolent, and narcissistic spirits. These spirits are causing the rise of this lawlessness in humans. Anarchy is on the rise all over the globe... Anarkos is becoming stronger and stronger." He paused to let that sink in.

Mel continued, "You have already encountered one human host that is being used."

"Do you mean Mr. Anarchy Rules?"

"Yes, Chris. His name is Joshua Smitely, and he is possessed by many daimonions and is definitely being directed by a Daimones... even possibly Anarkos himself at times."

My mind was reeling over what he had covered and what he hadn't. It would take time to work through all of it.

My subconscious mind, though, was already on it. It had latched onto something he said and brought this to my attention. I hadn't caught the mention of '*Anarkons*' at the time he spoke it.

Had it been a slip of the tongue? I don't think so. Now what were Anarkons? Mel just slipped it in and skipped right over it, like it was of little or no importance.

He thought I wouldn't catch it. He was wrong.

"Mel, earlier you mentioned Anarkons."

"Yes, I did," he said matter-of-factly.

"Go on, spit it out, Mel."

"These are not humans inhabited by Daimonia. They are Anarkos's minions... monstrosities from the spirit realm brought into concretion—in your world." He let that sink in for a few seconds before continuing.

"These creatures are unholy and defy nature. If a normal human sees one of them, their rational mind will interpret the creature as a gorilla, chimpanzee, or orangutan, something on this order that makes sense to the person."

Without warning, Mel ended our talk. "Take care."

"Mel... Mel, wait... wait! There are monsters out there... controlled by Anarkos!

"Don't you dare leave. I have..."

As he was fading out, I heard him say, "Chris, you have enough for now. Use what I have given, become experienced with it, make it your own."

Mel left me hanging... again. I would just have to struggle through with what he chose to reveal. I hoped it would be enough to keep me from getting killed.

The shopping network came back on. The host was describing a cell phone. It had GPS, unlimited minutes, unlimited data, unlimited messages, and coverage anywhere. No unauthorized users could use it, it was unbreakable, it never needed to be charged, it worked anywhere, and it couldn't be lost. That was what the man said. *I think I could use a phone like that.*

I looked over at the others. "I think it's time to get some sleep. Tomorrow, we will head out to Salt Lake City to find Camp Aharonite."

My sleep was pleasant and uneventful. No dreams, or at least none I could remember. I awoke with Tassi's head on my chest. She was never very far from my side; the others were always near too. I might not notice the other three, but they were keeping close tabs on me also.

I awoke to the smell of breakfast. I am going to enjoy having Momi around. I guess I wouldn't miss my mom… Jennifer as much. I laughed inwardly as I thought, *I have two mommies… moms.*

There was a knock on our front door. Well, it was really just a cutout in the wall. I went downstairs to see who it was. Since I had no idea what lived around our pad, I was cautious. Tassi was right there with me as usual.

I peered out the door. I didn't see anyone. Tassi nudged me in the stomach with her nose. I looked down at her and saw a package on the ground. The label on the package read—get this—Ezekiel Shopping Network, and it was addressed to Chris Gahrlan. I hadn't ordered anything, and besides, who had delivered it? I didn't think UPS delivered here. I laughed to myself when I thought of a possible name for this delivery service—APS: Angel Parcel Service.

I picked up the package and took it to the kitchen. Momi had breakfast on the table, and it smelled delicious. It was some sort of fluffy egg omelet stuffed with cheese and various vegetables I wasn't even familiar with. On the side of the omelet was poi, that Hawaiian staple. Poi is a thick paste made of ground-up and boiled plant roots. It tasted pretty good with the omelet. The poi had a nutty bean flavor that was unique. I didn't ask Momi whether he had gone out and scavenged for our food or if everything was from our kitchen.

Momi looked at me and pointed at the package. "What's that?"

"I don't know. It came overnight from the shopping network," I said.

"Open," he said rather excitedly.

I ripped open the package; inside were three cell phones.

Momi grabbed the red cell phone. "Red my color."

I picked up the blue one, since blue was my favorite color. I turned it on. The screen came up instantly and displayed a picture of Tassi and me. She was in my arms, and I was falling backward. This was just before I had carried her through the portal into the House of Orion. Who had taken the pictures? Did we have paparazzi stalking us? Very creepy.

I browsed through the phone. It looked like everything from my old phone was transferred over. I dialed my mom's cell number. The last cell phone in the package began to ring. I grabbed the pink phone and answered it. I was on the other end. Earlier, I had not been able to call my mom from my old cell phone because of no reception. Now the problem wasn't reception any longer but that her cell phone number was already transferred to this new pink cell phone. No touching base with her for a while.

Momi was all excited. "Look, look." He waved the red phone. It had a close-up picture of him rubbing Roscoe's neck for his home screen.

"That's your phone, big fella. Well, maybe not... it could be Roscoe's."

He laughed as he punched the touchscreen. My phone began to ring, so I picked it up. Momi was on the line, saying, "My phone, my phone!"

I smiled as I said "Aloha" and ended the call. I didn't want to use my minutes too fast! Wait, I had unlimited minutes.

For being here in the future, Momi seemed to be pretty much up to speed on the tech side of things, although on the language side, he was a little behind the times.

Momi left the room and shortly came back, carrying my backpack and two large red duffel bags that he had prepared for our road trip.

I asked, "What's in the bags?"

"Clothes and most important needs." He chuckled.

"You mean necessities."

"Yes, necessities. I bring food."

I laughed. "You truly are a mommy."

He just looked at me puzzled, then tossed the backpack to me and picked up the bags. "Go now," he said.

We walked through the cave toward the far side. As we got closer, I could see another wall had been activated. The Land that Time Forgot with its expansive grass prairie and huge trees was now visible with a stylized golden "M" portal front and center. Mel had left me hanging on what the "M" stood for... that's Mel being Mel. I was not going to let that bother me or take up any more thought. On the bright side we now had two portals; how koosh is that! The others had already arrived at the forest portal and stepped through. I was lagging behind.

"Wait for me..." I yelled as I vanished within the portal.

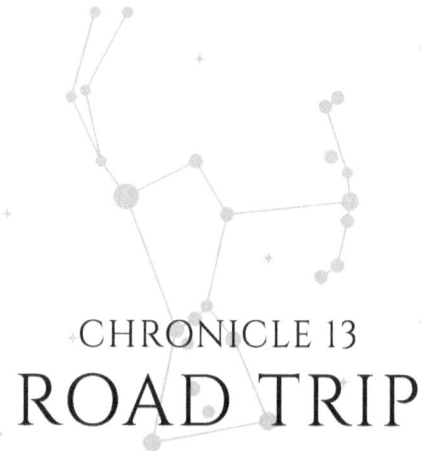

CHRONICLE 13
ROAD TRIP

I WOULD NEVER GET USED TO limbo land. A trip through it left me a little lightheaded and nauseated. Well, if you traveled through space and time, you might feel that way too. I shook it off and surveyed the forest we had entered. The others were up ahead; I needed to catch up.

Tassi was leading the way. I quickly caught up to her. She probably did know where to go, so I just followed. We were weaving our way up and down through various ravines and crossing a few small streams, leaving the river far behind us. Tassi stopped and sniffed the air; I guess she was trying to get her bearings and decide where we needed to go next.

I looked at her. "This is going to take an awful lot of time to get to Salt Lake City. It'll be months."

She gave me a contemptuous glare.

Then Momi spoke up. "Almost there."

"Almost where?" I retorted.

Tassi turned three-quarters of the way around and headed up a small ridge. When we got to the top of the ridge, I looked down. There at the bottom was a dirt road. We followed it as it weaved its way through the woods.

Up ahead, I saw something fairly large, off to the side of the road. It turned out to be a vehicle, a full-size van.

Momi ran up ahead of us, yelling, "Wheels. My wheels!"

By the time I arrived, he was in the driver's seat and had it started. I let the wolves in, and no sooner was I in the front passenger seat than he piped, "Buckle up. I drive." And off he drove.

I looked at him in shock. "You can drive?"

"Pahli... Barry showed."

I shook my head and thought, *Maybe you know how to drive, but do you know the road rules and driver etiquette? Do you have experience driving in traffic? Do you even have a driver's license?*

As if he read my thoughts, he reached into his pocket and pulled out a plastic card and waved it at me. "Driver's license."

"Oh," I said in astonishment. That was all I could get out. At least he had answered one of my concerns.

He had only been here a month, was from more than a hundred and fifty years in the past and expected me to believe he could drive in traffic. Had he ever seen another car? Or, for that matter, a highway? How about a freeway?

Momi briefly looked at me and grinned. "You give directions. You directioner." He laughed.

I didn't think that was a real word but played along. "Your directioner doesn't know where Camp Aharonite is or, even worse, where we are."

Momi looked at me. "Use phone."

I humored him. Well, we did have an unlimited data plan. I took out my phone and googled driving directions for Camp Aharonite. To my amazement, it worked. The phone knew where we were, it used the built-in GPS and... somehow knew the location of Camp Aharonite. I didn't think Camp Aharonite was publicly known or even had an address for that matter. I shook my head, confounded, and just accepted the fact that it worked.

It wasn't long before we pulled into a gas station of a small town. Momi pulled out another plastic card and swiped it at the pump. "Debit card." He grinned. He started to say something more.

I spoke up. "Yeah, yeah, Barry showed."

He nodded happily.

We motored off, following the directions. To my surprise, Momi seemed like an experienced driver. We were coming up to the next city when Momi pointed out signs for a county park.

He spoke up. "Stop at park. Eat time. We grill out."

We drove down a dusty gravel road that meandered through a rather dense forest with large, moss-covered boulders strewn here and there. It followed a small stream with all its twisting. Whoever had made this road must have been drinking the night before, been devoid of all common sense and reasoning or been just plain unscrupulous. They could have made a straight road from point A to point B, only a quarter mile, instead of an entire mile or more of a twisting and winding road going back and forth, hardly getting anywhere. More than likely, the construction firm just wanted to bilk the county taxpayers out of their hard-earned money. I'm kidding. It was a very scenic drive.

The woods finally opened up to a large meadow. A banner hung over the road, tied between two stately pine trees. It said, "Welcome, AIR."

What did AIR stand for?

There were cars and trucks parked along the road and into the front section of a meadow where a large crowd of people were milling around numerous tents and an outdoor stage.

Momi parked the van and said, "Let's go see."

I opened the side door and was going to tell the wolves to blend into the woods. I didn't need to say anything; they were gone, disappeared, becoming virtually unnoticeable. I caught a glimpse of movement here and there, but then, I knew Tassi and the girls were out there.

Momi and I followed a group of people. A foreboding feeling welled up inside me. I said to Momi, "I don't think we should be here."

Momi didn't react but rather just motioned with his hands. "Have food."

"Did you hear what I said?"

He didn't respond; his mind was totally engaged with getting food. Momi took off, making his way through the people.

I stayed where I was as people just walked around me. It was as if I wasn't even there or more like I was a boulder or a tree that they had to avoid. These people seemed like they were brain-dead. Had we just walked into a convention for zombies?

I saw Momi making his way back through the crowd. People were recognizing him and saying their pleasantries. *What's up with that? Am I not even here?*

A sudden chill went up my spine. I was starting to put two and two together... and it came to more than four. There was a very strong and active Daimonia presence here. That was what I was feeling, and that was why I was being avoided or cold shouldered. Darkness recoiled from and abhorred the light... and I was the Orion, Bearer of Light, Dispeller of Darkness.

Momi came over to me while scarfing down a burger. He had six or seven more on several plates with loads of fries.

"How did you get that?" I asked.

"Have plenty of cash." He waved a wad of money he had in his right hand as he balanced the plates of food in the other hand.

"Put that away," I said. "Do you want to get ripped off?"

He had a blank expression on his face. The linguistic barrier... Momi being from the 1850s had popped up again.

"Get mugged," I tried.

After I said that, he put the money back in his pocket quickly. "Mugged" must have been an old English word. Momi now knew that "ripped off" was equivalent to being mugged.

We fed our faces as we followed people heading towards a stage. There must've been at least a thousand people there. A band had just finished a song as a person walked across to the center stage. He began addressing the crowd. The man was flamboyant. Above him was a large banner that read Anarchy International Reformists.

Well, that clarified what the earlier banner had meant by AIR; it was an acronym.

My bad feeling about all of this was getting worse. There were active Daimonia here and none other than those that promoted anarchy. We were at the right place but at the wrong time. This was a perfect place to find at least one of Anarkos's Daimones, but I had no idea what to do once we found one!

It was not the smartest thing to do, but we continued moving deeper into anarchy by mingling our way near center stage. The orator was whipping up the crowd; he was very charismatic. What he said made no sense, but the crowd just hungrily devoured it. They were zombified.

I thought to myself, *You cannot have an anarchist society. It doesn't truly exist. It cannot exist. Anarchy is lawlessness. How can you have a functioning society without rules? It's all poppycock!*

But these people were buying it hook, line, and sinker, the sheer deception of Anarkos... yeah, no rules or ruler except Anarkos.

I started studying the charismatic man that was perpetuating this deception for Anarkos. Something seemed vaguely familiar about him. I studied his face more closely. My God, this man was the one I called Mr. Anarchy Rules. What a small world. Too small for me. There went having a peaceful picnic in the park.

His nose was pointed and had a slight hook to it, a hawkish nose. It was a little more twisted than when I had seen him last. Ha hah! I bet he had broken his nose when he took a fall on the asphalt outside the grocery store. His hair was still long and stringy, but now it was kept. Yep, he had washed his hair and tied it into a man ponytail. This was the same man, but where were his facial abrasions? He had taken a very nasty fall. Yeah, I bet they had probably been covered up by makeup. He wouldn't want to come out in front of his followers looking like he had been in a brawl.

All of a sudden, his eyes focused on me. There was a sudden glint in them, or should I say darkness. I saw a few facial twitches, and his body seemed to go slightly rigid in its movements. He, or whoever was in him, must have recognized me. Not good. Oh, so not good!

The man finished up his rally speech. The crowd was all hyped. He walked offstage, and as he did, I caught a glimpse of shadows around him. They had a slight greenish hue and were hovering above him, definitely not true shadows. These were like the ones near my mom fourteen years ago before she had inexplicably been hit by a semitruck. What was up with these weird shadows? Mel had never mentioned anything about them. He was tight lipped on the need to know. I think this was going to bite us in the butt and right now!

We had just stumbled upon a very, very strong Daimonia presence here… lots and lots of daimonions for sure. At the moment they were all doing their own thing and not being organized to any degree. Mel had explained that it took a Daimones to organize the daimonions. What a perfect opportunity for one or more of Anarkos's Daimones to be here and become active. I am being sarcastic.

Mel had given us the mission of hunting down and taking out Anarkos's Daimones. But he never covered how to find who they were inhabiting or how to take them out. This wasn't a need to know at the time. Training on this would be given in due time… probably at camp Aharonite… a little too late! We will just have to wing it, using what I have been taught so far.

A very disconcerting thought came to my mind… what if Anarkos himself was here? No time to dwell on this.

The man, Mr. Anarchy Rules was walking towards us, with three bodyguards in tow. He came up to us and, with a fake warm smile, extended his hand. I automatically shook it, and a sudden chill went through my body. He just smiled warmly and introduced himself as Joshua Smitely.

"New faces, new followers," he said. "Why don't you and your friend join me in my tent."

It was said as a nice invitation but had the underlying tone of more than just a request. It was a request that one couldn't not accept.

Momi was all bubbly, just talking away with Joshua. I was trying to figure out a course of action. Stress and its agitation seemed to negate my ability to think correctly, to logically analyze the situation. Nothing profound came to my mind. The only course of action I came up with was to scream and run. No, that wasn't a viable plan. I decided to do what came naturally to me: talk.

The conversation with Joshua was full of all the usual pleasantries and trivialities on the surface. But each of us was trying to get useful information covertly—without the other knowing. It was a subtle battle with words and no direct questions. I didn't know how much Momi was taking in, but I could sense his outward appearance of childlike exuberance was belying his real understanding of the seriousness of the situation.

Joshua and I goaded each other into giving out information that we didn't want the other to know. I believed I did this much better than Joshua. I gave him basically nothing. I told him Momi and I were two teenagers that had just met and decided on traveling around together, seeing the sights in New Mexico.

Joshua, like most bad guys, seemed to always want to impress their opponent. I liked that fault of giving out their plans, their agendas. Their need to show their superiority was their downfall... pride cometh before a fall.

Joshua described his idea of a society of freethinkers with no hindrances, no rules, free to think and to do whatever they pleased. There would be no government, no rulers, just everyone living in peace and doing their own thing. What really concerned me was how he had groups like this in all the major cities not only across our nation but overseas too. He also had many charitable and humanitarian organizations following seemingly different agendas on the surface, but with the main goal of perpetuating anarchy their true underlying motivation and mission.

Now get this: they were funded and organized by the same governments that they intended to topple. It was a sweet, devious plan. The first order was to topple the currencies of the nations of the world. Well, they were close to doing this already. Most nations were basically bankrupt already, just printing more money to shore up their countries. This was going to make the governments collapse into total chaos, not anarchy. I didn't think Joshua even foresaw this outcome. I was sure the Daimones clouded Joshua's mind from this fact.

Wow, that was so koosh, the knowledge and understanding of the situation was just there in my mind. That must have been revelation. I was smart, but to put that all together on how this was being done was beyond me. Hey, for the first thing I didn't follow the news. Now let me continue since I am on a roll with all my newfound knowledge and understanding.

They were using natural disasters too. Were all the floods, the droughts, the earthquakes, global warming, the polar vortex, and the epidemics, all natural? Maybe or maybe not. In any case, they were being used to bring about anarchy and chaos!

Then we have the societal crises: the banking and stock market collapses, the housing collapses, the utility company collapses, the food shortages, and especially the defunding of our police, firefighters, and military. That was too many things fueling or spreading anarchy—well, more like chaos—to just be happening all on their own.

Joshua's eyes started to become fixated, and a darkness came over him. I didn't know how to describe it other than to say it just seemed darker around him than in the rest of the tent, even though he was standing in the sunlight.

I grabbed Momi's arm and quickly ushered him outside, giving our goodbyes on our way out. We needed to get out of there quickly. Something bad was happening, and I didn't want to stay around.

Even before we left the tent, I could feel the temperature suddenly drop. It felt downright chilly, and if it continued dropping like this, it would be cold enough for it to snow! I didn't know how this was possible. It had been hot, ninety-some degrees, when we arrived.

We moved quickly. Once we were out of the tent, I thought the temperature would be back to normal, but it wasn't. It became harder moving through the crowds too. Some of the people were even impeding us. Someone or something… the Daimones were starting to direct the people. It was obvious we had walked openly into the enemy's camp. Yes, most of these people were just influenced, but some were completely under the control of the Daimonia. These evil beings had taken up residency within them. Ugh! That gave me the shivers just thinking about it—these slimy, putrid, vile creatures living inside human beings. Well, okay, they didn't have any physical form, but inherently that's what they were: slimy, putrid, foul, decaying… Oh, you get the idea.

The crowd stepped up its hindering and started to surround us. Something within me—that small, still voice—said, *Stand your ground*. Well, I listened to that voice. There were just too many of them; escape was no longer a viable option.

Things were getting dark for us, and what I mean was that it actually was getting dark! The weird thing about that, the sun was still shining brilliantly in the sky with no clouds. And the temperature was continuing to drop too!

Momi bumped into me and knocked me over. I should have told him I had decided to stop running. He was going to help me up, but I waved him off. I raised myself into a sitting position, much like the lotus position in yoga but not as formal.

A crowd started forming a large circle around us. Just before it closed the last opening around us, four shadows sprinted through. It was Tassi and the trio. They growled menacingly and formed a circle around Momi and me.

The crowd backed away from us as the wolves continued to growl and spring forward at them. We now had some breathing room, maybe twenty yards of clearing all around us. It looked like some of the people had broken ranks when the wolves advanced toward them. There must have been enough fear of being shredded by wolves to break the spiritual influence of the Daimonia. The inhabited ones did not flee, but they did back off slightly.

The people that had broken free of the influence probably wondered what they were doing. Mel had said they would not remember being controlled or why they were doing what they were doing. That was the truly scary part.

It didn't look as if we were going to get through their ranks even with my fierce friends, but that wasn't my plan.

Momi looked down at me. "Why stop?"

I looked at him and said, "We're standing our ground."

He looked directly back at me. "Why sitting?"

I laughed. "It's an expression for staying put... not retreating."

"We fight," he said.

"Yes. It's getting too dark to be running anyway." It was like dusk now.

Momi looked puzzled. Then he replied, "It sunny, not dark."

Now I was puzzled. "Is it not cold?" I asked.

"Cold?" Momi repeated questioningly. "No. It hot, much hot." Momi looked confused, and so was I.

I looked around me. Was I going insane or dying? What was happening? Then it dawned on me that I was seeing and feeling spiritually. Momi was my ground to this world. He saw what was going on in the physical realm. I was seeing into the spiritual realm. Was that why I had Momi? To help me stay rooted and know what was happening in the physical?

The Daimonia were bringing spiritual darkness, and with that came the spiritual cold. The effects on the physical mind were first a clouding of the thoughts then the flooding with evil ones. In the second stage the spiritual cold kicked in with numbness causing the eventual lack of any mental control of one's thoughts and actions. The Daimonia were now in control. I'm a total noob to all this...

God had imparted the knowledge and understanding of what was occurring. And the insight... for me to figure out a course of action.

To combat and overcome the Daimonia, I would focus on light and with it, warmth. This took getting calm and peaceful. I needed to have spiritual peace to manifest spiritual power. When one is under attack, this is easier said than done. I had to rely on Momi and my friends.

The crowd was getting restless. Well, they were more like a mob. They attacked!

The wolves kept lunging at them, but the mob just continued pressing forward.

I saw Momi throw his weight. The attackers bounced off his belly. He even grabbed many by the hair and then either slammed them together or just flung them to the ground. Momi was some kind of fighter. Well, more of a brawler. He had no actual fighting technique, just brute strength, weight, and sheer determination. He even used his fists as clubs and thumped them on the head. They just crumpled to the ground, but others sprang up in their place. Sometimes he smothered them in a huge loving embrace till they slumped to the ground. It was kind of comical, his fighting style, but it was effective, especially with the enemy swarming us.

The wolves were throwing their weight around t00, flinging themselves either at shoulder height or at the knees. They were taking the mob down in droves. The wolves were not trying to kill them, and neither was Momi.

The mob, on the other hand, was not so nice. Their intent was to seriously harm or even to kill us. They were all in a frenzy with no concerted control, just entirely a free-for-all, in taking us out. That was good for us, because we attacked with a coordinated effort and with just four, were able to keep the mob of hundreds from closing in.

Tassi stayed back and kept anyone that got through away from me. She was aggressive and very vicious looking with her fangs bared and saliva flowing. Even some of the totally possessed people turned and hightailed it out of there instead of going through Tassi.

I didn't know how much time my friends could give me. All of this was happening in mere seconds. I needed to get peaceful. How?

I grabbed whatever rocks were around me. Thank God there were rocks. I found four smooth, relatively round rocks right by me. A coincidence? I didn't think so. If you remember, a still, small voice had told me to stop right where I was and stand my ground.

I started juggling the four smooth rocks, tossing each one into a medium-sized arc, watching them ascend and descend. I was in the battle and yet I wasn't.

Juggling brings me peace by allowing me to disassociate myself from my surroundings. Running also brought me peace, but here running was not an option. There just wasn't enough room. Running in a small circle wasn't going to cut it.

The juggling worked. I still perceived things going on around me but with more clarity than before, yet I was totally detached from them. I became very serene, a gentleness and warmth seemed to spread out from me. I was emanating waves of peace. Many of the mob just stopped, looking confused and dumbfounded. They shook their heads and just walked away. The ranks of Joshua Smitely were thinning.

Those that stayed became more vicious, more frenzied, and started to recklessly fling themselves at Momi and the wolves. There were just too many attackers. My circle of protection started to shrink. The yelling and screaming along with the continual onslaught of the attacks of the mob started to wear away at my peacefulness and detachment.

A voice cut through the din, a feminine voice, soft and soothing like my mother's. It was one I recognized, even though I had only heard it a few times and very briefly: Tassi's. I focused on her voice and called out to her. To my amazement, she responded.

I am here, Chris.

Hearing her voice helped me regain my peace. I felt that spirit peace emanate from my being again, even stronger this time. I felt empowered and not alone. Tassi was with me.

The crowd of people became less frenzied. Well, peace is the opposite of frenzy and being out of control. Spirit peace, that peace that comes from God, is stronger than the kind of peace you can get on your own. It even brought more clarity to my mind. I knew what to do next.

I started thinking about light. A subdued white light began radiating from my body. The ground beneath me and the air directly around me became increasingly warm. The air started to crackle as it grew intensely hot. The darkness and the cold began to retreat, but then they held. It was a battle between light and dark, between hot and cold, between life and death.

Now it was strange that my thoughts kept going to my meteoric descent of the other night. It was as if I was there again, rocketing through the earth's atmosphere with flames swirling around me.

I decided to focus all my spirit will on the flames. The yellow, orange, and red flames started turning to bluish white. I could feel intense heat as they continued to grow brighter and stronger, collapsing inward around me and then suddenly reversed, expanding forcefully outward. It was as if I was a star going supernova.

Tassi shouted, and I could feel her spirit presence embracing me, smothering me. I was out of control.

Tassi and the wolf trio yelled in unison, *"Chris, stop!"* They enveloped me in an overwhelming spirit power hug of containment.

I blacked out.

Nothingness...

I TAKE A SABBATICAL

I AWOKE TO A BLACK-SAND BEACH with aqua waves gently tickling my bare feet. It was a place I knew very well, my peaceful place. The sand was soft and warm, tenderly hugging my feet. The water was pristine, with calming waves gently lapping the sand.

One lone majestic palm tree provided shade, with a large beach towel spread underneath. A cool sea breeze blew with a hint of sea salt and yes... no bugs! The sky was a beautiful evening blue, with a few fluffy white clouds riding on the currents of gentle breezes.

The sun had almost departed, surrendering brilliant hues of red, orange, purple, and pink, as an ushering in of the evening. It was a breathtaking sunset.

Chris... Chris?

Who was interrupting my peace? I called this my peaceful place for a reason. No distractions, no cares, no worries, nothing to do but relax and enjoy the sunset. In all fairness, though, I needed a friend, a little companionship, someone I could open up to... a person. This time, I needed not to be alone in my peaceful place.

Chris...

It carried a sense of urgency, a sense of sadness. The voice was now distinct and clear. I knew that voice... Tassi.

I am here, I called out.

Chris! Chris. The voice now carried tones of elation and relief.

The air started to shimmer in the distance, similar to heat waves rising off a hot desert floor. The distortion started taking shape. Slowly but surely, I saw a human form develop. Not just any human—it was a young lady that appeared!

I had been thinking of a friend, a companion, someone to talk to... Momi. But that was not who appeared.

She ran to me and gave me a gentle but powerful embrace. She released her hug, took a step back, looked directly into my eyes and smiled with relief. There was no mistaking the sentient being those brilliant-blue eyes belonged to. Only one: a certain wolf. This had to be Tassi. She was stunning as a human, with radiant platinum silver hair cascading down her shoulders lightly caressing the small of her back. The metallic-silver hair was another dead giveaway of the identity of this young lady—actually, teenager. What other creature had I ever seen with metallic-silver hair—actually fur?

"I thought... *we* thought... we had lost you," Tassi softly stated.

"What happened?" I asked.

We walked over and sat on my beach towel underneath the lone palm tree.

"Chris, you are unconscious, totally shut down! You are barely breathing, pulse virtually nil, no mental activity, no spiritual activity. For all intents and purposes, you are dead!"

"What? I only remember to the point of all of you shouting in unison, 'Chris, stop!' What happened?"

"Chris, I, or we, have been trying to break through spiritually for hours! You have retreated to your subconscious, and it has put up a barrier that was imperceptible and impenetrable till now!"

She unfolded the events.

"Chris, you were radiating a bluish-white light, causing the darkness and the cold to retreat, but then it held. It fought back, overcoming the light. The light then started to pulsate and coalesced into a single symmetrical sphere that hovered over your head. This sphere of pure spirit energy continued to shrink until it became almost too small to detect, then it rapidly expanded, exploding out-ward with waves of intense illuminous energy.

"You were going like supernova! Well, maybe not the energy of a supernova, but still an immense amount of power. Chris, I've been around the power released by solar flares, and what you were unleashing was on the same order..." She shook her head. "And you were able to absorb this amount of power too!"

Tassi continued, "The destruction would have been devastating in both the spirit and physical realms!

"My link with you allowed Nila, Kora, Cami, and me to enfold the energy back into you. We didn't know if you would survive. Chris, you accepted and drew this energy into yourself. Only a small shock wave of energy escaped, enough that everyone and everything in the park just crumpled to the ground... except the five of us."

Tassi didn't have to say it; I just knew she was in awe of what had just happened. The raw power I unleashed scared me... but what scared me even more... not being able to control it.

"What you were able to do... and survive. You were just sitting there, staring straight ahead with eyes that were like two brilliant-blue sapphires, looking very peaceful, and holding the four smooth stones in your hands. You did not move, and your breathing was imperceptible to the naked eye. My sensitive nose picked up on that you were still breathing. You continued to emit a faint, almost im-perceptible amount of carbon dioxide... along with minute traces of raw onion breath—from those hamburgers you just ate! That meant you were still in the land of the living, at least in body."

Tassi must have caught my dumbfounded look and pressed her hand to my forehead.

See.

There was a flash of white, and I was there, observing what had happened. A tiny speck of light hovered over my head, and then suddenly intense brilliant concentric rings of white light radiated explosively outward. Then just as suddenly they collapsed upon me and winked out. A flash of luminous energy emitted from me like a hiccup. Everyone around crumpled to the ground except my friends. Momi came over and picked me up, my body limp in his arms. He carried me through the field that was now littered with bodies of all those that were being used by the Daimonia.

We even came to an unconscious Joshua Smitely, his face contorted into a grimace of unbelief. Tassi checked Joshua and a few others at random. They were exhaling minute amounts of carbon dioxide. They too were alive. Tassi wasn't able to sense if I had expelled the Daimonia or if they were still inhabiting their hosts but comatose like their human counterparts.

It was quite a struggle for Momi, walking over and around the bodies, trying not to step on them. We finally made it to the van, and Momi gently laid me on the back bench seat. We were now on our way to Camp Aharonite.

There was another flash of light, and I was back.

"I have been at your side for hours, trying to reach your spirit, to no avail, until now."

Tassi looked around. "This is a very beautiful place but kind of sparse. All you have here is a tiny island with one large palm tree surrounded by ocean and an unending sunset."

"Hey, I have a beautiful sand beach, a soft, gentle sea breeze, and no bugs!"

"Is that all you do here, just sit under that palm tree and veg out?"

"Yes. Need I do anything more to be relaxed and peaceful?"

Tassi then looked down at herself. "Wait... What am I wearing?"

I smiled. "It seems to be the 'in' fashion for spirit beings this year. At least you're not wearing fur!" I chuckled.

Tassi was in a celestial-blue Hawaiian flowered shirt, white chino shorts, and to top it off, a white Angels baseball cap. Was this my subconscious's doing or someone else's? She studied her face with her fingers and whipped her hair over her right shoulder. She gently ran her fingers through her hair. She then looked at me.

"Nice job."

"What?" I said quizzically.

"You have me as a human female." She laughed.

"Hey, I'm unconscious, in a coma. I didn't consciously think of bringing you here or what you would look like in human form. And you are a female wolf... a human female body would naturally make sense."

She chuckled at my defensiveness.

I continued. "Moreover, my subconscious only transformed your other *female* wolf's physical characteristics into what their human counterparts would likely be."

She gazed into my eyes. "I am pleased with the form. You added nothing to your liking?"

I looked right back into her eyes and said with emphasis, "No, I don't think my subconscious exaggerated at all... how you would look as a human. Your stunning, brilliant-blue eyes, platinum silver hair, and light complexion would be a given as your core human features. You do have a broader chest, bigger butt, skinnier waist, smaller nose, higher cheekbones, and longer legs than the average female Mexican gray wolf, so you would be above average in these areas as a human female."

She smirked, struck a pose like a model, then smiled and said, "I do look good for a human female... a teenage girl."

We both broke into laughter.

"You do know this is not my true form? And... I'm no teenager!"

I spoke up in a warm, gentle tone. "This is an appropriate form... a person of like age: to be that friend, that companion, that someone to talk to, while I'm comatose."

"This place needs a feminine touch, a girl's touch."

"I thought you said you're not a..."

She placed a finger on my lips, letting me know to stop talking.

The area began to shimmer all around my tiny island, and a mist developed.

We walked along the ocean's edge, shrouded in mist, allowing the warm ocean water to caress our feet.

I began to hear the sounds of life, no longer just the ocean waves and gentle breeze but now the chattering and singing of birds and animals.

The mist dissipated, and we were now on a large, lush tropical island. I could even see majestic mountains in the distance.

Tassi laughed at my consternation. "Your peaceful place can be anything you choose."

"Then how can you change it? This is *my* subconscious, *my* thoughts, *my* imagination."

Tassi turned. "We are linked together."

I looked at her. "Well, it's official: you have ruined my peaceful place. Now it's like a vacation hotspot!"

Tassi laughed then continued, "You can imagine whatever you like. Your subconscious mind is active and operating even when you're unconscious."

"So I am imagining having this conversation."

"No, this is real, Chris."

"I thought I was just bantering with my imagination!" I looked at her. "Do you know what I am thinking? My inner thoughts, my feelings, my desires?"

"Chris, I only know those that you are actively thinking about. Your spirit has projected your thoughts. You are vocalizing them spiritually."

I gave her a quizzical look.

"Let me put it like this: you're talking out loud spiritually of what you're thinking."

"Do you mean to tell me that I wasn't imagining that it seemed like you, Nila, Cami, and Kora were listening in on my thoughts?"

"We weren't invading your mind. We can't read minds. You were projecting your thoughts spiritually, or better put, talking to us unknowingly."

I started to turn many shades of red and purple. This was really embarrassing. Nila, Cami, and Kora also knew my private thoughts!

"Chris, only those you thought about."

"You even heard what I just said to myself."

She smiled. "Your spirit is very strong, and you are unlearned in controlling what it projects." She stopped and turned toward me so we were face-to-face. "Chris, don't block us out. We do not think less of you. We are very privileged to know the true Chris Gahrlan."

"How much have you heard? How much have I projected?"

"We have heard basically all your thoughts since shortly before we met."

I stammered, "Wh-What's basically all my thoughts?"

"Your thoughts that we decide to pay attention to… Now, talking about us wolves as being noisy sleepers, howling, whining, yapping, and yipping—you're like that awake or asleep." She stepped closer to me. "Don't stop or change your openness even when you get the ability to do so."

"Why haven't I heard you gals?"

"Your mind is always in a state of agitation, commotion—it interferes with your spirit."

"I'm hearing you now."

"Yes, you are. We are actually conversing spiritually in your subconscious. You are at peace. Your spirit is not being superseded or suppressed by your conscious mind."

"That's why you haven't talked to me before?"

"Yes, I could only get one or two words through to you."

Then it dawned on me. When I juggled, I got peaceful and disassociated myself. That was when I had heard Tassi at the park.

"Chris, the more often you are at peace and your spirit is unhindered, unfettered by your mind, I believe you will start hearing my thoughts. Your spirit and my spirit are linking—bonding. I will hold nothing back from you, Chris. I will become as open to you as you are to me."

"How about with Cami, Nila, and Kora?"

"You are and will be very close to them too, but I believe it will take a more active decision to project thoughts to one another. Ours is a blending. We are separate but also yet one. This blending, though, is somewhat uncomfortable, or should I say disconcerting, to me!"

"Uncomfortable... disconcerting—how so?"

"Being exposed to emotions. Yours! Spirit beings like me... well, we don't have emotions. Now, to clarify, there are many types of spirit beings that do have emotions. They were *designed* to have them. But Cherubim were never... designed to have emotions."

"You are a Cherub?"

"Yes, Chris, I am." She looked around at our peaceful place then back at me. "Now, let us enjoy this peaceful tropical island."

She led us away from the ocean, inland. We followed a path that wound through the lush tropical foliage. I could hear water pounding and splashing. The path opened to a beautiful waterfall, probably seventy-five feet tall, with its water cascading over large black boulders into a beautiful, serene pond.

She gazed at her reflection in the placid waters at the edge of the pond. Then she stopped, turned toward me and hesitated.

"What is it, Tassi?"

"Chris, your spirit is already picking up on my thoughts!" She continued before I could say anything. "You may not be consciously aware of it, but your subconscious is."

"What makes you believe that?"

She pointed at her reflection. "Because... because that was how I envisioned myself as a human, except for a few minor tweaks. Your subconscious mind took from my mind how I saw myself as a human and added a few more curves... an hourglass figure!"

"Stop! Hold it. You have envisioned yourself as a human... a female, no less!"

She laughed, and before I could inquire more, she jumped into the pond, pulling me with her.

"Hey! We didn't change into swim—"

We splashed and frolicked in the beautiful warm water. Then a sudden chill came over me. Were there any creatures lurking in the water?

"Only if you imagine them," Tassi playfully said as she splashed me.

It was weird yet kind of koosh having someone answer my thoughts. It was nice and peaceful here. I enjoyed Tassi's company; it was easy being myself around her. That was a moot point because I couldn't hide anything anyway. My spirit projected everything that popped up into my mind.

Speaking of thoughts popping up, what had Tassi said a few minutes ago about when she first heard my thoughts?

"Yes, I did say shortly *before* we met."

"You do know that feels a little creepy, you finishing my thoughts."

She gazed at me. "Do you want me to stop?"

I didn't even hesitate with an answer. "No... It's just that I sometimes forget you're always with me."

Tassi continued, "I, or should I say we, picked up your thoughts soon after your arrival. You were really in a state of confusion. Your spirit projected your thoughts quite powerfully. That was what drew the four of us to you."

She continued, "Arthoxos and the other wolves must have noticed us leaving and decided to follow. We led them right to you."

"Who's Arthoxos?"

"He was the daimonion that possessed the male alpha wolf you defeated. We had been gathering intel for weeks concerning the sudden increase of Daimonia activity in this area... when you just popped in. We heard you spiritually. Your spiritual babbling caught our curiosity, and we had to check you out."

I quickly interjected, "What do you mean, my babbling?"

"Your thoughts at first were truly in disarray."

"Well, anybody would be if they found themselves instantly transported to who knew where!"

"Chris, what caught our attention was that your spiritual babbling and speaking... was that of angels!"

"Whaaat...!"

"Yes, you were speaking a language of the angels."

"Did Arthoxos hear me?"

"If he did, he didn't understand what you were saying."

"But you understood me," I quickly retorted.

"Chris, like any language, you must know it to understand it. You were speaking a very old language, one of the first spirit languages, one that very few know... the language of the Cherubim."

"What really are Cherubim?"

"Cherubim are guardian spirit beings. We are the guardians of God."

"What? God doesn't need guardians."

"You are right, Chris. When the Bible talks about us as being guardians of God, it doesn't mean that literally. How should I explain... We are like border patrol agents. We enforce and protect the spiritual and natural laws that God set up to separate the two realms—the Spiritual and the Physical. What I don't understand is how you can speak not only the old language of the Cherubim but many other Cherub languages. Only angels are fluent in a language of the angels, unless God is energizing a human spirit to speak it, but God isn't energizing you. You have spirit, Chris. But you are not an angel, not a spirit being. You shouldn't be able to speak Cherub!"

"Is that why we have bonded, or intertwined spiritually as you call it?"

"Chris, I think there's something deeper than speaking Cherub that has brought us together and unified us. We enjoy something that is truly unique, a uniting of two beings from two different realms. I don't know how to explain it, other than relating it to the human... male–female relationship. But for us angels, there isn't a male or female. Chris, we complete each other, just like a man and a woman. Each brings unique physical and emotional attributes to their relationship.

"You and I bring the attributes of the Physical and Spiritual realms together." Then she dove under the surface of the water.

I felt something grasp both my ankles. Immediately, I found myself yanked under the water. I repelled upward with a quick single thrust of my legs and arms to resurface, sputtering and coughing. Tassi laughed then flung herself at me. I caught and tossed her up over my head. She made quite a splash on reentry. We wrestled and tussled in the water till we were both exhausted.

"How can we become exhausted when it's only in our minds?"

Tassi smiled. "Your mind, whether conscious or subconscious, if it's not being controlled, will accept information and stimulus as being real, as if coming from outside itself."

We swam together, enjoying the peace and tranquility. Finally, we plopped ourselves down on the pristine black sand that surrounded the pond. We were both wearing fashionable swimwear. The Hawaiian theme had popped up, as usual. Tassi had a black one-piece arrayed with white, blue, and red flowers interspersed with green palm leaves. My swim trunks were white with stylized palm trees in a light gray. My subconscious was working overtime.

Tassi laughed. "No, Chris, the Hawaiian theme and swimwear was my doing. We did need something more appropriate for swimming."

We were *living in the moment, enjoying the moment, being the moment.*

"Yes, we are," Tassi replied to my thought.

Both of us relaxed and shortly dozed off. We awoke at the same time, which was just kind of freaky. And how can one sleep when one is already unconscious?

"Chris, in the subconscious anything is possible." She yawned and then jumped up, pulling me up with her. "Let's take advantage of the situation. We can do some combat training."

I looked at her, puzzled.

"All this"—she spun around slowly—"is perfect. We can get months, even years of training in a matter of hours."

"How so?" I replied.

"In the subconscious, time is not constrained. It is not a minute-for-minute representation. Haven't you ever dreamed? An entire day can be experienced in a second, an entire lifetime in a night."

She piped, "Let's do it. First, a clothing change, then some stretching."

I laughingly retorted, "Definitely a feminine trait... always thinking of what to wear!"

"Chris, we need the right clothing to spar in."

I found myself sporting a long-sleeve gray compression shirt with black compression pants. Tassi was wearing a blue shirt with black pants. I hoped this tight-fitting clothing was moisture wicking. I was sure my subconscious was going to have me sweating profusely.

Tassi was like my mom: she did all that freaky yoga stretching, not the normal stuff but the contortionist-type yoga moves. She even did that pretzel move with both legs behind her neck while sitting.

I gave her a smile then teasingly said, "Can we get on with the training?"

"Chris, you need to do stretching too."

"Why? Isn't this just in our minds? I'll just envision myself as being warmed up and all flexible like."

"Seriously, like I mentioned before, our minds are going to accept the stimuli as real for the most part. We can bend the rules, the physical laws, but we have to remember the fact that even if this isn't real, our bodies think it is. Otherwise, we could be in for some serious hurt."

After my stretching, we started some light sparring moves, like blocking, throwing kicks, and punches.

"Are we ready yet to do some actual figh—"

I didn't even finish before Tassi was in the air and had both her legs wrapped around my head.

I immediately jumped up in the same direction of her takedown. Otherwise, she would have taken my head off. A slight exaggeration, but I wasn't going to find out how my subconscious would respond. As we were in midair, I curled into a ball and went with Tassi's momentum. At the bottom of the arc, she was resting on my shoulders. I rotated till my feet were toward the ground. When my feet hit the ground, I sprang upward and, at the same instant, flung her off my head.

She had not been expecting me to make a countermove or one with such force. She went flying backward. Tassi was very agile and landed on her feet, but before she could regroup for another attack, I had already thrown a low roundhouse kick, sweeping her off the ground.

She landed on her back, and I was immediately on top of her with an elbow to her neck. In a real fight, I would've crushed her windpipe. That would've been all she wrote for my attacker.

Tassi smiled. "You are much more than you appear to be, Chris Gahrlan." And with that, she flung her hips upward, throwing me over the top of her head.

I did a tight somersault with a half twist in midair and landed on my feet in a crouch position. She completed a backflip with a similar half twist, and we were face-to-face in crouching stances. Tassi stood up, and I followed suit.

She smirked. "Enough of the hand to hand! Let's see how your sword skills are."

Before I could say anything, we were both outfitted in padded defense jackets and leg armor. If my memory served me correctly, the padded jacket was called a gambeson. It had long sleeves and reached past my butt in length. The padded leg armor...

"Yes, Chris, they are chausses. Now choose your weapon."

I looked over to my right. There on the ground was an array of weapons: long swords, short swords, battle axes, shields, and even long-shafted weapons.

Tassi selected a long sword and shield. I did the same...

We continued to spar with swords, swords and shields, two swords, battle axes, and shafted weapons. It seemed like days—or was it months? —that we practiced. Time is rather quirky in the subconscious. Actually, I couldn't really tell how long. In the real world, we wouldn't have been able to do what we were doing.

Tassi held up her hand. "Stop. Enough."

We were both drenched in sweat. That was how real it all was to our minds. But with that said, I never even got hungry, thirsty, or needed a nap.

"Chris, your swordsmanship is far beyond your years. You exhibit many of the known styles, and you combine them into new moves fluidly. Your dual sword technique is so deceptively graceful yet so deadly. Also, your pole weapon skills are next to none!"

She hesitated then continued with a note of sadness in her voice, "Your style and ability with the sword remind me of a certain spirit being I was very close with. He was by far the most skilled..."

"Who, and what do you mean by *was?*" I asked.

"Chris, he no longer exists. We will talk about this another time."

With that said, she continued, "Your subconscious allowed us to spar in real time, holding nothing back, not limiting our speed, quickness, and strength. This was like actual combat, without getting seriously bruised, injured, or killed."

I looked at her. "I don't know about you, but I feel like a Mack truck rolled over me and then backed up and did it again."

"When you wake up, you won't have any bruises."

"I don't know about that. I think my subconscious took this as being real."

Tassi laughed. "We did overdo it."

I brushed a few strands of her hair from her face. "I was fighting for my life, but then I forget, you wolves play extremely rough."

A phone started to ring.

"What's a phone doing in my peaceful place?" I quipped.

Tassi smiled and pointed at my waist.

I looked down. There, pushed into my shorts, was my blue cell phone. I hadn't put that there.

"This can't be in my subconscious. I didn't imagine or think of my phone." I pulled it out and hesitantly put it on speaker.

"Wake up!" a voice yelled. "It's time to get up, Chris!"

It was Momi. Before I could answer...

CHRONICLE 15
CLOWNING AROUND

I AWOKE SPRAWLED OUT ON THE back seat of the van. Momi was driving. Tassi and I were nearly nose to nose, with her staring intently into my eyes. The other three were looking on.

Momi peeked over his shoulder. "You back, really back. Phones awesome."

"Yep," I said lukewarmly.

Hey, haven't you ever been woken up from a dream all confused and disoriented, not knowing for sure whether you were still in a dream or actually back in reality? Well, that just happened, and "yep" was the best response I could muster.

Nila, Cami, and Kora came over and welcomed me back. They nuzzled, chewed, and clawed at me. Yes, I said chewed and clawed. Wolves and their tough love!

Now a disquieting thought came to my mind. Maybe I was imagining what had just happened, or maybe it was just a dream.

Tassi shook her head from side to side.

I gave her a light rub between the ears as I sat up. I searched the pockets of my shorts and started rummaging through my backpack.

Momi took a quick look over his shoulder to see what I was doing. He said, "Look for something?" Then, before I could answer him, he grabbed some objects off the dashboard and tossed them back to me.

"These do," he said.

I caught them. They were the four smooth stones I had used earlier to get peaceful when the mob was attacking us.

"Yes, thanks, Momi." I started juggling and thinking of my peaceful place. It wasn't long until I was there, but it was no longer *my* peaceful place. It was the vacation hotspot as I now called it, *our* peaceful place.

I walked the beautiful black beach, feeling the warm gentle ocean breezes.

Tassi, Tassi, I called out. *Can you hear me?*

Yes Chris, I can hear you.

This isn't or wasn't my imagination. I truly can converse with you?

Yes Chris, you can.

Tassi, I do have a beef with you. What you said earlier isn't true. I do feel sore after our subconscious sparring.

She laughed. *I guess my being a Cherub didn't help either. If I wasn't wearing fur, the black and blue bruises my body is sporting would be quite noticeable. Our subconscious minds must have taken the stimulus, to some degree, as real. It did stop short of giving us sprains or broken bones.*

I chuckled and changed the subject. *How come you're not here?*

You mean in imaginary physical form.

Yes, I said.

You just wanted to talk and know that you were not just imagining it all. Chris, I don't want us to be caught up living in your mind. We can talk spiritually. That's truly real.

I breathed a sigh of reluctant agreement. I stayed in our peaceful place, sitting on the beach, watching the beautiful sunset that continued to change but never actually set. I was at peace.

Then I heard Tassi, *We are at peace.*

I was enjoying the moment. Finally, I willed myself back into the present and found myself juggling. I continued to juggle, performing minor tricks with the stones, like spinning them and juggling them under and around my legs or around my neck and then under each arm. I am quite masterful at juggling and could be a professional performer. When I was a young boy… whoa, I'm not quite fifteen, and I'm talking like an old man! What I mean is that at the early age of seven, I envisioned joining a circus when I grew up and traveling the country, doing my juggling act.

That dream died one day. I remember it quite vividly. It still gives me the heebie-jeebies thinking about it. Jennifer had taken me to a circus, a huge circus. It wasn't one of those little circuses that showed up in your town for three or four days, with one elephant, a few horses, some clowns, a magician, and a flying trapeze duo. We had driven to a large city. It seemed like it took all day to get there. I don't even remember the state we lived in at the time, let alone the city we went to. This was a huge circus that was in a city for months. It even had a lion tamer with not one but eight lions and a white tiger. To top that off, there was even a so-called lizard man and a bearded lady—imagine that!

We went to a clown show; it was funny and even had poodles dressed up like little clowns doing tricks and walking on their hind legs. They selected around ten kids out of the audience. I happened to be one of the chosen ones. I got to help hold the hoops that the poodles jumped through. A small clown gave me a flaming torch and allowed me to help him start some of the hoops on fire, which the poodles proceeded to jump through. That was cool, or should I say hot.

The creepiness started after the clown act. It seemed wherever we went, I would see clowns watching us, even following us. Every time I would try to point them out to my mom, they would disappear. I counted four small clowns around my size, and if this was not bad enough, a big clown appeared. How could Jennifer not notice him? This was downright scarieee. The big clown towered over everyone. He looked to be ten feet tall. The worst was yet to come.

It happened when we were standing in line for the next juggling show. Jennifer was holding my hand as was usual when we were around a lot of people. A man pushed between us; couldn't he just have gone around? More people filed between us. We only got separated for a moment, but in the pushing and shoving of the crowd, I lost sight of my mom. The clowns took this opportunity to make their move.

The little ones started to surround me. I dashed through the sea of people, trying to get away. I heard my mom calling my name, but her plea was drowned out by the din of the crowd. The clowns continued pursuing me. They were hunting me down!

I tried to move in a circle that would bring me back to my mom. This all happened in a matter of seconds. Then I ran into the big clown, the monster clown. He had bright-orange hair that stuck a full foot straight out the sides of his head. He was bald in the middle, but his baldness was painted white. Large red circles around the eyes and the lips made him look like he was always smiling. His nose was the shape and size of a tennis ball, but instead of the traditional happy and playful bright red color, it was a glossy dark green, giving him an overall scary appearance. He grabbed my arm then smiled big, showing his teeth. That was what really sent sudden chills of fear through my body. They looked like the flat triangular teeth of an old-style bear trap and glistened like shiny metal.

I pulled away from his grasp and ran right into a young man and his family. The man looked down at me and asked, "Are you lost, little boy?" He gazed toward the monster clown then back at me. "Yeah, clowns give me the creeps too."

The mother softly spoke. "Dear, let's find your mom and dad." She gently grasped my hand, and with their two little boys in tow, they led me away.

It was especially crowded that day, and we couldn't help but bump into people. Who or what we bumped into next could have been right out of the deepest, darkest jungles of Africa. A wild man, he was tall, dark, and lithe, with stringy, unkempt long black hair that flowed over a fur pelt draped across his shoulders. The man truly had a wild-animal look. His two different-colored eyes, one dark brown, the other light blue, enhanced the wild effect. Did they have a wild-man act at this circus?

When I looked back over my shoulder, the monster clown and his four little cohorts were just watching me. Or were they watching the wild man? I looked over at the wild man. He was intently glaring at the clowns. I don't think he liked clowns either. But was something more going on between the wild man and the clowns? Curiosity got the better of me, and I peered back at the clowns. They now looked as if they were frozen in time. Only their eyes moved, darting erratically back and forth. Terror radiated from their eyes. I kept my head down as I turned back. I was in no way going to look the wild man in the eyes.

We continued our struggle through the crowds, and in a matter of minutes, I was reunited with my mom. The rest of the day, Jennifer held my hand so tight it would turn blue at times. I didn't see the clowns anymore that day, but I didn't stop looking over my shoulder either. To this day, I don't like clowns or circuses. I'm not afraid of clowns, but they all seem to have that sinister expression, even though they're smiling. Anyone that hides behind a mask of paint must be hiding something.

Sometimes thoughts just come into my mind, and sometimes I think they come for a reason. I don't know whether God sends them to prepare me or if it just happens coincidentally. The more I live, the less likely anything seems to be a coincidence. Today was going to further engrain this view.

My reminiscing was interrupted by Momi.

"Hungry. Stop… eat?"

"Yes, we can stop and eat, Momi."

"State Park up ahead. Can grill there," Momi said enthusiastically.

I was already learning that a big part of life, a really big part for Momi, was food!

"Do we have to stop at another park? The last one, we barely got out alive! Can't we find a restaurant to eat at?" I whined.

Momi replied matter-of-factly, "Wolves eat with us at park, and we can sleep there."

I shrugged. He had a good point; we needed to eat and find a place to sleep. No sirens went off in my head warning us to stay away; that was good. But shortly after we took the turnoff to the park, my stomach started to churn. It became queasy and knotted-up; hunger wasn't causing the stomachache. Something... was going to occur at this park, and it probably wasn't going to be good either. Mel said to take challenges on, overcome them and become greater. *Here we go again!*

Why couldn't God just talk to me, tell me what was going on? I know, I know, God expects us to live our lives, to use what we know, and then, if necessary, he will help us. I didn't know if my knotted-up stomach and the reminiscing about circuses and clowns would be much help. It was just a heads-up, a warning to be vigilant, to be on guard. Something was going to happen, and it probably involved Daimonia. I already had my belly full of them, and I wasn't even trying to find them.

Accidentally bumping into them earlier at the Anarchy International Reformists convention had now put me on their radar. Not good, way too soon to be thrown into the frying pan. Big Mel in our last so-called training session nodded in agreement when I stated, '*I, or should I say we, won't need to pursue them, they will pursue us.*' Hopefully I bought us some time before they would find us. I had not given the Daimonia that were active during my conversation with Smitely any idea where Momi and I were traveling to.

Our need right now was getting to Camp Aharonite intact... alive. Mel said I would receive training there.

Momi drove up to the drive-through window at the ranger station. He purchased an Arizona State Park pass and an overnight camp stay. How fortunate someone cancelled their campsite reservation... not! The attendant said, "Don't feed the bears."

Momi smiled and nodded.

We drove in and found our campsite. It was secluded, far away from all the others and had a big firepit. We ventured into the woods to find fuel for our fire. The three girls took off in the direction Momi went, bounding off to who knew where.

Tassi went up ahead of me, disappearing into the shadows of the forest. I felt alone, even though I knew she wasn't far away.

I heard a snap then a crunch; I whirled around, facing the direction of the sounds. There, looming not ten yards away, was a clown. A ten-foot-tall clown! Not good.

Now, talk about being startled. Okay, someone, somebody, or even God gave me a heads-up about clowns. Yes, it probably did help keep me from totally freaking out. Still, I wasn't expecting to see a ten-foot clown in the middle of the woods.

I just shuddered. I didn't like clowns.

The clown came out of the shadows toward me. I got the shock of my life. It had orange hair that stuck straight out from the sides of its head, a green nose... it smiled, showing large, shiny triangular steel teeth. The teeth were menacing. The clown was menacing. It was the same clown from my childhood!

It lumbered forward.

I dropped my firewood, keeping one branch to use as a club. I swung at the clown's head. It just swatted the branch from my hands. Now I was weaponless. I gave it a flying kick in the stomach. I just bounced right off, rolling to the ground. It was glaring down at me. I gave a low roundhouse kick below its knees. Ouch! I felt like I had connected with a tree trunk. My kick, though, had enough power to unbalance the clown. It came crashing down; the noise reverberated through the woods.

This clown was large and heavy.

It gave a deafening roar as it shook its head and rolled over on all fours. The clown roared again and then stood up, grabbing me in a big bear hug. The embrace was crushing me. I gave a headbutt to its big green nose. To my surprise, the clown released me. I crumpled at its feet.

Tassi came charging out of the shadows. She flung herself at the clown's head, forcing it to stumble backward. Tassi landed on her feet.

I shouted, "It's about time!"

Just then the others arrived. Momi yelled, "Bear!"

Nila, Cami, and Kora snarled and lunged at the clown. It batted them away; this clown was strong.

I scrambled away and sat down, watching the battle. I reached into my pocket for my stones and started juggling. I needed to be at peace to think clearly, and so far juggling was the best way. This clown was most formidable. Why had Momi said "bear"? I surveyed the ongoing battle disassociated and unconcerned. I focused on the clown. It began to shimmer and waver in substance, taking on the form of a... bear.

I was battling a bear!

A very large bear and one that was inhabited by Daimonia. They must've clouded my perception, which, in turn, deceived my mind. How did it know of my extreme dislike of clowns and especially this exact clown from my childhood?

I brought my thoughts back to the fight. I concentrated on the clown bear, willing my mind to see the true reality, the spiritual reality. Gradually I began to see shadowy forms hovering in and around the bear. The best way I can describe them is like apparitions: they were there yet not there. The more I willed myself to see spiritually, the more the shadows became separate from one another and took on faint hues of orange, green, and red. They were morphing in size and shape constantly but still radiating those slight hues of color. The reddish-hued seemed more substantial and gave off a stronger aurora; these must be the dominant Daimonia present.

As I concentrated on these reddish forms, a word popped into my mind.

Majoriteen.

What was a Majoriteen? Was it a name for a type of Daimonia, for a group of them, or an individual? In any case this bit of information would be useful for my plan. If the Daimonia could cloud my mind, then I could cloud the bear's mind through it. Now I did not know enough about the Daimonia to attack them directly, but I believed I could do it indirectly through startling them. I would momentarily startle the Daimonia then scare the bear. This is where knowing the name comes in.

Now, you are probably thinking, "Hey, Chris, the fight is already over after all the time you took coming up with this line of attack." No, the battle was still going on. It was time to attack Majoriteen, the main demon or demons, the red apparitions. Now that I thought more about this, I should've gone through the weaker ones. Well, I was going with what had been revealed to my mind, and that was Majoriteen.

I yelled, "Majoriteen!" The bear hesitated.

Mel was right, knowing the name of your attacker does give you some influence, some control over it. In this case for a very brief moment. I immediately pictured fire in my mind and focused it on and around the red apparitions. It wasn't any old fire but that which was near and dear to my heart, the flames of my meteoric descent to Earth. They were still very vivid and real to me. I could even feel the intense heat upon my body. That was how strongly an imprint of the incident was seared into my mind.

The bear immediately stopped the attack. It turned, dropped to all fours, and then proceeded to roll on the ground, trying to squelch the flames. The bear rolled a few times then hightailed it out of there with the Daimonia in tow.

I yelled after it, "Majoriteen, you're fired." Hah, get it? Pretty clever pun—*fired*, for *you are out of here.*

Reveling in my victory was short-lived. *The forest was on fire!*

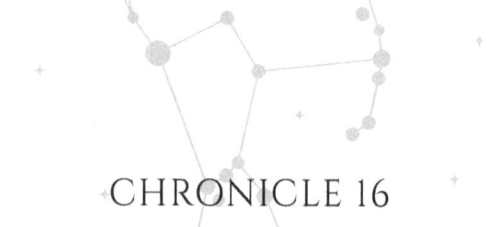

CHRONICLE 16

DINNER SERVED

I HAD STARTED A FOREST FIRE in a state park! Not good. Oh, not so good. I was going to be fugitive No. 1 in Arizona. Chris Gahrlan the arsonist! I had only tried to cloud the bear's mind with the illusion of fire, the same way the Daimonia had clouded mine with that of a scary clown. But the fire wasn't an illusion!

I came back to the now. Momi had taken off his shirt and was smothering the flames. Nila and Cami were using their bodies to extinguish them by rolling over and over. Tassi and Kora were putting out those the bear had started as it ran through the forest. I took off my shirt and blanketed the many small pockets of flames around me.

It took nearly half an hour to vanquish the fire. My shirt was smoldering. I threw it to the ground and stomped on it. The damp forest floor subjugated the heat. If it hadn't been for the dampness of the foliage and the ground, the fire would've escalated.

I could see where the fire had initially started. The ground and all the vegetation were scorched in a five-foot radius. The bear had done a good job of putting out some of the fire. It hadn't been doing this out of the goodness of its heart but was trying to save its own skin. The bear used the stop, drop, and roll method of smothering the fire.

I had set its fur on fire. That bear must have had very oily fur. The oil fueled the fire, which was very fortunate for the bear. The fire lived off the oil, only singeing its fur slightly. This is the same principle as a burning candle: the wax fuels the flame, leaving the wick only slightly charred as the melted wax is drawn off the wick, fueling the flame.

The bear did start numerous fires in the forest in its hasty retreat. Not all the flames were quenched by the initial rolling on the ground. Every now and then, it would do a stop, drop, and roll, trying to put out flames that recurred in its fur.

Momi walked up to me and patted me on the shoulder. "You toasted bear good. Bear not come back."

I laughed. "Thanks, Momi. Let us gather up some wood and make us another fire."

Momi gave me a stare of disbelief.

"Come," I said. "We will start a cooking fire at our campsite."

Momi breathed a sigh of relief. What really gratified me was that Momi would follow whatever I said. He trusted me implicitly. If I wanted to start another fire, he would help start another fire. Momi knew I had knowledge and understanding that he did not comprehend yet, that went beyond the five senses. Momi would be there through thick and thin. He would be my worldly stalwart. If I stumbled, he would be there to pick me up.

When we arrived back at camp, we had a guest. You would think that by now, nothing would shock me. Wrong! I dropped my firewood, and my jaw dropped with it.

"Hi, kid." Barry's face lit up with a big grin.

Momi took it in stride and greeted Pahli, greeted Barry.

Tassi and the other three wolves weren't surprised either. Well, they had probably smelled Barry from a hundred feet off.

I shook my head, picked up my firewood, and dropped it near the firepit. Barry already had a nice fire going.

"Why are you here?" I inquired.

He looked at me. "I'm always where I need to be, son. Right now, that's right here."

"How did you find us?"

"That was easy, my boy. You left a trail of bodies!"

"Whaaat?" I blurted.

Barry winked at Momi and continued. "You left a whole field of bodies, nearly eight hundred!"

I looked at him incredulously.

He continued, toying with me. "Both you and your mom are keeping the police and news people busy. Jennifer trashing a filling station and kidnapping a woman. You taking out an entire peaceful assembly of people." His face was solemn, but a trace of a smile appeared, and then he broke out laughing. "What really led me to you was the GPS on your phone." He smiled even bigger, like the Cheshire Cat. "Technology. Ain't it great!"

He must've seen the expression of concern on my face. "Everything is being taken care of."

I forcefully took a deep breath. Barry hesitated, allowing consternation and curiosity to build.

He then continued. "Our people are already on it, doing a containment story, like we did for your mom's station incident." He saw my countenance of puzzlement and bewilderment. "All your questions and concerns will be answered in time. Just know that we have people on it. You're not alone in this. You have support. The incident at the AIR convention will be reported as 'Entire convention of people collapsed due to contaminated water and extreme heat. No fatalities. Everyone is recovering. The event is postponed.'"

I relaxed a little. I knew—or was pretty sure—I had not killed anyone. My concern was the news: manhunt for teenage terrorist in progress with my picture plastered in every post office and police station in the country.

"Hey, ready, is it? Hungry. Eat now?" Momi interrupted, his hunger getting the best of him.

Barry had three large coolers beside him. He proceeded to take out large slabs of beef and put them on spits over the fire.

"You have enough food there to feed an army," I said.

Barry chuckled. "These wolves are high-maintenance creatures." No sooner had he finished that statement than he was surrounded by three snarling wolves. "They have attitude too," he exclaimed.

Tassi was by my side with a very stately, proud look. Barry held up both hands and waved the wolves to back down. "Okay, okay, I was just jesting. You know, Chris, that these are not really wolves."

I looked Barry in the eyes. "Yeah, I figured that out a while ago."

Momi spoke up. "Wolves not wolves?"

Barry continued, "These wolves are Cherubim that have taken on physical form in the natural world. They do not inhabit or possess, like the Daimonia. They are now physical creatures in this world that must follow the natural laws. Tassi and the three cannot take on another form, like being human. They are not shapeshifters." He paused to let it sink in. "They will remain in the form of wolves."

Barry glanced at me quickly, studying my facial expression, looking for a reaction from me. Did he know how I envisioned Tassi as a human... and that we talked to each other? Could he hear my spiritual chatter?

No! formed in my mind. It was from Tassi, a forceful thought. She had been able to overcome the commotion of my mind.

He smiled then continued. "Cherubim have a predetermined physical form for the natural world. If they are to be a wolf, they are a wolf; a lion, a lion; a human, a human. But they cannot change what they are. Tassi and the three had a mission here on Earth. It seems your missions have intertwined. To have not one but four Cherubim at your side... that is something very unique." He hesitated and shook his head. "And yet there's something even more to this situation than I am aware of."

My wolf friends made a series of soft snorts similar to human snickering. Barry inclined his head to the side, as if straining to hear. Did he pick up on their curt wordless response? I just laughed to myself. My friends did have attitude—lots of it.

Barry jumped up, startling me, but the wolves didn't even twitch. He ran over to the cooking fire.

His concern over burning our food to a crisp was not necessary. Momi had taken upon himself to be the interim chef while Barry and I were talking. Momi had even roasted corn and made a salad.

Barry shrugged and patted Momi on the back. "Thanks," he said.

We ate our meal in silence, gorging ourselves on the food.

I was quite hungry. Did fighting spiritual battles drain you physically? I didn't think so. I couldn't possibly eat that much food to replenish the spirit power I had released... in knocking out more than eight hundred people. My hunger was probably due to all the physical exertion in trying to stay alive.

I heard a noise behind us and turned around. A man was walking toward us. As he got closer, I saw that he was a park ranger.

"Hello, folks. How are you doing this evening?"

I quickly but nonchalantly looked around. My wolf friends were gone. They were scary quiet. Most likely they had disappeared before the ranger was even close.

Two more rangers came up the path. The pair started poking around our campsite.

Barry spoke. "Can we help you, rangers?"

The lead ranger turned to Barry. "We are trying to track down the individuals who torched part of this forest earlier today."

The other two rangers came up to Momi and me and looked us over.

One pointed at me and spoke up. "Sir, these two boys' shirts are smudged with soot and have burn marks."

The lead ranger came over to us. "You boys carelessly start a forest fire?"

"No sir," I replied. I thought to myself, *That's a true statement. We were not careless, and we didn't set the forest on fire. I set a bear on fire.*

I thought I heard a chuckle in my head. Was that Tassi?

Barry broke the interrogation. "The boys used their shirts as hot pads, carrying the scorched spits from the campfire."

The lead ranger shook his head, and a small grin came onto his face. "Quick thinking, Barry."

"I thought so, too, Bill."

They laughed and shook hands, pulling each other into an embrace.

"How long has it been, Barry?"

"Many, many years, Bill. Far too many."

I jumped in. "Okay, what's going on, Barry?"

"These men are on our side, Chris."

I inclined my head, not fully comprehending.

Barry smiled. "They are Aharonites."

"Oh, that's so helpful. Who or what is an Aharonite?" I huffed.

"Like I mentioned before, we have support. *You* have support. Your questions will be more fully answered at Camp Aharonite."

Bill came over and shook my hand. "Sorry, kid, but I couldn't resist having a little fun. Anyway, that was some fire you started."

I looked Bill straight in the eye. "I didn't set the forest on fire. I set a bear on fire!"

Bill looked at me then back at Barry and started laughing. They both laughed. Momi couldn't hold back a giggle. The other two rangers seem to be enjoying it too. The laughing turned contagious and overwhelming. I couldn't remain solemn and broke out into laughter too.

When everyone was finally laughed out, I recounted what had happened. Barry listened intently, analyzing and evaluating.

Bill stood up. "I hope I never have to face a ten-foot clown or, for that matter, an angry bear. We will write up in our report that a lightning strike started a fire, and a group of campers were able to put it out."

They said their goodbyes and left.

No sooner had they left than my four friends showed up. Boy, they would make great ninjas. They were whisper quiet.

I gave Barry a stern look. "How did you know about the clown attack and the fire?"

"I didn't know about the attack till you told your story, but I knew something had happened by the look of you two."

I shot him a glance back.

Barry continued, "You two were definitely playing with fire. You both have soot smudges and smell of smoke."

I looked at Momi and myself. Yeah, we had an encounter with fire.

We cleaned up camp, then Momi and I went to the camp shower facilities. The men's showers were basically open stalls which had some skimpy shower curtains that gave a little privacy but not much.

I heard Momi give a shout. "Whoa." He was in the next stall.

I then felt something furry brush my legs. Nila had come into my shower stall. Momi must've had the same surprise from one of the other wolves coming in on him. I looked at Nila and saw that she was soot ridden from the fire too. I lathered her up and rinsed her off. When I was finished, she tilted her head upward toward me.

I patted her on the head. "You're welcome, Nila."

With that, she squeezed out of the shower. No sooner had she left than Tassi nudged her way in. I lathered her up and rinsed her down too. Then a thought came into my mind: I was in the nude! I could feel my cheeks turning red.

Tassi inclined her head upward and shook it gently from side to side.

"I know, I know," I said. "Even if Cherubim aren't male or female, you took on a human female form in my subconscious."

Tassi gave a soft, high-pitched whine. I knew she had heard and understood. My soul, so to speak, was bare to Tassi and the others.

All my thoughts were spiritually transmitted to them, so what was the big deal about being physically bare?

Tassi gave another whine. I softly rubbed one of her ears. "Yeah, I won't change being totally open to you and the others."

She nudged me, telling me it was time to finish up. The wolves had it easy. They just shook themselves off, flinging water everywhere, and were ready to go. Momi had brought towels, soap, shampoo and even a change of clothes for both of us. I didn't know where he'd found everything, but it seemed he was prepared for this road trip of ours. Momi was my mom away from Mom. We were now both wearing jeans—our shorts had gone bye-bye for now.

Barry greeted us with a smile when we arrived back at camp. "You two, or should I say all of you, look much cleaner now. Let's sit around the campfire and chat."

Barry absentmindedly tended to the fire as he spoke. "Chris, one of those Daimonia knew you. It must've been around when you had your clown incident as a boy. It recognized you today and projected itself as something you feared or disliked."

I responded, "Why?"

"You're quite different than the normal human."

I shrugged as if to say to go on.

"They sensed you being different." He put another log on the fire. "Chris, have you heard the term 'familiar spirit'?"

"Yes, mainly from books and movies. It's a spirit, a demon that helps and attends to a witch or sorcerer."

"That's a common conception for familiar spirit, but the true or accurate one in real life is its familiarity, its closeness, its association with a person."

Barry leaned forward. "Think of it as family, your family spirit... they do not come alone. Where there is one, there are many. They become thoroughly knowledgeable about a person's life and family. Now, I prefer to use the word 'Daimonia' instead of the word 'spirits.' Many people, too many, think spirits are the dead living without a body, so-called ghosts. The dead are not living. There are no ghosts. It is just a Daimonia pretending to be the dead person. They are familiar Daimonia, totally intimate with that person's life. They may even have been around for generations of that family. These Daimonia will move with that family, and some will even tag along with the children as they leave the house to live on their own."

He locked eyes with me. "Chris, most people are not inhabited or possessed with the Daimonia, but they are being very closely scrutinized and observed by them, by familiar Daimonia. This clown bear, as you refer to it, must have Daimonia that were at the circus. It knew of your incident with the circus clowns, even the monster clown. It may even be one or more of the Daimonia that were hunting you that day."

That just sent a cold shiver down my spine. "They know everything about me!"

"No," Barry said. "You do have Daimonia that have observed you from time to time but no familiar Daimonia."

"Whew! Wait... wait... how do you know?"

"That is for another time, Chris."

I shook my head; at least I didn't have any Daimonia family. I breathed a sigh of relief. This was short lived. The clown bear incident popped up in my mind. "We have to leave immediately," I blurted.

Barry shook his head in an exasperated manner. "No, Chris. Remember, these Daimonia are in a bear."

"So?" I retorted.

"Chris, bears do not have the mental capacity for speech like humans. That bear and the Daimonia inhabiting it can relate very little to other Daimonia. Humans that are inhabited by Daimonia are the ones to be truly concerned about."

"Toast marshmallows?" It was Momi, his insatiable appetite resurfacing already.

I laughed. I was glad that Momi was by my side. He kept things fun and light. When the weight of the world is on your shoulders, so to speak, it's nice to have a reprieve from reality at times.

A few days ago, everything had been normal. Now beings from another realm had made a crowd of people turn all zombie-like and attack me. They made a bear appear as a ten-foot clown, a menacing monster clown that wanted to use me for fodder. What would be next? It was just insane. I pinched myself. *Ouch!* No, I was not dreaming.

I let my mind wander to my peaceful place just for a moment. Tassi's head lifted, and she looked directly at me with her brilliant-blue eyes.

Together.

I heard the word *together* in my mind. Tassi had spoken to me; we would be together in this.

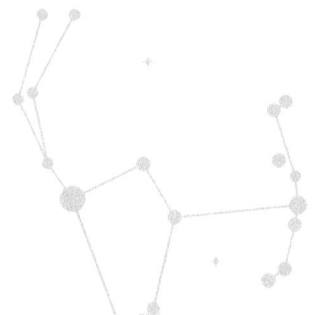

THIEVERY BY FUR

B ARRY LOOKED AT ME, TILTED his head, then looked at Tassi. He raised his eyebrows then brought his attention back to me. Had he heard Tassi say "together"?

He shrugged and then said, "Let's call it a night. I will see you guys off in the morning."

Momi already had the sleeping bags laid out near the campfire. He was always on top of things. I turned back toward where Barry had been standing. He was no longer anywhere to be seen. That was just freaky. He always seemed to show up when he was needed and disappear when not. Like Barry would always say, "I am always where I need to be."

I took out my four smooth stones and started to juggle. It wasn't long before all my cares and concerns were gone. I called out to Tassi spiritually.

I'm here, Chris.

Did I hear you say "together" now twice?

Yes, Chris.

How come I heard you the second time? I wasn't peaceful then. My mind did wander... I lapsed into daydreaming for a moment.

That's the key, Chris. Your mind wasn't totally absorbed in thought processes. It still took effort for me to get that one word, "together," through to you. Your spirit is getting stronger in communicating. It is learning how to connect with your mind. Just like a child learning to walk; the child tries to stand and move its legs, and the mind and body build the correct neural pathways to the limbs. Your spirit is doing just that. Right now, it's building the spiritual neural pathways to your physical mind. Soon, we will be able to talk spiritually anytime, without you going to your peaceful place.

I was glad I didn't have to figure out how to speak spiritually... I didn't even need to learn Cherub. That was good enough for me.

Then I remembered what I had wanted to ask. *Tassi, does Barry hear us?*

I don't think so, but I believe he surmises that you and I can communicate.

Oh, you got that impression too. How about Nila, Cami, and Kora—do they still hear me?

Your spirit is no longer projecting your every thought randomly. Only when you make a conscious effort to them will they hear you.

That's not the case between you and me?

No, it isn't, Chris. I still hear all your thoughts just like they were my own. We seem to be intertwined spiritually... linked together.

Why's that?

I don't know, Chris.

Is it because we befriended each other? No, that can't be it either. I'm friends with Nila, Cami, and Kora too.

Chris, I was drawn to you spiritually before I even knew you, and your spirit was drawn to mine. I think that's why we have so strong a bond in the physical world. Like I mentioned before, Cherubim don't have emotions, but I'm starting to! I'm forming a theory that because I am linked to you spiritually, your human emotions are coming across too, adapting and intertwining with my spirit. My physical form of a wolf was manifested by my spirit, so it shouldn't be the cause of my experiencing emotions. Cami, Nila, and Kora haven't experienced emotions, and they have the same physical construct of a wolf.

What do you mean by physical construct?

Chris, in simple terms, a biological robot. This wolf body is animated by spirit. My spirit is infused throughout this physical form and gives it life.

Do you eat, sleep, and breathe? Oh yeah, how can I forget, you gals eat like there is no tomorrow! And you are the noisiest sleepers.

"I am hungry!"

I hesitated. I had never heard that voice before. "*Who said that?*"

"Me. I'm hungry."

"Okay. Who's 'me'?"

"Kora. I am hungry!"

Tassi, I thought you said the others couldn't hear me.

No, I said you would have to intentionally direct it at them. Soon, you will be able to converse with them even when you are not completely at peace. Your spirit is learning very fast.

"Oh, this is so koosh," I said out loud. "*Nila, Cami, are you two awake?*" I spoke in spirit.

"*Yes.*"

"*We are now!*"

The "we are now" response sounded grumpy, perturbed. That had to be Nila. The "yes" response—that was Cami. It was gentler, more understanding. I didn't hear any flippant remarks back on what I was thinking. They couldn't hear my thoughts anymore. That was a relief.

"*Sorry for waking you, Nila.*"

All I heard back from Nila was a short, forceful exhale.

"*Good night, Cami.*"

"*Good night, Chris.*"

"*Good night, Kora.*"

"*I'm still hungry.*"

Yep, I had been right on the voices. This speaking by spirit was so koosh.

I had a peaceful, uneventful night until I was rudely awakened. Something had just walked over my stomach. Then noises of rummaging through our stuff broke the stillness. It was too dark to see clearly; the moon was obscured by an overcast sky. A shadowy thing scurried past me, then another one. It sounded like they were all over. Now, you would think I would be scared or at least concerned, but I wasn't. That small inner voice didn't sound an alarm, and neither was my stomach tied in knots. That was another telltale sign that something was afoot.

The commotion going on under the cover of a cloudy night was disturbed by a scream. Had that come from Momi? It was very high-pitched and would've put any falsetto singer to shame. Where were the girls? Nothing seemed to get past them, but even the scream hadn't sent them into action. I vaguely made out a large shadowy silhouette that seemed to be jumping up and down, swatting the air. It moved and sounded like Momi.

"*Go back to sleep. It's just critters.*"

"Who said that?" I blurted out. That voice was familiar. "*Nila, is that you?*"

"*Yeah, tell Momi to go back to sleep. It's just night critters.*"

"Whoaaaa!" Something had just run into the back of my leg, and another something scurried over my foot.

"*Chris, they're just... what do humans call them?... raccoons,*" Nila said, grumbling.

"Momi, they're just raccoons,"

"Raccoon. What raccoon?"

"Momi, they're just little night animals looking for food. They won't hurt you."

"Make go away. Can't sleep with raccoon around."

"*Will you two go—to sleep?*" Nila huffed.

"After I stoke the fire," I responded flippantly.

"Who Chris talking to? And what stoke fire?"

"*Go to sleep, you two!*" came another sleepy and very perturbed request from Nila.

It must have seemed strange to Momi, hearing some of my replies to Nila. Sometimes I forgot and didn't speak just internally in spirit to Nila but also spoke it out loud at the same time. This was all quite new to me.

"I'll explain later, Momi. Go back to sleep."

I threw some small branches and then some slightly bigger ones onto the few remaining embers. I bent down and blew gently on the embers until they came alive, glowing red-hot. I increased the frequency and intensity of my blowing until flames leapt forth, hungrily consuming the branches.

The fire bathed the surrounding darkness in light. I couldn't believe my eyes. We must have had the entire park's population of raccoons! The blazing fire had no effect on frightening them away. The little masked thieves just continued scampering about, searching for something.

I yelled for everyone to wake up. Tassi and the others didn't even twitch; they were in a deep sleep, totally oblivious to all the commotion. It didn't even faze the raccoons either. I even scathingly commanded Nila to get her lazy butt up, to no avail. Just moments before I had a very minimal conversation with a groggy and grumpy Nila and Momi in a frantic state, jumping up and down. What was up with everyone being comatose? I yelled within my spirit for the girls to wake up. I got a few lackluster yawns in response. I pictured and projected a bright intense light from my spirit into each of their faces—megawatts, like that coming from the lights of a football stadium. I even added the cheering of seventy-five thousand football fans.

On my third attempt, they must have gotten the full effect of being thrown right into the pending action of a Monday-night football game. The girls nearly jumped out of their skins. Nila was the first to respond. She gave a throaty, menacing growl, with the others adding their voices.

All four girls, along with Momi, were now attacking the raccoons. The girls tossed them out of camp, grabbing them by the scruff of their necks or by their tails. They crash-landed into the trees and the surrounding brush. It didn't take long before the rest of the raccoons hightailed it out of camp before becoming flying acrobats too.

"Thanks, girls. They were becoming a real nuisance."

I heard Nila in my head. *"Can we get some sleep now?"*

"Yes, Nila," I said out loud.

Momi looked at me quizzically. I shrugged and said, "I'll explain tomorrow. Get some sleep now."

I stretched out on my sleeping bag with Tassi and Cami beside me. I could feel a warmth and peacefulness envelop my mind; it was Tassi's spiritual presence blending with mine.

Sweet dreams, Chris.

Good night, Tassi.

"Good night, Cami."

"Good night, Chris."

Cami had responded! I was all ecstatic that it was getting easier and easier for my spirit to hear and speak with my friends.

The next thing I knew, I was awakening to the smells of breakfast: eggs, bacon, and pancakes being cooked over an open fire. Barry had returned and was cooking up a storm. Pancakes were flying off the griddle with Momi catching them on plates. The eggs came next and then the bacon. Barry would've made a great short-order cook. He was fast, and the food was very edible. We all ate till we were too full to eat any more. It seems you can always eat so much more when you're in the great outdoors.

Barry looked at Momi and me. "You two can do the cleanup. By the way, your camp looks like it has been ransacked."

I looked at Momi and then smiled back at Barry. "We had some unwelcome guests last night."

Barry's eyebrows twitched upward; I could see I had caught his curiosity. I related the events of the night—actually it was early morning.

Barry listened intently then asked, "Have you checked to see if you are missing anything?"

"No," I said.

Barry looked at me straight in the eyes. "Don't you find it rather odd that Tassi and the others slept through it?"

"Well... we did have a very hectic day, with the Anarchist International Reformists incident and the park fire escapade."

Barry spoke up. "Tassi, and the girls, they are Cherubim. Yes, in physical bodies but still spirit beings. They don't need to sleep."

"Are you saying someone, or *something*, put them into a deep sleep?"

Barry arched his eyebrows and gave me a slight wink as if to say, "Son, you're starting to catch on."

I shook my head gently from side to side, a couple of thoughts forming in my mind.

I spoke my current thought. "If the girls were induced into a deep sleep, no longer able or concerned about our protection, why didn't the enemy take us out?"

"Chris, not all Daimonia or spirit beings are your direct enemies. There are many who want you, some testing you, others waiting for you to do something, and some may even be helping you. When they feel the time is right, they will make their move."

"Yeah, that really answered my question. Now I just have more questions that need answering. Oh, oh, and why wasn't I affected? Why, why, why?" I blurted.

Barry gently touched my shoulder. "Chris, I don't fully know the answers."

"How about Tassi and the girls? Would they know?"

Barry's eyes had a glint of recognition; he looked directly into my eyes. "You can communicate... speak with them?"

A big smile formed on my face. "Yes, yes, I can!"

Barry shook his head, "I thought about the possibility but ruled it out. The likelihood of Cherubim speaking with a human... not happening. Their hanging around and watching out for you... should have alerted me otherwise. Cherubim are a very close group. They are not known to associate with any other spirit beings, let alone with a human! It's just them and God."

"*Bahh...*"

"*Hmmph!*"

"*What does he know?*"

"*Snob!*"

An influx of comments bombarded my mind from Cami, Kora, and Nila.

Tassi spoke to me. *Being guardians of the Physical Realm has its downside. We are not able to associate with other spirit beings.*

Tassi's remark to me of the Cherubim isolation from others brought sadness to my heart. But they befriended me... a mere human. Before I could ask Tassi about this, she continued, *Another time, I'll explain. Let's get back to the immediate situation; I do have a good guess as to who put us into a deep sleep... Nod!*

What is Nod? I asked.

Haven't you heard the expression "he nodded off," or "he went to the 'Land of Nod'"? These are referring to one going to sleep, going to the mythical land of sleep... the Land of Nod.

Just then, Barry blurted, "It's Nod."

I turned toward Barry. "Give the man a gold star."

Barry glared at me. "You already knew that, didn't you?"

"Yep," I said. "The hundred-dollar question, though, is why? And who is Nod working with?"

Barry answered, "Nod is doing her own thing. She doesn't work with others."

Tassi and the girls were now searching the campsite. They were sniffing around, poking their noses here and there—into places I wouldn't touch with a gloved hand, let alone push my nose into.

"What wolves doing?" Momi inquired.

"I think they're trying to figure out what the raccoons took from us."

Cami and Kora sniffed Momi up and down then sniffed his sleeping area. They finally became very interested in one of his extra pair of shoes. Tassi was sniffing my sleeping bag and backpack, while Nila started sniffing my pants leg. She didn't stop there; she continued up to my waist, then she stood up on her back legs, resting one paw gently on my shoulder while dropping her head to intently sniff my shirt pocket. Then she returned to all fours.

Nila spoke to me. "*What did Chris have in a shirt pocket?*"

"*Phone,*" I said to her spiritually.

Barry came over. "Chris, are you missing something from your shirt pocket?"

"Yeah, my phone. I didn't know I was missing it till Nila inquired."

"*What did Momi have in his shoe?*" Cami asked me.

I looked over at Momi. "Hey, Momi, what did you have in one of your shoes last night?"

He ran over to his sleeping bag and picked up his extra pair of shoes. He looked and felt inside both then turned to me. "Phone, had phone in shoe last night. Now gone."

Tassi and the others were already sniffing out the raccoon trails. The only problem was the scent trails fanned out in a crisscross hodgepodge from our camp. There were hundreds of raccoon trails, and most likely, they had passed the phones off to one another. It would take days to track our phones down.

"Hey, wait a minute," I said. "Why bother finding our phones? Won't they return to us anyway? The infomercial said they could never be lost, that they would automatically return to the owner."

Barry interjected, "Yes, they will eventually, but I have a strong suspicion that Nod had the raccoons also take other items with your spiritual scent on them. The phones won't reappear to you until the scent wears off."

"We have a spiritual scent?"

"Chris, your skin, hair, perspiration, all have been saturated by your spirit," Barry replied. "They probably took the towels you dried off with after your showers. They would contain dead skin and hair cells, along with plenty of body oils. Nod will have plenty of time to hack into your phones and gain some very valuable information. It will take the girls too long to hunt Nod down," Barry finished in a morose tone.

I blurted giddily, "Have no fear! Chris is here!"

Nila, Cami, Kora, and Tassi gave me glares. I quickly walked over to the van, climbed into the passenger side, and opened the glove compartment. I pulled out the pink cell phone then jumped out of the van, waving it enthusiastically and saying, "We will track them using the GPS. All our phones are interconnected."

Tassi and the others just shook their heads slowly.

Barry walked over to me. "We will have to be careful, Chris. Nod could be laying a trap for us. If Nod knew of the other phones, Nod probably knew of this one also."

"It's no trap," I replied. "Nod could've taken all of us out earlier. Nod is forcing or motivating us to come and find him or her... or it." I turned to Tassi. "Is Nod male or female?"

Tassi shook her head vigorously; I knew I had hit a nerve.

"Okay, okay, I'll refer to Nod as an 'it' for now. I do not know what Nod wants but I believe we must go to it. For some reason, Nod cannot come to us."

We used the phone's GPS to guide us as we trekked our way through the forest using the hiking and deer trails. We were making good time. We must have gone nearly ten miles and had not caught up to the raccoons. I couldn't believe raccoons could travel this fast and this far, even with their head start.

The trail finally opened up to a meadow. A large bird was circling high over a tall lone pine tree in the distance. The GPS signal pinpointed the tree as the location of our phones. It was a massive pine, a granddaddy of a tree, but it didn't look healthy. It had a pale, sickly green color to it. Everything around it had similar hues. Even the meadow surrounding the tree looked pale and dying.

The grass was mainly yellows and browns. Wait... the trees and vegetation weren't dead or dying. Now that I looked at it closer, it was as if everything was dormant... asleep. We were in the land of... the Land of Nod.

Then it dawned on me that I hadn't heard the others recently. How far had we traveled into this sleep zone? I stopped and turned around slowly. I didn't want to see what I had already surmised, but I had to know for sure.

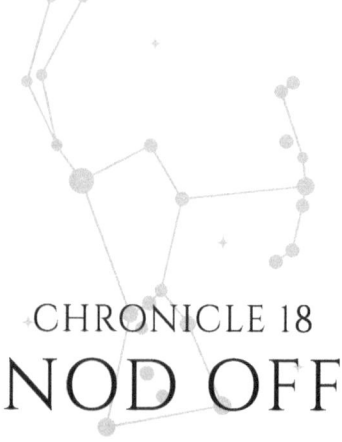

CHRONICLE 18
NOD OFF

MOMI WAS THE FIRST TO go. He was on his knees with his head down, arms hanging limp by his sides, snoring up a storm. Barry made it another fifty or so yards farther. He looked as if he had taken one last step and collapsed to the ground. His face mushed into the soft grass with his butt slightly raised into the air. It didn't look at all comfortable.

Nila, Cami, and Kora fared a little better than Barry, but they too, eventually succumbed to the slumber party. Each of them collapsed, with their front legs giving way and their forward momentum carrying them snout first into the dense carpet of yellow-brown grass.

I turned back around toward the stately but sickly-colored lone pine tree. There ahead of me was Tassi, still on all fours but with her head bowed toward the ground.

Tassi... Tassi, I called out to her spiritually.

She replied very faintly, *Sleepy.*

Tassi, stay with me, girl.

Trying but so very, very drowsy.

I was able to speak to Tassi without getting peaceful. Did this land of Nod calm the commotion of my mind or had my spirit become dominant? It was probably both. At least I didn't need to juggle.

I was the only one not affected by the sleep malady. I felt wide awake. Why only me? It seemed I was immune to the sleep-induced coma of the Land of Nod.

I walked over to Tassi and knelt. I gently cupped her head in both hands, lifting it till we were nose to nose, and looked directly into her eyes. She had a dazed, tired look on her face, as if she was soon to nod off. Ha-ha, *'nod off,'* ha-ha ... oh, I crack myself up sometimes.

I asked God for the correct course of action. Almost immediately, I felt a warm inner peace spring forth from within and with it a feeling of energy infusing my mind and body with vitality and vigor. I allowed the energy to continue to grow. It was like an underground spring with its waters bubbling up through the surface of the ground, water pooling upon itself until finally overflowing in concentric rings, overcoming the ground around it.

I knew God had answered me. Sleep was not something that you directly fought against. You prevailed over sleep by becoming energetic. Just like light dispelled darkness—vitality, energy, dispelled sleep. Nod was putting to sleep the mind and body by blocking or diminishing our biological... our physical energy, thus causing sleep.

I continued envisioning my spiritual energy as a spring of life-giving waters washing over and infusing vitality into Tassi's body. I could feel it flow out of me and into her. Alertness and aliveness shone forth from her eyes again. She was wakening!

Chris, thank you. A few moments later, her tone shifted. *Chris, Chris!*

I felt a closeness with Tassi like nothing before. I was experiencing sounds and smells that were immensely more stimulating than I ever had. My body felt different...the thick, coarse grass caressing my paws.

Chris! It was commanding yet pleading. *Chris! Chrissss!*

A searing burst of energy came with the last *'Chrissss'*. It jolted me back into control.

Chris, focus! Allow only your spiritual energy to flow, not your spirit into me!

I continued envisioning Tassi being energetic, bubbling with vigor and vitality. I no longer focused directly on the power or energy transferring to Tassi.

Chris, I am fully awake now.

It felt like someone was hugging me. It was a spiritual hug from Tassi.

Chris, your spiritual abilities seem to be on hyperdrive. It's like you're being energized, tapping power from any spirit being lulled to sleep by Nod. Tassi continued, *I did not think it was possible, the absorption of spirit, but you nearly assimilated my being!*

I heard a voice within my head. "*Well done, young one.*" The voice was warm, inviting, comforting. It could easily lull one to sleep... except for me, of course.

"*Release the others,*" I shot back.

The smooth, soothing voice gently responded, "*I have no direct control over my sleep inducement on living things. It is my essence; wherever I am, so also is sleep.*"

I went out on a limb and spoke. "*Nod, what do you want with us?*"

In a voice that was sultry and mesmerizing, "*It is only you I want, Chris.*" Hey, I was right on who was talking to me.

I heard Tassi's sarcastic thought, *Obviously it was Nod.*

I gave Tassi a mental shrug then replied back to Nod, "*Okay. What do you want with me?*"

"*Come closer and I'll explain.*" Nod could sense my wariness. "*Chris, my nighty-night personality doesn't affect you, so why not come closer?*"

"*Come closer to what, Nod?*"

"*To the majestic pine tree, of course.*"

I laughed within; that pine tree was anything but majestic.

Tassi and I continued walking toward Nod. We were at least a half mile away.

For some reason, Nod seemed like a she, even though Tassi had said spiritual entities didn't have a gender. Maybe it was because Nod's voice came across in a higher-pitched range... feminine.

Chris, it's your mind that is translating Nod's spirit speech into a feminine voice.

Yes, but my mind is translating it from what my spirit is passing down to it.

The notion of genderless spirits I'm going to have to refute. Spirit beings seemed to have masculine and feminine traits and emotions, so why not male and female spirit beings? Tassi had definite feminine personality traits as well as feminine emotions!

"Are you two giving me the silent treatment?"

"Nod, we are having a conversation..."

Tassi just ignored Nod's intrusion. *Chris, it's because our spirits are inhabiting a physical life form that we have gender traits.* Tassi objected to my unspoken thought of her becoming riled. *I am not getting agitated!*

You are a little touchy on this subject, undeniably overreacting like a female. I laughed inwardly. I knew males got touchy easily too. I was just having fun with her, ruffling a few feathers, or should I say fur.

Nod interrupted. *"This is very intriguing. I should be able to hear your spirit conversations. Even if I wouldn't understand the language, I should still hear you spiritually. It is one of my skills... the ability to eavesdrop on spiritual conversations even at vast distances."*

"I guess your ability to eavesdrop doesn't work on Tassi and me. Take a nap... we will be with you shortly!"

It seemed our thought conversations were private. They were not the same as spirit-to-spirit conversing of other spirit beings.

Only since you learned to control your spirit ramblings! Tassi piped.

Before I could come back with a quirky rebuttal, she solemnly asked, *Chris, do you think that was wise, telling her off like that?*

She'll get over it... after a little hissy fit.

I came back to our debate on gender of spirit beings. *Nod is a tree, and Nod definitely seems like a woman.*

Chris, a tree isn't female or male.

Okay, you have me there, but… explain why you four all have feminine Cherub names. You all reside in female wolf forms. You pictured yourself as a woman if you could take on a human form. Explain all that!

"*You two… enough of the silent approach with me,*" Nod tersely piped.

I was glad our conversations were private. We would have to get back to this discussion at a later time.

"*Nod, we will be with you shortly.*"

Tassi spoke. *Chris, do you think it's wise getting closer to Nod?*

No, but I really want to find out what she's up to and get our phones back.

I discreetly looked at my mom's phone. The GPS now indicated the other two phones were right where Tassi and I were standing. The phones must either be below us, buried or above us, in the air. I decided to look skyward, and that was when I saw this large bird spiraling downward. Tassi looked upward at the same time. You know, she did hear my every thought.

We both watched a very large bird, a man's height in body length, descending gracefully toward us. I would put it in the eagle family, a golden eagle. This bird, though, was not the normal color of a golden eagle. It was of a champagne gold color like that of a palomino horse. I have never seen or heard of a golden eagle that actually looked gold in color. They were always dark brown with just a slight gold sheen on the back of their neck and head. This bird was a rarity. What was its association with Nod?

I could now feel the beat of its wings as it hovered above us not more than fifteen feet above the ground. Its talons were clutching two objects, one red and one blue. The eagle released the objects. I instinctively caught one in each hand. They were our cell phones. It beat its wings vehemently, defying Earth's gravity, and slowly ascended back into the sky once again. I didn't believe eagles or birds this large were meant to hover. It looked like it took all its might to ascend back into the sky.

I smiled. Now I understood. I had been right: the raccoons had not traveled the ten miles to Nod in record-breaking time. The phones had been given to the eagle.

Tassi spoke. *Let's leave quickly. We have the phones.*

No, we must meet Nod and hear her out.

I still do not think that's wise, Chris.

It's not the safest course, but Nod has something to offer. It could be valuable to us.

I knew Tassi was not keen on my idea. It was as if she was shaking her head in disagreement. I was starting to feel her thoughts. In time, I would hear them as she did mine.

"*You two, quit all your jabbering and pick up the pace,*" Nod scolded.

You do realize, Tassi, that Nod gave the phones back as a gesture of goodwill. She is testing to see if we are willing to put ourselves on the line like she is going to do.

"*Yes, you are correct. It is apparent that Nod never intended to hack into the phones. She wants or needs you!*"

"*Will you two quit dawdling? At this rate it will be nightfall before you make it to me,*" Nod whined. She paused then continued, "*Chris, I need you to release me.*"

"*Why?*"

"*There are those that are going to use me to imprison spirit beings.*"

I gasped, and I felt Tassi tense up.

"Why me?"

"*You are not affected by my sleep-inducing effect. You can get close enough to me to cast me out of… my prison, this tree. I'm not your enemy, Chris, but your enemies are going to use me against you.*"

I hesitated before responding. "*You want me to cast you into the air?*"

"No, that would not be best."

231

Tassi interjected, *Chris, if you cast Nod into the air, she would just be dispersed. It would be very unpleasant for Nod, and she would just reform eventually.*

"*You want me to cast you into a person... into one of my friends? Or into an animal?*"

"*No, Chris. You see what effect I have on people, animals, or any living thing.*"

"*You want me to take you inside of me?*"

"*Oh, no. Anyone even remotely around you would then nod off.*"

"*What then?*"

"*Chris, I want you to cast me into a holding vessel.*"

"*Imprison you?*"

"*I am already imprisoned. I have no place in the physical realm.*"

I started feeling sorry for Nod.

Chris, there is a reason Nod was expelled from heaven.

Before I could inquire more about this statement from Tassi, Nod continued, "*I will give you the information on how to make a spirit-holding vessel.*"

"*What? I'm going to have to make this spirit prison too?*"

"*I'm going voluntarily. I am choosing my own form of prison.*"

Tassi chimed in, this time broadcasting herself so Nod could hear. "*I've never heard of a holding vessel for spirits.*"

I could almost imagine Nod smiling as she stated, "*It has never been done before.*"

There was a long, deep silence before Tassi retorted, "*It cannot be done! Only the Great Abyss that God sealed can imprison spirits.*"

Nod countered, "*My spiritual nature of sleep will make it possible. It has the ability to reduce, even negate, physical energy. Thus, it can be used to imprison a spirit being that is using a physical body or that's in a physical object.*"

"*Wait, you can negate the energy of atoms making up an object?*"

"*Yes, Chris.*"

Tassi shot back to me, *That is very seriously scary...*

Nod continued her explanation. "*It is actually going to be a containment vessel rather than a holding. It needs to contain the spiritual effects of my spirit. If it does not... I would put everything to sleep that's in proximity to it.*"

I had an inkling to take another look at my surroundings. I had seen this before, but I really didn't think anything of it till now. This Land of Nod had bodies of animals scattered within its boundaries. Most were small animals near the perimeter. Deer and faster animals or those that fell from above made it farther in. What was intriguing—strange, even—was that I did not see any skeletons or decaying animals.

I was interrupted by Nod. "*We must hurry!*"

"*Why?*"

"*There are those that are hunting you.*"

"*Tell me something I don't know.*"

"*They are starting to converge on you! They are near.*"

What? I thought to myself. Barry said it would take a long time for the clown bear spirit to relay my last known location.

The preacher, Joshua Smitely... Tassi posed.

That was hundreds of miles away.

Chris, maybe they are monitoring any intriguing news stories and came across our park fire incident.

Tassi, there are park fires all the time; what is so special about that one?

It was reported by the park rangers that lightning strikes caused it.

Well, I said, *lightning does cause many forest fires.*

Yes, it does, Chris, but there were no reported storms anywhere near this park... and these purported lightning strikes also happened in close proximity to Nod.

Tassi, we didn't even know about Nod till today.

But Chris, they did.

Nod broke the silence. "*Are you two done talking to each other? That is so not polite having your internal private conversations... while I'm waiting.*"

I liked Nod. She seemed genuinely friendly and sincere but much too talkative. Yak, yak, yak—she could talk you to sleep. That would get on my nerves after a while, the unceasing chitchat from Nod.

I wouldn't trust her, snipped Tassi.

I playfully replied, *I'm getting vibes of jealousy.*

I'm not jealous. Cherubim don't have emotions.

Let's nix that all-encompassing statement. A certain Cherub now has emotions and is developing more. I quickly continued, *Tassi, she won't replace you as my best and closest friend.*

Chris, I know that. I am concerned, not jealous. She has fallen from heaven. She is not on God's side. I don't like you getting close to her. That could and would be dangerous!

Nod spoke with great annoyance. "*I hope I'm not interrupting… Actually I do. We must hurry! They could trap all of you here with me.*"

I didn't like that prediction at all. Being trapped in the Land of Nod would really put a damper on my social life; I didn't even have any good books to read. What would Tassi and I do all day? Just walk around? We were impervious to the sleep syndrome. I didn't think I could revive the others; it had been the linking of our spirits that allowed me to free Tassi from Nod's sleep effect.

How about eating? Would we just have an insatiable appetite but never waste away? Oh, I forgot, we did have plenty of wild game that was just sleeping. What would happen when that was gone? Back to being hungry all the time, waiting for some unlucky animal to enter the sleep zone? That would be a terrible fate for both of us.

We increased our pace to an all-out run and arrived at Nod's tree within a few minutes. To my astonishment there was a sleeping person leaning against Nod.

"Who is that? And how long…" I blurted out.

Tassi replied, *Oh, that's Rip Van Winkle.*

Be serious, and where are you getting all this worldly knowledge from?

From your memories, of course!

Nod answered; she was unaware of Tassi's flippant response of Rip Van Winkle. "*That is a test subject, to see if my sleep abilities can imprison spirits inhabiting a physical life form. As you can see, it worked,*" she said rather resentfully.

I looked back over the meadow; Nod's ability to incarcerate spirit and physical beings was very effective. Nila, Cami, Kora, Momi, and Barry were out cold. I felt nothing from them. I could not even sense their spiritual presence.

I walked over to Nod with Tassi close by my side. I tentatively reached out and touched Nod, expecting to be entwined by her branches or by her roots shooting out of the ground ensnaring me. Nothing of that sort happened. She was pleasant to touch. Her bark felt velvety soft and cool. I could feel power flowing beneath my fingertips. It felt like a torrid river was flowing beneath her bark.

Nod spoke. "*Chris, take your knife and slice a piece of my bark off just below the cambium layer.*"

"*How did you know I have a knife on me?*"

"*As a tree, I may not have eyes and ears or a physical mind, but my minions do.*"

Tassi expounded for me, *Chris, that eagle, those raccoons, and even Rip Van Winkle over there, plus how many other creatures we don't even know about, act as her liaisons to the physical world.*

"*How big a piece should I take?*"

"*An inch wide and four or so inches long should suffice.*"

"*Suffice for what?*"

"*This will give enough of my spirit to energize the containment vessel.*"

"*Is the cambium layer where your spirit resides in the tree?*" Teaching time! The cambium layer is only one or two cells thick, less than a sheet of paper, and is the only living part of the trunk of a tree.

"*Yes, Chris. My spirit resides where there is life in this tree, and as you have noticed, the effects of it are far reaching.*"

I sliced a piece, with the cambium layer, that very thin bright-green layer just below the bark.

"Chris, you must leave soon! The enemy is almost complete in forming a perimeter around what you call the Land of Nod. Follow Ghris. He will be your guide."

Before I could even ask who Ghris was, I heard a series of yelps and barks much like that of a dog. They were coming from above. Tassi and I looked up... far in the distance a large bird was heading our way. What bird yelped and barked like a dog?

Tassi laughed. *This bird does! And he is the same one that dropped our cell phones to us.* Tassi had eyesight far better than a human... than me. I could only make out that it was a large bird. It didn't take long, and Ghris was directly above us.

"Nod, can you ask Ghris if I can strap a cell..."

Before I even finished my request, Ghris was spiraling downward toward Tassi and me. He swooped down just above our heads. I jumped backward so as not to be knocked over by the flapping of his wings. He landed a few feet in front of us. This bird was intimidating and majestic. A predatory bird that stood nearly as tall as me and was champagne gold in color with a brilliant sheen of 24 karat gold along the edges of his feathers. He peered menacingly at us, as if he was deciding whether we were prey or that he would honor my request.

Nod informed me that Ghris accepted. I secured my mom's phone to Ghris's leg. It took the donation of a sock and both shoelaces from the being who slept at the base of Nod's tree. This would allow us to track Ghris if we ever lost him.

Ghris knew enough not to stay long in Nod's sleep domain. No sooner had I completed securing the phone than Ghris took a few steps back and sprang upward as he beat his wings forcefully, lifting majestically but slowly into the air.

He circled above Nod's tree and gave a few yelps, then he dived directly at us, veering off at the last second. I stumbled backward onto my butt and Tassi dropped to her stomach. He vigorously flapped his wings and ascended quickly in a direction angling northwest behind Nod. The pressure of the air turbulence from the flapping of his wings plastered us to the ground. This bird would be something to reckon with if it decided to attack you.

"*Go now! Follow Ghris!*" Nod barked.

I spoke up. "*Where are we going, and how do we make the containment vessel?*"

"*I will fill you in on the way.*"

Tassi and I started off at a fast-paced jog. We looked up now and then to keep track of Ghris.

Nod commenced filling us in. "*You will go to Salt Lake City, to the artisan district. There, search for a Venetian glassmaker, then follow my instructions on making the vessel.*"

"*What instructions?*"

"*I will send them to your phone.*"

"*How can you send... you have no computer, no internet, and no hands!*"

"*Chris, you will find there is more to Nod than just my sleep ability. Even though I am stuck in this tree... in this place, I haven't just been idle with my time. I have acquired a vast amount of earthly knowledge and understanding. I hold online degrees in computer engineering, computer architecture, and computer information systems and a master's in computer security and cryptography, along with many other fields.*"

"*But how could you ...*"

"*My resourcefulness and adaptive intelligence have empowered me to overcome my physical restrictions... limitations. I have been on Earth longer than I care to remember and been imprisoned in some form or nother.*"

"You still didn't really answer my question— and what is this adaptive intelli..."

Tassi interrupted. *I have lost sight of Ghris. We need to pick up our pace... let us just focus on getting out of here*, she implored.

We ramped up to a very brisk run, maybe I should say an outright run. I no longer heard anything more from Nod; we must have gone beyond her range of spirit communication. We kept on in the direction last seen of Ghris. Hopefully he was waiting for us. I was feeling the koosh.

Tassi interrupted my koosh. *We are out.*

We were now back in the land of the awake, back in the green. The pale-yellow meadow had returned to a lush green. It didn't take us long, and we came to the fringe of a surrounding woods. That was when it happened... out from the shadows they appeared!

CHRONICLE 19
SHISH KABOB

Now, if you wanted to have a full-on fright, this was it. Two creatures stood in front of us while three others came from behind to block any possible retreat. I don't use the word "creatures" lightly. They could have been straight out of a horror flick. I don't believe they were of this world.

The best way I can describe them is as an assemblage of some of our Earth animals and insects. Yes, I said insects too. Their bodies, legs, and arms were like those of a gorilla, but the resemblance to one stopped there. They had a tail like that of a scorpion. Now, scorpions with a three-inch tail are scary enough, but try to imagine a four-foot scorpion tail with the last foot being the stinger.

It even got more gruesome. Each creature's face was humanoid but with lionlike features. A nose, or should I say a lion's snout but flatter, more pushed in like a bulldog's. They had lionlike eyes and ears. Did I mention some had a lion's mane but a much shorter version. The mouth was bizarre. The best way I can describe it is as being like the mandibles of a praying mantis. To complete the ensemble, the hideous creatures had wings like a bat, all leathery like. There was no way these creatures could fly; their wings were not large enough to support flight. Maybe they allowed them to glide, but even that would be questionable.

These things reminded me of the creatures from gargoyle lore. Gargoyles seem to show up in all cultures, under different names, but still gargoyles. Have these creatures been seen by humans throughout the centuries? Is that where the myths and lore of gargoyles sprang from?

These monstrosities also reminded me of the creatures mentioned by John in the Book of Revelation: the creatures that came out of the Great Abyss in the Last Days. I hoped these weren't the Last Days; that would just be a total bummer. I hadn't even gone out on a date yet. On the positive side, I wouldn't have any more homework. Now that I thought about it, these couldn't be the Last Days described in the Book of Revelation, because my big brother—Jesus Christ—hadn't returned for all his brothers and sisters. Whew! That was a relief. I had so much yet to experience in this earthly life.

Tassi, are these creatures the Anarkons that Mel spoke about?

Yes, Chris, but now is not the time...

I was brought back to our current predicament by a low, throaty growl from Tassi. She was in full battle mode, no longer cute and cuddly—as if a wolflike creature ever could be. We were now back-to-back. She was facing three Anarkons, while I faced two.

I slowly reached behind my back and withdrew my knife. I brandished it toward the two Anarkons, waving it from side to side, trying to instill some fear into them. It didn't work. In unison, the two made hideous coughing noises... no, not coughing. They were laughing at me. How rude and insensitive! Didn't they know that could mentally scar a teenage boy's psyche? What bullies!

I now had a strong suspicion that my knife would not have much effect on them. Did they even have blood to bleed?

I spoke to Tassi. *Should we run or fight?*

It might be best to live to fight another day, Chris.

Then I remembered Big Mel's advice: "Don't run from your challenges; embrace them. Whatever the enemy throws at you, overcome and become greater!" He was not saying that you needed to be totally victorious but that you had grown, become greater. Now, this advice was based on the premise that you survived to fight another day.

They had us well surrounded… we would have to fight our way through them. Before I yelled my battle cry, "Attack! Take no prisoners!" Tassi already knew and lunged at her three.

I threw myself at the closest Anarkon in front of me, knocking him into his comrade. In essence, I was trying to make this fight a one-on-one, to hinder the second opponent till I dispatched the first. It was much better odds, one against one.

I brought my knife down in a slicing arc across the Anarkon's neck. It just glanced off with a screeching sound much like when you dragged your fingernails across a chalkboard. *This isn't good*, I said to myself. *Well, let's try another approach. If this creature's hide is like armor or a bulletproof vest, then it must be attacked straight on for any chance of being pierced.*

I tried jabbing straight on but still couldn't penetrate the creature's hide. More force behind my thrust was needed. I leaped upward into the air and came down with all my weight bearing behind the blade. Success! It went straight into the creature's chest all the way up to the hilt, hopefully where its heart was—if it had a heart. I ripped it back out using the saw teeth on the top edge of the knife. The gaping wound was quickly filled with a black, ooze-like substance. I immediately did this two more times, with one being into the neck and directed upward toward the creature's brain. The wounds were quickly filled by the black ooze, the Anarkon's blood. They didn't seem to cause any lasting damage!

I still had his partner pinned under him along with both of their scorpion-like tails. I wouldn't want to be skewered by one of those. I was sure the stinger would inject some type of venom that would be not only fatal but excruciatingly painful.

I had to try another approach; this slicing and jabbing with my knife wasn't cutting it. I would have to…

Tassi responded to my train of thought before I even finished. *Chris, they didn't bring any weapons we could use against them.*

Oh, didn't they? I grabbed and yanked free the tail of the Anarkon on the bottom then twisted it around and thrust its stinger into its partner's side.

It pierced the creature's hide! I was immediately startled by a bloodcurdling scream. What came out of the creature's mouth was not the scream of an injured animal but that of a young girl. It just froze me to the quick. I immediately recovered, knowing that it was a clever ruse. This was no human girl I was fighting. I girded my mind with the truth: these were unholy creatures.

I thrust the stinger a couple of more times, now into the center of the Anarkon's chest. It started convulsing violently, withering with extreme agony and pain.

I rolled off, no longer able to stay on because of its violent spasms. It gave one last convoluted spasm, heaving it off its partner. Then it began to shake and shudder vehemently. The spasms stopped, and it became deathly still. I watched as the creature dissolved into a pile of black, tar-like ooze.

What a stench this ooze gave off as it soaked into the ground, leaving just a slight scorched trace to the ground's surface. This vile creature's bodily fluids must have been very acidic or caustic to burn the surface of the ground. I wasn't going to get close to it to check it out. Even though I was curious, I thought better of it; the smell was just downright nauseating. Besides, I didn't have the time; I had one more to dispatch.

I took advantage of the other Anarkon's momentary shock at seeing its comrade's demise and flipped the creature over onto its stomach. I only had a few seconds before it would realize what I was up to. The first Anarkon I had disposed of by stabbing it through the chest with the other Anarkon's stinger. I must have penetrated its spinal cord. Scorpion venom from another scorpion of the same family is fatal if it's injected into its nervous system. These creatures were similarly affected... thank God.

Now a scorpion is immune to its own venom unless injected into its nerve plexus, the largest cluster of nerves located at the base of its tail. I expected this would be the case for these creatures too. I had a problem... just like for a scorpion, this Anarkon's stinger couldn't reach the base of its tail! My adrenaline was pumping full on, but it still took the throwing of all my hundred and fifty pounds to break its tail at the stinger segment. In a life-and-death struggle, one becomes mighty strong. Now with the stinger flopping loosely, I was able to force it into the creature's nerve plexus.

It was like riding a broncin' buck. I rode it out till its spasms ended then jumped off. I watched the creature dissolve into a black ooze that the ground consumed thirstily. This was very unsettling but at the same time satisfying.

I turned my attention to Tassi. She had dispatched two of these unholy monstrosities in a similar manner. While the last Anarkon faced Tassi, I came from behind and grabbed its tail, which Tassi had already snapped at the third segment. Tassi lunged at the Anarkon, forcing it backward as I thrust its stinger into the base of its tail. It gave off a high-pitched, childlike scream, not unlike the others, as it went into ungainly death throes.

Tassi and I backed away to stay clear of the creature's stinger.

Good job, girl.

No sooner had I finished congratulating Tassi than I heard what sounded like the cavalry coming.

This cavalry wasn't for our side! The Anarkons had reinforcements stumbling and fighting their way through the woods. They were forming a pincer movement that was forcing us back toward the Land of Nod. Now, I am a good military strategist. No, I haven't been through a military academy. I'm too young for that. My military expertise is from combat video games. Yes, that's right. I have fought more battles than many a military commander has in their entire lifetime. So, what if mine are all virtual? It's still experience. I have fought in hundreds of battle scenarios and historical campaigns. Hey, I'm an armchair military expert.

The only counterattack we had was to punch through before they completed the pincer. Tassi was already on it. She charged the weakest point. All I could see was fur and teeth, a silver blur that was here, there, everywhere. She had the enemy in disarray, even attacking themselves. She was in the midst of them, and then she wasn't, leaving them combating one another... till they came to realize what she had done. I started on the perimeter, hacking and jabbing, but for the most part just trying to keep up with the silver blur.

We had broken through and now were out of the woods. This was not ideal, being back in the open, since it left the enemy the ability to attack us on all sides. It didn't take long, and we were surrounded by too many of them for the two of us to handle.

Then, out of the clear blue sky, came a fierce battle cry, a high-pitched scream, followed by Ghris bulleting down at an unearthly speed. His wings were plastered against his body, his feathers ruffled in the turbulence as if they could be ripped off at any moment.

Ghris was not slowing down; he started spinning like a projectile. The next thing I saw was Anarkons being thrown into the air. Ghris had cut a swath through their ranks. Those that were thrown even took out more of their own. Ghris made a strike; he toppled almost the entire group of the creatures like bowling pins.

He had cleared an unobstructed twenty-yard-wide path. Tassi and I did not wait for the dazed Anarkons to reassemble their ranks. We ran unhindered. It was at least a quarter mile until we met up with Ghris. He was standing upright but swaying ever so slightly. He was probably very, very dizzy and must have had one koosh of a headache. The slightly dazed and glassy, unfocused look was a tell-tale sign he wasn't all there. Ghris was stunned. He was down for the count, totally vulnerable to attack.

Suddenly, the ground seemed to boil around us. Out from it arose more Anarkons. Their wings were not useful for flying, but they gave decent camouflage allowing them to blend into the ground. I should have noticed the unusual bumpiness of the ground around us, but when you are running for your life, you have other things commanding your thoughts.

One Anarkon arose behind Ghris, intending to skewer him in the back. I leapt over to Ghris, swinging my knife in a downward arc and intercepting its stinger. Success! It was short lived; the ground beneath my feet shifted, and I stumbled forward off of a hiding Anarkon. What were the chances of that? Before I could take corrective action, it brought its stinger into position to strike.

It was all blindingly quick.

This was a moment when muscle memory and instinct took over. There was no time to think; the body just responded to the input from my five senses through my subconscious. I parried the stinger like it was an opponent's sword. Ghris had taken flight. The creature feinted right and grabbed me as it pivoted behind me. I swung my knife in an arc downward behind my back, toward the creature's belly. It gave me a bear hug, thrusting my knife deep into its belly. It was not a good move on my part. My knife didn't do any life-threatening damage to the Anarkon.

For me it was a life-threatening move! I was caught in a painful bear hug with my fighting arm now pinned behind my back. It thrust its stinger into my abdomen. The pain was intense as venom flowed. Tassi quickly threw herself at the three Anarkons she was battling. They fell to the ground in a tangled heap. She was over by me in the blink of an eye with her jaws tightly biting down on the tail of my Anarkon. It momentarily eased its bear hug, enabling me to extricate my right hand with the knife from between us. I grabbed the stinger with my left hand and brought my knife down with a sawing action between the tail and the stinger. I had to saw my way through, severing the stinger from the Anarkon's tail. Tassi flung the Anarkon to the side.

The flow of venom into my body stopped by severing the stinger from the tail. I was the Anarkon's shish kebab a la carte. The stinger had to be left in; if I pulled it out, I would most likely bleed to death. I could feel the venom spreading out from the entry point. The stinger had missed my spine, otherwise it would've been good-bye, Chris. Its effect was excruciating pain, then tingly sensations, then numbness and then no feeling at all. I could only feel from my waist down and from my rib cage upward.

The creatures kept coming.

Fighting was extremely difficult. When you can't feel your midsection, it's difficult to coordinate your upper and lower body. Each seemed like it was doing its own thing. When my upper torso moved right, my legs moved left. It was just plain frustrating and a very unnerving situation to say the least.

I continued to fight.

Tassi and I were holding our own, trying to make our way to the next section of woods.

Tassi spoke. *I am with you, Chris.*

It then dawned on me; my ability to continue to fight was Tassi's spirit joining with mine. She was bolstering my spirit to counter and slow the spreading of the venom. It was contained to my midsection, but for how much longer?

Tassi shouted in my mind, *Chris, give your spirit direction!*

Give my spirit direction? How about... keep me alive!

Of course I didn't want to die, and I did not want to be turned evil either! I spoke this internally and willed my spirit to hear and do it. How it was going to do it, I had no idea. That was all the direction I could give it.

When you have tried all you can do and you don't know what more to do, then you go to the one who always knows what to do.

"Dad! Dad? I need help! Hello? Overwhelming Anarkon army—humanity's stopgap... dying here! HELP!"

I was starting to lose all feeling and ability to control my body. It became increasingly difficult to think straight, and what little coherent thought I had left was becoming animal like. My thoughts turned to ripping and shredding the intruders.

I fought to my last ounce of strength till I could do no more. I dropped to my knees as all consciousness left me.

I MEET MY MAKER

I AWOKE AS A RATIONAL THINKING human. Maybe I jumped the gun. I was thinking normally... like me. There was just one teeny-weenie problem: I couldn't feel my body. I had this sensation of weightlessness. It was as if I was floating, but not like floating in the air or on top of water. This floating felt like I was a bubble trapped deep underneath the water, trying to rise to the surface but not having enough buoyancy. I can tell you, the situation was quite unsettling!

I screamed. No sound. I couldn't even hear that annoying ringing in my ears I had whenever it was extremely quiet. Tinnitus is the medical term. I got it after a really bad ear infection. It is a lingering reminder not to blow my nose too forcibly when I have a head cold. Well, let's not get into that discussion. Back to where I was, wherever that was.

This was starting to get scary. Was I dead? Was this death?

A powerful but gentle fatherly voice interrupted, "No, son, you are not dead."

It didn't sound like my prankster angel buddy, Mel. I took a shot in the dark. "Is that you, Dad?"

"Yes, Chris."

Now, I have always felt close to my Heavenly Father, but I have never had a real, audible conversation with Him. Oh yes, I heard from God via that still, small voice. You know, that mental inkling that I was being told something.

"Chris, you know you're not dead."

"Yes, I know. When you're dead, there is no thought, no knowledge, no wisdom."

My mom and Pastor Dan, who I considered my earthly dad, had taught me that from the Bible: that when you were dead, you were dead. You were not floating around somewhere. Hey! I was floating...

"Chris, your soul life has not gone back to the ground, nor has your spirit returned to me. If you were dead, this would be so."

No, I am not doubting God. I just like talking things out.

"Chris, you have developed your spirit well. It won't give you up! It's tenaciously holding onto physical life for you."

"I'm just this floating bubble somewhere. I hope I don't pop!"

I heard a deep, rumbling chuckle. "Chris, you are after my own heart, and you have a sense of humor in everything too."

"What, God has a sense of humor?"

"Of course I do! Have you never seen a duck-billed platypus? Or how about the macaroni penguin? What about goatees on every goat? If that's not a sense of humor, and at the same time, proof that there is a Creator... a God. Chris, life can be serious enough. That was why I formed, made, and created so much beauty in the world and, oh yes, humor to go along with it too."

"So, what is going on, Dad? Where am I? What am I?"

"Chris, you and Tassi were spiritually trying to contain the onslaught of the venom. Then you gave direction to your spirit..."

"Not to turn me into a bubble!"

Yes, I just did that, cut *God* off in midsentence, cut the Creator of the heavens off. Hey! I feel comfortable in my Heavenly Father's presence. I can be myself, me being me, even if I am just a floating bubble. God's Word states we can stand before Him, in His presence, without any self-inadequacies, sin, guilt, condemnation, and so forth. So that was what I was doing.

"Chris, didn't you tell your spirit to protect you from being turned evil by the Anarkon's venom?"

"Well, yes, but…"

"Chris, your spirit can never be contaminated, never be inhabited by evil or anything else. You are born of my seed. You are my son by spirit. This can never be changed or undone. You have my spirit genetics."

"You mean I'm a demigod?"

"Well, Chris, everyone that is born again, is born of my seed—is a demigod."

Oh, that just about burst my bubble. I heard a low rumble—God chuckling again. Yes, I did make a pun: burst my bubble. Get it?

"I have many sons and daughters; all have callings. You have a unique one." He let that sink in then proceeded, "You've chosen to accept yours—to be the Orion, the Bearer of Light." There was a lengthy pause, letting me know what he said next was very important.

"Chris, remember this: *a heart of light prevails.*"

"Are you giving me a heads-up about what I'll need to do? How do I even do that?"

God just continued. "You truly will and have already shown demigod-like powers."

"If I am a demigod, I'm not doing so hot. I'm just this floating bubble!"

"You're not just a floating bubble, Chris, but millions, or should I say trillions, of floating bubbles."

"What?" I blurted out in exasperation.

"Chris, like I mentioned earlier, your spirit didn't protect itself from being turned evil… because it can't be turned evil."

"What *did* it protect of me?"

"It protected your soul life! What makes you… *you*: your thoughts, your memories, your emotions, your will—everything that's you. Soul life is not just in one part of your body, just like your spirit isn't. They are both intertwined throughout, down to the sub-subatomic particle level. Think of your soul and your spirit as being composed of cells—Soul cells and Spirit cells. Your spirit protected each and every soul cell, the accumulation of what makes an entire soul—an entire you! For your spirit to do this without my intervention is phenomenal! To fuse soul life with spirit life! It would be a hard thing for God to do."

"But nothing is too hard for God... is it?"

"Chris, I'm just trying to give you a perspective of how immensely difficult it was for your spirit to do such a thing!"

Then I remembered something else very, very important. "Hey, Dad, what about my body? Can I get it back?"

"Your spirit protected that too! Remember, soul life is in the blood, and blood gives physical life to the body. Your physical body is now energized by spirit, and spirit energy is now sustaining each of your physical cells by that joining, that fusing, of your spirit and soul life. Yes, your heart is not beating. There's no blood flowing, no breathing, no brain activity, but your body is alive. Everything is being held in a state of suspended animation... sustained by your spirit."

I breathed a big sigh. Yeah, okay, I couldn't really breathe a sigh, being trillions of bubbles. "You don't know how relieved I am knowing I'm not going to be Bubble Man forever!"

God chuckled again. "Chris, you truly have the heart of God. That was what your soul life embedded to your spirit, giving it the impetus and ability to do what it did. That is having koosh."

God used my word, koosh!

He chuckled. "Chris, you truly live life to the koosh."

I laughed. He'd used it again!

My Heavenly Father continued, "This and other qualities of your soul developed and brought your latent spiritual abilities into concretion."

A thought suddenly popped into my mind. Why was this the first time I was having a real one-on-one conversation with God, man to man? Okay, okay, I know God is not a man, but you know what I mean.

"Chris, the human mind is always busy, busy, busy. People just can't hear me with all that mental commotion going on. They just can't get peaceful enough."

"Oh, I get it now. I'm just trillions of disassociated bubbles. How can I not be at peace?"

God laughed. "Chris, right now, your spirit and soul life are fused, unified. You are now a spirit being, disassociated from your physical body. There is no warring between the physical you and the spirit you. You have a full, unfettered presence with me. That is why we can have this one-on-one conversation. You can have a conversation with me when you are back in your physical body. It can be done. Moses did it."

"Wait... Moses, was he an Orion?"

God continued, "Chris, I will allow you..."

I interjected, "One wish!"

God chuckled. "No, but I will allow you one question. You can ask anything, and I will answer."

"There has got to be a catch," I said.

"No catch, Chris. Ask anything."

Then it popped into my mind, that silly age-old question.

Before I could say anything, God answered. "Of course, Chris. The chicken came before the egg."

"Hey, that wasn't what I really wanted to ask. But you knew that anyway, didn't you? That was why you gave me one question I could ask unconditionally about anything!"

"I am God... I am all-knowing. But for you, it's not good to know what may or may not happen. That could alter the course of the future for the worse."

Before I could say anything else, God spoke commandingly, "Chris... AWAKE."

I felt like a bubble—or rather, many disassembled bubbles—being inexplicably drawn together in a swirling vortex of liquid and then forcibly sucked into a long narrow passageway and finally spewed out into a vast chamber. It was like being a bunch of cleaning bubbles in a slowly flushing toilet, swirling around and around and then finally being sucked tenaciously out of the bowl through a long drainpipe to finally be emptied into the vast city sewer system.

My physical sensations started coming back first. My entire body went from numbness to an acute tickling sensation, to a painful pricking, to normalcy. Next came my hearing from total silence to sporadic buzzing, much like a bunch of annoying flies whizzing around, to a jumbling of noises, to coherent sounds intermixed by sporadic spoken words.

I was becoming aware of a conversation. Don't you just love it when you come into a conversation that's already begun, not fully cognizant of what is being discussed? I missed bits and pieces, but what I caught of the conversation got my dander up.

"...the boy is not with the living... will use... instead of the boy... dispatch the wolf... find the mother..."

I felt a protective rage starting to develop deep within my being. I became mentally aware of my situation. I was slumped over, encircled by the enemy. They thought I was dead. They were in for a big, big surprise!

I could feel energy intensifying within. It kept growing and welling up, much like a torrential rain filling a reservoir past its capacity—to failure... *the dam burst.*

Power just flowed out of me. It was all a blur. All I could remember vaguely was dispatching the enemy. I saw a dazzling array of flickering colored lights like those at the end of fireworks, twinkling vividly and finally fading out to darkness. I felt totally alone.

Then I heard a noise behind me. I slowly turned around. There, standing on all fours... a majestic wolf. Was it another enemy? I still had feelings of contempt and loathing but was able to resist the urge to just take this wolf out and ask questions later.

As I stared at the wolf, I heard within my mind, *Chris! Chris! Is that you?* in an urgent but questioning tone.

Then, a flood of—memories, thoughts, and emotions bombarded my mind. I started piecing together what just happened, but there was a large gap in my memory. I had no recollection whatsoever of when I was in full power mode. I remembered the starting and the ending of it, but nothing in between, nothing of what I had done when I was unleashing my power against the Anarkons.

A scary realization occurred to me: was someone or something controlling me? God said I couldn't be turned evil... but could I be controlled or used for evil?

I came back to normalcy. Well, at least normalcy for me. There in front of me was Tassi. Why had I not recognized her a moment ago?

Chris? A soft, questioning plea from Tassi.

I replied hesitantly to Tassi, *It's me... I think!*

Just then, an unsettling thought came to my mind: *Maybe I became an Anarkon!* Chills just went through my body. I didn't tell my spirit to stop me from turning into some grotesque creature.

I heard Tassi laugh. *No, silly boy! You are still a boy, or should I say a young man.*

"Whew!" I sighed with relief. *Do I look the same? Am I the same person?*

Relax, Chris. You look the same.

Then it hit me. Tassi hadn't answered my second question: was I the same person? Don't you just hate that? When you ask a person multiple questions, they always, always pick only the first question to answer. Do they forget you asked more than one question?

Chris, you are not the same person. Tassi dropped her eyes to focus on my stomach.

I looked down. My shirt was tattered and stained black around the black hole where I had been skewered.

"My... my... blood is—is... black... like- like... the Anarkons'!" I stammered out loud.

Chris, it's not all that bad. You cannot bleed to death anymore.

Oh, that's just comforting. But am I still human? I lifted my shirt, rubbing the caked black blood, my blood, from my stomach. To my amazement, I was totally healed! I was a quick healer now. Well, that was a positive to dwell on, but I didn't think I was a normal human anymore.

Chris, you were never normal. Before I could say anything, she continued, *do you think any normal human can run as effortlessly as you can? Never tiring, no muscle fatigue. All you need is food and water now and then.*

Do I still have the same insides?

Tassi hesitated before saying, *No. Do you think your black blood is just a color change? Chris, your spirit needed to make some modifications or adaptations to keep the Anarkon venom from killing you. You are still human. Your physical body isn't what really makes you human.*

"What?"

Chris, look at me. I am in the form of a wolf, but I am not a wolf and never will be. I am and will always be Cherub. It doesn't matter what construct—what body—I am inhabiting. Tassi looked around. *Chris, we need to get going.* Seeing I was still in distress, she said softly, *You are still Chris... the Chris that I know!*

These words from Tassi were comforting, but I was not totally at ease with what I had become.

My mind was still racing a mile a minute, thoughts popping in and out. Was my enemy, mankind's enemy—Anarkos—making me into his antithesis? Had Big Mel somehow foreseen this? Did being brought back to life from being born dead make it easier for my spirit to transform my physical body?

We took off running toward the north. I felt great. Running was effortless, like it had always been. At least that hadn't changed.

Something started gnawing at my mind, but I couldn't put my finger on what it was. Then it hit me! It was like the time when I was sitting on the overstuffed couch with my mom in Barry's apartment. This time, though, the world hadn't gone all black, at least not yet.

It was happening again...

JENNIFER TAKES TO PEN

J ENNIFER FELT LIKE SHE WAS being zapped, like she had grabbed a frayed lamp cord. A series of electrical jolts swept through her body from her head down to her toes. She gave a slight startled scream. It wasn't all that painful, but the tingling sensation was not pleasant either. All eyes in the classroom became focused intently upon her.

Jennifer felt a sudden, overwhelming need to write. She was already taking notes for the Spiritual Concepts, Constructs, and Connections class at Camp Aharonite. Jennifer started penning as quickly as the words formed in her mind. She gasped. Now everyone in the classroom, including the teacher, gathered behind her, each riveted on what she was writing so hastily.

Chris's body finally succumbed to the Anarkon's venom. He slumped to his knees, head down, arms hanging limply at his sides, eyes shut. There was no breath, no sign of life in his body.

Tassi gave out a pained howl of grief. She bolted through the group of Anarkons that had surrounded her to reach Chris. As the Anarkons clustered around Chris, Tassi ferociously kept them at a distance, snarling, snapping, and lunging at them. She had put up an invisible barrier that they could not penetrate. Each lunge caused the Anarkons to stumble back, as if an invisible hand had punched them. They continued to attack, wave after wave. Tassi's counterattacks though, started to wane. The invisible punches became less and less powerful. Tassi continued to retreat closer to Chris with each advancing onslaught.

Then an abrasive voice pierced the battle clamor. It was menacing and reptilian-like with a slight hiss at the end of each word.

The man spoke commandingly, **"Ana molecheta cha."** *The Anarkons immediately stopped.*

Out from the shadows of the woods, he had appeared with an Anarkon of stature by his side. The man was staring at Chris, but his mental focus was somewhere else. He was deep in thought. He had black hair tied in a short ponytail, his face was pockmarked, and he had a slight twist to his nose like it had been broken recently. His attention then came back to the situation at hand. He had decided on his next course of action.

The man spoke to the Anarkon at his side. "Regent, have all but twenty of your force return to the perimeter around Nod. Let no one in or out."

The man looked at Tassi and Chris then glared icily back at the Regent. The Regent hastily relayed the orders, and twenty Anarkons remained around Tassi and Chris.

The two walked closer but kept a safe distance of twenty feet or so.

He spoke. "It is finished. The boy is no longer with the living."

Jennifer stiffened. "No, it cannot be," she said, sobbing.

Jennifer continued to write.

The man looked directly at Tassi and shook his head slowly from side to side. In a mocking manner, he spoke to Tassi. "You are just realizing how useful that boy could have been." He continued to cut Tassi with his words. "I see the light hasn't fully turned on in that tiny brain of yours. Isn't it a shame that we are relegated to using physical bodies to function in this realm?" He kept on goading and mocking Tassi. "Yes, because you are able to link with him spiritually, it allowed you to use your spiritual powers, unhindered by the natural laws of this realm. He was already gone when you set up that barrier and expelled my Anarkons."

Jennifer let out a cry of grief but continued writing.

"It was only a lingering trace of his spiritual essence that opened the door and allowed you to tap into the spiritual realm! Imagine harnessing the full power that boy was capable of unleashing in this realm! Oh, no matter. If we couldn't have him, we weren't going to let you!"

Tassi snarled and leapt toward him, only to be tackled by four Anarkons.

He laughed menacingly. "That was a really feeble attempt. Already lost the will to fight without your pet boy. That will make it easier for us to dispatch you. We don't know how you joined with him, but we will find out."

He kept on baiting her. "Maybe we can use the girl, his mom, in like manner. Her body was never found. She could still be alive."

Before he had finished his threat, Chris's body twitched.

The Anarkons near Chris and Tassi took notice as a series of twitches went through his body. Chris's head slowly began to rise; the Anarkons started moving away cautiously, not turning their backs on him.

Smoothly and effortlessly, Chris stood. The air around Chris crackled with power. Anarkons started stumbling and colliding into one another. They sensed the urgency of the need to distance themselves from Chris.

His eyes were still shut. Slowly, Chris removed the stinger from his midsection. A black ooze filled the void in his stomach. His eyes suddenly opened, an intense brilliant blue, like that of two supernovas. Then, like a solar eclipse, they turned black. Even the whites of his eyes became black. The man smiled. He turned quickly and retreated toward the woods with the Regent close behind.

The remaining twenty Anarkons were not far enough away. Chris moved immensely fast and impaled the closest of the Anarkons with the stinger he still held. A dark-purplish light emanated in outward rays from inside the creature's body. It screamed as it exploded into tiny bits of colored light, like that from fireworks on the Fourth of July. The heat given off was intense. Fortunately, it only lasted a fraction of a second; otherwise, everything would've been vaporized in the immediate area.

Chris continued methodically attacking, dispatching the remaining Anarkons in like manner.

*The Anarkons were in a total frenzy. They tripped and even threw other Anarkons toward Chris, trying to save themselves. Tassi just watched, stunned, as Chris turned into a killing machine with only one objective—**destroy every last Anarkon**.*

He moved with lightning speed and machine-like precision, anticipating their every move. The Anarkons were dripping in fear, and Chris seemed to feed off their fear, even becoming more powerful and more determined not to let any escape his wrath.

Chris annihilated all twenty Anarkons. He then turned his attention toward the forest. Two runners could faintly be seen scrambling for the safety it could provide. His protectiveness mounted again. Chris pointed at them with the scorpion stinger he still held in his hand. Energy shot forth. It was not the crisp and sharp, brilliantly white jagged lines like those of lightning. These were invisible, leaving only a wispy and feathery trail of purplish-black haze. It left a lingering sweet smell in the air of ozone being vaporized.

The energy bolts struck the edge of the forest with a tremendous thundering sound, vaporizing a swath of forest just in front of the two runners, the escapees.

He had missed!

The intensity of the energy bolts shook the ground with such force that they were knocked to the ground. One was a man, and the other was an Anarkon. Only charred remnants of that section of the forest with wisps of smoke rising into the air remained.

They got up quickly and switched direction, stumbling and scrambling to make it into a section with trees before Chris could release another bolt. He tried, but the power dissipated as quickly as it came.

Chris then turned his attention to his immediate surroundings. There, off to his left, was a majestic wolf. He showed no signs of concern, no trepidation, no fear. He looked at the wolf with contempt and loathing, just as if it were an Anarkon.

*Tassi felt she was in imminent danger! She shouted Chris's name spiritually with as much power as she could. "Chris! Chris, is that **you**?"*

Chris's demeanor softened. Recognition came into his black, pure-black eyes. Slowly, the blackness ebbed, giving way to his normal green eyes. Tassi breathed a sigh of relief.

She tried again, this time gentler, slightly hesitantly. "Chris?"

Then, like a dam breaking: memories, thoughts, emotions, all flooded Tassi's mind. Their link was restored! Tassi knew Chris was back... She knew what he was thinking. Everything was back to normal. Well, not everything...

Jennifer stopped writing when nothing more came to her to write. She was mentally and physically fatigued but at peace. Chris was alive and well—or was he? Jennifer threw the doubt out. Tassi had said she felt the old Chris, knew his every thought. It must be so. But what had Tassi said at the end? "Not everything."

Ms. Cozzi came over to Jennifer, gently pushing her way through the perplexed students. She put her arm around Jennifer and looked at the other students. "Class dismissed." Then, as students filed out of the room, she added, "Class, your homework assignment: a two-page report explaining the spiritual constructs and connections aspect of what just took place."

She led Jennifer out of the classroom and down the hall to her office. There was quite a commotion in the hallways as the students began to mingle with the other classes that had just finished too. They finally made it to her office. Ms. Cozzi looked at her door and timidly turned the knob. She stopped and backed away.

Ms. Cozzi looked at Jennifer. "There is a light on in my office, and the door is unlocked. I didn't leave it that way!"

"Maybe it's maintenance repairing something in your office," Jennifer reassured her.

Ms. Cozzi rather hesitantly opened the door. There in the office was a man Jennifer knew. He was sitting behind Ms. Cozzi's desk. Jennifer smiled. He had made himself at home, leaning back in the chair with his legs draped over one corner of the desk.

He immediately stood up, rather shakily, as if taken aback, but he quickly regained his composure. A warm smile spread across his face. "Jenn... Jennifer, you are looking well," he affably said.

Ms. Cozzi spoke up. "Barry? What brings you back to Camp Aharonite so soon? Oh, and don't say 'I am alwa—'"

"But I *am* always where I need to be, Ms. Cozzi!"

Jennifer laughed. Good old Barry. If you could actually say old. He didn't look a day over forty, but he gave off an air of being much, much older.

Barry motioned for Ms. Cozzi to seat herself behind the desk. He then pulled up chairs for Jennifer and himself. He put both elbows on the desk and rested his face in his hands. Barry looked directly at Ms. Cozzi with puppy-dog eyes. "Now give me the whole scoop on what's been going on here."

Ms. Cozzi laughed. Barry pretended he was a big kid in detention, trying to soften up the teacher. He then lifted his head from his hands and leaned back in his chair. "Okay, Teach, spill the beans."

Ms. Cozzi gave a quick synopsis of what had gone on since his last visit and then went into what had just happened. Barry's eyes grew large as she read what Jennifer had written in the classroom.

He became serious. "Jennifer, God has called you to be a Seer."

Ms. Cozzi interrupted. "No, Barry, a Seer foretells the future, whereas what Jennifer did was the work of a Recorder."

"Aaah, aahh. Right, right, Ms. Cozzi," Barry agreed.

Jennifer was intrigued. "What's a Recorder?"

Barry kept silent and allowed Ms. Cozzi to answer.

"A Recorder is a man or woman God has called to record certain information and events chosen by Him. Barry is a Recorder."

Barry's eyebrows and facial muscles twitched, and he quickly responded, "Your definition of a Recorder is very incomplete. There is much more to being a Recorder than just writing what God wants saved."

"Oh, I know, Barry. She will learn all the particulars when she is formally taught."

Barry remarked, "I have never ever seen or heard anyone being able to record in such detail and length their very first time! For God to work within you like this without any formal training is remarkable, young lady. Your ability to control your mind not to wander or waver, especially when the account to record is so very close to you, is just phenomenal." Barry hesitated to allow what he said to sink in.

He continued, "You truly are a chosen vessel of God. The gifts and calling of God are irrevocable. Whether you choose to accept and perform your calling or not, God will never withdraw it."

Jennifer almost spoke up, but the word "no" formed in her mind. She decided not to relay the thought that had just dawned on her. Pastor Dan and his wife, Sandy, as well as others, had taught and worked tirelessly with both her and Chris to develop a deep trust in God. It allowed them to control their minds and foster great Godly love and peace. He was preparing them to handle their callings, if they chose to accept them.

She and Chris had already given themselves to do God's will, whatever God would call them to do. If that meant being a Recorder, so be it. Now, why she wasn't to relay this new understanding to Barry and Ms. Cozzi, she didn't know.

Barry didn't seem to notice Jennifer's lack of a response. He continued, "What you are given to record is not only for God's people but for you personally. Jennifer, you must study the knowledge God had you record thoroughly. He will then unfold Godly understanding and wisdom that will help you and mankind."

Ms. Cozzi interjected, "Barry, is this why you are here, to help Jennifer? No... no, that's not it! You didn't even know about Jennifer's ability to record. You are here because *it's* occurring now!"

Barry motioned with both hands, beckoning for her to proceed.

"What you informed us about the last time you were here... is happening *now!*" Ms. Cozzi couldn't contain herself. She blurted, "A convergence is forming, one of immense proportion and magnitude… one that could be used to release the imprisoned Daimonia from the Great Abyss!"

Jennifer gasped, and Barry just about fell over. He had been balancing on the back legs of his chair. The chair seemed to have slipped out from underneath him. It fell to the floor. Barry, with the agility of a cat but not the grace, caught himself. His hands flailing, he managed to grab Jennifer's chair and Ms. Cozzi's desk, stopping himself from joining the chair on the floor.

Jennifer and Ms. Cozzi laughed. Barry was a sight, nearly doing the splits. He quickly regained his balance, pulling himself up smoothly. He did a quick bow and picked up his chair. Barry sat normally this time.

Ms. Cozzi shook her head and, with a smirk, said, "Good boy. I hope you learned your lesson of why we sit properly on a chair."

Barry smiled. "Touché, Ms. Cozzi." Then he became serious. He hesitated, inhaled deeply then slowly exhaled to regain his composure. "Now… this convergence hasn't come and gone like normal. It's continued to build in strength and intensity!"

Ms. Cozzi cut in. "Barry, are you thinking what I'm thinking?"

"Ms. Cozzi, I'm not a mind reader!"

She continued, "This convergence is of such magnitude and duration that it will perhaps produce a trove of unparalleled Facsmeres!"

Barry elaborated, "Jennifer, when a convergence—an intersecting of the spiritual and natural realms occurs—conditions arise that make it possible for the formation of Facsmeres. And because of this unusual convergence, the Facsmeres, as Ms. Cozzi suggests, may be very numerous and unique."

Jennifer asked, "Like the one of Chris and Tassi, you have in your bedroom?"

Barry's face twitched ever so slightly. He looked at Ms. Cozzi. "Would you care to elaborate, since you teach a class on Facsmeres?"

"Barry, I teach a series of classes on Facsmeres!"

"Just keep it short and sweet." He laughed.

Ms. Cozzi began, "Facsmeres are a spiritual aberration that manifests in the physical realm in what we call raw or wild Facsmeres. They come in geometric shapes similar to snowflakes but are translucent and much larger, usually the size of a quarter. From a Facsmere, a trained Recorder can glean and save historical information on events past, present, and future regarding God's people and mankind. A Recorder is able to save this knowledge in a construct we call a Facsmere, an actually finished or refined Facsmere. What looked like a painting you saw at Barry's depicting Chris and Tassi, is a finished Facsmere."

"Facsmeres are like diamonds," Barry added. "You have rough or natural diamonds, and then you have the cut and polished diamonds. The rough diamonds don't look like much; just pale, dull, oily lumps of glass that most people wouldn't take notice of. Now the cut and polished diamonds show their brilliance, their true nature; they are prized and sought after. The same is true of raw or wild Facsmeres and their finished or refined versions."

Ms. Cozzi continued. "Only God's people prize Facsmeres, whether raw or refined. The Daimonia have never shown much interest in Facsmeres."

Barry, with an excited tone in his voice, jumped in. "Except to hinder, aggravate, or stop God's people, the Recorders, from finding and possessing them."

"But now that will change!" Ms. Cozzi exclaimed.

Barry stiffened slightly then looked at Ms. Cozzi and nodded toward her, giving her the okay to elaborate.

She cleared her throat and said, "Barry informed the Aharonites just a few days ago that changes have occurred with the Facsmeres. The Facsmeres are more than just a historical time capsule. They can now be used to communicate with the past, present, and future. The ramifications are immense.

"Think about it. The Daimonia could use them to plan their attacks... prepare the past, coordinate the present, and inform the future. It would be devastating!"

A slight series of shivers went through Barry's body.

Ms. Cozzi looked at Jennifer. "You are a key!"

"What?" Jennifer exclaimed.

"You seem to be the only one that can activate a Facsmere as a communication device. We have tried and failed here at camp to duplicate what you were able to do with the Facsmere at Barry's apartment."

Barry looked Jennifer directly in the eyes. "Girl... you and your son... are the cause... of the change in the Facsmeres and... this unusual convergence."

"What!" Jennifer blurted.

Barry took a deep breath and exhaled slowly. "We have never had anything like this happen before. You and Chris seem to be the keys in all of this."

Jennifer was exasperated. "How do you know it is Chris and me that... that are the cause of all this? How about Anarkos? He brought forth a haboob and raised up his Anarkons!"

"That might explain the convergence, but the change in the Facsmeres... is tied to you and Chris."

Jennifer spoke up. "Oh, you mean when I heard Chris say 'Mom' or when that wolf, Tassi, invaded my mind."

Barry nodded in agreement and then inhaled deeply before he spoke out. "It's time to coordinate an effort to find the convergence's epicenter and any natural Facsmeres... before the Daimonia!"

He paused to let the gravity of what he just said sink in before continuing, "We will give Jennifer a field assignment."

Ms. Cozzi responded, "Do you think that's wise, since she's such an important key?"

"They don't know she's alive." A slight smirk formed on his lips. Jennifer took notice. She couldn't put her finger on it, there was something amiss with Barry. He didn't seem quite his usual self. What was going on? Barry proceeded, "If we keep enough Aharonites around her, the Daimonia won't be able to pick up her human or spiritual scent... and she will remain incognito."

He didn't wait for a reply and continued, "Besides, I don't think we have a choice. If I am right that Chris and Jennifer are the cause, then she might have an affinity to the convergence and the Facsmeres it might produce! She's maybe the only one who can find them before the Daimonia."

"But, Barry, we don't even know where to start looking," Ms. Cozzi blurted.

"Aahh, I think we do," Barry said, wagging a finger. "The region where Chris put to sleep more than eight hundred people."

"What!" Jennifer shouted.

Ms. Cozzi spoke up. "We'll cover that another time, Jennifer."

"Barry, do you really know that's where the heart of the convergence is?"

"No, but for as long as I have been a Recorder, I have learned to move forward with the information and understanding I have. God will then provide revelation if necessary."

Barry reached over and gently patted Jennifer on the shoulder. "Chris has been doing remarkably well." He drew in a breath then continued, "I think Chris manifesting such immense spiritual power in a relatively short period of time has caused this unusual convergence to occur between the spiritual and natural realms. This convergence is not retreating. It's becoming a gateway between the realms!"

Jennifer was exasperated. Barry gave her a sympathetic look before he spoke. "Jennifer, both spiritual events are involved. But I think Chris's is where we should start. All I truly know is that you and Chris are very important in what is unfolding."

He looked at Ms. Cozzi. "Instruct the Aharonites to assemble."

FRED

BARRY WALKED OUT OF THE main meeting hall in the center of Camp Aharonite. He was pleased with how everything was developing. The Aharonites had decided to send out seven teams of eight to ten people. Nearly everyone was still inside the meeting hall, working out the details, except a few security guards doing their rounds.

He chuckled to himself. The security people were a mere formality. They were more maintenance or groundskeepers than guards. The camp really did not need to be guarded. It had two Cherubim and was shrouded from any physical perception. Even from an airplane or satellite telemetry, all that could be seen was a rock-strewn canyon that was densely populated with canyon maples, firs, and aspen trees. There was only one entrance to the canyon, and that was imperceptible too.

Barry slowly turned around, surveying the camp. He marveled at the eclectic architecture of the buildings in the camp, which depicted various styles and time periods. The number and size of the buildings could support a large town, yet there were maybe just two hundred Aharonites here at any one time.

He didn't know the reason behind the diverse architecture and why an entire city was hidden, unknown to the world. How had the Aharonites accomplished this? Maybe the two camp Cherubim had built it. No, he knew that wasn't true. God hadn't even zapped the Ark into existence for Noah or had his angels do it. Noah labored for a hundred years to build the Ark. God didn't interfere in the struggles of man; rather he supplied what was needed for man to accomplish it... with just a little Fatherly help now and then.

He walked toward the parking area, and as he approached a car, his facial features began to waver. Suddenly, standing there was a young man of about twenty-five with bright-red hair and a lightly freckled face. Fred was bewildered; he didn't remember coming to Camp Aharonite. Why was he dressed in a colorful Hawaiian shirt, tan khaki shorts, and neon-blue sneakers? He didn't even own any clothes or shoes like this.

Fred hurriedly opened his car and got inside. He buckled up and looked into the driver's-side mirror. Why was his hair spiked up? He used both hands and frantically messed up his hair, so it fell over his ears and forehead in a rough, moppish way. He sat there in his car, totally confounded; his mind was racing a mile a minute. Was he supposed to be here today? He took three very slow deep breaths to help calm himself down.

Now he muttered under his breath, "Think, Fred, think. Was I scheduled to be at Camp Aharonite today?"

Slowly, recollection came back. Yes, yes he was. Fred breathed a sigh of relief. He was here to perform some minor software updates on the camp's network servers. He was a pretty good IT tech and was thankful for having been recruited—or should he correctly say rescued—by the Aharonites. They had delivered him from a continuing downward spiral into the imprisoning depths of despair.

He had never truly been satisfied with life and had hit the lowest low point. He had recently lost his job in the IT department at a major global corporation. The Aharonites met him when he was flipping hamburgers at a fast-food restaurant and staying in halfway houses. Life held no purpose or meaning for him. It had been just day-to-day drudgery for mere existence. He even gotten himself involved in a radical group called AIR—Anarchist International

Reformists, they called themselves. At the time, it sounded good to him: no government, no hierarchy of society, no rules or laws, or very few, just everybody doing their own thing.

The inspiration and guidance had come from Joshua Smitely. He called himself the Reformist and was a very charismatic and persuasive individual. Everything he said at the time made sense, even the idea of an anarchist society. He propounded that anarchy was based on the principle that all people had equal rights and equal status. There were to be no formal leaders, no government, no formal law enforcement, and best yet, no income taxes! The people as a whole would take care of anything that needed to be addressed, either in small informal groups or through the society as a whole.

The fundamental principle for anarchy to be sustainable was based on this rendering of the golden rule: "Do unto others as you would have others do unto you." Joshua taught his followers that if each individual and the society as a whole honored this rule, anarchy would thrive and become the dominant society in the world—a new world order.

The spread of anarchy was well on its way already. Joshua had groups of anarchists all over the world, and their numbers were growing rapidly. The majority of people were becoming increasingly disenfranchised with their current governments. Whether they were young people right out of college, those already in the workforce, or retirees, they felt abandoned. Joshua spoke directly to their needs, wants, and desires, and promised that they could all be fulfilled by an anarchist society! It was as if he had them bewitched. Anything he said about anarchy, they hungrily devoured and accepted.

Fred snapped out of his reminiscing. How long had he been just sitting deep in thought? He started the car and proceeded out of Camp Aharonite. It was as if someone or something didn't want him to concentrate or remember what he had done today. Now what was the first thing he had done? He didn't even remember getting out of bed. He had a big, big, big… problem, he didn't remember anything of this day!

He brought his mind back to the now as he was just entering the mouth of the canyon to exit. He didn't even know whether he was still on Earth or in another dimension when he was at Camp Aharonite. It became so quiet. The only noise was that of the car engine. He really did need to get a new muffler.

He gripped the steering wheel tightly and kept his foot on the gas pedal. It probably didn't matter what he did, but it made him feel more in control by acting as if he was. On either side of him sheer vertical walls as smooth as glass ascended out of sight. The passageway eventually became a series of curves for a time before it went completely pitch-black. The headlights of his car were to no avail. There was nothing but absolute blackness and, to top it off, no sound at all! He couldn't even hear himself breathe. Did time stand still in here, wherever or whatever "here" was? All he knew was that he never was late coming or going from camp.

As he continued to drive, the absolute darkness finally gave way to the midmorning sun and the dirt roads winding through the foothills of the Wasatch Mountains surrounding Salt Lake City.

He breathed a sigh of relief. No matter how many times he went through this, he never got used to it.

Fred felt his body tense. Then a low rumble from the pit of his stomach emanated from his mouth like the sounds of thunderous waves crashing against a rocky shoreline. The harsh, guttural, and thundering sounds rose to a crescendo and then, in rapid staccato, came crashing down. His ominous laughing reverberated through the midmorning tranquility. It sent icy chills to the very heart of his being, totally incapacitating Fred.

Arthoxos reemerged and looked into the rearview mirror. Fred's facial features were stern and hard, his eyes cold and uncaring. Even Arthoxos marveled at how a red-haired, freckle-faced, wimpy boy could turn so callous looking. Arthoxos grinned. How weak-minded these humans were, so easy to inhabit and control. Even that wolf he had inhabited had fought him for control constantly until that wet-behind-the-ears boy—Chris—had killed him, trapping Arthoxos in the wolf's lifeless carcass.

How humiliating it was being defeated by a mere boy. The boy didn't even have an inkling of how powerful and dangerous an enemy he had vanquished and then so trivially discarded into a rushing river, to be quickly swept from his memory. Oh, that boy would remember and pay for his haughtiness. Arthoxos would be patient, knowing that their paths would cross again.

He just needed to keep to the mission. Everything was going as planned. Arthoxos would plant a few false memories for Fred. Then he would let Fred reemerge, not knowing anything was seriously wrong. Fred would go on with his pitiful life as if nothing was amiss. He would remember waking up, doing his morning routine, arriving at Camp Aharonite, working all day, driving home, and then vegging out while watching TV after eating Chinese carry-out.

Arthoxos drove the car down the winding road into Salt Lake City, reveling in how well he had impersonated Barry. He had spoken like Barry, walked like Barry, behaved like Barry, and, for brief time periods, seemed as if he really was Barry. That last part was disconcerting even to Arthoxos. Would he become a twin of Barry if he impersonated him too long or too many times? He had been kind and loving... giving such proper and profound advice, and information to Ms. Cozzi and Jennifer. He had been comforting and encouraging, as if he was the real Barry. Even that reminiscing to himself about Noah and how God worked with man—that was not of a Daimonia. The thought sickened Arthoxos and made him a little jealous. As soon as God made humans, God hadn't been as invested in heaven as he was in the world of man. What did God see in these pathetic weak-willed creatures? He amused himself with some of Fred's memories and added a few of his own to occupy himself while he drove.

It only took forty-five minutes to come to his destination, a large hotel on the northeast side. He pulled up in the hotel's overflow parking lot. AIR was drawing huge numbers of followers. He had to walk three blocks, sporting a flamboyant Hawaiian flower shirt and neon sneakers. How did Barry think anyone would take him seriously? Or was that his purpose? Even more so, who would take seriously a timid-looking, red-haired, freckle-faced young man wearing those same ridiculous clothes? Arthoxos always wanted to project an image of respect. No, of dominance.

He arrived at the penthouse suite on the upper level of the hotel. Arthoxos entered the room without knocking. All the curtains were drawn, and the lights were dimmed. They were evidently expecting him. How? This was disconcerting. He wasn't even sure if he was going to report back today or anytime soon for that matter. He just felt he needed to show up, almost like he had been constrained to. It was too dark in the room to make out any of the faces, but he was able to count six individuals. He knew one was Joshua Smitely by the way he moved. The two that flanked him must've been his bodyguards. The other three were probably a secretary, an advisor, and a personal attendant.

A low, reverberating voice rumbled through the room. "You decided to report back. A smart decision on your part."

The power and ferocity of the voice stilled even Arthoxos for an instant. The voice was reptilian in nature—alligator-like. It was low, gruff, and guttural, ending many a time in a short but powerful hiss. The hiss was not unlike that of a human with one mighty bad chest cold, inhaling deeply. He could not tell which person the voice of Kakos emanated from.

"Everything go according to plan?" the cold-blooded voice hissed.

"They knew nothing of the boy," Arthoxos retorted.

"Did they suspect an impostor was in their midst?"

"No, Kakos. Not even the two Cherubim perceived the deception."

"Two Cherubim… Camp Aharonite is far more than it appears."

Arthoxos smiled inwardly. If Kakos only knew what he knew! He had already decided not to give out any more information to Kakos than was absolutely necessary. He waited in silence long enough to be back in control of the conversation. He was very good at instilling a dominating presence, too. Well, at least he used to. Kakos had made that difficult, giving him a human host that was physically all but intimidating and even more so when wearing these ridiculous clothes! He would turn that around on Kakos; he would use Fred's nonthreatening appearance to his advantage.

"New developments have arisen," Arthoxos said commandingly.

Kakos did not respond; he awaited Arthoxos's elucidation in dead silence. Arthoxos grabbed a chair, roughly placed it in the center of the room, and rotated it so the back was facing the six. Then he straddled the chair, leaned forward, and crossed his arms over the top back of the chair. He played the tough guy part to a tee, even though outwardly he looked like an adolescent momma's boy. Arthoxos was not going to be threatened or toyed with by anyone—not even by Lord Kakos.

Kakos was the Daimon Lord of Chaos. He promoted and lived off disorder, confusion, and turmoil. Kakos seemed to be growing more powerful and more demanding each time they met. When he now spoke, Arthoxos felt disorder and turmoil rise in his body. He had not felt this before from Kakos. Then it dawned on Arthoxos... Kakos was subtly manipulating and twisting the AIR people into disseminating chaos more than anarchy. He was having Joshua sow elements of discord, confusion, and turmoil into the anarchy ideology. It was devious and subtle. Most people already equated anarchy and chaos as nearly identical concepts. A little tweaking here and there, and he now had chaos being promoted. These chaotic feelings from the AIR people were feeding and energizing Kakos, making him more powerful than ever before!

An epiphany—a realization came to Arthoxos. *Kakos, you have usurped Anarkos's organization! AIR is now yours!*

Where was Anarkos? Then it dawned on him that Kakos had been impersonating Anarkos for some time, maybe years. That body that Joshua Smitely had dumped nearly three years ago in the Land of Nod... could that have been...?

Arthoxos felt the discord and turmoil becoming even more intense in his being. He now had to focus his entire concentration on fighting it to retain control. Kakos must have been getting irritated with his delayed response. Good.

He steeled his gaze in the direction of the six then spoke. "Lord Kakos." Immediately, the disorder and turmoil inside him dissipated. *Great*, he thought. *I'll play along being subservient to Lord Kakos for now.*

A low, nearly imperceptible hiss resonated in Fred's mind. *Kakos inside Fred's head!* It was so obvious, so clear now to Arthoxos. He hadn't been aware of it till now, till Kakos chose to reveal himself with that alligator hiss!

"I see from your facial expressions that you now truly understand the situation: that you are not in control. You are *mine*, Arthoxos! Your thoughts, your actions, I can influence and manipulate. The question then arises, are they your thoughts or my thoughts?"

"I have snitches within," Arthoxos said under his breath. He felt several cold shivers run up Fred's spine. *That's right, snitches, I'll get you! Kakos won't be able to protect you. You cannot hide from me for long. I know where you live!*

Arthoxos decided not to respond to Kakos's show of power and his verbal digs. "Lord Kakos, the information I have obtained is most valuable."

"You'll receive what we agreed upon when it is finished." Kakos menacingly hissed, "Are you not satisfied with the down payment? Have I not given you a young human host, fairly smart, and very weak willed? Is that not what you requested? Besides, I have equipped your host with six lesser daimonions at your disposal."

Arthoxos thought to himself, *No, they are there for Kakos to monitor and control... the Arthoxos.* He would work on singling out the daimonions one by one, starting with the weakest and forming an alliance to oust Kakos. The strife and disorder daimonions that

Kakos planted within Fred were the strongest. They were causing much discord and turmoil within him.

"Arthoxos, do not think of not fulfilling our arrangement or betraying me! The consequences would be dire..." Kakos simply let the threat trail off.

Arthoxos was testing the waters to see how much information was being given to Kakos. It seemed Kakos wasn't going to let on how much he had actually heard, but Kakos was definitely being informed to some extent. This was intolerable! He would have to be careful about what he thought. Then it occurred to him that he could stop the flow of information. He had to... no, he had better not think any more about it till later, when he was farther away from Kakos's presence.

"Arthoxos, you should be beholden to me. How long do you think you would've been able to sustain yourself in the putrefying remains of that dead wolf? Stranded, just hoping for a receptive host to eventually come along. Your other alternative, not much better, was to transfer yourself to whatever rock the carcass happened to be resting upon."

He hissed, "What, then, wait for some unsuspecting rock hunter to add you to his rock collection? What would be the odds that he would be a receptive host? You would have found yourself sitting among his other rock specimens, minimally radiating your animalistic spirit, waiting and waiting for some unsuspecting host to come to the rescue. You would most likely have been self-imprisoned for a millennium until your daimonion life force finally ebbed and you reemerged in the absolute void... the Great Abyss, from which none have ever returned!"

Kakos hardened his intent toward Arthoxos, malevolence rising in his voice. "It was not by chance that you ended up in a human host so quickly. I have been watching and looking out for you for quite some time. I even allowed you to make a very equitable arrangement with me... when you weren't even in a negotiating position."

"Thank you, Lord Kakos. You have been very generous!" Arthoxos figured abasing himself would appease Kakos for the time being. He would not win a fight against Kakos at this time. The AIR supporters in such close proximity were empowering Kakos like high-octane fuel to a race car.

"Lord Kakos," he continued, "I have found out that Facsmeres have morphed!"

"Explain."

"They can now be used as communication devices not only in the present but in the past and the future." Arthoxos paused to let it sink in... "There is a drawback, though."

"Go on, Arthoxos, get to the point."

"Only three beings have been able to operate them to communicate: the boy, his Cherub, and his mother."

"Why am I not surprised that the Facsmeres' transformation is connected to that *boy*... Chris?" he hissed in an icy tone of disdain and loathing. "Go on, Arthoxos, get to the pièce de résistance."

"The mother, Jennifer, is alive and at Camp Aharonite." Arthoxos left out the fact that Jennifer had been called by God to be a Recorder.

"How opportune," Kakos said malevolently. "She can be used to control both her boy and the Facsmeres!" Kakos's voice held a new intent. "Arthoxos, it is time to lure Jennifer out of camp and capture her."

"I have already taken care of it, Lord Kakos."

Kakos suddenly hissed then spoke in a subdued but menacing tone. "We have an uninvited visitor in our presence! Who dares to intrude?"

CHRONICLE 21
THICKER THAN BLOOD

N OT AGAIN! I SHOOK MY head in disbelief. Being transported to who knew where and at any time was nerveracking. I was in a dark room, and all I could see was the silhouettes of six people. One of them sitting in the center of the room spoke.

"Lord Kakos, I have found out that the Facsmeres have morphed."

"Explain."

I tried moving my head to see who that individual was talking to. I couldn't move. This wasn't right; something was amiss. Now that I thought of it, how come I wasn't lightheaded or nauseated? I always felt that way after a jump. Then it occurred to me that I had not been transported. I was somehow listening in on a conversation. That was just freaky and felt a little defiling. I thought to myself, *Maybe I shouldn't continue eavesdropping*, but my curiosity had been piqued. Who was this Lord Kakos, and what was a Facsmere?

I brought myself back to the now. How much of the conversation had I missed?

"Go on, Arthoxos. Get to the point, *hisss*."

Arthoxos! He was the Daimonia that had attacked me. He had inhabited that alpha wolf. I could still remember the intense malevolence radiating from the eyes of that dead wolf. I shuddered. It still gave me the jitters just thinking about it, and all I did had been for self-preservation.

"Go on, Arthoxos. Get to the pièce de résistance."

"The mother, Jennifer, is alive and at Camp Aharonite, Lord Kakos."

Hiss. "My suspicions were correct... she is alive. Excellent. She can be used to control both her boy and the Facsmeres." *Hiss.*

No... No... Not a chance, I said to myself.

"Arthoxos, it is time to lure Jennifer out of camp and capture her."

Oh, no you don't.

"I have already taken care of it, Lord Kakos."

Just then, I felt a presence of something or someone trying to break into my mind, shouting!

Chris, Chris... Chris!

Then a far more intrusive voice hissed, *"We have an uninvited visitor. Who dares to intrude?"*

My name was called again, more urgently. *Chris, Christopher!*

I was brought out of whatever I had been snooping on, to find myself still running with Tassi as if I were on autopilot.

All right, all right.

Chris, you were not responding, and I couldn't hear your thoughts!

You didn't need to be shouting.

I wasn't shouting. I was just trying to break through to you. It's like you disappeared, but you were right there beside me physically. Chris, why did you hiss at me?

I didn't.

If not, you—who hissed? And who is the uninvited visitor?

The uninvited visitor would be you! I think you gave us away to the enemy.

Gave us away? To who?

Tassi, I don't really know what happened. All I know is somehow, I found myself listening in on a conversation I don't think I was meant to hear. It was between a Lord Kakos and Ar—

Kakos is involved?

Yes, Tassi. He was the one that hissed at you! He and someone he called Arthoxos were discussing—

Arthoxos was there too?

Will you quit interrupting me? This Lord Kakos and Arthoxos were discussing using my mom to control me and something called Facsmeres. They have set a trap to capture my mom!

Chris, she will be safe. Camp Aharonite is impenetrable.

Tassi, they have already set the bait to lure her out of camp.

Chris, we can change our plans and go to Aharonite first.

A multitude of thoughts swirled within until peace embraced me. I had reached this decision... *No.* I paused then declared, *Tassi, this fight is thicker than blood.*

You may be the Orion, but you are still your mother's son.

I know. Even as the Orion, I will always love my mom and protect her. But right now, the enemy will not and cannot afford to hurt my mom.

Chris, you are wiser than your years, but I still don't think a quick stop at camp would cause any harm.

Tassi, it may be a ruse. We need to free the others from the Land of Nod. This may be part of their strategy. It's only you and me right now. What better time to try to take us down?

Chris, I do not believe they set this whole thing up. It was not by their design that you heard what you heard. We at least now know a few of the adversaries we are going up against and a limited scope of their plans. I did botch things up by spiritually barging in. They now know that somebody heard their plans. They will be wondering who it was, how much they heard, and how they were able to do it.

How did I do it?

I don't really know, Chris. It's possible it was a vision or maybe a new ability of yours. Whatever it was, it's going to cause them some consternation.

Tassi, this was just like at the grocery store! No... I only heard it in my head that time. Or was it his head?

You are referring to hearing the discourse inside Joshua Smitely's mind between him and a menacing presence with a reptilian voice?

Yeah, a.k.a. Mr. Anarchy Rules. Lord Kakos's voice sounds eerily similar! Was Lord Kakos controlling Mr. Anarchy Rules? Hissss... his words drip with power... hissss! I mocked. *Why is it, all the inhuman bad guys have reptilian voices? And what's up with the hissing?*

Tassi chuckled. How could a wolf chuckle?

Chris, you know that was a mental chuckle and that I am not really a wolf! I am a spirit being in the form of a wolf. If I had a brain with the mental capacities of a wolf, I would not be able to hold much of a conversation.

Oh, I am just razzing you.

Chris, it just occurred to me... you did not have a vision. They felt your presence, or should I say my presence, when I broke through to you. You were there in spirit somehow. I believe it's an innate ability that you possess.

When did I receive it?

I do not know, but it is similar to what happened with Joshua Smitely at the grocery store. Chris, there is another that has a like ability.

Who?

Don't you remember, Chris?

You mean Nod.

"She did tell us that she has the ability to eavesdrop on spirit conversations."

What does this mean, Tassi?

We will just have to wait and ask Nod.

Are we going to run all the way to Salt Lake City?

No, silly boy. Ghris will take us to a highway; from there, we'll try to hitch a ride.

It would've been much easier just circling back to our van, I complained.

Chris, have you ever driven?

I just rolled my eyes. Tassi didn't have to see me doing this; she always knew my thoughts and emotions.

I rest my case, Chris. Besides, they might be expecting us to come back to the van.

Tassi, hitching a ride with a wolf—that's so not going to be easy.

Chris, most people won't see me as a wolf.

Yeah, they are going to see you as a dainty Chihuahua.

People will see me as what makes sense to them for the circumstances, like a dog.

Yeah... a Chihuahua. I snickered.

Tassi ignored my humor and continued her explanation. *That's just how the human brain works, interpreting and comprehending the external world according to that person's view of reality, at least the reality they have been conditioned to. Something will work out, remember... God is on our side.*

We were still running north. Running felt great; I felt an inner strength that I never had before. I had always been able to run effortlessly and never ran out of breath, but now, I felt powerful, like I could carry a person under each arm and not lose stride. It was so koosh.

Then a silly thought came to my mind. *I bet bugs won't even bite me, let alone bother me.* I could hear Tassi chuckle in my mind.

Chris, I don't want to interject in your reverie, but we have to stay focused here.

Hey, I'm just following what Big Mel encouraged me to do: Live the moment. Enjoy the moment. Be the moment.

Chris, we have to stay vigilant. They could be planning another attack.

I motioned with my hand upward in a dramatic gesture and with a flippant, authoritative tone, "The eyes of heaven are ever watching." Then I continued in my normal voice, "Ghris will let us know, way in advance of any formation of the enemy. If he's anything like a real golden eagle, he can see a rabbit twitch its tail at over a mile."

Tassi conceded, *At least we now know who and what we're up against.*

Hey, do you think my spit is poisonous scorpion venom?

No, silly, your saliva is not. Now please quit with the Anarkon humor.

I stiffened slightly, becoming serious. *I'm not becoming an Anarkon, am I?*

No. You're just experiencing some minor side effects. The increased amounts of nutrients and oxygen carried by your new blood is just giving you a natural high. You are like a kid on a sugar rush, one that has eaten a whole bag of candies and guzzled down a couple of sodas.

Okay, my mind is on a high, but what other side effects am I going to experience? Wait. How do you know so much about this alteration of my body, soul, and spirit?

Chris, our unique bond, that linking of our spirits and minds, is still there. Your entire being is completely open to me. We are one yet independent of each other. This independence allows me to notice the changes that you may overlook or are not even aware of.

I reached out for a closer spiritual bonding with Tassi. I had to make a real mental and spiritual effort to be close with her. I was always open to Tassi; she heard all my thoughts, felt all my emotions. Nothing of me was hidden from her. I didn't know whether it was me or if it was because she was a Cherub that I did not hear her thoughts continuously. She was not a totally open book all the time like I was to her.

Now Tassi was going through some changes of her own too. She was starting to develop emotions, even though she totally ignored them.

I do no such thing!

Yes, you do!

I do not!

Yes, you do!

Chris, grab hold of your mind and focus.

I now heard her inner thoughts and felt a warmth embracing my being. My mental commotions subsided. I was at rest. I could hear Tassi's heart beating and even her blood flowing through her body.

What kind of blood did she have?

Keep your focus, Chris. Wait, you're hearing it... this is something else!

What do you mean? Is this another side effect?

I wouldn't consider this a side effect. It is a new ability. Many animals have exceptional hearing.

Yeah, like I want to hear someone's bodily functions... ten feet away from me. How about hearing someone belch from across the room or being able to eavesdrop on a conversation some twenty feet away?

Hearing conversations at a distance might be useful, Chris. Your improved hearing, though, is not what is really bothering you, is it? she asked softly.

Tassi, you already know the answer to that.

Chris, you won't grow a scorpion tail or become a hideous creature.

How do you know?

Because the Anarkons are animated by Daimonia, and therein lies the problem. The evil of the Daimonia is so pure it eventually corrupts, contorts, and twists anything physical into a malformed, misshapen creature corresponding to the spiritual nature of the evil.

So I won't eventually morph into...

Correct, the key is what is animating the body or construct. Your life force, Chris, what animates you, that soul life and spirit, is still from God.

Tassi, how do you know?

Because we are spiritually linked together. I would know if you were animated by evil. You are animated by the light, by spirit from God.

Wait, is this why God spoke to me?

God spoke to you?

Yes, Tassi, He said I could never be turned evil.

That's what I've been trying to explain to you, Chris. Now, you could be influenced or used by evil, but you can never become evil... be transformed into an evil being.

What about when I go Anarkon? I go entirely blank. I don't remember a thing.

When you go Anarkon, it comes from the Dark Realm. The intense animosity, hatred, fear, seem to overwhelm your mind... at least for now. Chris, you have the ability to conduct and direct spirit power originating from the Light Realm or the Dark Realm.

You are a multipowered being. Think of yourself like a conductor of electricity. You are the transmission line, the conduit. It doesn't matter what power plant is generating the electricity. It just flows through you and is directed by you. In this analogy, electricity is spirit energy, and the power plants that supply that energy are from either the Light Realm or from the Dark Realm.

Now let's see if I have this right. You're telling me that spirit energy, or any energy for that matter, is neither intrinsically good nor evil?

That's correct, Chris. How it is used, that's what makes it good or evil.

We were interrupted by what sounded like a piercing car alarm.

Tassi nudged me mentally. *Look upward.*

Ghris was circling above us. I should have known that the screeches were none other than Ghris getting our attention. Golden eagles make a variety of sounds, but one of them, a series of high-pitched screams, does kind of sound like an ear-piercing car alarm... and Ghris did shriek just like one.

Ghris flew a diagonal line from us to slightly eastward. He flew back and forth along this line three times and then plummeted out of sight. Bird down marked the spot. Ghris must have found a road.

We took a bearing and then proceeded toward that vicinity. It was still a dense forest, so we only knew the general area where Ghris went down. Tassi chose to stay on the present deer trail headed in that direction. We trusted Ghris that this trail would lead us to him and the road.

It was time to pull out my cell phone to see just where we were and how far we had gone. I stumbled head over heels and shredded a few bushes before landing on my butt.

"Tassi! Don't stop on a dime like that!"

It can be a problem when someone knows what you are going to do before you even do it.

"Tassi, you know I can't stop as quickly as you!" I huffed out loud. I took a deep breath then stood up and brushed myself off.

I reached into my pocket, grabbed my phone, and selected the GPS app. I hadn't used the GPS before because it wasn't useful in mapping a route through an undeveloped area; it only showed roads, not deer trails. Trying to trek through this tree-infested, mountainous terrain without using trails would be insane. Ghris was taking us the quickest and shortest way to Salt Lake City with his aerial view of the terrain, roads, and deer trails. We had already run for nearly three hours, and my GPS app calculated thirty-eight miles from our original position. Wow! That was around twelve miles an hour. That was booking it, especially through this type of terrain. From the GPS, I could see Ghris's route was 380 miles shorter than if we had traveled by road.

Since Ghris was now grounded, I decided to use the GPS locator to pinpoint the location of my mom's phone. I had set the parental GPS location to *on* for her phone just after leaving the Land of Nod. Ghris was so kind as to allow me to attach my mom's phone to his leg. The hot-pink phone accented his stunning yellow leg. Just kidding; his legs were gnarly, and those two colors, to me, just clashed. He wouldn't win any fashion contests.

When I activated the parental GPS locator on my phone, my screen went blank. What was up with that? The phone was rebooting. Come on now! My home screen came up shortly but not the one I had had before. Now it showed Tassi and me looking up at a beautiful, lush, majestic pine tree—Nod's tree. Well, maybe in her wildest imagination. Nod's tree in reality looked anemic. The once-majestic pine tree was sparsely decked with yellow and brown needles, not beautiful like the screen now depicted.

I swiped the home screen. An app started running. Just for a split second or two, it flashed the letters NLS.

"What's NLS?" I muttered out loud.

"Nod's locator system," a sultry feminine voice said in my head.

Chris, I do not know what NLS is. What prompted this thought of NLS? Tassi questioned.

That wasn't you that just spoke to me, was it?

Chris, I didn't hear anything.

This was freaking me out. *Who just spoke to me then?*

"I did. I am NOSI."

What or who is a Nosi?

Tassi looked at me quizzically. *Chris, I don't know anything about a Nosi.*

Well, someone or something is talking to me.

It isn't me.

Then who, Tassi?

The soothing feminine voice spoke again. *"To answer your question, NOSI is an acronym for Nod's operating system interface."*

I didn't wait for her to continue. *You are like Siri, the personal digital assistant for the iPhone?*

"I am far more than a digital assistant," she said in a rather offended tone.

Tassi broke in after considering the bits and pieces of the conversation relayed by my thoughts. *Nod has commandeered your phone. She is not to be trusted. It would be best to leave Nod where she is and turn that phone off. We should immediately turn around and get our friends out from her sleep-inducement land.*

Tassi, I think we should help Nod. Someone or something is already using her.

At first, I felt murmuring come from her, but then she replied, *Chris, now that I think about it, you are right. If we have Nod, then it will stop them from using her against us and slow down whatever they are orchestrating. Chris, you are a formidable tactician.*

Tassi. Like the old adage, 'Keep your friends close but your enemies closer.'

"*Nod is not your enemy,*" Nosi quickly added.

I don't think I like this Nosi listening in on everything we say, Chris.

Nosi responded, "*I awaken upon phone startup, or my name being mentioned. I sleep when asked.*"

Tell her to go to bed, Chris.

Tassi being privy to my every thought could piece together what Nosi only spoke to my mind. She was not thrilled that she could not hear Nosi.

I held up a hand and looked directly at Tassi. "First, I want to try out Nod's locator system."

Tassi huffed but sat on her haunches and waited.

Nosi, show the location of Ghris.

A map showed up on my phone's screen with a projected route from my position to the country Greece, the one across the ocean.

Tassi giggled. She saw through my eyes the land of Greece. Remember Ghris is pronounced like Greece.

Shortly the screen changed. Tassi wasn't giggling now. A new map appeared. It showed Ghris's location on Highway 191 at three and a half miles as the crow—or the eagle—flies.

Nosi spoke. "*You gave Jennifer's phone to Ghris.*" Before I could ask her how she knew that, she continued, "*You activated the parental GPS locator for Jennifer's phone. A logical assumption would be that since you're looking for Ghris's location, then Ghris must have Jennifer's phone.*"

Tassi, she can think and even has a sense of humor.

That makes me even more wary of her, Tassi cynically replied as she took off following the deer trail again.

The brush and plant life started to be increasingly more prolific. We were getting closer to the edge of the forest. I quickly glanced at my phone. We only had a quarter of a mile till we met up with

Ghris. The upper part of the map on the screen now showed Salt Lake City, with a small dot in the northeast part of the city, labeled Nacamichi's.

What's Nacamichi's? Sounds like an Italian pizza joint.

Nosi spoke up. *"Nacamichi is Japanese, and he doesn't make pizzas. He's a Venetian glassmaker."*

A Japanese Venetian glassmaker! I quipped.

"Chris, a Venetian glassmaker uses the techniques and glass formulations of the ancient Venetians."

I know. I am just having a little fun with you. Is he the one that will make Nod's containment vessel?

"Yes, Chris."

How long will it take him to make this vessel, Nosi?

"I have no time projections. It has never been done before." Nosi continued, *"Maybe we should change plans and go to Camp Aharonite first. It's near Salt Lake City too."*

Tassi was listening in on my thoughts. *Chris, what is this "we" stuff from Nosi? And how did she know Camp Aharonite is near Salt Lake City? This Nosi has been listening in on us the whole time! What a sneak. Nosi should be called Nosey!*

"I am no such thing!" Nosi replied rather tersely. *"I was just awake. It's not my fault you two talk a lot."*

Tassi, is it just me, or does Nosi display emotion in the tone of her voice?

Chris, she's just a computer program.

"I am not just a computer program, and I do have feelings!" Nosi stated rather tersely.

Okay, okay! Let's focus on what is relevant at the moment. To go or not to go, that is the question, I said rather dramatically.

Okay, Shakespeare. Tassi laughed.

Since making this containment vessel could take a while and we have relevant information about the enemy that the Aharonites do not have, Camp Aharonite first it is!

Chris, look. Tassi mentally nudged me.

I took notice that the trees waned to scrub brush and sundried grass. We took a few more twists and turns, and there it was: Highway 191.

Ghris was perched on a dead pine on the other side of the highway.

"Now all we need is a ride!" I said out loud.

Then I heard the noise of vehicles approaching to our left. I could see nothing but the sharp bend of the road.

Be patient, Chris. You have above-human hearing, Tassi said softly.

I waited and waited. Then lo and behold... bikers!

CHRONICLE 22
HELL'S ANGELS

THE BIKERS LOOKED LIKE A rough and tough gang. Calling them a gang might be a misnomer; they were more of a motley group of rough-and-tough lowlifes. Now, when I use the word "bikers," I was not referring to the pedal variety. These were motorcycle-type bikers, and they rode custom choppers, not off-the-assembly-line motorcycles.

Nosi jumped in. *"This type of motorcycle grew into its own around the mid-sixties. They are motorcycles with very long front forks, skinny, oversized front wheels, extra-long handlebars, oversized loud engines, low-to-the-ground frame, sissy bars, front-mounted foot pegs, and far-out paint jobs accented with lots of chrome."*

Thanks for the info, Nosi.

These choppers were as motley as their riders. Some were modern and geometric, some ornately decorated with skulls, some with wild animals, some with Cherubim, and some just classic vintage.

Their riders' apparel was as varied: from classic biker leathers to faded and torn jeans, to western style, to punk, to an all-out formal tux. Some wore helmets, some did not. We saw one with a cowboy hat, one with a leather aviator helmet and goggles, and two with bandanas.

They were now stopped along the roadside, about a hundred yards from Ghris. He was a majestic creature. Ghris could capture anyone's attention, even a bunch of weird bikers!

This is our ride, Chris!

You've got to be kidding! Where are you going to fit on a motorcycle? I wagged my finger at Tassi.

Chris, we need a ride. Don't be so particular.

Tassi, they look like they could be part of the notorious Hells Angels biker gang. My mother would not approve of me hanging around this group. They didn't look like the type of people you would want to meet in a dark alley.

"*Today, most bikers are not part of organized gangs,*" Nosi interjected.

She continued with her two cents. "*Chris, you are thinking of the Hells Angels of the 1950s and '60s that spread fear, destruction, and anarchy by terrorizing entire towns. This was done by what the Hells Angels call the one-percenters. The other ninety-nine percent were far less evil, and many were even law-abiding. Today, they are a global business organization doing charitable and social work. But many consider this a front for the one-percenters to operate a crime syndicate that's dangerous and still spreading anarchy.*"

We finally must have arrested their attention. The bikers turned and stared at us.

Tassi, if we have to fight our way out of this...

They all started waving enthusiastically and shouting warm greetings. Outward impressions are not always indicative of the type of person, just like judging a book by its cover is not always indicative of what's inside. You can select a book by its cover, but you should only judge it by its contents. It's the same with people.

We exchanged pleasantries and introductions. Their appearances were just that: appearances.

These were not tough, rugged, or bad people, not with names like Betty Jo, Bubba, Haas, Sue—Sue was a guy—Yogi, Estelle, and Edison. It was quite clear after the introductions that they were just role-playing rough-and-tough bikers. All were in their late forties or early fifties, starting to show graying hair, aged faces, and extra weight around the middle. This was by no means a nasty biker gang.

Bubba, their leader, was a big—and I mean a very big—man. He must have weighed more than four hundred pounds and towered nearly seven feet. For all of his largeness, Bubba walked and spoke softly. He reminded me of Pastor Dan, a big gentle man, but Bubba was just two sizes larger.

Bubba spoke up. "It looks like you went through quite an ordeal." He pointed at my bloodstained and tattered shirt.

I did not know what he thought the black splotches on my shirt were. They were blood—my blood… but not normal human blood.

Bubba continued, "Before we left on our cross-country road trip, all of us had this feeling it would lead to a wild adventure. I believe you are this wild adventure."

He looked at the other bikers, pausing on each one, before continuing, "We will take you anywhere you need to go."

The others nodded that they approved.

Sue spoke up. "We were heading to Salt Lake City for the big bikers' convention, but I guess that can wait."

Yogi then added, "We can always make the next one, if it has to be."

Estelle interjected, "We will take you anywhere but Hawaii. Our bikes don't do well on water."

Everyone laughed. Even Ghris gave his two cents, with three long high-pitched chirps. They sounded like shrill cackling laughter.

Bubba asked, "That eagle yours too?"

"No, Bubba, the wolf and the eagle decided to join me on my trip. They are friends."

Edison spoke up. "That is no eagle." Then he pointed over at Tassi. "And that is definitely no wolf. You call them your friends. They are not mere animals, are they?"

I changed the subject. "Tassi probably won't do well riding on one of your bikes."

Haas chuckled.

Betty Jo spoke up. "Mae can ride with me, and Tassi can ride with Noah."

I looked around. "Where are Mae and Noah?"

"They stayed at the last diner a little longer. They should be here any time now," Bubba replied.

Seconds later, I heard the sound of a vehicle, a loud, rumbling noise coming from the direction of the highway. Haas walked out onto the highway and started waving his bright-red bandanna like an official at the Indy 500 waving the checkered flag for the last lap. Out from the tree line curve, a motorcycle appeared with two riders, one in a large sidecar.

I told you this was our ride, Tassi giddily mused.

You sound so excited.

Chris, I've never ridden a motorcycle before. Your memories and emotions of being on a motorcycle are exhilarating.

Tassi, you do know you're not going to be on a motorcycle but riding in a sidecar?

I smirked in amusement. Tassi being so thrilled about riding in a human contraption was beyond me.

Edison pointed a finger at me. "You are in communication with that wolf... with Tassi. Aren't you?"

I shrugged.

Bubba intervened. "Mount up, people."

That was perfect timing.

"Chris, where are we taking you?"

"Somewhere in the Wasatch foothills of Salt Lake City, Bubba."

"Wait!" Sue spoke up. "You don't exactly know where you're going?"

I held up my cell phone. "I have a GPS locator app running."

Edison peered over my shoulder, scrutinizing my phone. "I've never heard of a Gabriel VII cell phone. Who makes it?"

I shrugged and responded, "I don't know. I ordered it from one of those late-night TV infomercials."

Edison's eyes narrowed, and he cocked his head. "Wait, wait a minute. There's no cell signal out here. How are you getting one?"

"This is a satellite phone," I quickly replied. "I get a signal anywhere."

"Not so fast. That was a good comeback, but..."

"But what?" I retorted. He was starting to get on my nerves.

"I work with NASA as a consultant. They called me a few days ago. It seems some anomaly in space is interfering... with all satellite communications."

I stared back at him quizzically.

"And it is growing stronger. If it continues, all our cell phone communications will eventually go down too.

"Chris, I am an astrophysicist."

Betty Jo interrupted. "He's one of the best in the world. He's the foremost scientist in the field of dark matter and dark energy."

Yogi broke in. "Most scientists study things that are actually there."

Sue interjected, "Just because we can't see it doesn't mean it doesn't exist."

"Yeah, like there are dark photons too," Yogi countered.

Edison continued, "This anomaly has something to do with dark matter and dark energy."

I replied too quickly, "You mean spirrrrr... it, matter and spirit energy."

I figured I might as well say the whole phrase, since I'd brought attention to my initial blunder of saying "spirit."

Edison's eyebrows twitched, and I could see curiosity in the eyes of the others.

Bubba saved the day again. "It's best if we get started now. Chris, you ride with Betty Jo, and Mae can ride with Estelle, allowing Tassi to ride with Noah."

I looked at Bubba. "I need to take care of something first."

He chuckled. "Chris, we all get the call of nature. We did ours at the diner's restroom a piece back."

293

I smiled, but instead of walking into the forest for privacy, I walked some two hundred feet toward Ghris. I needed Ghris to do something for me.

Tassi spoke to my mind. *Try speaking to him spiritually.*

How do I go about doing that? I don't even know what spirit language he speaks, if any.

Chris, you seem to innately possess some of Nod's abilities. Maybe you can speak bird too! She giggled. *Now get peaceful and try. It's better than doing some sort of silly sign language to a bird.* She laughed. I received vivid images of me doing comical hand and body gestures to get Ghris to understand me.

I even laughed. *Tassi, you are truly being humanized.*

I'll take that as a compliment, even though it comes from a human.

Not a bad comeback, though lacking a bit of zing to it.

Chris, just get peaceful. The bikers are waiting.

I looked over my shoulder. They were all watching me.

I closed my eyes. Tassi and I became one. It was only a matter of seconds when I heard wings flapping and felt a blast of wind against my body. Upon opening my eyes, I found myself staring directly into Ghris's blue eyes. He was an enormous bird! Blue eyes...

Chris. Stay focused.

I closed my eyes, pictured Ghris, and then began speaking. It was rapid staccato bursts of chirps and clicks, in rhythmic waves. This was unlike any language I had ever heard.

I asked Ghris to search for my mom and deliver to her the cell phone that was strapped to his leg.

His response came back immediately in chirps and clicks, almost before I finished speaking. I understood clearly what he said: "*I will, young one. Send picture of Mom.*"

How do we do that? I asked Tassi.

Picture your mom as you speak to Ghris. The mental picture will be anchored with the words that you speak.

I gave him my mom's last known location... the Wasatch foothills of Salt Lake City.

I visualized her walking, jogging, and I threw in a close-up of her talking and making all sorts of flamboyant hand gestures. The hand gestures should help identify her even at a great distance.

I felt a strong wind and the soft touch of feathers against my face. I opened my eyes and saw Ghris steadily ascending skyward. Before he disappeared from view, he said, *"Done. Will find young one and Cherub after finding Mom."*

The ride was uneventful except for Tassi and I still being one with each other. I felt the thrill and excitement she was enjoying. The sounds, smells, and visual sensory input were intoxicating... they were coming from Tassi.

You are enjoying my superior senses right now. In time you may develop more of the Anarkon senses and abilities.

What, there are more coming? Not just my hearing?

Chris... I said "may." I don't know all the Anarkon abilities you will develop or how they will come in. In this physical realm, I am like you or any human. My knowledge, understanding, and wisdom come from my mind or revelation from God.

You mean it's different in the spiritual realm?

Yes, Chris. We have access to the spiritual there but not the physical. God has access to all realms... He knows all.

Do you lose it—the knowledge, the understanding, the wisdom—when you go from one realm to the other, Tassi?

For the most part yes. We spiritual beings do retain what we have made our own. Now, we can link to the spirit realm, like you can, but we lose that full access of spiritual knowledge, understanding, and wisdom when in the physical realm. An analogy that you can understand would be like having to download information on a computer instead of already having it in computer memory.

We started slowing down. At least four hours must have gone by. I had been too into the serenity and oneness with Tassi to have taken any notice of time or realized we had entered the outskirts of Salt Lake City. But something arrested my attention when we pulled up to the motel...

CHRONICLE 23

LUL

I T LOOKED LIKE WE HAD pulled into a biker convention—motorcycles galore. The motel was an old army base where sixteen barracks had been turned into sixteen motel units. Each had four rooms to a side and every room its own door. There were no hallways to enter a room, which would make it convenient for taking Tassi in and out.

We all dismounted near a unit nestled among the trees at the far back of the complex. Another enhancement to my body, like Tassi's construct, was no muscle soreness or fatigue... that was koosh. The others had to stretch and walk off the stiffness from the long ride.

Bubba sauntered over. "Noah and Mae will check us in. We'll stay here tonight." He looked at Tassi then back to me. "This motel is biker friendly, and Tassi can come and go rather easily without being noticed."

Betty Jo piped up, nodding in agreement. "We're surrounded by woods, and seeing a glimpse of a wolf would not cause much of a commotion."

"Where is she?" Estelle inquired.

"She was right among us yet walked away without us even taking notice," Edison remarked.

"All wolves are ninja-like," Yogi added.

"She's not a wolf!" Edison barked.

"We will check in and then eat," Bubba said, changing the topic.

"Can we eat at the Hogs Haven?" Haas implored.

"We can't take our bikes. They will get stolen or stripped down," Noah exclaimed.

Mae piped in. "We can take the bus. They're still running."

"The bus stop is like five blocks away from Hogs Haven. We would have to walk through the worst part of town," Mary Jo excitedly stated.

Sue countered, "There are nine of us plus Chris and a wolf. We look like a biker gang not to be tangled with."

Edison shook his head in exasperation at Tassi being referred to as a wolf.

We walked from the motel a few blocks to a convenience store and caught the 727 city bus going to 142nd Street and Kilaire Way. Mary Jo had not been exaggerating when she'd said we'd be going through the worst part of town. Only one block from where we were dropped off by the bus, the city turned from a normal thriving and safe environment to an impoverished and menacing one. The businesses and apartments were run-down, streets and sidewalks were in disrepair, and people stayed behind boarded-up windows and locked doors.

Evening here was not a time of quiet and rest. Shouts of anger, screams of fear and pain, dogs barking and growling, and the steady hum of machinery from seemingly deserted factories permeated the night. Bubba informed me that this section of the city, nearly thirty blocks in all, was a city in itself. It was run and inhabited mostly by the lowest of the low. It was a safe haven for any criminal. If the police ever entered, it was only by day, and then with ten or more squad cars and a SWAT team.

We made it through unchallenged and unscathed but not unnoticed. We were being watched.

Mary Jo gave a sigh of relief as we entered Hogs Haven and blurted, "You were right, Sue. We fit in as a gang not to be messed with! The menacing biker outfits with studs and chains all made it."

"I think Bubba made it. His largeness makes most people think twice about challenging us," Mae interjected.

"Noah and Haas are no small fry either!" Mary Jo chuckled.

"I'm glad it was night, and they didn't see our grays. We are no longer in our prime," Estelle put in.

They all laughed.

Noah and Haas clapped me on the back. "Boy, let's find a table and eat."

Noah and Haas were no slouches when it came to size or eating. They were both daunting men, towering near six and a half feet tall and weighing nearly three hundred pounds, with appetites that matched their size.

Food is good, Chris, Tassi informed me. She was outside the restaurant, keeping watch.

How do you know?

I played the hungry dog to one of the kitchen help. He was outside eating his supper.

You probably just scared the living daylights out of him.

I did no such thing. She feigned offense. *I can look cute and needy when necessary.*

Yeah, just like a full-grown tiger can!

Chris, how can such squalor and decadence exist in a beautiful city?

Someone is probably paying off city and state officials.

It was so koosh being able to talk with Tassi; it was as if she was always by my side. It was no different than internally talking to myself.

Really, Chris!

You know what I mean.

Haas nudged me. "Aren't you going to have seconds?"

The food was remarkable for a place called Hogs Haven. You would think a restaurant with such a name would serve basic, down-to-earth food, like meat and potatoes: roast beef, meatloaf, stews, etc., all served on paper plates with plastic utensils. Not so.

"Hogs" is slang for "motorcycles." The place was a haven for bikers, but it was a five-star restaurant foodwise! The atmosphere and clientele... not so much.

Tonight was Bavarian night, and the menu comprised food like you would have at an upper-class German restaurant. What was out of place was the absence of fine china and crystal glassware—anything breakable. Everything was stainless steel—the plates, the flatware, and the drinking glasses. They also looked worn and abused, as if they had been used for something other than just eating!

The clientele here were bikers and white-collar workers for the most part. The terrific food brought in even some high-society people, if they were daring and had bodyguards along. The restaurant was located just inside the safe haven for criminals, the lawless territory... what we had just walked through.

Tassi gave me a heads-up that an unsavory group was entering the restaurant. I'm not talking about the rough and dangerous biker type. What came through the door looked like death warmed over. Their skin was a pale, off-white color, and their eyes were glazed over as if they just had awakened from a deep sleep or were on mind-altering drugs.

Nosi piped in, *"Those are Hypnos."*

What are Hypnos?

"They are people who are home to a type of Daimonia that dull or numb the mind and senses of a person. The Hypnos when active cause others around them to become complacent or inactive... in essence, the rational thinking part of the mind is numbed or put to sleep. These people then become very suggestible, easily influenced... a state of susceptibility."

Like that of one who is hypnotized, I said.

"Yes, Chris, that's why they are called Hypnos."

The atmosphere in the room seemed to change almost immediately from a loud and active, bustling environment to one of quiet and inactivity. A sullenness or coldness had swept over the restaurant. Many now started taking notice of us, while others seemed oblivious and uncaring about what was happening.

Tassi could see through my eyes. *Chris, it is getting icy in there. Danger is imminent! I come!*

No, Tassi.

Chris, the Hypnos effect is allowing the more dangerous Daimonia to gain control of the people they are inhabiting. It seems someone is manipulating the Hypnos effect to orchestrate an attack. I bet it is against you and our new biker friends.

Tassi became increasingly alarmed. *Chris, this is oh, not so good! Many of the bikers here are very bad people! The Daimonia residing within them are seriously dangerous and now have complete control over them!*

I took a quick glance around the room. Bubba and the others seemed indifferent. At least they were not belligerent. Good. The Hypnos were having only a minor effect on them; at least no menacing Daimonia were taking control of my friends.

My immediate response was to juggle. Yes, I said juggle. I gathered up six of the stainless-steel plates near me, shaking any food from them. It didn't seem to bother Haas and the others when I did so. Juggling the six plates did draw the attention of the Hypnos, though.

Smiling, I flung five of the plates in quick succession when they reached the bottom of the juggling arc. I forgot about my newfound strength. Oops! My bad!

Each of the Hypnos I targeted went flying backward, taking out anyone who was behind them. They were knocked out cold, all five of them. I hoped I hadn't broken too many bones.

The atmosphere in the room changed as the people came out of their stupor, slowly regaining control of their minds and bodies. It was as if they were awakening from a nap, a little groggy and foggy in the head.

"Well done, boy!" a voice said from behind me. It came from a red-haired, freckle-faced young man at the bar.

I didn't hesitate, letting fly the sixth plate. It winged true to its target. The man flew backward against the wall behind him, taking out an entire group of rough- and tough-looking bikers.

The red-haired young man at the bar shook his head and then smiled. "Boy, you are going to pay dearly for taking him out. Doing it with a dinner plate, a dirty one at that! How humiliating and degrading!" He then grinned.

His voice and tonal inflections sounded familiar. I had heard him before, but where? Then it hit me: I had heard him when I had eavesdropped on Kakos and...

"Arthoxos!" I said out loud.

He gave me a slight nod. "Boy, if we were not on opposing sides, I could learn to like you."

I felt a large hand grasp my shoulder. I turned. It was Bubba. He gently hustled me out the back, with the others following. We had to weave in and around people. Small altercations were arising, and chaos was commencing.

We made it outside, with Bubba, Haas, and Noah shoving and tossing people out of our way.

Tassi was waiting for us. *We should move quickly,* she said within me.

No sooner had she finished than out of the darkness stepped a young woman barring our path. She was solemn, eyes glazed over, and had a pasty dead white complexion. Her hair was jet black, stringy, and cut shag style just above the shoulders.

She spoke within my mind. It was a voice devoid of emotion—monotone but somewhat hypnotic. "*Mom is correct. You are a fascinating creature.*"

"*What? I'm a creature now?*" I huffed. She didn't respond to my intentional snide reply.

Nosi broke in. "*This is Lul... Nod's daughter.*"

What's up with this mom and daughter stuff? Spirits... Daimonia don't have progeny.

Tassi answered. *Chris, remember what Barry explained. Daimonia that are similar like to hang around one another. Some of these associations develop into groups, not unlike a human family, taking on the nature and traits of—parents, siblings, aunts, uncles, and even cousins.*

When Tassi and I spoke to one another, as I mentioned before, it was like when a person talked to themselves internally. No one else heard them or should be able to hear them, and Lul was no exception.

Lul continued, *"May I call you Chris?"*

"You're going to anyway," I quipped.

She smirked. *"My mom said you were very up front, even confrontational."*

"I'm just a lovable teddy bear with sass!"

"Your humor mirrors those qualities too! Are you oblivious to the danger you just came from? And the danger right in front of you? I could turn your friends here against you." Lul pointed at them.

"What's with all the hand motions but no talking?" Edison demanded.

Bubba silenced Edison with a big "Ssshhhh."

Edison couldn't contain himself. "Are they talking? I don't hear anything! Is that just some sort of strange sign language? Is it mental telepathy?"

Haas interrupted Edison. "No. They are communicating by spirit."

"Oh, that's helpful! Am I the only one that doesn't know what's going on?" Edison whined.

"Sssshhhh!" Bubba huffed.

I responded to Lul. "Since I am so up front, what do you want?"

"My mom sent me to—"

"Spy on me?"

"No. She has enough allies that keep her well informed. I am here to watch out for you. Mom knew you would get yourself into trouble."

Before I could respond, Tassi stated, *Nod already knows you all too well.* Then she chuckled.

Lul continued, *"I will slow them down. When things do not go as he plans, he has a tendency to go berserk."*

I answered, "Well, he is Lord of Chaos. That would be a likely reaction."

"How did you know that was Kakos you took out?" Lul asked, somewhat impressed.

"Kakos likes to be in the fray. He feeds off of it. And that red-haired young man that spoke to me, he'd be too obvious. Kakos likes to be behind the scenes, unnoticed."

"My mom was right when she said you are far more than your years."

Tassi broke in. *"Lul, we need to get going... Now!"*

"Won't Kakos know that Lul is helping us out?" I voiced.

Lul responded with a cold smile, *"Kakos usurped my Hypnos. He will pay dearly for that,"* she said icily. That sent a chill down my spine!

She then walked through our group and entered Hogs Haven. Immediately, all hell broke loose inside.

HUNTED BY BADGEE

L UL PROTECTED OUR FLANK. SHE made it very convincing that she was ticked off at Kakos. Tassi responded to my thought, *Chris, she was not acting.*

We headed back the way we came. It was the shortest and most direct route back to the bus stop. It seemed all too quiet. There was no yelling, no screaming, no sounds of life. Not a good sign! Tassi had already split off, blending quietly into the shadows of the night. The only sign of life was a solitary large bird circling high above in the moonlit sky. I focused my gaze on the bird. What kind was it? Suddenly my eyes zoomed in, and I could make out the features of the bird rather easily even with minimal light. It was an abnormally large raven. My eyesight was vastly improved over that of a normal human!

Tassi gently spoke. *Your vision is becoming like that of my construct, better than that of an eagle's daytime and an owl's nighttime vision. Embrace your new transformations. Accept them and master them, bring them under your control, and adapt them to your liking...*

I interrupted. *Tassi, something is certainly not right.* I slowly turned around. Where did they go?

There was no one to be seen. How do you lose nine people, especially as big as they were? I could've sworn I had heard them walking, stumbling at times, and talking just a moment ago.

Should I come?

No. It's best if we stay separate. I may need you as the cavalry. I will backtrack, checking the buildings that we passed by.

Be careful, Chris. It is you they want!

I know. That's why I'm having you hang back. You can come to my rescue if needed.

I started checking out the buildings by jumping straight upward and peering in through the windows. It took a minimal flexing of my calf muscles, more like a spring upward than a jump, to propel myself ten to fifteen feet upward to the window ledges. It probably looked comical from inside, seeing a head popping up, peering in through the windows.

At times, I held onto the window ledges with one hand while my other hand rubbed away the grime and soot enough to peek through. I went from building to building on both sides of the vacant street we had walked along.

It was strange; from the outside, the buildings looked vacant, but inside, it was another story. Many were warehouses, neat and clean, with crates stacked upon crates and things neatly tarped. Some of the buildings were factories still producing something. Machines and assembly lines pumping out products. It was like the street I followed, seemingly unused. I bent down and took a closer look at the road. Its surface was well-worn, and I could see tread marks that had cut through the dust and grime. It was still being used!

I came to a building with a rusty old steel door hanging slightly ajar. What a coincidence.

A trap! Tassi said.

It was as if Tassi was by my side. She saw, felt, and knew everything I did. Of course, she wasn't by my side.

I am close enough.

It's not a trap, Tassi. It's too obvious. It's an invitation.

An invitation to a trap, she quipped.

305

You have me there, but my curiosity is piqued, nonetheless. I want to know what's going on. Besides, I'm not going to leave my new biker friends.

Chris, you may put your new friends in more peril than if we just sneak away and continue on to camp.

You may be right, but there is no guarantee they wouldn't be hurt. Let's have some fun, meet our new friends, and see how they want to play.

Going through the open door was too easy and outright no fun. I jumped up to a window ledge then swung upward to another line of windows, then propelled myself off the window ledge straight upward. The force crumpled the ledge. My bad! There went a stealthy entry.

I shot upward nearly twenty feet and landed gracefully on the rooftop. That was so koosh! I could get to like doing this parkour thing.

Chris, you're not doing well at the element of surprise.

No sooner had she said that, than I was surprised. I jumped back, nearly falling off the edge of the roof. A very, very large raven had swooped past, grazing me with the tip of a wing. Whoa! This raven-like bird was nearly the size of Ghris! Was it the same raven I'd spied earlier in the distant night sky? Was it stalking us?

Nosi broke her silence. *"Ravens are an imminent sign of death to follow, a harbinger of war, an attendant to evil, a disguise of Lucifer."*

Tassi followed my thoughts. *Chris, I wouldn't put a lot of stock in superstitions and folklore about ravens, but it may be a guard, informing of intruders.*

Then I should make a spectacular entrance.

Do you think that is wise? You don't know your—

We will find out!

I ran over to a rusty, broken-in steel door that led inside. With a forceful jerk, I broke the remaining hinge easily. I proceeded to vandalize the factory by throwing it forcefully through a large skylight in the center of the roof.

The glass and the steel framework went crashing into the factory. If the people inside had not heard me before or had not been informed by the raven, they surely knew I was here now. I counted one, two, then jumped. I didn't want to beat the glass and steel to the floor. But… I didn't think about landing on the glass or steel jutting up.

It was a little late for second thoughts as I plummeted downward. Had I made too quick an assessment of my new body's capability? It was at least a fifty-foot drop… was I capable of landing uninjured from such a height?

It is surprising how many things one's mind can think of in a matter of mere seconds. I thought of a myriad of scenarios that might happen, and one of them was landing on my head. They make it look so easy in the movies. Let me tell you, your upper body is heavier than your legs and feet. Guess what that means. Yeah, your body wants to rotate so you are falling head first.

I instinctively threw out my arms and, with aggressive muscle control, shifted my weight to remain upright. Hey, was that why many a superhero had a cape? No, it wouldn't allow them to remain upright. I don't believe it would have enough surface area to be functional, but it did make them look cool.

I landed with a slight bend to my knees among the twisted steel and shattered glass. What a koosh entrance. This body was remarkable!

Nosi piped in, *"Using the equation for free fall: velocity equals the square root of twice the gravity constant times the height. Plugging in your estimated height of fifty feet indicates you were travelling at 56.58 feet per second or 38.6 miles per hour when you hit the floor."*

Tassi sighed. *You should have put her to sleep!* I just smiled inwardly.

What Nosi said put me in awe. This Anarkon-based body, my new body, was able to absorb the momentum of a nearly forty-mile-an-hour sudden stop! Probably even a lot more! I'd barely bent my legs. How koosh was that? I wondered if I could fall from an airplane and walk away uninjured?

Chris, you're not trying that out! Tassi said testily. *Now focus. You have walked, or should I say jumped, into danger.*

In the shadows among the crates and tarp objects, I could sense life... breathing... and boy, did they smell! My new senses of hearing, sight, and smell were kicking in. My mind was not yet fully capable of analyzing all the new sensory data, but Tassi's was. She was with me. It was becoming easier and easier to link with her.

Are you ready, Chris?

You know I am!

A flood of processed sensory information became readily accessible to me. There were twenty intruders within a 150-foot radius. Yes, they were the intruders. They were intruding on my life! I knew where each bad guy was, what position they were in, what they were wearing, what weapons they had, even what they had eaten at their last meal.

Tassi! Are you in the building? That was a rhetorical question. I knew exactly where she was.

I should've known that it wasn't just my sensory input that was providing such great intel. She was using sensory input from both of our positions. Tassi's mind was somehow able to extrapolate our limited sight input using the sounds and smells from both of us, producing enhanced visual images as if we could see them directly. It was like having multiple drones providing real-time surveillance video with sound.

I knew the exact position of all twenty in our vicinity, plus four more! The four more were Bubba, Haas, Mae, and Sue. Where were the other bikers?

They took them toward the hallway that leads to the front of the building, Tassi replied. She knew our biker friends by smell.

Bubba, Haas, Mae, and Sue had five bad guys in their vicinity; two were women. Yes, Tassi and I could tell by their scent. Women have a distinctive smell from men, and it's not from their perfume.

Nosi cut in, *"Males and females of any species have differing amounts and types of hormones that lead to the differing scent between the two sexes."*

They were on top of two crates at forty-five degrees to my left. I did not need to look in their direction; Tassi was providing this information from her vantage point.

My head was making small but perceptible movements while I rotated in a complete circle. I probably looked like a robot.

Chris, you don't have the ears or the nose to pinpoint position without moving your head and body. At least not yet.

What do you mean, not yet?

I am just joking. At least I don't think you will.

Tassi, that's not very comforting.

Chris, we will cross that bridge together.

I better not turn all freakish looking!

Didn't we already cover this? Bring your thoughts into subjection. Dwell on what you want, not on what you don't want. Or you may get ...

Okay, okay. I know the principle. What you consistently dwell on becomes what you believe, and what you believe eventually becomes reality.

Back to the now.

It was stimulating, even intoxicating, the sensory information that Tassi was providing.

She chuckled. *Who do they think they are fooling?*

I laughed. Oops, it was out loud. My bad.

I instinctively took the psychological edge my outward laugh provided—a slight hesitation of a bad guy near me. He slumped to the ground quietly, guided by my hand.

This was one that Tassi chuckled about, using a so-called scent killer or scent blocker spray. Many hunters use them, especially deer hunters. It only blotted out his human scent, but he still left a scent from the scent blocker!

I darted in and out among the crates, taking them out one by one. I did it in a random pattern to build upon their uneasiness. Let them worry about who was going to be my next target. My speed made it seem like there was more than one of me.

When you're in a fight, controlling or manipulating your enemy's emotional state is pivotal. If my enemy is not becoming apprehensive... then I resort to bantering. Yes, I talk to them. Actually, it's more of a sparring with words. It really does agitate them, keeping them from being focused.

The smell of their uneasiness was getting stronger. They started moving from their planned positions.

I took out four more, allowing them to give out a shout as they collapsed to the floor. After a few more had fallen, all hell broke loose.

Shots rang from all corners of the building. The lights suddenly came on!

A deep, guttural voice commandingly broke the chaos. "Stop! He is to be taken alive."

I made more noise on purpose, taking out two more. Again, shots rang out, followed by more bodies slumping to the ground! I looked toward the man in charge. He had two female archers by his side that had taken out those that had fired the last round of shots. Their lifeless bodies joined the others on the floor. I could smell power emanating from the direction of the man in charge. Could I really smell power?

Yes Chris, you can smell physical and even spiritual power!

The power I smelled was sheer raw animal power. And it wasn't coming from the one in charge. It was coming from someone or something behind him in the shadows!

The man in charge spoke again. "Come forward, boy. Give yourself up. We are done playing around."

He stepped forward. The man was dressed in black, with a black hood covering his face. He reminded me of how TV portrayed ninjas. I do not know whether real ninjas dress like that or not.

He grabbed someone from behind one of the archers and dragged the person out in front. He held Sue around the neck! The man leaned over to the archer nearest to him and stripped an arrow that was notched on the archer's bow. He forced the tip of the arrow to Sue's heart.

"Now, boy, you will surrender. I have three others if his death doesn't mean anything."

I moved forward quickly, taking out two more without concern for the noise they made falling to the floor. I bounded upward over three crates and stood directly in front of Sue, all within mere seconds.

Before what was happening and going to happen registered with the man, I had already lifted Sue upward and to the right. In a flash, the palm of my free hand rammed the arrow that the taller man held to Sue's heart. It went through both of them with the arrow tip protruding out of the back of the man.

Sue's eyes grew wide as he touched the blood around the fletching of the arrow protruding out of his chest, then they closed. Both men slumped to the floor, loosely connected by the arrow. The eyes of the man glinted with astonishment then closed. I quickly moved between the two female archers and took out the two male ninjas guarding Bubba, Haas, and Mae.

Pure, unadulterated, savage power still emanated from the shadows behind my friends. I placed myself in front of what projected this pure animal power. The two female archers just stood there with bows drawn... not at me, but towards what was lurking in the shadows!

A man stepped out of the shadows, a wild man. He was tall and lithe with intense eyes, one blue and the other hazel. He had long wavy jet-black hair that rested upon a badger pelt draped over his shoulders.

Ahhh, I knew this dude. Yes, he was now sporting a thick, well-groomed beard and was ruggedly but cleanly dressed in all black. He was definitely the man that had icily stared down the clowns that were hunting me seven years ago at the circus. He still gave off a wild animalistic presence. And there was no mistaking those two different-colored eyes. Of course, the badger pelt sealed it. This was the same man!

He grinned and nodded in approval. Did he know I recognized him, or wasn't he going to let on that he knew? Just like I wasn't. He wasn't.

"You are not hesitant to do what is necessary, even if it means taking out one of your own. You fight with the tenacity and determination of a cornered animal. Excellent!" He held a strip of white cloth above his head.

"Truce," he said as he waved it. Then he released it to quietly flutter to the floor with the slumped ninjas. The two female ninja archers backed off together, and now their bows were hanging limply by their sides.

He walked past me to the two female ninja archers. They stood unmoving, as if frozen in place. This was just like what happened to the menacing circus clowns of seven years ago! Had fear seized the two? Or something fear itself feared? All they could do was watch and wait.

Standing between them, he placed a hand on each of their shoulders and gently pulled them close to him. Each tried looking at him, but they could only move their eyes rather warily through the eye slits in their hoods. Their eyes started darting back and forth erratically. The two sensed imminent danger but were powerless to do anything. He smiled and looked directly at me... then he snapped their necks as easily as snapping his fingers. He allowed their lifeless bodies to crumple to the ground.

I looked at him questioningly, keeping my poker face on, not reacting in any manner.

He raised his eyebrows then spoke in an ominous menacing tone loud enough for all to hear. "Now I am the only bounty hunter here!"

I didn't think any of the remaining ninjas lurking in the shadows were going to object. I looked directly into the bounty hunter's eyes. "Who would put a price on my head?"

He laughed. "Pup, you amaze me and amuse me. But that is for you to find out." Then he continued, "I love the thrill of a good hunt, and I think you'll be quite the hunt."

"What do you mean, 'will be'?"

"You have not grown into your full potential... what you are capable of unleashing. It would be over too quickly—no more tracking, no more strategizing, no more chasing. Where's the fun? Besides, the price on your head is not worthy of you."

"How much am I worth?"

"Your present bounty is of no importance. It will soon skyrocket."

"Why?"

"After such destruction."

"What destruction?"

He didn't answer. I guessed he meant the taking out of the bounty hunters.

"So, if I understand this, you are going to let me leave—my friends, too—and without a fight."

He nodded.

"Then you're going to hunt me when the bounty is high enough."

"Yes, but it's not just about the bounty. You must be at the peak of your abilities. You're still in the pup stage. I will be patient while you mature into your full fighting and bounty potentials."

"Is that wise, letting your quarry become even more formidable?" I didn't wait for him to answer. It had been a rhetorical question. "What's with wearing a badger pelt? Did you kill it with your bare hands at the age of five?" I sarcastically joked.

He smiled. What was up with the smiling? His smile was threatening. Now that I thought of it, it seemed more like an animal baring its teeth before it attacked.

Then he spoke. "This was my first kill, at the age of ten. I was hiding in his burrow. He dragged me into his living chamber to finish me off."

The bounty hunter needed to lighten up a bit.

"Do they call you the Badger?" I said mockingly, having fun. "Oh, oh, the Badgerman. No, no, Bad... gee!"

"Pup, I have killed men for less. You are good, trying to bait me into a fight right now. That will have to wait. You and your bounty are not ready yet. Killian is the name, big game and bounty hunter extraordinaire." He paused then seriously said, "It's been rumored that you are the Orion, the mighty hunter."

I smiled, waited a few seconds then responded. "My first kill was an alpha wolf with just a knife, at fourteen."

He nodded in approval. "It was what put me onto your trail. That was no ordinary wolf. You dispatched Arthoxos! That was quite a feat for one so young and probably no prior fighting experience. I have taken his skin only once."

Looking directly into his eyes and with authority, I spoke. "I *am* the Orion! And I may take up hunting a certain bounty hunter."

"That might be very interesting; I've never been hunted before," he said without any trepidation.

Tassi broke in. *Chris, we have a limited window of time. We need to get going!*

It's only been a few minutes, Tassi. Everything is going better than we anticipated. I don't want to come off as being in a hurry. He may become suspicious. Besides, he may know what is going on here.

"Hey, Badgee, I'm curious. What's in the crates?"

Chris, we already know that. We can smell it.

"Pup, I'll play along. It's no skin off my nose. These factories are producing weapons: guns, explosives, vehicles—all military grade." He waited, letting it sink in, then continued, "Some of the buildings are more akin to labs. They are producing street drugs like PCP, MDMA, LSD, meth, even synthetic marijuana."

"For what purpose?"

"Pup, I'm just a freelance bounty hunter. I just happened to notice. All this is of no importance to me!"

I turned my back on Badgee and started walking away.

"Pup, you are bold and brash."

I held up my arm above my head with the back of my hand toward him and gave a slight gesture, indicating my unconcern. "Badgee, I've accepted you live by a code of honor. Besides, I am yet a pup with too low a bounty."

Walk away to fight another day was my course of action. Sue and the ninja leader needed medical attention, and soon. Further Bubba, Hoss, and Mae would become casualties.

Tassi agreed then added, *Killian is much more than a mere man. He snapped the necks of the two archers easily.*

Nosi squeezed in, *"That would take the strength of an orangutan... six times that of a very strong man using both hands!"*

I shook my head. *Thanks for the comparison, Nosi.* Badgee would be a handful even with my new Anarkon strength and abilities.

I ushered the bound and gagged Bubba, Hoss, and Mae toward a hallway. They went reluctantly, leaving Sue's lifeless body.

Tassi, doesn't this all have the earmarks of...

Yes, Chris, this would fit Kakos's M.O... Weapons, drugs, all used to promote chaos.

We met Tassi down the hallway at a room where my other friends were bound and gagged. Tassi and I led all of them out of the factory through a series of twists and turns down numerous hallways. It was as if we knew exactly where to go. Well, we did. We just backtracked on the scent trail that had been left when the bad guys, the ninjas, had brought my biker friends here.

I reveled in my improved sense of smell. *Dogs have it so great with their keen sense of smell. What a rush!*

Chris, God designed it that way. Hormones and other chemicals are produced, giving dogs a sense of accomplishment, pride, happiness, excitement.

So that's why they're so into it, sniffing and tracking, even week-old scent trails. The animals that left them are long gone, and yet they are as excited as if the animal was just there.

Yes, Chris, but ours is so much more... being enhanced by our spirits, our linking, our intellect! For us, it can be intoxicating.

We had just made it outside when I heard a series of low rumbles emanating from within the building. I dashed back inside and bounded through the maze of hallways. As I entered the main part of the warehouse, I could see my buddy Badgee had started a series of fires before he left. He also must have disabled the sprinkler system. It wasn't coming on.

I made it back to Sue and the ninja leader. They were still sprawled on the floor, connected by the arrow... still alive. I decided to separate them by breaking the arrow. But wouldn't you know, the arrow shaft was not wood, like in the movies. It was a graphite composite, much harder to break.

The flames continued to escalate, and things started to explode.

I took out my very sharp knife and, with my newfound strength, severed the arrow shaft without too much difficulty. I hefted Sue and the other man, one on each shoulder. Their weight wasn't the problem. Trying to balance their bulk and squeeze through the doorways was the problem. To make it through the doorways, I had to shift one in front of me and squeeze on through, then shift that one back on my shoulder. I probably looked pretty klutzy.

Finally, I made it out of the building. There was not much time. Tassi herded the others, and we ran down an alleyway. We were only a few blocks away when the factory erupted in a series of explosions. This wasn't the end of the destruction; more buildings were destroyed as we made our escape. Had Badgee blown up all of Kakos's factories and labs?

Now I knew what Badgee had meant by his statement earlier: "After such destruction, your bounty will go up." I was sure I was going to get blamed for all of this. Even the killing of the ninjas!

The ones I took out I had only rendered unconscious. Kakos would definitely be peeved at me, and that was an understatement.

I proceeded to undo the duct tape from around my friends' hands while I explained the situation. They pulled off the remaining piece from over their own mouths.

Hoss spoke up. "Sue and this other guy are still alive?"

"Yes," I said. "They fainted at the belief I had dealt a lethal thrust. I aimed the arrow above their hearts and between their main arteries and veins. Internal bleeding should be minimal... as long as the shaft is not pulled out."

Edison interrupted. "How were you able to do that?"

I didn't answer Edison; he always asked way too many questions. Father had guided my hand.

Bubba spoke up. "Edison, you and Mae, stay here with Sue and the other. You can join the rest of us back at the motel." Edison was going to complain, but Bubba cut him off. "Edison, the two of you don't look like gang members or lowlifes, especially the way you're dressed. The authorities will accept your stories." Mae was already on her cell phone, calling for an ambulance.

"What are we going to tell them?" Edison whined.

"You and Mae will come up with something, hopefully something that won't land you two in jail."

Noah playfully slapped Edison on the back. "We'll visit you and Mae in... the big house." He laughed.

Edison rolled his eyes.

Mae had finished her call and spoke up. "Edison, you are a scientist, and I am a teacher. We both have backgrounds that won't cause anything to come up on the authorities' radar!"

"Oh, all right," Edison grumbled.

Nosi spoke up in my mind. "*Sue and the other have a ninety-three percent chance of a full recovery.*"

"*How do you know?*" I inquired.

"*I pulled up some medical anatomy charts and tables with blood-loss statistics of various wounds. The arrow went between the aorta and the superior vena cava at roughly thirty-five degrees.*"

I thought about asking Nosi how she knew the path of the arrow, but thought better of it.

Tassi implored, *Just put her to sleep.*

The rest of us headed back to our motel, leaving Edison and Mae to meet the ambulance and authorities. We didn't seem to have anyone following or watching us. I figured Badgee had something to do with that. The reason I thought so was because every so often, we would come across someone slouched over or a group of people sprawled out on the sidewalk, like druggies or drunks who had passed out. It just seemed like too many of them, and they were all in the direction we were going! Coincidence? I don't think so.

Chris, use your sense of smell.

Tassi's bringing it to my attention was all that was needed. I could smell, or should I say, I consciously took notice of the scent trail left by none other than Badgee. I knew it wasn't coincidence; at least my subconscious mind was on duty, registering it all.

Nosi spoke up. "*Chris, your conscious mind is not set up to register your enhanced Anarkon senses without conscious effort. Your conscious or reasoning mind would be overloaded. On the other hand, your sub-conscious mind is collecting and sifting through all your sensory stimuli, and if danger is perceived, your conscious mind will be alerted.*"

I relayed this information to Tassi by thinking and mulling it over. I had developed this habit early on after becoming aware of Nosi. It kept Tassi always in the loop when Nosi spoke.

Chris, ask Nosi how she knows all this.

"*Nod has imbued me with all her knowledge, understanding, and wisdom of both the natural and spirit realms.*"

Tassi spoke up. *Chris, I do not trust her. She knows way too much. If it were just Nosi and me, I would be concerned, but I have you.*

Tassi let out a mental sigh.

We made it to the bus stop unhindered, due to Badgee. We caught the last bus back to our motel. Everyone said their good nights.

We left early the next morning, after a big breakfast of course. Mae and Edison weren't detained too long the previous night by the authorities and were able to get enough Z's.

We had been motoring through the Wasatch Mountain switchbacks for quite some time with Nosi guiding us. The constant thrum of the motorcycles' engines and the rush of the cool, clean mountain air were comforting and invigorating. Nosi informed me that we had made it to our destination. I told Bubba and the others to stop.

Tassi and I got off. I thanked my biker friends. We walked off, taking the left fork in the road, which was a dirt road, for about a quarter of a mile. It ended abruptly at the base of a hill. I could sense our biker friends watching us from afar.

Tassi and I walked right through the rock-strewn hillside!

CHRONICLE 25
CHERUBIM ABLAZE

I WOULD PROBABLY NEVER GET USED to limbo land. The utter darkness and complete sensory deprivation were just so unnerving. We must have been walking for at least twenty minutes since passing through the hillside. It truly got on my nerves.

I held onto Tassi's neck fur, not that I needed to. Tassi and I were still linked, so I was not alone. Would we ever get out of limbo land? Or would we be lost walking forever? That would be a total bummer.

The total darkness finally gave way. We were now in a very dark passageway that was a series of curves. It started becoming lighter. I could make out sheer vertical walls, smooth as glass, ascending out of sight on either side of us.

Bamm! We were out of limbo land and into a sparse, arid desert.

We had walked at least a few miles when they suddenly appeared. Now, this was quite a sight! Up ahead, blocking our way, were—get this—two gigantic flaming swords. When I use the term gigantic, I mean *gigantic*. They must have been fifty feet tall. The swords were dodging and parrying one another.

Less than a week ago, I might have allowed this to blow my mind. Now I took it all in stride. I was no longer just Chris Gahrlan, teenage boy. I was the Orion, mighty hunter, bearer of light, and just all-out butt kicker. If this was some kind of test or indoctrination, I was going to ace it.

Hey, what were two gigantic clashing swords compared to a talking constellation, wolves that were really Cherubim, a ten-foot monster clown, or Anarkons, those hideous misshapen insectoid creatures? Oh, and how about a possum the size of a small elephant? It hadn't been even a week. Bring it on!

Chris, you see the positive in everything.

My mom brought me up that way. She taught me to see the positive *in* everything but... not the positive *for* everything. Bad things do happen, and one should not want or rejoice for the bad, but one can find the positive in the bad and make it into something good.

"Halt! Who goes there?"

Chris, we should stop walking and respond to the request. They are probably having difficulty in recognizing whether you are of the dark or of the light.

Who are they? And do I look evil... a dark one?

Chris, they are two Cherubim that guard Aharonite.

What, you mean Cherubim look like gigantic swords?

No, Chris, Cherubim do not look like swords.

I am just having fun with you, Tassi.

Chris, you should take this more seriously.

Tassi, do they recognize you as a Cherub?

Yes, they know who I am.

Then they should know that you would not be with a dark one.

It may not be that simple...

Why is that?

I heard in my mind what sounded like a sigh with a note of sadness to it. *Chris, I studied and trained under one of the greatest military spirit beings that ever was...* She hesitated. *He turned traitor... and became a dark one.*

You trained under Lucifer? I razzed.

She ignored my jest to get her to go into more detail. I didn't press the matter any further. She would share more when she was ready.

I continued to walk closer to the two flaming swords. They seemed to be clashing even more violently. Sparks rose high into the air from the crushing blows of the two swords. They were becoming more agitated. Good.

Had I pitted one Cherub against another? It seemed that way.

We were now roughly a hundred feet away. There was no intense heat—actually, no heat at all—from the mighty flames. I looked toward the tips of the two swords and said out loud in a formidable commanding tone—if a teenager ever could sound formidable—"I AM ORION, BEARER OF LIGHT, MIGHTY HUNTER, SUBDUER OF DARKNESS. ALLOW US ENTRANCE!"

Tassi was sitting alongside me now. I placed my hand on the back of her neck, gently furling and unfurling my fingers in her soft, dense fur.

Did I go overboard on the introduction, Tassi?

It sounded a little sappy, somewhat comic bookish.

You didn't have to use the same words I was thinking!

Chris, I rely on your thoughts and memories. I'm not of your world; it is alien to me. Nearly every time I respond, I take a crash course on your thoughts and memories pertaining to the subject, then I formulate a proper response.

Is that why you sound so much like me?

I try to put my own spin on it when I can. Our unique link is what makes it possible for me to understand, communicate, and act as a peer. She paused. *No, Chris, you don't have to be concerned about me becoming you. I still am retaining my unique personality and individuality but as if I were a person of your age and—*

We were abruptly interrupted by the gigantic swords. "You dare address us in such a manner? You are but a whelp. How outlandish a claim; there has been no Orion as young as you. We do sense that you are unique… born from the dead, yet not of the dead. This is a quandary. Only one we know would even think about doing such a thing."

"Melchizedek!"

Now it was my turn to interrupt. "You mean Big Mel," I quipped.

"What audacity, using a nickname for a celestial being."

I shot back, "Are you two going to introduce yourselves?"

"Shall we humor the whelp? We are Swen and Vwen, guardians of Aharonite."

"Now, that wasn't so bad!" I said rather sarcastically.

"This whelp likes to play. Doesn't he know the seriousness of his situation?"

"Swen, you need to lighten up. I like the boy. I could sense he was of the light when he first arrived."

"You could do no such thing! We still cannot sense anything spiritual of him. He stands before us, neither of the light nor the dark."

"Swen, I can, too, sense he is of the light."

"No, you can't."

"Yes, I can."

"Oh, Vwen, you just think he is of the light because of his playfulness and a penchant for humor."

"Swen, when have you ever known evil to be playful and humorous?"

"Brother Vwen, you have just lost your acumen for discernment."

"I have not!"

"Enough, Vwen. Since the boy likes to play…"

I chimed in. "*Oh, I've grown from a mere whelp to a boy!*"

"Well, boy, let's see whether you're all talk or if you can back up your machismo. We will have a contest. If you win, you will have entrance to Aharonite, but if you lose…"

"I will not lose."

"Boy, you should want to know what will happen when you lose."

"Swen, it's probably on the order of eternal servitude or you want my firstborn."

"Boy, your arrogance is going to get the best of you."

"It's not arrogance, Swen. I need entrance. And if I don't agree with your terms, I don't get in. Besides, I never like to focus on what I might lose, so I am better off not knowing."

"Then it's agreed. Approach."

Chris, I do not think this is such a good idea!

"Boy, if you are thinking Melchizedek… Big Mel… will come to your rescue, not a chance. Hahhh… hahhh." His sarcastic laughter shook my very essence. "You've just entered our domain! Big Mel? Hahh… He can't help you here!"

Chris, I have a bad feeling about this.

Tassi, are you acknowledging your emotions?

Chris, this is not the time or place for… Chris! Chris! I'm no longer by your side!

"Tassi stays outside. No pet Cherub allowed! This is going to be a duel, boy!"

"If this is a duel, then according to the Code Duello—that's *dueling rules*, Swen."

"Don't condescend to me, boy."

I continued as if I hadn't heard him. "According to the Code Duello, since you challenged me, *I* get to pick the weapons."

"Oh, all right, boy."

Vwen interceded. "How about chess or a game of one-on-one, like basketball?"

"Vwen, this is a duel. Those are games. Let the boy pick."

"Swen, I choose swords."

Chris! You are walking right into his strength!

I know, Tassi. Seeing two huge flaming swords dueling would make that very likely.

"Good choice, boy," Swen barked roughly.

I then watched incredulously as the two gigantic flaming swords transformed into two giants fifty feet tall with swords all of twenty-five feet long.

"Now, boy, you must defeat both of us in battle."

"Isn't that two duels?!"

"No, boy, you will battle both of us at the same time."

"Is that even considered a duel? That's a trio duel... no, I have it, a *truel*."

"Boy, are you going to banter all day or fight?"

"I do have a minor concern, Swen."

Chris, this is more than just a minor concern. Swen is stacking everything in his favor.

"Boy, what's your concern now?"

"According to the Code Duello, the challenger must provide the challengee the weapon the challengee chose if the challengee does not have one."

"Why all the verbiage? Just ask for a sword."

"The challengee is requesting of the challenger that the challengee needs a sword to be provided by the challenger, since the challengee does not have one."

"Enough with the challengee and challenger stuff, *boy*."

Chris, you are really agitating Swen.

That is part of my strategy, Tassi.

But, Chris, Cherubim don't have emotions.

Tassi, Swen is getting hot under the collar. He has definitely been around humans too long. He has caught the human malady—emotion. I laughed.

Tassi internally just shook her head.

The two giants stepped away from each other, revealing a massive boulder jutting out of the ground. Swen pointed at the top of the boulder—it was more like a large oblong rock pillar—with a sword stuck in halfway to the hilt.

"There is your weapon, boy."

Vwen immediately spoke up. "Swen, no being has ever been able to pull Amme—"

"Don't say that traitor's name, Vwen."

"Well, no one has been able to claim his sword since the Great Fall."

I could hear Tassi gasp in my mind.

Tassi, I need to know, was he the spirit being you trained under that went bad?

Yes, Chris.

Do they know you two were very close—connected in spirit?

Only Nila, Cami, and Kora know.

I smiled. *This is so koosh.*

I could feel Tassi questioning my excitement. Then it dawned on her. *Go for it, Chris!*

It seemed I enjoyed goading Swen a little too much; I liked getting under his skin. But in my defense, I tend to do that when I'm going to "truel" two giants.

"Swen, what is that? Excalibur? Come on. Get a little more imaginative."

"Boy, where do you think man got the idea of a mighty sword in a stone from?" snorted Swen. "If you want a sword, boy, take it. All the Code Duello states is that the challenger needs to provide the weapon of choice if the challengee doesn't have one. It doesn't say *how* the weapon of choice needs to be provided. I provided you a sword. Well, a sword in a huge boulder, a sword no spirit being has ever been able to pull out, let alone a mere boy! But that is not my problem."

Then Swen laughed. The ground shook as he broke into spasms of laughter.

I walked past the two giants and stood in front of the natural rock pillar. It was roughly twenty feet in diameter, five feet high and green in color, not unlike jade in its raw natural state.

I started slowly walking around the pillar. I made one pass then two passes... I was at peace. Tassi and I fully merged. I began to speak in a language unknown to me but one I'd heard before.

"Boy, are you speaking to the sword?"

"Swen, the boy is speaking in the old language! Listen to him!"

Swen lowered his head to hear better. "It is the first language of the Cherubim! What is that boy up to?"

I continued speaking; the words flowed easily across my lips. They started exuding power. The power began to resonate through the sword in rhythm with my words.

"Chris, just focus on speaking. Do not think about the meaning." Tassi began speaking the language in unison with me.

I did not remember how many times I had walked around the pillar when my body suddenly stopped.

Seven times, Chris. Now jump.

My body responded. I cleared the top of the pillar easily and landed on one foot, gracefully transitioning into a walk. I felt powerful, even more so than the first time Tassi and I had merged. The addition of the Anarkon abilities was phenomenal—to jump six feet straight upward from taking a step! That was so koosh.

Walking up to the sword, I knelt in front of it. I raised my arm and grasped the pommel of the sword as if I were going to draw it out of a scabbard. Tassi and I were still speaking together, and the words continued to flow. I could almost make out their meaning, but again, she exhorted me to focus on speaking only.

The power that resonated in the sword flowed into me. It was peaceable and gentle, easily entreated. It reminded me of water from a cool spring bubbling up into a quiet pool that quenched one's parched lips as they caressed the pool's surface.

I began to lift my arm, and the sword started to rise.

"That's not possible!" shouted Swen. "Only a spirit being can possess it, and at that—a Cherub! For a mere boy to wield a weapon of such power..."

I could hear Tassi exhorting me. *Stay focused on the sword.*

I grabbed my mind and forcefully concentrated it on the sword then continued raising my arm in a smooth upward motion as I slowly came to a standing position. This sword was not made for a human. It was nearly six feet in length and probably weighed at least forty pounds. The pommel was made for a hand twice the size of mine, for a being that stood at least ten feet tall.

"That sword is made for a Cherub, boy! You have no right to wield it."

"Swen, you conferred that right to wield it when you presented it to me. You and Vwen are Cherubim, are you not?"

"He is right, Swen. You gave him the legal right to try to wield it."

"Oh, close it, Vwen."

I liked Vwen. Swen was okay too. He just had issues with humans.

Tassi chuckled. *Chris, you're all heart.*

I tilted my right wrist and brought the sword horizontal at eye level. It was light as a feather for me. I brought my left hand up a foot away from the tip, gently resting the blade in the palm of my left hand. Hey, I didn't want to spoil the moment by cutting myself and bleeding all over.

Chris, you heal too quickly for that now.

I released my grip on the pommel and allowed it to rest in the palm of my right hand. I could feel Tassi's approval in my mind. I was glad we could talk to each other without anyone hearing us.

And know each other's thoughts, Tassi chimed in.

You always know mine.

You know my thoughts, too, when we are fully merged, like right now.

Yes, I know. It makes me fully complete, and I'm honored to know the thoughts of a Cherub.

I came to a kneeling position with both arms still holding the sword slightly outward from my body at eye level. In the old language of the Cherubim, I spoke out loud. "Thank you, Father, for the ability to wield this sword in truth, might, and mercy, bestowing glory to you, Father."

As I was finishing saying "Father," the sword began to shimmer. Right before my eyes, it reduced to a more manageable length; even the pommel now fit my hand.

I stood up, holding the sword high, pointing it toward the heavens, and said, "This day, I dedicate this contest to you, Father.

"Now let's kick some Cherub butt!"

Before I could enjoy the moment or study my sword further, I felt a blast of wind. My muscle memory took over—or was it Tassi's? I instinctively jumped backward off the pillar, doing a midair somersault, and landing in a crouch some fifteen feet away. Where I had been standing, the sword of Swen cut a six-inch-deep gouge from edge to edge through the top of the stone pillar.

"Swen!" I chided. "What a cheap move from a Cherub!"

The ground shook with a mighty tremor from the blow, with aftershocks following. The aftershocks, I soon noticed, came from Swen repositioning himself for another swipe. I was getting under his skin.

I feinted right, took two large steps toward Swen, and feinted left. Then I sprang off my right foot. I propelled myself toward Swen's legs at calf height. It was a thirty-foot jump, and I was still in the air! As I passed through Swen's legs, I twisted my torso upward and brought my sword across the back of his right ankle, slicing through his Achilles tendon.

He bellowed in pain. "Boy, I'm going to—"

Then I felt a mighty wind coming toward me. I couldn't believe how well attuned I was to my opponents and my surroundings. I believed Tassi was relaying this information and helping me with my moves.

Yes, Chris, I am.

It was just pure koosh! We were independent in body and mind but acting as one.

Without hesitation, I stretched my body out and allowed the momentum of my sword swing to spin my body out horizontally. At that very moment, a huge sword sliced right above my out-stretched body, cutting both of Swen's legs! The noise he made was earth-shattering.

I spun out on the ground, immediately pushing off with my left arm and planting my feet on the ground. My momentum lifted my upper body, and I was now back in a fighting stance, with my sword in an upright position, ready to parry. The only problem was that Swen and Vwen were behind me. How embarrassing.

I did a quick upward hop and twisted a hundred and eighty degrees clockwise. I was now facing them. To my amazement, Swen was still standing, with his legs intact.

"Vwen, you did that on purpose!"

"No, Swen, the boy is just Cherub-quick."

I was looking toward Vwen but keeping Swen in view when I saw writing appear on the side of the pillar nearest me. Part of the face of the pillar was now smooth where the writing appeared.

<u>Boy</u>	<u>Swen & Vwen</u>
III ~~IIII~~ ~~IIII~~	0

Vwen spoke. "The boy gets three points for a major hit to a limb and five points each for two life-threatening hits."

"Vwen, that was *your* sword blow to both my legs, giving the boy ten points," Swen said, a touch irritated. Well, maybe more than a touch.

"Swen, the boy is an exceptional fighter. I haven't seen moves like that since Amm… since the traitor."

"Boy, don't listen to Vwen."

"Well, he is, Swen! Anyhow, Chris, you have thirteen points. The first to twenty is the win—"

I knew immediately to flatten myself to the ground.

WHOOSH.

If I hadn't been kissing the ground, I would've been cut in half by Swen's sword. I then rolled to the side. Where I had just been, Vwen's sword struck, embedding itself deeply into the ground. I quickly resumed a standing position.

"I told you, Swen, the boy seems to be able to anticipate our strikes."

"Vwen, you were just slow on your swing."

"I was not. What about your missed swing?"

"Are you two going to continue to bicker or fight?" I sarcastically quipped.

"Vwen, we should resume our normal Cherub size. The boy is not daunted by our Titan size. He is taking full advantage of our slowness."

"Yeah, when you have bodies that large, it's easy to read your body language. One would have to be slow *not* to be able to see it."

"Boy, your audacity is going to be your downfall."

"No, Swen, it will be yours."

The two giant visages shimmered, shrinking in size. Now standing on either side of me were… still two giants.

"Okay, boy, let's see how you fare fighting normal-sized Cherubim."

I guessed normal size for them was like ten feet tall. That was still a giant in my book.

"Swen, does it still take two Cherubim to fight one boy?" I was still having too much fun goading Swen. It was causing him to make rash moves. He was becoming more and more reckless. Maybe my scheme was working too well. If he ever got the chance, he might kill me or, at the least, severely disfigure me.

Swen suddenly charged me like a frenzied bull on steroids. I succeeded in countering the charge and the vicious blows that followed. This infuriated him even more. He continued advancing, forcing me into a seemingly reluctant retreat. His sword strikes got closer, and three even made contact with my arms.

Swen smiled and roared, "Three points for the Cherubim!"

Swen had forced me into backing toward Vwen. He took advantage of the opportunity and advanced quickly to sandwich me between the two of them.

Vwen was just starting to thrust his sword toward my back for a kill strike. I brought my sword under my left arm and behind my back to deflect Vwen's strike. This left me seemingly totally vulnerable to a frontal attack by Swen. He immediately took advantage of the opening to charge and run me through for a kill shot to the heart. My timing had to be precise.

"*Jump, Chris!*" Tassi implored.

I was already springing into the air at the *J* in "jump." I did a backward midair somersault right over Vwen's body. I saw him look up in utter disbelief.

It was over in an instant as Swen's sword impaled Vwen right through the lower abdomen.

I landed in a fighting crouch. I had done it again—my backside was towards them. I quickly spun around so I was facing them. The force of Swen's charge carried the two a safe distance from me.

I glanced over at the pillar. Ten more tallies appeared on my score, for a total score of twenty-three. I had won the battle against two Cherubim.

Swen quickly extricated his sword from Vwen rather callously. Vwen took a little time but stood up, unharmed, as I had anticipated. The two Cherubim didn't have anything to lose except maybe their pride. I wasn't sure how I would have fared with similar blows. They were Cherubim, while I was... somewhat human!

Swen snarled, "Boy, it's not over yet!"

CHRONICLE 26
THE EQUALIZER

THIS WAS GOING A LITTLE overboard. Gaining entrance into Camp Aharonite took defeating two Cherubim. I had just defeated Vwen. Now...

"Boy, it's you and me. Mano a mano," Swen barked.

Chris, I think you overdid it by riling up Swen by pitting the two against each other.

Whatever gave you that idea?

That was my strategy: to make it personal, keeping them from coordinating their attacks and more than likely getting in each other's way to get to me. It had worked too well. Swen was out for blood—my blood.

As I was contemplating a strategy to beat Swen, or to just stay alive and in one piece, my sword suddenly started shimmering. I quickly held it in front of me, getting it away from my body, but at the same time not letting go of it.

The sword started transforming right before my eyes. It had now become a long rod with both ends sporting wicked, two-foot-long double-edged sword blades. The sword had become an eight-foot pole weapon! For lack of a better name, I decided to call my sword the Equalizer, since it had become a weapon that did equalize my reach... to that of a Cherub. Both Swen and Vwen had at least a three f00t longer reach.

I did a couple quick spins with a few jabs, complete with turns and a forward thrust, followed by a rear upward thrust behind my back and a full spin with two frontal parries. I brought the Equalizer front and center then proceeded with a clockwise baton spin that ended with a quick thrust of one end into the ground.

I was now ready to battle Swen. I held my weapon with my right hand, and with my left, I gestured for Swen to bring it on.

He did not hesitate. He charged straight at me but then veered off around the pillar. Now, if he was thinking of surprising me, it wasn't going to work. The rock pillar was only waist-high on him.

"What are you doing, Swen? You know I can see you."

He then ducked down behind the pillar. When he came back up, he had a big grin on his face. The grin was scary, a bit disconcerting in that it was one of those fake, contorted grins. It was nearly as bad as the painted-on smiles that clowns wear. Clowns are just the creepiest, though Swen came in a close second with that twisted grin of his.

When he came around into full view, I found out why he was smiling. Vwen must've dropped his sword behind the pillar when he left the contest. Swen now had a sword in each hand.

Speaking of Vwen, where was he?

I took a quick look around, moving just my eyes. I did not want to give Swen an opening. There, off in the far corner of my vision, I could see Vwen standing near Tassi.

Vwen was talking to Tassi. I listened in. "*The boy is much more than he appears. I like him.*"

"*His name is Chris, Vwen.*"

"*Chris's fighting style mirrors yours, Tassi... and the traitor, the Fallen One... the one I can't mention by name.*"

"*Does it, now?*" Tassi said rather coyly.

"*You are connected, linked with that boy... even now! He's hearing everything I'm saying, isn't he?*"

Tassi did not respond.

Vwen continued, "*I do not understand how this is possible, but it would explain Chris's fighting style and ability, since you trained under... you know who. It does not explain his phenomenal strength, speed, and agility!*"

"*Vwen, enough talk for now*—it's starting."

Swen clashed his two swords together as if he was sharpening their blades.

"Boy, let's see how well you fare one on one."

"Swen, this reminds me of David and Goliath. You *do* remember what happened to Goliath?"

Swen huffed and then attacked, his two swords slicing menacingly through the air. A normal human would have only seen the swords as a blur and heard them like twin props of an airplane revving. I saw each sword move distinctly as if in slow motion, as well as heard their distinct sounds. I could track both swords' movements relatively easily.

I thanked God for my new Anarkon senses and abilities.

My help too!

That goes without saying, Tassi! You know when I say 'I,' it means 'we.'

Swen was such a show-off. He was doing sword katas—a series of choreographed sword movements and maneuvers—which were extremely intricate and dramatic. I stepped forward and quickly thrust the Equalizer first into his right sword kata and then the left. They both abruptly halted, one after the other. The force was tremendous, like stopping twin 150-horsepower outboard motorboat propellers at full throttle. My body and weapon transferred the force back into the ground. Had I struck on the upward swing of either of Swen's swords, I would have been flung high into the air. That would not have been good, being at Swen's mercy. Swen didn't have any mercy.

I smoothly released the Equalizer with my left hand and brought it vertical with my right, lightly touching one of the blade tips to the ground and smiled.

"Two points for Chris," Vwen yelled.

"Vwen, we don't need a ringside announcer."

"I like the boy, Swen. Don't kill him."

"Vwen, if he bests me, he will live. Otherwise, Melchizedek will have to find another!"

Swen wasted no time; he charged with an increased intensity and zeal. Even with my new heightened senses it was now harder to distinguish and anticipate the slices, the thrusts, the jabs, and the feints. The strokes were delivered with such power and ferocity that if my timing and countering were not precise, I would be chopped meat or flung helplessly into the air.

Chris, you really ticked him off by abruptly ending his showing off.
I just couldn't resist, Tassi.

Swen brought both swords together and took a ferocious sideways swing at my middle. I was slow in anticipating the move. All I could do now was block. I quickly pushed the Equalizer into the ground in front of me, clenching it with a hand near each end. The force of Swen's blow was enormous. My feet and the Equalizer dug a trench nearly fifteen feet long. I found myself almost up to my knees in the ground before I finally came to a stop.

Swen came barreling at me, knowing I was at a complete disadvantage. What to do when you're stuck in the ground with a raging ten-foot giant commencing to slice and dice you into sushi? What to do?

Timing and being at peace are everything in moments like this. I waited till he was almost upon me. I was already deeply crouched, and at the precise moment, I forcefully sprang upward, freeing both myself and the Equalizer. I propelled myself over Swen. He jumped upward to counter, baring both swords, dicing my inner thighs as I tucked and rolled in midair. I had to grit my teeth. That hurt like hitting my funny bone—times ten! The shooting pain incapacitated me for a short, almost unbearable few milliseconds before fading to numbness. That was not the end—it came back with vengeance of an agonizing wincing pain which thankfully ebbed away rather quickly.

I brought the Equalizer behind me in an upward diagonal slice to Swen's chest. Because of Swen's jump and him leaning backward to connect with me, my slice entered slightly below his rib cage and ended upward through his heart. He crumpled to the ground. Swen was down for the count. He remained deathly still for a few moments then struggled to collect himself in a crouch with his head down.

Vwen yelled, "Ten points for Chris! Three for Swen."

Swen growled. "Whose side are you on, Vwen? The point scoring seems to be rigged."

"Chris dealt a killing blow; yours was mere superficial lacerations."

Swen slowly stood up, still collecting himself. He was unscathed, of course. I was already on the ground in a fighting crouch but with my back to Swen.

What was up with that? My ability and timing seemed impeccable except that more often than not, I landed from a jump with my back toward my opponent. Swen thought I was doing this on purpose, just toying with him.

"Boy, what audacity... showing me your backside again. Do you not consider me a worthy opponent?"

Tassi always had my back, and in this case, she literally did. Instantly, I had full sensory input from her. It was as if I was in her body and saw from her vantage point. Tassi was in a position to see what I physically could not. I could now see Swen perfectly even though I was facing away from him.

I could not help myself. Still with my back to him, I lifted my left hand high into the air, gesturing for Swen to bring it on.

Chris, you need to stop antagonizing him.

But Tassi, it is so much fun... and makes him more reckless.

Swen charged at my backside, his twin blades cutting the air in violent, sharp, furious, short strokes. He was anticipating that I would move out of the way, but I stood my ground. At the last fraction of a second, I fell forward, rotating my body. I brought the blade of the Equalizer that was touching the ground upward with a quick, powerful slice. As my back just started to touch the ground, I extended my arms, propelling the blade toward his chest for another kill strike.

Swen was quick! As my blade started penetrating his chest, he rotated and flung his body to the side. He continued to make two complete sideways twists, contorting his body into a fighting stance as he hit the ground. It was like watching a piece of rubber flex and bend. It was not humanly possible, but then Swen wasn't human. He was able to deliver three scathing blows to my sides in the process of evading my kill strike. The pain from the blows was as if someone had taken a blow torch to my sides.

Vwen yelled, "Five more points for Chris, for a total of seventeen."

Swen roared, "Hey, what about my three blows?"

"Six for Swen, for a total of nine."

Now, I don't think it was my imagination. Swen seemed to be slower and not as powerful after each major strike to his body, especially from the last two. Had I actually hurt the Cherub? He did have bursts of quickness, but that was what they were: short-lived bursts. My sword blows were weakening Swen. His speed, quickness, strength, and energy no longer seemed unending.

Chris, what are you thinking?! This is surely not a good idea.

Tassi, it will be over soon.

For whom, Chris? You do know Swen has the advantage of longer reach when you are using a sword.

I'll stay just out of his reach, or I'll get inside... his speed, quickness, and strength are second to mine now.

The Equalizer began to shimmer. This time, I did not hold it away from my body but held the shaft firmly with both hands. It morphed into two identical swords. I now was holding an Equalizer in each hand! Way, way koosh.

"Swen, the boy's mastery of the sword's capabilities is remarkable. It's as if he's wielded it before."

Swen ignored Vwen's comment. "Okay, boy, you are good with the long weapon, I'll grant you that. Let's see how you fare with two swords."

Now, Swen didn't know I was ambidextrous, and not only that, but I could use both arms completely independent of one another. I used to practice for hours upon hours juggling five items with each hand and interchanging the items back and forth without even thinking. I would say my juggling had prepared me for this day.

Tassi snickered. *Your endless hours of video gaming have also helped.*

Yes, Tassi, I can confidently say my avid enjoyment of role-playing fighting games also prepared me for this sword battle.

I really enjoyed those swashbuckling games. I was glad of the experience I had gained in sword fighting... mastering two swords, even if it was only virtual experience.

Chris, our practice sessions at our vacation hotspot have strengthened and reinforced your combat skills. It was like six months of actual sword and hand-to-hand combat. And our link, our oneness... you have complete access to all my sword-fighting skills and abilities.

Swen didn't delay any longer; he had re-energized. He came at me hard, relying on brute strength and quickness, usually attacking from the front with bold and even brash moves, always advancing.

He fights like Nila, Tassi uttered.

Yes, I did envision Nila as headstrong, bold, and brash, an out-for-blood type of fighter too. I, on the other hand, liked to use cunning, finesse... and of course, some misdirection with a little chitchat. I enjoyed joking and kidding around.

"Hey, Swen, how long have you been a security guard for Camp Aharonite? You and Vwen must have done something awfully bad to get this job assignment."

"Boy, you better just concentrate on fighting."

I countered with my own frontal assault, both blades slicing and jabbing at Swen. He countered these with a little more effort than usual. I went left; he went left. I went right, and he went right. He was slower now, from just coming at me hard. It was time to get inside of Swen's reach, where I would have the advantage. Now with a few more mental jabs to keep him off guard, I would make my final move and end this.

"Swen, you are following my lead. We would make great dance partners. Do you know the female part of the tango?"

Vwen spoke. "Swen, Chris's mastery of the dual swords reminds me of you know who."

Swen just huffed and strutted forward with both swords slicing toward my head. I blocked them by bringing both swords vertical above my shoulders. Then I quickly dropped to my knees with both sword tips slicing Swen's body on the way down. Before he could counter, I brought both swords between his legs, crossed my wrists, and with the back of a blade against each of his calves, I stood up, forcibly sweeping Swen off his feet. He came crashing down hard on his back.

"Two points for Chris, for a total of nineteen, one point away from a win!" Vwen blurted excitedly.

Immediately, I hurled myself into the air over Swen. He sliced upward, cutting deeply into both my sides as I sailed over him.

"Five points for Swen, for a total of fourteen," Vwen announced.

I called to the Equalizer to become a pole weapon again. Of course, I didn't speak it out loud; I didn't need to give Swen a heads-up on my next and final strike.

To my amazement, it transformed into the pole weapon nearly instantaneously. That was so koosh! I thrust the Equalizer downward toward Swen's chest for a kill strike. He had already started to roll out of the way, but he was too slow and too late. At the last second, as I descended from the apex of my leap, I pulled back slightly. The Equalizer still pierced his chest. It was just not the fatal strike through his heart as I originally intended.

I didn't know what another fatal blow might do to him. Would he come out unscathed? His recovery from the last one had seemed very slow. Maybe Swen didn't have mercy, but I did.

I deftly landed on my feet, pivoting to face Swen. He was very, very slow in getting up; he seemed to be slightly dazed.

We had both gone into our fighting stances, weapons ready, when Vwen yelled, "Chris is the victor!"

"Vwen, you don't have to sound so thrilled."

"I do like the boy, Swen."

"I like him, too, Vwen."

"Wait a minute, just hold on. Swen, you were out for my blood, even to end my life."

"No, Chris. I—or should I say we—made it appear that way."

"What? This was all a ruse?"

"No, not all of it. You had to believe it was a real fight so you would hold nothing back! Chris, the only thing that was a ruse was my animosity toward you, that I was even out to kill you. You would not have been permanently harmed."

I glared at Swen. "You mean that twenty-five-foot sword blow from you would not have cut me in half? It put nearly a half-a-foot-deep gash into a solid-stone pillar!"

Swen laughed. "It would not have severed you."

"We made it appear as a big gash in the pillar," Vwen chuckled.

"Well, that explains everything!" I huffed.

Vwen continued, "Quintarium is a quasi-phased light substance. It exists yet doesn't exist in both the spiritual and physical worlds."

"Oh, that makes it ever so clear. Thanks!"

Swen interjected, "Chris, our swords and yours are made of Quintarium. Well, that's not entirely correct. Ours are a composite with a small amount."

Vwen blurted, "Yours, Chris, is pure Quintarium. More than all that is known to exist. And... and..."

"Spit it out, Vwen," I said.

"Chris, no one knows how *you-know-who* forged a sword out of pure Quintarium. It cannot be altered from its original state of small grains, the size of grains of sand."

"Ooh, how could I have been so addled? We have swords made up of some kind of light matter that phases in and out... a shifty light that appears physical yet not physical."

Vwen continued, "let's suffice it to say that Quintarium affects the energy of things and most dramatically—spirit energy."

"So you're telling me it has little effect or no permanent effect on physical things but attacks the spiritual?"

Swen replied laughingly, "Yes, Chris! I'm still intact, even with you slicing off my body parts! Your sword saps a lot of spiritual energy, being pure Quintarium. I'm weaker and have aged a few millennia!"

Swen had a sense of humor. Nothing would ever be the same.

I looked over Swen and myself. Our clothes even remained untouched.

"Chris, we held nothing back. You bested two Cherubim. I would not have believed that possible."

I felt a firm but pleasant nudge. Tassi was physically by my side. Swen and Vwen must have lifted the barrier.

Swen continued, "Even from the very beginning you were more than we expected. Seeing Vwen and me as two flaming swords at the entrance to Aharonite shows remarkable spiritual maturity."

I inwardly smirked. *I actually saw them in their skivvies!*

Tassi chuckled.

Swen hesitated, looking at me quizzically as if he'd heard Tassi's chuckle, then continued, "Most spirit-filled humans see us as some kind of stone statues if they see anything at all."

Vwen cut in, "And to be able to fight a Cherub, let alone two, in a no-holds-barred match? Incredible! We did not anticipate you being able to do what you did, even with Tassi's help."

Swen continued. "We thought we would have to coddle you in a fight. No mere human would ever have even a remote chance against a Cherub. You put that in doubt when you sprang on top of the pillar from a walking step. You were full of surprises... with you speaking the old language, and removing the sword from the pillar, and… it accepting you, as its wielder! Then when you were able to handle the strength, speed, and quickness of a Cherub, we knew we had a fight on our hands."

"I was just toying with you, boy, when I offered you a sword fused to a pillar of rock. I figured you would give it a couple of good yanks and then give me a tirade on how it was unfair. Many have tried through the millennia to become its wielder but to no avail. It's been accepted that only the sword's original wielder would ever be able to wield it. And he is no more."

I glared at Swen and Vwen skeptically. "Are you telling me you were not anticipating any of this?"

"Chris, we only expected for you and Tassi to grow in your union by depending on one another and working together. We just wanted both of you to get more fighting experience together in a somewhat controlled situation. But we did not believe you would have even a remote chance against us."

I heard Tassi in my mind. *I knew nothing of this, Chris.*

I know, Tassi.

Then it dawned on me. "Swen, you keep using the word 'we'. I have a gut feeling this means more than just you and Vwen."

They both grinned.

This had all the makings of…

I yelled it out loud. "Mel!"

CHRONICLE 27
TV REALITY STAR

I FOUND MYSELF ON A BEACH—A pristine *black* beach.

Not as nice as our solitary place, Tassi quipped.

We were still linked. She was with me and I with her, though physically she was not. I could see through her wolf eyes, Swen and Vwen standing by the green pillar... and I was also there. Yet I was on a beach too! This was a vision, and I had Tassi along for the ride. This was so koosh.

The waves gently caressed my bare feet as I beheld the beautiful sunrise. I looked myself over. I was sporting khaki shorts and a black flowered Hawaiian shirt. To top that off, there was something on top of my head. I reached up and ran my fingers over it. That something was a baseball cap with a large stylized embroidered letter *A*.

Chris, this does seem like a certain someone's playful tomfoolery.

Yeah, you're right. Now we just have to wait for him to show up. He'll probably do it in some dramatic and flamboyant fashion.

No sooner had I said that than lo and behold, a gigantic tsunami was heading right towards me. Now you would think I would have been ready for Mel's arrival, but I never knew if or when or how he would show up.

Tassi, can one get hurt in a vision?

She didn't answer. *Chris, look closely at the top of the wave.*

There, on top of the hundred-foot-plus wave, was someone on a surfboard! As the tsunami approached, it quickly reduced in size, leaving Big Mel to glide in. At the last moment, he did a full quarter turn, flipping the board on edge to drench me thoroughly from head to toe with a giant wall of water.

"Mel, did you really have to soak me?"

He smiled and did a quick bow.

"Hey, what's with almost getting me killed by two Cherubim? Whose side are you on, anyway?"

Mel let me rant and rave. I went into a little tirade for a minute or two. He knew I needed to get it off my chest. "You feel better now, Chris?"

"No! I'm still a little miffed with you." I crossed my arms, tapping one foot like an angry parent. "So, Mel, you were behind all of this?"

"Yes, Chris, this was conceived to help you continue to grow toward reaching your full potential. This was an in-school session with a little hands-on training."

"A little hands-on training? You almost got me sliced and diced!"

"Swen and Vwen were not trying to kill you, Chris."

"It sure looked and *felt* like Swen was trying to!"

Mel shrugged. "I'll admit, he got a little carried away."

"You think so?" I snipped.

"Chris, it had to be real to you and Tassi. What you two have—a linking of spiritual entities—is remarkable. But it is far more than just a linking. It seems you can merge together as one being yet still retain complete independence. It's a conundrum. This scenario was to give both of you more experience in building this unique symbiotic relationship through a real battle experience. At the time, Swen and Vwen were your enemies, or at least you believed that to be true."

"Mel, I'll have to give both Swen and Vwen A's for outstanding acting."

Mel chuckled. "Chris, you rose to the occasion. Whatever they came at you with, you overcame. You became greater. You are phenomenally resourceful and adaptive; that shone through as you exploited Swen and Vwen's weaknesses in whatever form they chose. Whether they were enormous or just normal size, you found a way to exploit it to your advantage."

"Mel, at their normal size, they were still the size of Goliath!"

Mel just ignored my little dig and continued. "You allowed, or should I say *used*, your enemies—mock enemies—to make you into their most formidable foe."

"Isn't that what you taught and encouraged me to do from our first encounter?"

Mel smiled warmly. "You did good, Chris. You didn't run from this challenge; you embraced it. Although I never envisioned the events that just enfolded."

"Swen and Vwen were just to fight you in a hand-to-hand contest."

"Mel, they made it into a winner-take-all battle to the death."

"It was never intended to get as heated as it did, but Chris, when you pulled that sword out, it escalated. That was not part of the script. Swen and Vwen had to knock it up a notch. They started taking you seriously. Cherubim are… competitive. They take combat very seriously. You were shaping up to be a real opponent with many surprises."

"Mel, wouldn't an Orion be able to stand against a Cherub?"

"Chris, you didn't use the attack powers of an Orion. We knew that with Tassi, your fighting skills and battle tactics would be phenomenal, but your having the speed and strength of a Cherub was not anticipated. We had no idea that your body had become a spirit construct. It wasn't till we noticed traces of black on your shirt, black blood, that we put it all together—that it was your blood and that you had become an Anarkon Archetype!"

"An Arche… what?" I stammered.

346

"An Archetype, Chris. It means a facsimile or prototype based off of something that came before. Your spirit construct is adapted or modeled off the Anarkon spirit construct."

"I am a *version* of an Anarkon?"

"Yes... well... the... "

"Mel, just spit it out."

"Chris, the Anarkon is actually a modified Lucinion construct."

"What do they look like?"

"They are one-toed two-legged creatures."

"Mel, that's really helpful."

"Chris, they are an assemblage of a horse, a lion, a scorpion, and human."

"Wait, wait! Do they have a tail of a scorpion like an Anarkon?"

Tassi chimed in. *Chris, you will not morph into an Anarkon or Lucinion. You have spirit from God. You are of the Light. Light is energizing your construct, like we already went over. Not darkness.*

"So, what is a Lucinion construct, Mel?"

"Chris, the *what* is not what's important but the *where*—where they come from."

"Mel, just get to the point. Wait, just wait... the Lucinions are... Luci... Lucin... Lucif... eer... are Lucifer's! Right?"

"You are correct, Chris. Lucifer formed the Lucinion constructs and held them in stasis for his eventual conquest of the physical realm."

"You've got to be kidding! These monstrosities were going to be Lucifer's fighting force? They are but grotesque, misshapen monstrosities!"

"Chris, that was just what Lucifer wanted: hideous, malformed creatures to do his bidding."

"Why?"

Mel sidestepped my question. "That will be for another day, but they are very powerful and formidable warriors. The Anarkons in their own right are too. Look at your Anarkon enhancements: quickness, speed, strength, and regeneration—like that of God's

Cherub construct. Chris, you defeated two of God's most formidable Cherubim, Swen and Vwen."

"Mel, the Anarkons are not so great. I held my own against four of them when I was just a mere human."

"Did you now?"

Tassi, is Mel implying that someone or something orchestrated my body being transformed into a spirit construct?

I believe he is.

Mel continued after letting his response sink in. "We thought they were all destroyed by Michael or imprisoned in the Great Abyss along with the Dark Ones."

"You mean *the* Michael? And who are the Dark Ones?"

Tassi replied. *Yes, Chris, Michael the warrior angel. One of God's two remaining archangels. The Dark Ones are Lucifer's seven most powerful, most trusted, and most evil—Daimon Lords!*

I was glad she explained because Mel wasn't going to. He just did his usual and continued with his current train of thought. "It looks like Anarkos must have absconded with some of Lucifer's Lucinions during the Discontentment."

"What's the Discontentment?"

Mel decided to appease my curiosity... this once. "Lucifer didn't just decide to commit high treason on a spur-of-the-moment decision. It took nearly a millennium before he and others completely corrupted themselves. The Discontentment was a period of serious turmoil leading up to the Great Battle that resulted in the Fall of Lucifer and one-third of God's angels. Before this, Lucifer was perfect in all his ways until iniquity was found in him. God created Heylel—Lucifer, as you know him—in perfect beauty and full of wisdom. In the presence of God, none could be compared to Lucifer's beauty and brightness. He was even called the Brilliant One—by *God*. Lucifer reflected the light of God like a myriad of diamonds, rubies, emeralds, and sapphires."

"What happened?"

"As you are aware, God allows free choice, even for spirit beings. This means he had to create the potential for evil."

"You mean God made evil spirits?"

"No, Chris." He seemed downright saddened by my question. "God didn't create or make anything evil; only the *potential* for evil was available. Lucifer and other angels found a way to corrupt their spirits to the antithesis of good—to evil. Chris, do you know what Lucifer's true name, Heylel, means?"

"Noooo… Oh, oh… Evil One… Mr. Nastiness… Dark One!"

"Chris, it means Morning Star, Shining One… Bearer of Light!"

"What? Mel, that's what Orion means!"

"Chris, the Orion fills the gap left by Lucifer."

"So, what does an Orion, a Bearer of Light, do?"

"Chris, first you must understand what light truly is. Do you remember our earlier conversation on light?"

"How could I ever forget? I became like a fiery meteor plummeting to Earth shortly after. You said you were going to tell me what light truly is after I had experienced more of my journey. This, so far, is definitely not a journey; this is a fight. No, a battle… no, a war."

"It is all part of your journey, Chris. It is not one as in traveling from one place to another but of traveling to your full potential. You have grown, adapted, overcome… you have become so much more than I ever imagined. You are constantly advancing from strength to strength. You are becoming the enemy's worst nightmare."

"This is truly a journey! A hero in the making."

He let that sink in. Mel was right. I had almost thought of this journey as a curse, but it wasn't. I had an opportunity to do good on a massive scale. And I was still alive!

"Now, Chris, to the pièce de résistance… What truly is light?"

"Mel, that's what you are going to tell me."

Mel laughed. "Chris, you already know the answer!"

I pursed my lips, annoyed, but racked my brain... "I know God states that He is light... sooo that means everywhere I see light... I am seeing God?"

"Not quite, Chris. You are seeing the *effects* of God. In the first chapter of Genesis, God said, 'Let there be light.' This whole chapter is talking about restoring the Physical Realm, the Physical Universe as you know it. Chris, doesn't it seem strange that God would say, 'Let there be light' when He is light? He's already there!" Mel laughed.

"Wait, Mel, just wait. Did you say restoring the Physical Realm? That means... it already existed and... and something happened to it."

Mel continued as if he hadn't heard my question. Oh, he could be so infuriating. "Light in the physical realm is the manifestation of God's Essence, Chris."

"Ooooh, that's just plain..."

Tassi's voice came to my mind. *Chris, the first Earth, was devastated by the battle, the fall of Lucifer and one-third of the angels.*

What? You mean there is a second Earth?

I'll fill you in later. Right now, just pay attention to Mel.

Mel continued. "Think of it this way, Chris. There is... let us call it Spirit Light, and there is what you know—physical light. In the spiritual realm, there is Spirit Light, and it is God. In the physical realm, you have the concretion, the manifestation of Spirit Light: physical or natural light. It's that simple, Chris."

"Yeah, right!" An angel was talking about complex realities of the universe as if it was some simple school lesson.

"God is everywhere. Spirit Light is everywhere. It is what keeps everything together. Without it, the physical realm would not exist. Even your scientists calculate the physical universe as having only five percent of the energy and matter necessary to keep everything together in existence. There's ninety-five percent missing! It has to be there, but they can't detect it. They only see its effects.

"They call it dark matter and dark energy because it's invisible to them... it is Spirit Light. Your scientists know that without this other ninety-five percent, the planets, stars, galaxies, and even electrons, protons, quarks, et cetera, would not stay in their trajectories. God—Spirit Light—is what is supplying the necessary energy and matter to keep the physical realm in existence.

"In the physical realm, you see its concretion as physical light, but physical light is more than just the visible light you see. It is all of the electromagnetic spectrum and *more*. Now this is where it gets even more interesting; the photon which your scientists call light as it behaves as a particle... has infinite energy."

"Mel, how can a single photon have infinite energy? How?"

"Because it is the manifestation of Spirit Light... God."

"Oh, of course. How could I have not known that."

Mel disregarded my sarcasm and continued. "All physical matter can be made from light, from photons: gold, uranium, diamond, oxygen. Physical light is just a shadow of its true essence, Spirit Light. Even in the darkest regions of space, there are over a million photons present per cubic meter. Chris, there is so much more Spirit Light present than physical light, in this emptiness. You are never alone. Spirit Light is always present. *God* is always present!

Chris, you are the Orion, the Bearer of Light! The light you bring is Spirit Light, far more powerful than its shadowy counterpart, physical light. Chris, the light you bear or bring is not always zapping the enemy with bolts of light or supernovas, but also in words."

"What?"

"Chris, Jesus Christ made water into wine, fed five thousand people with five fish and a loaf of bread, walked on water, and commanded violent storms to be still. He even dispelled evil spirits, the Daimonia, by the words he spoke. This is bringing or bearing Spirit Light too. Remember..." Mel paused, conveying the importance of what he said next. "Sometimes there's a need to fight, and sometimes there's a need to speak."

And I had a need to speak. Well, ask a question, and it wasn't about Mel clarifying what he had just said. Actually, I had a lot of questions, but one was at the forefront of my mind.

"Mel, what's up with this sword?"

He grinned. "Chris, that sword is the key..." His voice tapered off as he vanished. The vision ended. I was no longer on the black sand beach.

Are you kidding me? Mel had done it again. He'd left me with more questions than I had before.

Tassi laughed. *You gotta just love Mel!*

Yeah, right. More like grow to be ever increasingly frustrated by him.

I found myself looking at Swen and Vwen, who were kneeling. Even on their knees, they still towered over me.

Swen spoke. "Chris, you truly are the Orion. God's ways are unfathomable. But choosing a teenager! I did not... *we* did not think... But God is never wrong. You even showed mercy when it was not deserved. Your last strike could have been a fatal one, but you pulled back, softening the blow."

Vwen spoke up. "Very commendable, Chris. You might have scattered Swen's spirit to the cosmos. It would not have been fatal as in forever, but it would have taken him a millennium to recompose."

Swen and Vwen both arose and gave me a great big bear hug, lifting me off the ground. They put me down gently, both grinning. Swen grasped my shoulder with his large hand and said, in a gentle but authoritative voice, "Chris, this sword and these two Cherubim have chosen to stand with you. We are *ever bound* to you."

Tassi internally gasped!

Swen and Vwen bowed their heads then looked at me. "Your request to enter Camp Aharonite is granted."

They turned and walked away. The two Cherubim began to shimmer. Their visages became like mirages, and then they vanished altogether.

Tassi excitedly spoke. *Chris, you have not only gained their respect and friendship, but you have gained their loyalty... forever! No Cherub has 'ever bound' themselves to any being other than another Cherub!*

Aren't we bound? Nila, Cami, and Kora too.

Yes, but our situation is quite different... we are spiritually connected. Deciding that was enough talk, Tassi said, *Come on. Let's head to camp.*

I hadn't noticed till now that a road had appeared beneath our feet, stretching forward and behind slightly to our right.

This is hunky-dory. Which way to camp?

You know, for a millennial, you sure don't speak or act like one.

"I was raised on old TV shows, books, and music—1960s and earlier. They are more wholesome, family oriented, and more God respecting than today's depravity."

I had lost all sense of direction. The valley walls stretched all around us. I didn't have the foggiest idea which way we had even come in. I started walking in the direction I was facing. Every so often, I would look behind me to see if the entrance to camp appeared in that direction. This time when I turned back around, wouldn't you know it, right there, in front of me, not more than a hundred yards ahead, was a large sign over the road that read Welcome to Camp Aharonite.

I don't see anything but the sign! Swen and Vwen are just toying with me... again! I yelled, "I'll get you guys back!"

I felt—or did I hear it? I think it was a soft rumble, like that of thunder in the far-off distance—probably Swen and Vwen, laughing. I smiled and shook my head gently.

The valley stretched outward in all directions, ringed by mountains in the distance. Tassi brushed up alongside me. I heard her in my head. *Chris, are you going to just keep carrying that sword around?*

I had the flat of the blade resting gently on my left shoulder while I held the hilt in my left hand. *What am I supposed to do with it? Stick it back in a large rock? Maybe hang it on the wall in camp? Put it in my pocket?*

Yes, that's a good idea.

What is?

Put it in your pocket.

Yeah... oh... maybe I could have it transform into a pocketknife.

Such a smart boy you are.

Now, now, Tassi, watch the sarcasm. I heard her snicker.

I brought the Equalizer front and center, visualized, and spoke forth, *Pocketknife.* The sword shimmered and shrank immediately. It caught me off guard how quickly it shrank. I fumbled, trying to catch the sword—knife—as it continued to shrink.

Tassi was laughing at my comical antics. It looked like I was trying to hold onto something that was extremely hot. I made a last-ditch effort, tumbling forward, catching it in my left hand just before it would have hit the ground. I came to a sitting position on the ground with my legs sprawled out in a contortionist way.

I heard clapping and two awed voices exclaiming, "Sword turned pocketknife!"

I looked up. There in front of me were two young men, all smiles. I brought myself to a standing position by drawing my legs together. I rose smoothly and effortlessly, like someone very strong had grabbed me by my hair and lifted me up with a swift powerful upward motion. I pocketed the knife nonchalantly as I gazed upon the two young men.

They both blurted together, "OORIONNN!"

I extended my hand to the closer of the two. He was shorter than the other by at least a foot. He couldn't have been more than five feet tall and looked to be in his mid-twenties and well-fed. He grasped my hand with both of his and shook vigorously.

"Welcome, Orion, I am Jorge," he said with a slight Spanish accent.

The other man stepped forward, towering over the shorter man. He looked twentyish, rugged, well put together, soldier-like. He grasped my hand with a powerful grip, gave a quick up-and-down shake, and released. "Em Petrovich, sirr."

Jorge spoke up. "Call 'im Vic. He's too Russian already."

"Em not Russian. Em Slovakian. But Vic... Vic gwood, I like. Jorge zinks em too regimented, too military, too Russian-like. He vatches too many moovies."

He straightened up and brought his heels together with a crisp thud and saluted sharply. They both laughed.

I smiled. "Call me Chris. Orion is too formal. Besides, I would like to keep that just between us. How much did you two see?"

Petrovich—Vic—said, "Zeen whole thing."

"*Everyone* saw everything!" Jorge added.

"What do you mean by 'everyone'?"

"Entire camp zee," Vic responded.

Jorge continued, "Chris, your arrival was unexpected... unauthorized. This had never happened before. Someone or something had gained entry through the portal. The entire camp was put on high alert."

"Securrity cams tranzmitted everything. All camp vatched!" Vic blurted.

Jorge continued, "Chris, your entrance was impressive! You, with a wolf pelt wrapped over your shoulders and a wolf by your side, brazenly announced you were the Orion and commanded the Cherubim to give you entrance to Camp Aharonite!"

"Zhought you toast!" Vic piped up. "Zhen challenge Cherubim ta fight! Again, toast! Zhen pull sworrd out of rock... maybe not toast!"

Jorge continued, "Chris, we saw the fight... mainly a blur. You bested two Cherubim; they conferred their loyalty on you and granted you access to camp."

Jorge and Vic did a playful bow and waved us forward. "All Camp Aharronite awaitz, Sirr Orion!" Vic said in a dignified manner.

Tassi, I feel like I am in a TV reality show with no script! What if I had to go... relieve myself?

Tassi laughed. *They would have gone to a commercial break.*

Jorge and Vic headed toward the sign, toward Camp Aharonite. They must have felt Tassi and I were not right behind them. They stopped and turned around. I was sitting on the ground cross-legged, and Tassi was sitting on her haunches beside me, looking all majestic.

CHRONICLE 28

VYXKRY

JORGE AND VIC STARED AT me questioningly.

I looked up at them. "I need some time to process… think through all of this before we enter camp."

They both nodded then, without saying anything, came over and sat down in the sand. I rummaged through my pockets till I had found where I had haphazardly tossed it. Taking out the pocketknife, I carefully began scrutinizing it. The knife looked like a normal six-function knife with a blade, a slotted and a Philips screwdriver, a pair of scissors, a file, and a toothpick. I thought to myself, *How's that the key? Mel said the sword was the key. But a key to what? Maybe I'm supposed to use the toothpick to pick a lock. What lock?*

Oh, I know. "Equalizer, turn into a key," I implored. Ahhh, nada… nothing happened.

Chris, I know you are just playing around, but the Equalizer is no toy. It's a powerful sword, a powerful weapon.

Tassi, that's it!

What is?

What you just said.

Tassi mentally shrugged.

Mel said the sword is the key. That means we have to start at it being a sword.

Chris, do you really think you are going to get answers from a sword? What, are you going to ask it questions? Tassi chuckled.

Something like that.

I visualized the pocketknife as the sword. The Swiss Army knife became less substantial, transparent, then it stretched and elongated till it morphed into the Equalizer. It was a stunning sword, fashioned out of a metal-like substance...

Quintarium, Chris.

Thanks, Tassi. That's really helpful!

I held the hilt in my right hand with the tip end of the sword resting gingerly in the palm of my left hand. I didn't want to slice through my hand. Not that it would do permanent damage, but it would hurt... a lot.

The sword was a brilliant translucent silver with all the hues of the rainbow morphing in synchronous waves along its entirety. It was mesmerizing watching the different hues dance in and along the length of the blade. I could have easily lost myself in the sword. It took a substantial mental effort to force myself to look away from the blade.

Tassi, how long was I transfixed on the blade?

A long time, Chris.

How long is long?

I'm not real good with human time increments, but I would say... two, maybe even two and a half days.

Days! It felt like only a matter of seconds.

Chris, I had to spiritually jolt you in order for you to break free. Then she laughed. *You were only mesmerized by the sword for a few minutes.*

I breathed a sigh of relief. *Tassi, I'm not sure I like some of the human qualities you are exploring.*

You know, "I am, and forever will be, your friend." She laughed. Chris, *you have a lot of not so useful knowledge in your mind but so much fun.*

That's not quite a verbatim quote of one of my favorite movie lines.

Chris, I like to put my own spin on things. Besides, I like the way I said it even better.

I gave her a look.

And no, Chris, I will not take the humor to the degree Mel does.

We both laughed.

I lowered the sword and rested it across my knees. I gently ran my fingers lightly over the blade. It was cool and yet hot to the touch. It was as if waves of cold and hot intertwined within the sword but did not merge; they remained separate. Was this the manifestation of the physical and spirit properties of the sword? I bet the cold represented or embodied the physical side and the hot the spirit side or light side.

I stopped and pushed down on the blade with my fingers. It was solid. I pushed harder.

Chris, I don't think that is—

I was struck by an intense white light as my fingers penetrated the blade. It was like a star going supernova.

Then everything went black.

Absolute darkness.

Total nothingness!

I immediately withdrew my hand. I was still sitting on the sand, and my fingers were all intact. I shook my head. "Was that a vision of being annihilated?"

I do not know, Chris, but I would advise you not to proceed any further.

Tassi, the sword is the key.

I heard her sigh. I pressed firmly with my fingers again. They penetrated the blade. So far, no supernova again. I moved them along the sword ever so slowly. A series of images flashed in my mind, but they were much, much more than just images. There were sounds, tastes, smells, and feelings associated with them. These were someone's or *something's* memories.

I paused the movement of my fingers, and a memory popped up. It was clear, vivid, and all too real, nothing like my memories, which were vague and surreal. It felt as if I was there, experiencing it, just like the being who had lived it!

The being was moving fast through the vastness of space. And I mean fast, like in light-years per second. We were speeding through quadrants of space faster than the blink of an eye. There was just something that didn't make sense... then it dawned on me. This expanse I was seeing was not normal space. It was not black and speckled with bright white dots of stars and galaxies.

Tassi spoke up, seeing the memories with me. *Chris, you are seeing the spirit realm!*

It was white like our daylight and speckled with vivid colors ranging through the entire spectrum.

Chris, you're seeing it as best as your human senses and mind can grasp.

How do you see it? Can you show me?

Since I am in a physical construct, I see it as you do.

I thought as much. I remember our conversation about spirit beings in the spirit realm having access to the knowledge and understanding of God. Tassi, is that why God banished Lucifer and his angels to the physical realm?

Yes, Chris. In the physical realm, they can't tap into the knowledge and understanding of God, and their spirit powers are very limited.

Do the colors and shapes I'm seeing mean anything?

Being in the physical realm, I no longer have full access to all my spirit memories and understanding of the spirit realm. But to the best of the limited mental capacity I now have, and the revelation I just received, the purple shapes would form black holes and the white shapes, wormholes in the physical realm. The other colors and shapes would be other universes, spirit entities, dimensions, and... spirit elementals.

What's a spirit elemental?

We will go over that another time. God gave me a limited amount of revelation to answer your questions. I need time to try to jog my memory. For now, pay attention.

The spirit being was moving in and out of and sometimes even through the various colors. Suddenly, he... I'll just call him a "he" for simplicity... made a ninety-degree turn downward, right into a brilliant white shape—into a wormhole. Everything became jumbled and distorted. Then there was nothing but brilliant white.

Don't tell me he got annihilated. How can you get destroyed more than once?

Chris, just be patient.

The brilliant white light became dark and murky. I felt the sensation of being submerged in some type of fluid.

Tassi, is this water?

Yes. It's an extreme expanse of water. God calls the Deep.

You mean there is like an ocean in space!

Yes, there is. Your questions can wait. Pay attention, Chris.

Now he was moving through the water as if it had no resistance. Then he emerged into the blackness of space with stars, galaxies, planets, asteroids, and comets... wait, what?

Yes, Chris, the Deep separates the physical realm from the spirit realm.

You mean there is an ocean that separates the two realms?

You're catching on, Chris.

Before I could inquire more on this, the being traveled right through a star then a few planets and even through asteroid belts. *Stop, stop... Stoppp! How can he be doing this? Spirit beings can't function like this in the physical realm.*

They can't, Tassi agreed. *Something far greater than any spirit entity is helping him.*

What or who can function like this in the physical realm?

Then it dawned on me.

Yes, Chris. God.

The being stopped and looked directly at a tandem black hole then turned completely around.

You've got to be kidding. He was now looking at the Orion constellation. This was my universe! And right where I had met Big Mel, though at that time, I had called him Orion.

He moved toward the constellation and proceeded directly to Orion's belt. Three stars made up the belt. He went toward the center star, a brilliant white-blue supergiant. The being was super close. I could now only see the three stars that made up the belt. Then, out of nowhere, a very large hand appeared. Oh, so koosh— this must be the hand of God. The being stood roughly in the center of the palm... of God!

A mighty anvil and hammer appeared in front of him.

I couldn't contain myself. This was so koosh. God and the being were going to forge something. *I—I bet a sword!*

Chris, just watch.

Tassi, this is so very, very koosh!

Christopher! Pay attention!

Another large hand appeared with a small pile of rocks. These rocks disappeared and reappeared, disappeared and reappeared...

Tassi, that's... that's Quintarium, I bet. God is supplying Quintarium ore.

The hand with the ore went right into the center star of Orion's belt. After quite a spell, it emerged as a large blast furnace, which parked itself on the other hand in front of the being. I bet the blast furnace contained a small portion of that white-blue supergiant's core. It must have been millions of degrees Fahrenheit.

Nosi broke in. "*Chris, I do not have any data on the core temperature of this star, but your sun's core temperature, which is a much, much cooler star, is roughly 27 million degrees Fahrenheit.*"

Tassi, it takes well over 27 million degrees to melt Quintarium!

If that's what your digital friend says. Tassi still seemed to have it in for Nosi.

I guess I'm just too trusting.

Yes, Chris, you are.

The being took out a pair of tongs and used them to pull out a crucible from the blast furnace. He skimmed off the impurities with what looked like a large butter knife. The being purified the Quintarium seven times by reheating and reskimming it.

A voice that sounded like many thunders and many waters at the same time spoke; it was the voice of God. "I will now imbue the pure Quintarium with some of your spirit... Amemnon."

I knew it! I just knew it! This being was the one and only Amemnon. I didn't hear a peep from Tassi.

Amemnon then cooled the liquid Quintarium to a solid. It didn't take long. He was in space at absolute zero degrees Kelvin.

Nosi spoke. *"That is minus 459.67 degrees Fahrenheit."*

That just gave me the shivers. At even just minus sixty degrees, you'd freeze your face off in a few minutes.

Amemnon proceeded to hammer out the solidified Quintarium into a thin sheet on the anvil. He folded the sheet lengthwise and hammered it thin then folded it widthwise and hammered it again to the same thickness. He did this process seven times while heating and cooling it in between each hammering.

Now he reheated it again, but this time, he started forming it into a shape. It took lots of hammering and reheating and hammering. He used various hammers and other tools to form... a sword.

Tassi, didn't I say he was going to make a sword?

Then I noticed changes were being made to the sword. It looked like a finger but with no hand. It must have been the finger of God that was detailing the hilt and the blade. God even honed the blade with His finger! It was a magnificent sword, with exquisite artistry. The hilt depicted a fierce hawk-headed man for the grip and pommel, standing on a withering serpent for the crossbar.

Tassi, these are constellations prophesying the one who will ultimately defeat Lucifer, the great dragon—the Orion.

I knew the names and relevance of these constellations from my first encounter with Mel. He had said this information would become useful to me, and he had been right.

Is this the weapon for the Orion?

Chris, I do believe so.

Does that mean Amemnon was the first Orion? She did not respond. *Tassi, I don't think Amemnon went bad.* I knew that she was trying to make sense of all this. *Tassi, what about the Equalizer? It doesn't look like this.*

Before she could respond, the invisible finger of God etched something on the blade. Amemnon was looking directly at the writing, but I couldn't make anything out.

Tassi, what did God write on the sword? Did you see what he wrote? Why can't we see what God wrote?

Chris, it is not for us to know at this time.

The voice of God interrupted us. "It is finished, Amemnon... Vyxkry is ready."

With that final revelation, the memory ended.

The Equalizer must be Vyxkry! I said assertively to Tassi. *It must have been Amemnon's sword. It was the one I pulled out of the stone pillar. It has his memories.*

I looked at the sword resting on my knees. The pommel wasn't that of a hawk man, nor was the crossbar that of a withering serpent.

Jorge and Vic were watching me intently. They had no idea of what was transpiring.

Tassi, this sword has got to be Vyxkry. It has to be! But it sure doesn't look like it.

Chris, did you think of asking it?

Now come on, Tassi, that would just be so lame. The sword already accepted me. Oh, all right. Sword, are you Vyxkry? Identify yourself!

Nothing happened.

Well, that didn't work. Maybe, just maybe, I needed to officially accept it. I held the sword in front of me at eye level with outstretched arms and spoke internally. *Vyxkry, I am the Orr...ion...*

The sword transformed before my very eyes...

CHRONICLE 29

THE FALLEN

I POSSESSED VYXKRY, THE SWORD OF Amemnon! So very koosh! I rested the sword back across my knees.

So, was that the key? Knowing the sword was Amemnon's?

No, Chris. Many know that sword was Amemnon's. Many have tried in vain to possess it for millennia. If anything would be a key, it would be knowing that God and Amemnon forged the sword or that it came from the future or knowing the true name of the sword. But I don't think any of these are the key. Chris, all these truths are still important and will come into play sometime.

All right, I said, a little disappointed. *Let's continue our journey in finding the key that Vyxkry holds.*

I excitedly moved my hand along the sword, pushing fairly hard with my fingers. Another memory popped up. It was quite a zinger. Amemnon was in the midst of a great battle. This was a spirit battle in the spirit realm.

Tassi, this is so... so...

I know, Chris, it is koosh.

This is so very—

Chris, stop, you're hyperventilating.

The memory I was experiencing was so wild and fantastical that it was like being in a dream where anything is possible.

Your mind is interpreting the spiritual realm in terms of what it can relate to.

This was my mind's take on the memory...

Two opposing sides were arrayed against each other, the Light, or the good side, against the Dark, or the evil side. When I or Amemnon looked at the Light side, the beings or entities were bright and vibrant; they radiated a goodness, a kindness, a joy... whereas the Dark side, like the name implied, were beings or entities that were dark, twisted, and menacing, and they radiated intense evil... hatred... malevolence... pain... suffering...

Amemnon was looking at a really bad dude. He was humongous and looked like twin tornadoes, one funneling upward and the other one funneling downward. They were rotating in opposite directions with what looked like thousands of mini tornadoes spinning topsy-turvy throughout. I was glad Amemnon looked away, for the tornado-like structures projected pure hatred. I felt an unfathomable fear rising within me.

Lucifer?

Yes, Chris, this is what your mind is interpreting of what your physical senses are picking up of the spiritual... Lucifer being twin tornados.

You are experiencing the Great Rebellion of Lucifer and his angels, the Daimonia.

Tassi, Amemnon is on the wrong side!

She just sighed. *I know. I was there.*

But he was the one that made the Orion sword, Vyxkry... with God. He couldn't be bad!

Chris, need I remind you—Lucifer was at one time one of the three archangels for God... and he turned bad.

Tassi, he's the first of the Orions. He couldn't have gone rogue. Wait, wait. Did you say you were there?

Of course I was there... and some of it is now coming back to me. Amemnon's memories are triggering a restoring of mine—at least those memories associated with his.

Before I could inquire further, Amemnon turned. We were now viewing the Light side. He was looking at a humongous cylindrical pillar that was at least a mile high and a quarter mile in diameter. It was a translucent white light with rings of varying colors pulsating in brightness within. These rings were phasing in and out as they moved, spiraling upward and downward in an orderly fashion. I felt goodness, joy, hope when looking at this being.

Chris, this is Michael—the warrior angel, one of the two remaining archangels for God.

The two opposing sides were clenched in a horrific battle surrounding both Michael and Lucifer. This battle was taking place in three dimensions. It reminded me of one of those movies with the fighting in midair. Now, I don't even want to tell you what these spirit beings looked like. You might think I was on drugs, hallucinating, or just insane. But if you ever read the book of Ezekiel or Revelation from the Bible, then you have an idea of what I was seeing.

This is not what we spirit beings look like, Tassi interjected. *Your mind is representing what your spirit is picking up and can only put it into terms what your mind can and will accept, with ...*

I had to interrupt Tassi. *What are those?* I mentally pointed at beings that were huge and nightmarish, moving hard and fast.

Chris, those are Ninions. They are beings with immense understanding and wisdom.

Tassi, they look like humungous giants with eyes all over. Yuck!

Chris, your mind is interpreting their great spiritual depth and expansiveness as size and their perception, understanding, and wisdom as many eyes.

Why the thousands of eyes, Tassi? Why not a huge owl... owls are known for wisdom.

Chris, this is your *mind. We are experiencing all of this through your understanding. You see wisdom as many eyes because you are familiar with the saying "the eyes of your understanding" and the Bible verses equating eyes to deep understanding.* She let that sink in then

367

gave me a mental nudge. *Let's get back to the memory before we lose too much of what is going on.*

The battle looked chaotic on the Dark side, like a mob attacking… very little organization. On the Light side it was just the opposite. Neat formations of beings working in unison. Michael's forces were advancing; they were collapsing the Daimonia upon Lucifer.

Amemnon, whose memory we were reliving, yelled in a thunderous voice, "NO!" He then fought vehemently, attacking the retreating Daimonia.

Amemnon was acting as a barrier, prohibiting the Daimonia from withdrawing to Lucifer. They were either going to advance toward Michael's armies and fight, or they would suffer the wrath of Amemnon and fall by his sword.

Michael's troops stayed away from Amemnon and concentrated on the other Daimonia. Amemnon grew in size and strength with each fallen spirit being. Vyxkry was absorbing their spirit power and transferring it to Amemnon. The more blows from Vyxkry they took, the weaker they became, to the point that they faded into nothingness.

But for all of that, Amemnon couldn't stop the retreat of Lucifer's troops. Lucifer grew in size with each Daimonia that retreated into him. Amemnon turned his focus to what looked like a large wispy cloud that was also retreating to Lucifer. It was a sickly pale green. Amemnon blocked its path. He attacked with Vyxkry, slicing through the cloud-like entity with phenomenal speed. Amemnon became a blur as he attacked on all sides of the entity. It collapsed into a sickly pale-green winged steed. He grabbed its withered and tattered mane and swung himself upon its back. It snorted out a greenish-brown mist through its nostrils then proceeded into a bucking frenzy. Amemnon quickly subdued the steed.

He abandoned trying to slow the retreating hordes of individual Daimonia and concentrated his efforts on seven very large dark cloud-like shapes. They looked much like cumulonimbus clouds.

Tassi, are these the seven dark ones that are now trapped in the Great Abyss?

Yes, these are the most aligned, hated, evil ones that follow Lucifer... obediently.

Amemnon, with his steed, engaged the seven dark ones that were retreating to Lucifer. He fought them but to no avail; they were able to combine with the bottom tornado.

Off in the distance were some shapes that were very wispy, almost transparent, and seemed to have no beginning or end.

Tassi, what are those?

Those are Elementals.

Are you now going to explain what Elementals are? I implored.

Chris, we should pay attention to Amemnon's memory, but suffice it to say that Elementals are what spirit beings feed off.

What?

Spirit beings draw spirit energy from Elementals and become the kind or type of spirit beings from the very spirit nature of the Elementals they draw from. But the Daimonia... have morphed the Elementals' spirit nature to the antithesis, the direct opposite of its spiritual nature.

Tassi, you're just confusing me.

Chris, can't you wait?

No, I can't.

But I had to because something immense and cataclysmic was about to happen. I knew this from Tassi's thoughts. She had already experienced this battle many millennia ago.

Michael and his armies were advancing quickly. Only a small contingent of the Daimonia was left, impeding a direct onslaught from Michael and his armies.

Tassi, is Lucifer up to something?

Lucifer is always... up to something.

Michael and his armies suddenly stopped advancing.

Chris, he has just figured out that it was a trap. Michael now knows he should not have forced the Daimonia into Lucifer. They would not have gone on their own. Now Lucifer has immense power from all the spirit beings contained within him.

Tassi, that's it!

What is?

Tassi, Amemnon was attacking the retreating Daimonia so they wouldn't combine with Lucifer and increase his power. Don't you see?

She didn't answer. I let it go for now.

Tassi, at this distance, Lucifer could inflict massive damage to Michael and his armies. Why doesn't he attack?

Chris, Lucifer is setting Michael up. He is very deceptive and crafty, plus a phenomenal tactician, second only to Amemnon. At this point, we and Michael still had not figured out Lucifer's ultimate goal.

Amemnon moved quickly, and so did Lucifer.

Lucifer is now at the face of the Deep, Tassi stated.

It was transparent and radiated a beautiful soft, warm light.

Wait... Tassi, this can't be the same Deep! The Deep earlier was dark and murky.

Chris, the earlier Deep was after this battle, after it had been breached by Lucifer.

Wait a minute, this is so koosh. Amemnon went into the future to our present time period and made Vyxkry? Then he went back to the past and fought the Great Battle with a sword from the future.

Tassi mentally nodded in agreement. *God is light-years ahead and always has what is needed at the right place and the right time.*

Chris, haven't you read the first chapter of Genesis in the Bible? There were no stars, no sun, no moon, no constellations for the first heaven and Earth. The physical face of the original deep radiated a beautiful soft, warm light for this first Earth. That Earth became without form and void. It became useless... because of this battle—the Fall of Lucifer!

It was totally immersed by the waters of the Deep.

Whaaat! Tassi, wasn't that the flood in Noah's day?

No, Chris. That was only fifteen cubits over the tallest mountain. When the Deep was ruptured by Lucifer in the Great Fall, the first

*Earth was drowned in about 93 million miles of water that then...
completely froze.*

Wait, wait. It became an enormous block of ice?

*Yes, Chris. In the first chapter of Genesis, God restores the Deep. He
melted the ice first by calling in the Light. God said, "Let there be light."
Next, He separated the waters of the Deep from the waters on the Earth
with an expanse—what you call an atmosphere—and space, where the
sun and stars now reside. Then He gathered the waters remaining on the
Earth unto one place, letting dry land appear. God was restoring your
Physical Realm—your Universe... the second heaven and Earth. I will
explain more later. Let's watch now as this unfolds.*

*Lucifer had orchestrated his movements, or should I say retreat, to
the face of the Deep. Amemnon had positioned himself between Lucifer
and Michael.*

*Tassi, Lucifer is now trapped between the face of the Deep and
Michael's armies. That's not good battle strategy, getting yourself
trapped.*

*Chris, like I said before, this is just where Lucifer wanted to be.
Michael and we hadn't figured it out.*

What hadn't Michael and the Light side figured out?

Before Tassi could reply, Amemnon yelled, "NOOOO!" It was
a thunderous voice that stopped everyone. I felt a shock wave of
power that vibrated through my very essence... and this was just a
memory!

Michael paid no heed and unleashed a tremendous volley of
energy bolts at Lucifer. It was like thousands of lightning strikes
all at once. Vyxkry acted like a lightning rod, or should I say, spirit
energy rod. It absorbed and quelled many of the strikes. The energy
bolts not consumed by Vyxkry headed toward the face of the Deep.

Lucifer had struck out at exactly the same moment as Michael
did. But... he didn't strike out at Michael. He struck out at the face
of the Deep!

The combined spirit energy of Lucifer and Michael ruptured the
face of the Deep on the Spirit Realm side. It was so powerful and so

focused that it continued, completely through the Deep, shattering the face of the Deep on the Physical Realm side.

Chris, the breach was catastrophic to your world. It caused the entire Deep to flood the Physical Realm. This is where the first heaven and Earth get flooded.

The collapsing of the physical face of the Deep upon itself continued, creating a void.

This is the birth of the Great Abyss!

It grew like a fissure in ice, zigzagging frontward and backward from the origination point. This fissure though, according to Tassi, would never end. It continues to weave its way like an enormous snake throughout the two realms to this very day.

Where the catastrophic breach occurred in the physical face of the Deep is the origin of this void—the Great Abyss. It became a vortex pulling Michael and his armies towards its enormous maw to be consumed and entrapped in the Abyss. Lucifer's twin tornados, rotating in opposite directions, seemed to produce a countereffect to the pull of the vortex.

Tassi, was this Lucifer's ultimate plan—to have Michael and his army imprisoned in the Great Abyss?

Yes, Chris, and to have full access to your realm with his spirit power intact. Michael and the rest of us didn't realize till it was too late…

Tassi, Amemnon did!

She remained quiet.

Amemnon was being dragged into the vortex. Unlike Lucifer's twin tornado, he was not so spared from its tremendous pulling effect. Amemnon lashed out with Vyxkry toward the twin tornados; it became like an enormous whip. This whip was pure spirit energy and wrapped around the tail section that connected the two tornado-like structures of Lucifer. Amemnon pulled, and the energy whip grew and severed the two tornados. The one closest to the breach that contained the baddest of the bad Daimonia, the seven Dark Ones, began to be sucked into the vortex of the void. The other tornado was not far behind.

Amemnon's energy whip still had a grasp on the tornado being sucked into the vortex. The vortex's pull was too strong for Amemnon to escape. He started to glow and pulsate as pure energy like that of his sword Vyxkry, his whip. They merged together, and their combined energy began to swirl the tornado in the opposite direction of the vortex's rotation. The sickly green steed that he had put in submission took the opportunity in the turmoil and bolted. Amemnon and Vyxkry's energy enveloped the entire tornado, spinning it faster and faster. The rotational energy of the tornado countered the spin of the vortex, resulting in an immense implosion devouring the tornado and its inhabitants within the Abyss. The vortex ended, sealing the Great Abyss!

The sudden implosion caused an equally powerful explosive blast of energy which ripped apart Lucifer's remaining tornado. Lucifer and his remaining Daimonia were cast into the Physical Realm. The breach closed itself without the pull of the vortex. Michael and his armies were left intact in the Spirit Realm.

Tassi, see, see... Amemnon sacrificed himself to close the Great Abyss. He locked away Lucifer's top seven Daimonia in the Great Abyss, instead of Michael and his armies. He also scattered Lucifer and his other Daimonia into the physical realm... maybe not so good!

Tassi, Amemnon was—is—a hero!

Tassi sighed. *No, Chris. From Michael's and all the other angels', even my viewpoint at the time, he looked like he was trying to save himself. He is the Fallen, just like Lucifer and all the other Daimonia.*

But that's not true! We lived his memory.

Yes, Chris. Only you, me, Vyxkry, and God know the truth.

The memory ended.

CHRONICLE 30

I GO TO CAMP

J ORGE AND VIC SCRAMBLED TO their feet as I stood up. I took a
moment to steady my mind from just experiencing the intense
truths revealed by Amemnon's memories. I brought Vyxkry
front and center and pointed it toward camp.

"About-face. March!" I said in a joking tone.

Jorge and Vic both saluted, did an about-face, and marched forward toward camp. Vyxkry once again shrank to a pocket-size army
knife. This time I didn't fumble it but gracefully timed my hand
motion to the shrinking of the sword. It was strange; Vyxkry was as
light as any normal pocketknife its size.

Tassi, this defies the laws of physics!

*It only defies the physical laws, not the spiritual. Chris, spiritual
laws supersede the physical...*

Tassi and I were cut short in my lesson on spiritual laws.

The entrance to Camp Aharonite appeared in front of us. Clearly
a veil was lifted, a cloak of invisibility turned off. I was left speech-
less at what I saw.

Tassi quipped, *That never happens!*

Ooh, droll, very droll, Tassi.

The road we were on went through an archway cut through an
enormous, and I mean enormous, tree. It reminded me of General
Sherman...

Nosi chimed in, "*General Sherman is a giant sequoia tree in California's Sequoia National Park; it stands 274.9 feet tall with a diameter of 36 feet... but doesn't have an archway cut through it. That would be the famous Wawona in California's Yosemite National Park, which fell over in 1969. It stood 234 feet tall with a diameter of 26 feet and had a seven-foot-wide-by-nine-foot-high archway cut through it. Now General Sherman is ...*"

Thanks, Nosi, that's enough for now.

This tree made General Sherman look like a dwarf. It would take at least two General Shermans on top of each other to attain the height of this tree. That would be... yes, nearly six hundred feet tall.

Nosi interjected, "*The tallest recorded tree on Earth is Hyperion, at 379.1 feet in Northern California—*"

Tassi interrupted, *Chris, doesn't this tree remind you of—*

Yes, Tassi, I was just thinking along that same line of thought. This tree has a stature like the trees in the Land That Time Forgot, Roscoe's home. That is where everything was—is—humongous. Even the trees were on steroids.

On either side of this tree there were walls that stretched as far as the eye could see, with similar-sized trees every so often shooting skyward, reaching for the stars. The walls were all of two hundred feet tall, as impressive as the trees. They were smooth, glasslike, reminding me of jasper. The translucent dark-jade color shimmered with the hues of a rainbow. What was astonishing, too, was that the tree trunk was of the same crystalline substance but in a brownish color. It was a seamless, homogeneous structure, and yet the trees were alive. I could tell because we were walking on ground strewn with needles and pine cones.

Jorge and Vic seemed oblivious to the snap, crackle, and crunch of the needles and cones under their feet. They escorted us into the archway.

I was in awe! It was at least thirty-five feet tall and just as wide, with a depth that looked to be fifty feet. The walls were fifty feet thick! I slowly spun around while looking up. The entire inside of the archway was seamless from floor to ceiling. This was beyond awesome; it was super koosh.

Vic stopped and turned around when he noticed Tassi and I were falling behind.

"Vhat looking at?"

Jorge stopped too, and did an about-face then burst out in laughter. Tassi had sat on her haunches with her head upward as if she was howling. I was still slowly turning around while gazing upward. We must have looked very comical.

"What are you two doing?" Jorge hooted.

Tassi mused, *Chris, I don't think Vic and Jorge see it. The trees, the wall, the archway, are shrouded from their senses.*

Jorge and Vic had puzzled expressions on their faces.

I believe you are right, Tassi.

"Jorge, we are just stretching, getting the kinks out."

Chris, that was lame.

Jorge spoke. "We will be out of the Great Shroud soon. It shields the presence of Camp Aharonite."

I responded within myself, *Yeah, that's right, but it also shields a phenomenal crystalline wall and skyscraper-tall trees.*

Aharonite had at least four layers of protection. Was God expecting an attack someday? First, the portal entrance. Not anyone could find it or was allowed to enter it. Second, you have two Cherubim standing guard. Third, the Great Shroud shielded the presence and entrance to Aharonite. All you saw was a road meandering through the valley. Swen and Vwen probably controlled the shroud, whatever that was! Fourth, the wall—over two hundred feet tall and fifty feet thick. And the archway? I'm sure it had an equally impressive gate. Swen and Vwen probably controlled that too.

We emerged from the archway. What lay before us? Three Segways!

This is so koosh. I always wanted to try one of these. Tassi, you're going to have to paw it.

She laughed. *I'll be able to keep up.*

I jumped on the nearest one and began to...

Vic spoke up. "Taakes time ta learrn—"

Before he could finish, I was doing doughnuts around the two, hopping on and off, jogging alongside it, riding backward, just having a blast. I sped past them then reversed and motored slowly till I was alongside the two.

Vic and Jorge stood there with jaws dropped.

"What? I freestyle skateboard!" I continued past them, grinning. "Get the lead out and mount up, you two!" I then darted ahead, not knowing if I was going in the right direction.

They both hopped aboard their Segways and caught up.

The first part of Camp Aharonite was park-like: trees, flower gardens, ponds, fountains, statues, lampposts, benches, and even picnic tables.

Vic excitedly pointed at the first building we came to. "Securrity and maintenanz. Vwork there, Jorge an me."

It reminded me of a fire station from the 1900s, but it was not timeworn; it looked like it had been built yesterday. The structure was of fieldstones, going three stories high, with a prominent bell tower in the center ascending another three stories. Eight pairs of ten-foot-high arched wooden doors lined the front, with tall, narrow arched windows dotting the rest of the building.

We continued onward. More and more buildings appeared. They were of differing time periods and architectural styles, but what was even more curious was that they all looked recently built.

Jorge veered to the right. Up ahead of us was a very large picture-postcard, Gothic-style eighteenth-century brick building with a five-story tower front and center.

"That's our school and administration building," Jorge announced.

"You have a school?" I blurted. "Can't a person ever get away from school?"

Vic laughed. "Lot of schoooling at Aharronite."

Jorge added, "You probably teach some classes."

"I'm going to teach? I'm only fourteen."

Vic grinned. Jorge continued, "No one in Aharonite seen such fighting skills. You bested two Cherubim... Spirit beings. You are the Master Huntsman, the Orion, head of the Hunters."

"The Hunters? Who are they?" I questioned.

"Learrn more later," Vic quipped.

"That's been the story of my life lately."

They both laughed. "Velkom being Aharronite," Vic blurted.

We continued on, passing more buildings. They were beautiful and intriguing, buildings of the past, yet new. What purpose did they serve?

Tassi responded in my mind, *When the time is right, you will get the answers.*

"We here!" Vic and Jorge heralded in unison.

A dense forest of trees loomed before us with a winding cobble-stone road cutting through it. The trees made a beautiful canopy over the road. We motored on through, and eventually the trees gave way to an immense open area with hedges sculpted in shapes of animals and abstract objects. The area was dotted with a multitude of statues. When I looked ahead, I was awed to spy a castle right out of medieval times with a drawbridge and even a moat. I wondered if it held any deadly creatures like piranhas, alligators... oh, oh... sharks!

Tassi chuckled. *You have such a wild and gruesome imagination.*

We were being invited inside; the drawbridge was being lowered.

The stone edifice was massive. Four square towers that looked to be all of eighty feet high stood at each corner of a roughly fifty-foot-high wall that encompassed seven buildings surrounding a large central one.

Nosi chimed in. "*Castles consist of a fortified wall encompassing a heavily built central building called the castle keep. The castle keep was where the lord of the castle resided and was the largest, grandest, and most secure building of a castle. Castles were built around the fifth through sixteenth centuries in Europe and Asia. They were...*"

Thanks for the info, Nosi.

The keep was immense and taller than the wall towers. It was square with terraces and arched windows abounding on all four sides. At each corner of the keep round towers formed halfway up from which arched skyways extended to each of the four wall towers. The castle keep towers ended in bright-red-tiled pinnacles. The bright-red roofs were striking amid the white stone of the keep itself.

We slowed as we crossed the drawbridge into the castle. I was not expecting the hustle and bustle. It was like entering into the commotion and activity of daily life in a metropolitan city... without any cars, trucks, and buses of course. The people were just busy going about their normal activities—if living in a castle in this day and time could be called normal.

They were dressed in modern-day clothing for the most part. A few wore tunics, leather pants, and calf-high leather boots. As we passed by people, they acknowledged us with a quick hello or a nod, some with a slight bow. They did give Tassi a wide berth.

It is not I but you, Chris, that they are giving distance to.

Tassi, I'm only a fourteen-year-old teenager.

She laughed. *Chris, you are quite an imposing teenager!*

I saw through Tassi's eyes: a tall, lanky boy with windswept hair, piercing, brilliant-green eyes, a wolf pelt draped over his shoulders, and a sword in hand.

When did that appear? I exclaimed. *That sword has a mind of its own.*

Tassi laughed. *Chris, you were just contemplating having the sword in hand.*

I'm going to have to be careful when thinking about it. I do look a little more formidable with a sword, but my sneakers just don't cut it.

I stuck the sword behind my belt and through a belt loop. It wasn't proper, but it worked. Then I remembered what Jorge had said: all of Aharonite had seen and heard me calling out the Cherubim, pulling the sword out of the stone, defeating them in a sword fight, and even their giving allegiance to me, the Orion.

Tassi snickered. *I rest my case.*

I sighed. *There goes any chance of being a normal teenager here!*

Chris, you were never normal.

Thanks, Tassi.

That doesn't mean you can't have normal friends.

Oh, that makes me feel oh sooo much better; my normalcy comes from who I associate with.

Don't you feel like you fit in, that you are no different, when around them? You have already made two friends here that treat you as a peer.

Yeah, you're right. Vic and Jorge make me feel that way. Tassi, so do you... and you're a millennia-old Cherub!

Thanks, thanks a lot. You didn't have to throw in the age part.

Tassi, you don't show it, and you do act like a teenager. A human female one! I laughed.

She smirked inwardly and shook her head in response to my male humor.

We stopped as five young people ran over to us. Each went down on one knee, brought their right arm across their chest, resting a closed fist over their heart, then made a single short downward nod of their head. I instinctively returned the gesture while standing. The three boys and two girls then stood.

One of the girls pulled over her head an empty scabbard and presented it to me. "You can use this more than me. I don't even own a sword yet."

They then quickly jogged off. All were dressed similarly in tunics, leather pants, and mid-calf-high laced boots.

Jorge turned to me. "They Hunters."

Tassi added, *Paying their respect and fidelity... also making sure their leader doesn't trip over his sword.*

Ha ha, Tassi. I shouldered the scabbard on my back and sheathed the sword.

We continued onward toward the castle keep. Two large imposing arched doors opened, beckoning us to enter. They were easily twenty feet tall and a foot thick, ornately designed out of material that had the color and sheen of burnished bronze.

Inside, it was even more impressive. I was expecting it to be dark and gloomy, lit with mere torchlight, but it was not so. The interior was bathed in light from large rectangular windows around the perimeter of the room at ceiling level and circular skylights dotting the ceiling. I called them windows and skylights, but they were probably light fixtures of some type since all of them were equally bright and never varied in brightness.

The room we were in reminded me of the Sistine Chapel, with murals on the ceiling and walls. Scattered in between the murals were large tapestries hanging a few feet below the windows to a man's height above the floor. Statues, suits of armor, and weapons adorned the room.

Two young men came into the room and escorted me off. Jorge and Vic stayed behind, making themselves comfortable on two large, overstuffed upholstered chairs.

My escorts were Hunters. They were attired like the group of Hunters from before, and they saluted me in a like manner.

We weaved through rooms and hallways, eventually coming to a library. This was one koosh of a library. It was dodecagonal in shape, about one hundred fifty feet in diameter, with books all around, rising three lofty stories high. Each floor had six ladders attached to rails in the floor and trolley rails attached to the walls three-quarters of the way up. The ladders moved on a dodecagonal pathway around the room for each floor, giving access to all the books.

The floors were made of a transparent material that projected out from the twelve walls about thirty feet inward. Six transparent catwalks symmetrically spanned the open gulf from this outer dodecagon platform to another transparent dodecagon platform surrounding a bronze-colored open spiral staircase in the center of the room.

Gazing upward, I slowly spun around. What a magnificent library. The open architecture gave an almost unhindered view of being completely encompassed by three stories of books some eighty feet high.

What books did they have? Did they have a library catalog system—analog, digital?

We walked around the spiral staircase to the opposite side and went underneath it. The space was eight feet in diameter, and I could see straight upward some eighty feet. When we entered the center of the staircase, the floor began to rise. This was an elevator... in a medieval castle. Oh, so koosh.

We rose smoothly with only a faint noise that sounded like rushing water. I found out later that this elevator was hydro powered—powered with water. The entire castle was. The wall towers were actually water towers. Even the perimeter wall and the castle keep walls were double walled, with their interiors filled with water.

We ascended smoothly; first floor, second floor, third floor... not stopping.

The inside rails and spindles of the spiral staircase were all that enclosed us. The elevator rode on these rails. I should have called it a platform since it didn't have walls or a ceiling. I could see the books through the open spindles of the spiral staircase as we ascended.

The ceiling was fast approaching, and our escorts seemed unconcerned. The ceiling was not fully transparent like the floors but radiated a soft, opaque light. Tassi and I continued to look upward. We weren't slowing down!

CHRONICLE 31
BARRY FOR REAL

T HE PLATFORM CONTINUED RIGHT ON through! What seemed like a ceiling above was not. We emerged into a room directly above the library that had windows from floor to ceiling instead of books.

Our two escorts seemed to have wandered off. I walked to the windows in front of me for a view of Aharonite. Tassi stayed on the platform but turned so she was now facing the opposite direction. Through her eyes, I could see eleven people at the far side of the room. They were all standing by a large round table that seated twelve.

That twelfth seat must be mine!

Tassi chuckled. *No, Chris, that seat is mine.*

This room was the same size and shape as the library below, a one-hundred-fifty-foot-diameter, twelve-sided room. The people seemed to be studying me intently, quietly. Aharonite sprawled out below me: buildings, roads, maintained grounds, parks, and the wall we had entered through. But there was a shroud, a veil, here too, inside the wall. My curiosity was piqued. What was out there that someone didn't want us to see?

I spoke out loud for all to hear. "Father, open my eyes that I may see."

Nada, zippo. I saw nothing more than before.

I heard Tassi in my mind. *It is not the time for you to know what is out there.*

Nosi piped up. *"Camp Aharonite is surrounded by four walls, each roughly fifteen hundred miles long."*

"Fifteen hundred miles?" I accidentally blurted out loud. *Tassi, each wall is fifteen hundred miles in length! The walls would encompass like half the area of the United States.*

Nosi fact checked. *"Actually 63 percent—2.25 million square miles. The United States is 3,531,905 square miles."*

Nosi, I was just ballparking. Wait! How do you know about these walls?

"Nod is privy to much about the spirit realm."

Tassi interrupted. *Nod knows too much! She even knew the whereabouts of Aharonite!*

That's another reason why we can't let the enemy have or use her.

Tassi sighed.

There is something else, Tassi... someone is messing with me. This tidbit of info about the walls has made it worse. Now I know there is something really, really monumental out there! Aharonite is a drop in the bucket. What's out there to need that much space?

She just snickered.

A voice asked, "Son, what is fifteen hundred miles? Did God reveal what is out there? We cannot see or go past the shroud."

It came from one of the men at the table. I decided to ignore him and not answer. I was building an air of authority. I would be the one asking the questions.

Tassi, doesn't that table with seating for twelve remind you of the Round Table for King Arthur's Knights?

Yes, Chris, but I'm relying on your memory.

Nosi broke in. *"King Arthur is a medieval legend of Britain—"*

"Not now, Nosi."

All of the eleven at the table were old. Well, not all; two were in their late teens—my two escorts. Now I knew where they had wandered off to. They had taken their places at the round table. The others were four men and five women, ranging in age from their mid-forties to late fifties.

Tassi agreed with my thought. *Yes, Chris, take charge of this meeting. Prove to them you're not just the Orion, mighty Hunter, leader of the Hunters, but leader of all Aharonite.*

I continued as if they were not in the room, still looking out the windows in front of me. They say silence is golden; in my case, the silence was used to take charge of the situation, not to get peaceful and collect my thoughts. Here we had a group of mature people, experienced and accustomed to being in charge. Now we had Chris, fourteen-year-old boy, naive, wet behind the ears, an upstart, a newbie, one that was going to change all of that. You may think I was being too dramatic, but on the contrary, I was having fun. I just had to make sure I wasn't showing it.

Tassi snickered. *Really, Chris, having fun at a time like this!*

Yep. I figured I'd ramp up the fun and play with their minds... making it seem as if I had eyes in the back of my head! Tassi's eyes were my eyes too, and she was facing them. They didn't know I could see through her eyes.

I addressed the group with my back still to them to continue the suspense and air of mystery.

"You in the gray flannel shirt... tell me about yourself; name, current and past Aharonite positions with accompanying responsibilities. Proceed clockwise around the table and sit when finished."

When the two young Hunters got their time, it was comical. They were called Gilfrey and Godfrey, twin girls but not identical twins. Girls with boy names—what was up with that? Gil and Frey, as they preferred to be called, bantered back and forth, disputing or adding to each other's narrative. It must have been confusing when their parents called, "Gil... Frey." Would both come or just Gilfrey?

All were seated now. That had gone well. Everyone had followed instructions, and there were no dissenters. I stood there in silence, watching them through Tassi's eyes. I sensed something was amiss, but I couldn't put my finger on it. Tassi felt it too.

Chris, something very old is awakening.

Just once, just once, I would like things to be non-life-threatening!

Chris, you are the Orion, the Bringer of Light. When you are present, spiritual evil recoils. All God's people have this effect to some degree. Yours is just magnitudes greater.

That's soooo comforting, knowing anytime I am…

Chris, whenever WE are in the presence of evil, it will flee or—

Yes, Tassi, I know—fight! Why do I get the distinct feeling that in our case, it's most often going to be the latter?

I was just finishing memory pegging the eleven. I had learned this in sixth-grade English class. It was a technique to remember people's names. It was simple and effective: picture the face and repeat the name while associating it with a funny or exaggerated characteristic of the person that exemplified their name. For instance, the man in the flannel shirt—his name was Flaherty… flannel and Flaherty. It was not a perfect association, flannel and Flaherty, but it worked for me. Now I took a step further to remember not only their names but also anything else I had learned of them.

Still gazing out the windows in front of me, I started conversing with the eleven, using their names and information given. From the tone of their voices and body language, this impressed them: a boy that took charge and had some not-so-human abilities.

The news I received from the eleven was troubling. I already knew from my biker buds, from Edison, that some sort of space anomaly relating to dark energy, a.k.a. spiritual energy, was wreaking havoc on all satellite and cell phone communications. Soon, according to Edison's calculations, all wireless communications would be totally down.

This news was bad, really bad. The entire human race without cell phones and the internet! What chaos, what turmoil would ensue. People having face-to-face interaction!

Putting aside the comic relief, this was an ideal situation for Kakos to expand his power and influence. Could he rival Lucifer?

Tassi, is Kakos responsible for this anomaly?

No, Chris. Lucifer probably set up the conditions for this anomaly in his insurrection against God, but I am sure Kakos and Anarkos are taking advantage of it.

Speaking of Anarkos, where is he? He seemed so dominant in all of this from the very beginning! Now it's Kakos showing up everywhere.

I don't know, Chris. I am sure he'll show up at the most inopportune time.

The eleven had informed me that this anomaly was a non-dissipating convergence between the physical and spiritual realms. It was not closing. A singularity had occurred, leaving a gateway open between the two realms. If that was not bad enough, unbridled power was amassing. The current consensus of the Hunters was if this amassing of power continued, it could be harnessed to open the Great Abyss... releasing a full onslaught of Daimonia against mankind!

Tassi, why could it be used to open the Abyss?

I don't know for sure. I'm assuming this convergence is intersecting with the Great Abyss.

Tassi, this is where Lucifer's Dark Lords and other very nasty and vile creatures are imprisoned, and if they are set loose... it's not even the end times yet!

This was definitely not in my job description. I had been drafted to take down Anarkos's top generals. Now Kakos was involved and possibly Lucifer himself!

Are these some of the other tasks referred to by Big Mel?

Tassi chuckled. *Probably so.*

I'm going against Lucifer too?

Chris, WE are! And Lucifer is always involved in anything malevolent.

I turned slowly around and walked toward the eleven. I had a slight smile on my face and proceeded as if this news was nothing more than hearing about bad weather coming on the horizon. I had a great team: four Cherubim—no, make that six; I had almost forgotten about Swen and Vwen. Then I had Barry, Momi, the Hunters, and Nod.

"You have me too!"

Yes, Nosi, you too.

Chris, Nod?

Yes, Tassi. Having Nod with us is far better than against us.

Aren't you forgetting, Chris? We still have to break out Nod and the sleeping five.

The sleeping five... that was good, Tassi. You are learning to have fun communicating. They will have to remain in their beauty sleep a little longer in the land of Nod.

Chris, I don't think we have...

Tassi, we will take it one moment at a time. Live the moment. Enjoy the moment. Be the moment.

Right now, I was in the moment.

I reached the open seat at the table. None of the eleven objected as I was starting to sit.

Chris! Stop, stop!

What, what, Tassi?

You're going to look like a doofus. You're trying to sit with that four-foot sword hanging off your back, past your knees.

Thanks for the heads-up.

I slid the scabbard off my shoulder and smoothly withdrew the sword as I sat. I held it in front of me for all to see, the sword that for millennia, no spirit being, let alone a boy, had been able to wield.

Gil and Frey's eyes both grew wide as they gazed at the sword. They couldn't contain their excitement, blurting at the same time, "What's the sword's name?"

I smiled like the cat that ate the canary.

Chris, you aren't really...

In a somber tone, I said, "Excalibur!"

Seriously, Chris? Excalibur?

It will be Vyxkry's public name.

She just sighed.

Tassi, doesn't this castle, the round table, the seating for twelve, the sword being pulled out of a stone… remind you of King Arthur?

You know I am relying on your memory. She then chuckled. *So, you're playing King Arthur.*

Yep. He brought light to the Dark Ages! He probably was an Orion too.

Chris, he was a fictional person, a legend.

Or was he? I laughed.

I laid the sword on the tabletop. I felt a slight tingling sensation through my fingertips as they penetrated the tabletop's blue gem-like surface. I withdrew them slowly but discreetly. I hoped no one had observed what had just happened.

What's going on, Tassi?

I do not know, Chris. It seems Vyxkry is not affected, and neither are the others that are touching the blue surface of the tabletop.

For a brief moment, when my fingertips had penetrated the surface, I felt power radiating from within.

Chris, I sense Daimonia power. Don't touch the blue surface! The whites of your eyes were darkening. We don't need you to turn into Mr. Hyde!

The table was beautiful and mesmerizing; what a magnificent piece of craftsmanship. It had an intricately carved border that looked like ebony wood with exquisitely fine inlaid silver filigree. This border was a foot wide and encased a twelve-sided, highly polished, faceted dark-blue surface. It looked to be a gem—a humongous gem that was a mesmerizing deep blue, like looking into the depths of a placid ocean on a moonlit night.

Now what was up with this fascination for the number twelve? A twelve-sided library, twelve-sided council chamber with twelve windows, a table with a twelve-sided gem, seating for twelve…

Chris, the table has twelve ornately carved legs representing the twelve signs of the zodiac.

I rest my case.

Tassi had stayed on the platform in the center of the room. We thought it wise not to be together, just in case one of us needed backup. If it followed the recurring pattern so far, it would be me, needing the backup.

Tassi chuckled. *Trouble follows you, Chris.*

Only since I met you!

I brought the meeting back to the immediate topic. "When and where did you get this information?"

Ms. Cozzi spoke up. "Barry informed us weeks ago that something spiritual was brewing. Then yesterday, he arrived and informed us of all that we just told you."

My body stiffened, and so did Tassi's.

Tassi, this all happened yesterday! That means we have a fake Barry among us!

Yes, Chris, he couldn't be two places at once, asleep in the Land of Nod and here at Camp Aharonite.

This is going from bad to worse, Tassi. We have an anomaly opening a gateway between the spiritual and physical realms, a possible breach of the Great Abyss, and now the infiltration of Aharonite by Daimonia!

I stood up smoothly and effortlessly, pushing my seat back with my legs while being careful not to touch the gem's surface of the table. In a low, authoritative tone, I announced, "Daimonia have infiltrated Aharonite!"

"No...! Impossible...! Never...! Who...? How...? Can't be...!"

The affirmations of incredulity went around the table, followed by silence, then stealing glances, then directly eyeing one another.

Flaherty spoke up. "What do you mean infiltrated?"

In a gentle but confident tone I spoke. "The real Barry was not here yesterday."

Ms. Cozzi gasped. "What do you mean, the real Barry?"

"I was with the real Barry yesterday, and he is definitely indisposed for the time being."

Flaherty spoke. "How do you know that the Barry here was the fake one?"

"That's an easy question to put to sleep."

Tassi mentally giggled. *Put to sleep… as in to resolve and Barry asleep in the land of Nod. Clever Chris.*

Tassi, that was just for you. They won't catch the sleep inference relating to the situation of being indisposed.

"I've been surveilling Kakos recently and overheard a conversation between him and one of his henchmen, Arthoxos. This Arthoxos was to impersonate Barry and infiltrate Camp Aharonite."

Chris, do you sense it? Daimonia have stirred and then faded quickly.

Yes, Tassi.

Murmurs went around the table. "Kakos involved?" "No, he wouldn't dare." "Kakos can't." "Who is this Arthoxos?"

I waited till all were silent then smiled. "Arthoxos—I thought I had killed him. He and seven others attacked me."

Murmurs and coughs went around the table.

Tassi sighed. *Chris, you are having fun with them… aren't you?*

Am I? I'm just trying to get the infiltrators to show themselves.

Chris, it's working! The Daimonia are awakening again. You've got their attention. When they show themselves, it's going to be nasty.

"I should rephrase. I killed his host, which now keeps my shoulders warm." I gently caressed the pelt around my shoulders then continued, "Kakos must have provided him another host—an Aharonite—with the ability to impersonate the likeness of Barry."

Gil and Frey both leaned over the table to get a better look at the wolf pelt.

"Back to what I was saying… I overheard Arthoxos telling Kakos that he found Jennifer alive and well at Aharonite. That he had learned Facsmeres had morphed and that Jennifer and I could operate them… and how he had lured Jennifer out of Aharonite."

Tassi, the Daimonia presence in the room has faded again.

Yes, Chris.

Why?

I don't know, Chris… maybe it's something being said?

Ms. Cozzi broke in. "Barry fell off his chair when he first saw Jennifer. I thought we had just startled him. Then he always seemed to turn the conversation around to where we filled him in on what was happening at Aharonite... with Chris... with Jennifer. I now believe he was genuinely surprised to see Jennifer and was there gathering intel." She paused then continued, "He had me call for the assembly of Aharonites, where he orchestrated us to send Jennifer and most of Aharonite out of camp!"

Ms. Cozzi looked directly into my eyes and then, with a serious tone in her voice, spoke slowly with pauses, letting her words sink in. "His conversation and actions... support everything... that you... have just told us. I am sure of it now... that was Arthoxos... the fake Barry."

Tassi, the Daimonia presence is stirring again.

There was a moment of dead silence in the room. You could've heard a pin drop. Well, with my improved hearing, I could actually hear everyone's heartbeats.

Gil excitedly broke the silence. "So this Arthoxos posed as Barry?"

"Yes, Gil, I believe he did."

Tassi, the Daimonia presence has faded again.

Flaherty spoke. "They have found a way to mask their presence from our spirit detectors! Even mask it from the Cherubim!"

Tassi! Didn't Swen and Vwen sense us when we came through the portal?

Yes, they did. We are spirit beings energizing these physical bodies, giving them life. The Daimonia that inhabit or possess animals or humans are not the life source for that physical body... that is still soul life... physical life. But when they awaken or take control... that is when their spirit is energized.

Chris, when Daimonia or any spirit is dormant, not energizing, it is very difficult to sense without revelation from God. Case in point: the Daimonia and whatever else is in this room.

Frey piped, "Who is Arthoxos inhabiting to impersonate Barry?"

I spoke up. "That's what we need to find out. Start by looking at all the Aharonites that came here around the same time Barry showed up."

Gil remarked, "What if Arthoxos changes who he inhabits?"

I hesitated briefly before I hit them with a real zinger. "We have a much bigger problem than just Arthoxos." I set my eyes briefly upon each one of the eleven then spoke. "The infiltration of Aharonite is not limited to just the impersonation of Barry."

"What?" gasped the council members in unison.

Tassi's thought came to my mind. *The Daimonia presence has been off and on… now it's back on again. Chris, it must be something that's repeatedly being said.*

I think I knew what was activating the Daimonia presence. *Tassi, Arthoxos must be using some form of hypnosis.*

I believe you are right. It is a word or words being said that activates and deactivates their awakening… their energizing.

Tassi, I believe it's just one word, and I am pretty sure I know what word… Arthoxos is very full of himself. I spoke out loud. "Arthoxos."

The Daimonia presence disappeared. I said it again. "Arthoxos." The Daimonia presence was back! Ha, I was right. I said it again to turn it off. "Arthoxos."

Nothing changed. I said it again. "Arthoxos." The Daimonia remained active!

"Chris, you broke it. But being serious, Arthoxos had a limit on the number of times or just saying his name back to back was the final trigger for the Daimonia to remain active."

"Well, I guess we will just have to live with them, Tassi."

The eleven looked at me with confused expressions on their faces. I decided not to explain why I said "Arthoxos" repeatedly. It wouldn't change anything anyway. Now back to the current discussion. In a serious tone, I asked, "Did the fake Barry meet with anyone other than Ms. Cozzi and my mom—in private?"

There was dead silence for a short space, then both Gil and Fry were the first to respond. "Yes…" they said in unison.

CHRONICLE 32

MAJORITEEN

"HE MET A DOGGIE," GIL and Frey excitedly blurted. "Who or what is a doggie?" I implored.

Flaherty piped in, "It is a person that is inhabited by Anamai—animal Daimonia—that is trained to track spirit scent, not unlike a dog tracking physical scent. These individuals act like dogs in other ways too. That's why we jokingly call them doggies."

"Why bring a doggie into Aharonite?" I asked.

Ms. Cozzi spoke. "This doggie happened to sniff out your mom."

What! I said internally. I gathered myself and continued, "Is that wise—bringing Daimonia into camp?"

Flaherty responded, "We thought it was worth the risk. Doggies are inhabited by lower-level, nonaggressive, nonviolent animal spirits. These low-level Anamai have similar behavioral traits of dogs: submissive, obedient, playful, silly, mischievous, but mostly just wanting to please their master... upper-level Daimonia. We thought it best to bring this doggie to Aharonite along with your mom. The upper Daimonia, the Daimones, would not find out that your mom was still alive with the doggie missing."

I continued with my questioning. "What did Barry do when he met the doggie?"

Gil spoke up. "Nothing, really. He just looked at it intently, paced a few times, looked intently again, then left camp."

"But he came back to camp later that day," Frey quickly added.

"He did?" both Flaherty and Ms. Cozzi exclaimed in unison.

Gil piped. "We heard he visited the doggie five times that day."

"He did what?" both Flaherty and Ms. Cozzi said in shock.

Frey continued, "Gil and I were only on duty two of those times. Arthoxos took one Aharonite with him for each visit."

Tassi, did Arthoxos get these Aharonites possessed with some of the doggie's Daimonia?

Yes... and this doggie is unique. The Daimonia presences we feel stirring at this table are not mischievous, lower-level Anamai. *This doggie had some very evil, very vile, very nasty, and definitely not submissive Daimonia.*

Kakos is going all out, Tassi.

Chris, I don't think Kakos had this planned.

What do you mean?

Remember what Gil said earlier. Barry, or rather Arthoxos, looked intently at the doggie then paced then intently looked again. I believe Arthoxos was surprised to find a doggie here. He was studying it, deciding what to do, possibly communicating with it. He even left Aharonite then came back.

Maybe he left to report back to Kakos?

Maybe or maybe not, Chris. Arthoxos probably has his own agenda. He's not the usual docile and subservient Anamai.

Yeah. He is more like a belligerent, aggressive, psycho pit bull that's on the loose.

Tassi laughed then grew serious upon a realization. *Chris, he may even have transferred some Daimonia that were within him to those five Aharonites.*

Why?

Kakos is probably controlling him through Kakai that he infected Arthoxos with... to control him, spy on him, make him obedient.

Kakai? What are Kakai?

Kakai are Daimonia that cause and spread chaos—disorder, division, turmoil. The name is derived from Kakos... Kakai. Remember, Chris, the Daimonia don't really have any true or unending alliances with one another. That's at least a positive for us; we can play them off one another.

Tassi, it's time to flush out the Daimonia presence in this room. I think all five Aharonites that Arthoxos took with him to the doggie might be in this very room! The twins know who two are. Let's find out if they are council members.

Chris, be ready!

I spoke out commandingly to the twins, "Who are..."

Before I could finish, they struck. We were besieged by five clowns!

Clowns gave me the creeps, the heebie-jeebies. And these were no ordinary clowns; they were the five clowns of my childhood. Four of the clowns were small, around four feet tall. The fifth was a large, menacing clown, the monster clown!

He didn't seem all that big now, maybe seven feet tall.

You were seven years old then. Everything seemed bigger.

Tassi, I'm talking about the recent park incident.

Chris, those Daimonia were in a large bear. In the physical realm, Daimonia don't have the ability to actually morph or transform. They only project an image to the physical senses.

How do they do that?

They twist and convolute the light waves around a physical object, modifying or transfiguring the form of the original. They can't conjure up something that's too far or too different from the original.

Oh, you mean they can't make a person look or move like a truck... a monster truck!

Bingo, Chris. They would use a truck or a car for that. The person's mind does the rest. What the mind believes it sees, becomes the new reality.

Well, my mind was seeing the monster clown. He was large and had pasty-white skin with a blazing-orange, twelve-inch-high reverse

Mohawk, a dark-green tennis-ball nose, and a very large bloodred mouth filled with sharp triangular steel teeth. He grabbed me in a fierce bear hug. We were face-to-face. Actually, he was a head taller, so my face was pressed to his chubby neck.

This clown was quite strong, much stronger than any human. A normal person would have been crushed. I only felt a firm squeeze. Aaahh, a friendly, endearing hug. The embrace brought flashes of memories to mind of my clown escapade at the circus when I was seven. It hadn't caught my attention then, but three pale-green shadows had hovered near the clowns that day.

Another memory popped up. This was the park incident with my setting on fire the clown bear. Here, too, three greenish-hued shadow thingies had been present. They were interspersed among the more prevalent red-and-orange-hued thingies.

I heard a nasty laugh reverberate in my head, followed by a deep, guttural voice. "*We meet again, boy!*"

"*Majoriteen!*" I shouted spiritually.

"*Bravo, my boy! Was it the clowns that gave me away? Your vehement dislike of them is very apparent. I couldn't resist clowning around!*"

"*Very funny! A Daimonia with a sense of humor.*"

Another memory surfaced from fourteen years ago. I had seen Jennifer, my mom, get hit by a semitruck. Again, three green shadowy things hovered in the background.

"*You were there all three times.*"

"*Boy, what are you talking about?*"

"*You pushed my mom in front of a semitruck fourteen years ago.*"

"*No, boy, I don't remember ever throwing someone under a truck; that I would remember! It wasn't me. But that does sound deliciously fun.*"

As usual, I would have to wait on who or what was behind these greenish-hued shadows and how they related to me. I returned my focus to the current situation. Now, being super strong had its advantages, the downside being that I didn't want to seriously injure the person inhabited by these not-so-friendly Daimonia. I firmly butted my head into its flabby neck, connecting with something hard. A series of snap, crackle, and crunch noises ensued. Maybe a touch too hard. Tassi had been right.

Of course I was right.

Majoriteen had projected a larger, taller clown, but in reality, the host was my height. I had headbutted a face, not the neck.

Majoriteen released his grasp as he reeled backward. If he thought he was going to get away from me that easily, he was wrong. I leapt forward and came down into a slide, legs in front of me as if sliding into second base. I twisted on my left side and gave a roundhouse kick, sweeping him off his feet. Majoriteen went down like a ton of bricks. His head hit the floor with a resounding *wump*. He was knocked out cold. That was going to leave some nasty bruising and a fierce headache for that council member.

Tassi, this is difficult fighting the Daimonia and having to be careful to not seriously injure the host that is being used.

I think you will have to work on it. You need a lot of improving. This council member is going to be in a world of hurt.

Oh, give me some slack. And what's up with you just watching? I whined.

Chris, you told me to guard the platform to prevent anyone from escaping this room. Besides, the situation seems to be well in hand.

Gil and Frey had taken two of the small clowns out of commission. They had overpowered and hog-tied the two with their belts. It looked funny with the clowns squirming on their stomachs with their ankles and wrists trussed up behind their backs. It reminded me of calf roping at a rodeo.

Ms. Cozzi, Flaherty, and two other council members were embattled with the last two clowns. Unexpectedly, the clown visages wavered to human form but quickly re-morphed to... ducks. Beastie ducks!

They must have picked up on someone's dislike or phobia of ducks!

Nosi spoke up. *"Anatidaephobia: the fear of ducks, first coined by cartoonist Gary—"*

Nosi, we don't need a lesson on phobias.

She continued, *"Coulrophobia: the fear of clowns—"*

"Hey! I don't have a fear of clowns... just a seriously strong dislike. Do I need to turn you off?"

Yes, turn her off! Tassi implored.

There were screams and shouts of "I hate ducks!" "Ducks give me the shivers!" "Monster humanoid ducks are the worst!"

They were duck-like creatures with black feathers; oblong torsos and heads; mottled orange beaks fitted with two-inch-long razor-sharp triangular steel teeth; long, noodle-like, spindly orange legs; overly large webbed feet with long talon-like nails; body-length wings ending in five slim feather appendages that acted as thumb and fingers; and small, beady, pure-black pupils set into large oval white eyes.

The battle ensued. The council members, including the ones that were now beastie ducks, all fought ferociously; no kicks, no punches, no flips were barred. It was winner take all. They were all well trained in the martial arts. Ms. Cozzi used ki aikido, turning her attackers' strength and momentum against them. The others used more aggressive forms like karate, jujitsu, and kung fu.

Now something drew my attention to Majoriteen's host, which still lay motionless on the floor. Maybe it was that still small voice, or was it that nagging feeling that something did not add up?

Majoriteen seemed all too easily taken out. That was what was unsettling and kept me on peak alert. My ears picked up on it first, and yes, there was plenty of battle din, but I heard it... a very, very faint buzzing or perhaps a sizzling sound not unlike that of one of my favorite sauces, fettuccini alfredo, simmering ever so slightly.

Then it happened. Wispy, transparent red tendrils started emanating from Majoriteen's host. They were smoke-like vapors coming together, forming a thinly veiled red fog-like layer that hugged the floor as it drifted—no, more like was drawn—toward the two hog-tied council members still in the form of beastie ducks. They were not struggling anymore but lay motionless. Their visages began to waver and became human again as red tendrils started emanating from their bodies. These tendrils sought out and joined with the red fog-like thingy.

The others in the room seemed oblivious to what was occurring.

Tassi spoke. *Chris, your spiritual senses are much more heightened. The others cannot see what is spiritually happening.*

Tassi, is this Majoriteen recombining?

I think so, Chris. This would explain how Majoriteen avoided being discovered by the Aharonites.

How so, Tassi?

I believe he entered Camp Aharonite through the doggie lady and possibly others. He dispersed himself among many hosts, thereby watering down, or should I say diluting, his spiritual essence. All the Aharonites could sense at best were the low-level animal Daimonia. This doggie lady probably had the majority of Majoriteen.

I snickered at her choice of words, "majority of Majoriteen."

Tassi, you said others housed Majoriteen also.

My educated guess is that the fake Barry—Arthoxos—has been coming and going for a while now and infected others.

Then it hit me like a Mack truck.

Tassi, there are five council members infiltrated by Daimonia, and there are, or were, five clowns—one monster clown and four dwarf clowns.

All of Majoriteen is here at Aharonite and in this very room.

Good, very good thinking, Chris.

Majoriteen went for council members, but why? Oh... oh, I know—to gain access to this room. But why this room? What makes this room so special?

Chris, both you and I felt a foreign presence in this room, something we had felt earlier, something not coming from the council members, something not Daimonia.

That truth sent chills down my spine. I had a bad feeling that whatever or whoever it was… *wanted* me here too!

Chris, some of these questions are going to be answered very soon… the Daimonia are on the move again!

The red wispy fog sought out and coalesced at the feet of one of the uninhabited council members. Ms. Cozzi, Flaherty, and another council member were already cautiously backing away from this woman. They must have sensed something ominous was about to happen.

Tendrils of deep blood red snaked their way up the council member's legs from the cloud that was now a vibrant blood red at her feet. The tendrils spiraled upward, intertwining as they went. The council member's face showed sheer panic. She tried to scream, but no scream emanated from her mouth. Two of the snake-like bloodred tendrils slithered into her mouth, and the other three weaved upward, consuming the rest of her. The five tendrils had completely absorbed her.

Did I just stand there and watch… doing nothing to intervene?

Chris, we were caught off guard. The spiritual manifestation of the Daimonia and this entity was so quick and intense it lulled us into inaction!

One could say the monstrosity that was before me was human-oid. It stood erect and had a torso with two arms supported by two legs that ended in what could be called feet. It was a nightmarish caricature of a human female in a body-hugging bloodred diver's wetsuit. But this wetsuit covered her entire body from head to toe. I could still make out her facial features, but she had no actual eyes; only black orbs filled the hollow eye sockets. She or *it* had a nose but no nostrils, lips but no mouth, no ears, no hair, and hands that had no fingers.

It cocked its head toward me, and those black orbs fastened upon me. A sudden, cold, menacing laugh emanated from it, but there was no parting of the creature's lips. It was a masculine, deep, reverberating laugh that sounded spiritually within me. Majoriteen had always taken on a masculine appearance in our previous encounters. It was weird now that he was in a feminine physical form.

The room became malevolent; waves of rage, pain, suffering, killing, and destruction flowed through my being.

I heard in my head, in a low, menacing tone, "*I, Majoriteen, am complete! You are mine, boy!*"

Why, why, *why* did all the bad guys call me "boy"? Couldn't they come up with something more original?

Tassi interrupted my thoughts with a visual of what was happening.

I saw through her eyes. The entire room had become a site of carnage, of mayhem. All the council members, the ten that were left, were wreaking havoc, obliterating anything in their path. They attacked one another with the ferocity and venom of wild animals fighting for their lives.

The visual then went to me.

My face and body took on a cold, hard, and haggard appearance. My eyes were turning from brilliant green to black. Even the whites of my eyes were becoming black.

Raw, undiluted power surged from my being. The ten council members were lifted off the floor into the air and tossed aside harshly like baggage at the airport. They were flung against the walls and slid down to lie slumped, unmoving, on the floor in unconsciousness.

Majoriteen laughed. "*Yes, boy! Use your destructive instincts. Your thirst for carnage, rage, and hate has arisen. Embrace it.*"

Tassi yelled, *Chris! Chris, fight for control, or you will destroy everyone and everything in this room.*

Majoriteen stretched forth an arm with an open hand, beckoning with a tendril that formed a finger-like appendage.

Aahhhh, it was so inviting, so embracing, so enthralling. The raw power continued to build within me. Majoriteen nodded with approval. The air started to crackle and swirl around my being. Strong, forceful winds erupted like those of a gale storm, shoving the council members forcefully behind me and against the far walls of the room, leaving an unobstructed clearing between Majoriteen and me.

Tassi was unaffected by my rage-fueled acts of power. She lowered her head and gave an internal nod. She now understood.

I extended my right arm upward and relaxed my fist, uncurling my fingers, palm facing upward.

Majoriteen stiffened, his black orbs fastening upon me.

My eyes turned from pure black back to brilliant green. Vyxkry gently lifted off the table, hovered, and then smoothly rotated ninety degrees with the hilt facing me. It shot forward, rising gracefully as it sought me out. Vyxkry's hilt settled in my outstretched palm. My fingers closed around the hilt as I brought my arm forward and down, pointing Vyxkry directly at Majoriteen.

Yes, yes. Yes! I heard Tassi's relieved and excited words.

I moved forward with blinding speed, slashing and cutting through the air with beautiful but powerful, fluid movements. I was performing a kata, a set of choreographed movements in the martial arts. The twists, turns, ducks, blows, and pivots came with little thinking. It was like muscle memory, in which the body just took over and performed without conscious thought the routines and movements that were drilled in it through countless hours of practice. For me this was spiritual muscle memory taking over.

It would have made a great movie scene if shown in slow motion. To the naked human eye, it would have all been a blur. I covered nearly fifty feet in a zigzag manner, with hundreds of complex movements performed. Majoriteen was at the far end of the council chamber, still some fifty feet away.

Tassi chuckled. *You're enjoying yourself too much, Chris.*

I'm living the moment, enjoying the moment, being the moment!

I was not doing this for show, not for an audience. There was a reason for my grandiose performance.

I was fighting a spiritual enemy. With every stroke of Vyxkry, the spiritual darkness, that malevolent force of hatred, killing, and destruction from Majoriteen, was being absorbed. I was growing stronger while Majoriteen's spirit influence was becoming weaker. As I cleaned house spiritually with Vyxkry, I now perceived that something had clouded my mind! It had kept me from thinking about using Vyxkry far earlier!

Tassi, I could have prevented all of what happened, starting from the very first uprising of the Daimonia... nipped it in the bud!

Chris, both of us were dulled mentally and spiritually about even considering using Vyxkry... but this has worked to our benefit. Chris, you have now proved you can control and use the power from the dark side... without being controlled by the evil. Tassi let that sink in before continuing.

You are becoming a very powerful opponent... even without Vyxkry. Well done!

This prompted my mind to recall what Big Mel said from our first encounter, 'Whatever the enemy throws at you, overcome; become greater. Your enemies will make you into their most formidable foe.' This was coming to pass, but I wasn't going to thank my enemies for it.

Now my overcoming and controlling the power from the dark side did save many. The quick, powerful, and apparently ruthless taking out of the ten council members was the saving of their very lives. Then my second seemingly uncontrollable act of carnage and rage, the trashing the room, was really getting them out of harm's way. They were now at the back of the room, as far away as possible from Majoriteen. All were safe—unconscious, totally battered and bruised, but no longer under the controlling influence of Majoriteen.

Yet I was distraught, even with Tassi's praise. I felt as if I had failed.

Chris, she cannot be saved. Majoriteen has absorbed her entire being. There is nothing of her remaining.

Deep within my heart, I knew Tassi was right. She did her best to console me.

Her last remark hit home. *Chris, God has not asked or required of you to save or help everyone. Even God does not save or help everyone.*

As my heart was acknowledging this truth, my spiritual awareness sounded an alarm, or was it Tassi?

Chris, do you sense it?

I did. This was far from over.

CHRONICLE 33
THE AWAKENING

SOMETHING WAS NOW AWAKENING! IT was definitely not Daimonia.

Majoriteen shouted, "*No! ... Nooo!*" He moved away from me, backing up rather stiffly with somewhat jerky movements, as if he was fighting for control.

I commenced forward, this time performing another kata but with slower, more directed, more powerful sword swings and thrusts.

Chris, do you notice what is happening?

Yes, Tassi. This other entity and Majoriteen are connected. The awakening of it coincided with Majoriteen becoming complete.

Yes, Chris, but it is also evident that this other is becoming more powerful and... Majoriteen less. He seems to be fighting against it!

I added, *Whatever deal he made with it isn't going to end well for him.*

Majoriteen stiffly stooped down and picked two swords up off the floor.

Where did those come from?

I readied myself for Majoriteen's rageful charge. His black eyes became blacker if that was possible. They fastened upon my eyes. Just for a fraction of a second, I sensed a plea for help. Majoriteen asking me for help? Then waves of rage, murder, carnage, and destruction hit me.

I braced myself for a full-frontal assault. But Majoriteen turned and moved quickly away from me. The silver blur flew past. Majoriteen went sprawling to the floor with Tassi atop.

He flung her off and moved to the back wall—or was it the front wall of the room? In a dodecagon room, is there a front and a back? Anyway, he was near the window I had been looking out earlier when surveying Camp Aharonite.

I moved forward swiftly. Majoriteen was feverishly striking the window with both swords. I sensed an excitement—no, a hunger. It was coming from within the window!

Tassi hit Majoriteen hard, knocking him away. I was there, too, bringing Vyxkry down upon him. He stopped my downward slice to his head using a V formed by his two swords. This was just a momentary victory. Vyxkry continued through both swords, his head and exited his lower torso. He screamed in pain but was left unscathed physically yet drained spiritually. Vyxkry was absorbing spirit energy from Majoriteen, though it didn't seem to weaken him much.

The sword battle that ensued was vicious, with powerful, short, furious strokes. Majoriteen was fast, powerful, and brutal with no regard for whether he took blows or not. His swords must have contained Quintarium, which allowed him to block and parry with Vyxkry as long as the contact was short.

Tassi, why didn't Vyxkry cut through Swen and Vwen's swords like it can with Majoriteen's?

They are Cherubim, much stronger spiritually. But I can sense this other entity is beginning to energize Majoriteen, which may soon put him on the order of a Cherub spiritually.

I felt the sense of hunger from within the window increase. It was not directed at me but at Majoriteen. This other creature needed Majoriteen... wanted Majoriteen... craved Majoriteen.

Tassi went for his wrist, her jaws powerfully clamping around it, and dragged him to the floor. I immediately kneeled on his free arm, forcing it to the floor, brought Vyxkry down point first on his wrist then drove it to the hilt. Tassi at the same time bit down on his other wrist with all her strength. A series of pained shudders went through his body.

Majoriteen released the two swords to the floor. He heaved us off then flung himself at the window and furiously pounded it with his fists. His wrist seemed unaffected from Tassi's chomping on it; the entity was surely energizing Majoriteen. I grabbed and tossed him away from the window. He landed on his butt some twenty feet away. He was slow in getting up, and his movements were rather jerky and erratic, but this soon ebbed. He got his second wind and charged towards me, then at the last moment turned and bolted straight at Tassi. He vaulted off her back toward the top of the window. His fingers reached out, or should I say tendril-like appendages, to grasp what looked like sword pommels projecting out from the two top corners of the window. When he came down, he had a sword in each hand!

What had those swords been doing in the upper corners of the window?

Majoriteen forced a smile.

Chris, I think Majoriteen is fighting for his survival, but it's not against us.

Yes, I agree, Tassi. I was sensing that too! But what is the purpose of the swords in the window frame?

I think we will find that out soon, Chris. And… I bet the other two swords that Majoriteen had earlier were from the bottom two corners of the window.

Majoriteen halfheartedly started thrusting at the window with both swords. The window started showing stress fractures radiating out from the blows.

Chris, I am getting a strong feeling that the four swords were keeping something imprisoned within the window. And that something needed Majoriteen and a human soul to… awaken it, release it, and energize it!

You mean that creature is going to absorb Majoriteen?

Yes, Chris. I believe Majoriteen will be no more... just like the council member.

I shook my head incredulously. *That thing feeds off of... Daimonia!*

Tassi jumped and knocked Majoriteen away.

A menacing, bone-chilling laugh reverberated through the room, followed by *"YOu ARe ToO LaTE!"*

I charged and leaped. I wasn't going to allow whatever thing was imprisoned in that window to be unleashed into our world without trying something... anything... to stop it.

Tassi shouted, *"Nooo!"*

I impaled the window with the blade of Vyxkry. It did not shatter but held. My rash decision turned out to be the correct thing to do. But was it rash? I was peaceful at the decision I had come to in a blink of an eye—to thrust Vyxkry into the fracturing window.

I could feel power from me flow through the sword. We were healing the window. The fractures began fusing back together seamlessly.

Flashes of memory came flooding into my mind, and they weren't mine! I could not make heads or tails of the jumbled images and thoughts. This creature was truly alien in its thought patterns and memory. No sense of time, distance, even similarities; there was no something first or last, before or after, near this or near that, like this or not like this. Time was irrelevant, spatial reality was irrelevant, and associations were irrelevant. All these were nonexistent concepts to this creature.

What came flooding into my mind next was as alien in its own right. I now understood that day some fourteen years ago: the greenish shadows had not been trying to kill my mother and... stop me from being born. They had *instigated* the intervention of Big Mel and the beginning of me. The need for an Orion!

Before I could think about what was just revealed to me, I was hit with a blinding flash of power from within the window. At the same moment Majoriteen hurled himself at me, forcefully removing

Vyxkry and me from the window. We tumbled to the floor nearly thirty feet away.

Majoriteen went back to vandalizing the window with the two swords. The stress fractures came back. He had undone all that I had repaired. Tassi took him out again, but at the same moment, unbeknownst to us, a council member had risen. He was not far from the window. Majoriteen slid the two swords across the floor to him. The lone council member picked them up and threw himself at the window. There was a big thud as the council member and the swords embraced the window. The two swords pierced completely through the window. Fractures zigzagged outward from each sword in a spiral fashion until the entire window was composed of irregularly shaped dime-size pieces.

It suddenly exploded outward in thousands of shards, with the council member not far behind. He uttered no sound as he plummeted eighty feet to his death.

A wispy greenish vapor briefly formed what looked like a shadow of a human standing where the window used to be. The shadow slinked down into the room. It moved like a shadow, looked like a shadow, but there was nothing in this room to cast this shadow.

Majoriteen shrieked, "No!" He rasped, "Help me, boy!"

Red tendrils started emanating from Majoriteen as he lay on the floor, unable to move. They were being drawn into a black swirling funnel-like void that had appeared in the floor some six feet from him. Majoriteen was coming undone!

I attacked the shadow, which was a good fifty feet away from Majoriteen. The blows from Vyxkry had no effect. Tassi flung herself at the shadow; she encountered no resistance and ended up sliding into a wall some thirty feet away with a resounding thud. Majoriteen continued to lose more and more of himself.

A cold menacing voice resounded in my head. "Sabboth awakens! Majoriteen will be no more."

What was left of Majoriteen had no resemblance to the nightmarish form of a tall, lithe woman in a red diver's suit, now just a misshapen, twisted, and gnarled red mass. I quickly moved over to the swirling void. It reminded me of a tiny vortex, a tiny whirlpool with its top flush with the floor... I was looking into the maw of Sabboth!

I drove Vyxkry, point first into it, almost up to the hilt! The tendrils that were being absorbed immediately vaporized into puffs of wispy smoke. The humanoid shadow form of Sabboth shuddered. I had caused some pain to Sabboth!

What kind of grotesque creature is Sabboth? His body is disassociated from his mouth!

Chris, that is just how he has manifested in the physical realm.

The absorption of Majoriteen halted.

Tassi mentally nudged me. *Chris! You saved Majoriteen! But I don't think that was such a good idea.*

Tassi, at the moment, it was the only way to stop this... Sabboth from becoming more fully awake and more powerful. Majoriteen is a very formidable enemy, but I think Sabboth is a greater threat right now.

Something seemed not so right. Sabboth hadn't strayed much from his original location. Was Vyxkry holding him? Sabboth began behaving like a rabid dog securely chained. He, or it, tested the boundaries, sometimes rather vehemently, other times timidly—docile, even. Vyxkry was anchoring Sabboth, acting like a tether! It had taken four swords, an unknown containment material, and him being in a comatose state for his imprisonment! How long would Vyxkry hold him by itself?

Tassi interjected, *Chris... I believe Sabboth resides somewhere between the spiritual and physical. We are only aware of him because of the shadow he casts in the physical.*

Wait, wait... are you thinking he resides in what I call limbo land?

Exactly, Chris, that's my theory.

That's just hunky-dory. That means we have to go into limbo land.

No, Chris, the raid into limbo land will have to wait. We don't have the time or the knowledge to attack him directly... and come out alive.

If we can contain Sabboth in the physical again, it will once more imprison him in limbo land.

I'm already on it, Tassi.

I quickly picked up the other two swords that Majoriteen had dropped earlier. We had forced him into dropping them by nearly severing his wrists.

I turned to Tassi for guidance. *How are we going to find his other anchor points? And even if we do, we don't have enough swords. We only have three, and he was originally imprisoned with four... and what about a containment window? We don't have that either!*

Let's focus on solving the first problem: finding his anchoring points.

Okay. How do we do that?

Usually, Tassi and I conversed normally by just talking. It was a form of spiritual talking within our linked minds... like a person talking to themselves internally. But much of the time we just responded to the other one's thoughts, and that was the case now.

Smart thinking, Tassi, but do you think Sabboth will fall for it?

There's a good chance. His appetite is not fully satiated yet.

I backed away from Sabboth, brandishing the two swords, then turned around and walked to where Majoriteen lay. I transferred the two swords to one hand and reached down with the other.

Yuck! Yuck! Majoriteen was just... well... yucky! I didn't know what I grabbed of Majoriteen, but it was cool, slimy, and squishy! I dragged him rather callously and without concern.

I heard in my head a somewhat raspy and not-all-that-menacing or venomous voice. *"Boy, are you using me as bait?"*

Chris, other direction.

I turned and proceeded, not being in a hurry. Sabboth followed. Hopefully his other anchor points were within the tether length.

Tassi, your plan is working! I did my best to keep up appearances, but on the inside, I was ecstatic. He was acting like an animal with only two primal needs: to survive and to eat.

His hunger has gotten the best of him. Tassi chuckled.

Sabboth followed me like a dog following its master. Looking to be fed.

That was what we were relying on. Sabboth, without his connection to Majoriteen, was just a base animal, relying on animal instinct and reasoning. We surmised he needed Majoriteen to fully awake.

Tassi, we only have so much tether length. When will we know we are in the right spot?

When that *happens!*

A vortex ring in the floor appeared around Majoriteen, a swirling motion like a whirlpool within a narrow ring.

Majoriteen stammered, *"Boy, you better get me out of here!"*

"Maybe I'll just let Sabboth eat you!"

"You wouldn't do that... and that's going to be your downfall, boy—not being able to sacrifice the one to save the many. You can't even sacrifice one of evil."

"Majoriteen, are you really goading me into letting Sabboth have you?"

Tassi interrupted. *"Boys, boys!"*

The vortex ring started to contract inward. Sabboth was going to consume Majoriteen in one big gulp! I dropped the swords off to the side and, being careful not to step within the vortex ring, reached over and grabbed Majoriteen with both hands. I gave one immense heave. Majoriteen slid, tumbled, and scuttled out of harm's reach.

That was all too easy!

In a heartbeat, it became obvious why. I looked down. A second ring had appeared, and it encircled me. I found myself sandwiched between two concentric vortex rings. Now I was in jeopardy!

Chris, I think Sabboth laid a trap for us!

You don't say, I said sarcastically.

The swirling within the rings intensified, causing my feet to be drawn securely to the floor. I was trapped! Eventually, the floor would give way to a full whirlpool, a full-blown maelstrom, a point of no return. I would be drawn into the maw and heart of Sabboth.

I heard Majoriteen say, *"Boy, didn't I warn you that not being willing to sacrifice even one to save the many was going to be your downfall?"*

Majoriteen did not understand—I *had* to save him, not sacrifice him; otherwise, Sabboth would fully awaken. He needed Daimonia for some reason to do that. What his intent with me was, I didn't know. It obviously wasn't going to be good!

Tassi, that did not work out as planned.

Yeah, it sure didn't. Now Sabboth will probably become even more powerful from having you instead.

No, Tassi, I'll just give him an extreme bellyache. Now, get me out of here!

I felt pure, delicious power flow into me. I just loved it when Tassi and I fully linked. My body started to crackle with power. I was becoming sparky!

Chris, how can you make fun at a time like this? Concentrate, will you?

Tassi, power is flowing out of me. We are feeding Sabboth. Power down! The inner and outer vortex rings were shrinking. I was being squeezed!

I shouted, "Nooo!"

Tassi had flung herself at me. The impact slid both of us into the center of the two rings.

"That went well! Now we're both trapped!"

Tassi's force was mainly a spiritual blow that was concentrated at my feet and graduated upward. Tassi did not use her physical weight and momentum, propelled by spiritual power, to extricate me. That would have been like being hit by a Mack truck going eighty miles per hour. For those of you not in the know, a Mack is a rugged, heavily built semitruck.

I was now cradling Tassi in my arms. *Chris don't put me down! The closer to the floor we are, the stronger the pull.*

Yes, Tassi, I am well aware of that. I have found it a lot easier for me to move my head than my legs.

Nosi chimed in. *"It's probably similar to the phenomenon of the diminishing strength of electromagnetic radiation as the square of the distance. At two feet away from the source, it would be one-fourth. At three feet, one-ninth. At four feet, one-sixteenth. At eight feet, it would be one-sixty-fourth as strong—"*

We get it, Nosi, Tassi sharply replied to my mind.

Tassi, I have a plan! I closed my eyes.

Chris, are you going to sleep? That's a great plan.

Shhh. Shush, Tassi.

I focused spiritually on Gil and Frey. There was a spirit of slumber coming from them.

Chris, are you trying to wake them? Like you did me in the Land of Nod?

Tassi, you and I are linked together. I'm aware their minds would be fried if I directed that much power at them. No, I'm just giving them a spiritual nudge from the outside.

I envisioned brilliant sunlight shining directly upon their eyelids, as if they were looking up at the noonday sun on a clear midsummer day. Eyes closed of course.

I shouted over to them, "Arise, sleepyheads!"

Their eyes snapped open at the same time; both shook their heads and rubbed their eyes.

Frey mumbled, "Was someone trying to blind us?"

Gil blurted, "Who would do such a thing—shine such an intense light directly into our eyes?"

Chris, I think you forgot the part about their eyes being closed.

Frey grumbled, "All I see are black spots popping in and out."

"My eyes hurt," Gil added.

In a matter of ten or so seconds, their vision finally cleared up. They looked over at us and saw our predicament. Frey piped up, "Don't you two look cute."

"Will you two quit your jawing and get over here?" I said rather edgily. "Pick up the two swords next to us on the floor and thrust them into the outer swirling vortex, one on either side of us."

Gil and Frey asked no questions. The two thrust the swords as told. The outer and inner vortex rings stopped collapsing inward. I breathed a sigh of relief. How long would this last? Probably not long.

Tassi, the time is now.

I flung her upward and outward. Sabboth had been weakened to a degree by the two swords, and it was far less effort as I got Tassi over my head at the peak of my heave. The downward pull was drastically less at this height from the floor. Now was it one-sixty-fourth less as Nosi believed... maybe. Tassi made it free and clear. She did a few flips in the air, not by her own choice, yet landed gracefully on her feet like a cat. The swords, though, didn't weaken it enough at floor level for me to jump free.

Within moments of Tassi's escape, all hell broke loose.

Tassi, Frey, and Gil had their hands full, and so did Flaherty and Ms. Cozzi, who were just stirring from their slumber. The other council members, the five that had survived, had gone berserk. That just goes to show you that who you hang around with affects your behavior. I had my suspicions about who the bad cookie was: Majoriteen.

Chris, I found Majoriteen... or what's left of him.

Tassi was looking at a puddle of reddish-brown ooze. It was just nasty and gross.

Tassi, I would wager he is inhabiting one or more of our berserk council members.

"*Boy, it's Sabboth causing this chaos,*" Majoriteen voiced. "*I would be more concerned about Sabboth. He's comin' for you!*"

Majoriteen's warning was a little on the late side. Sabboth was no longer tethered; he had escaped. That was the least of my troubles. The floor I was anchored to was all but gone, except for a remaining remnant that precariously held me up. The two vortex rings had given rise to a full-blown maelstrom, and I was in the center of it!

All eyes in the room were riveted upon me. The chaos paused to watch my imminent demise.

I knew from Tassi to look up. There, directly above me, was Sabboth. He seemed to pulsate with different shades of black and subtle hues of putrid green. Frey, Gil, Ms. Cozzi, and Flaherty all cried out. Then I was gone—devoured into the heart of Sabboth!

DOGS LOOSED

T*ASSIII!!* WAS THE LAST THING I heard from Chris. Our connection with each other was now gone! No longer did I sense any presence of him, just nothingness. We had been planning to escape together. Chris was to go near supernova, hopefully annihilating Sabboth, with me pulling him back just in the nick of time. Had I lost Chris like I'd lost Amemnon?

Majoriteen had been wrong. Chris had sacrificed the one for the many. He gave himself up, without a fight. Sabboth was gone, and we were all safe, but for how long?

The price was too high.

Did Chris surmise something, something at the last moment, that would defeat Sabboth? Did it involve going into the heart of Sabboth? What made Chris believe he would not be assimilated as easily as Majoriteen?

The extreme feeling of heaviness, of frenzy, of chaos had ebbed. I slowly turned in a complete circle, evaluating the situation, not wanting to focus on what had just happened to Chris.

I hesitated a moment, gazing at the place where the floor had swallowed Chris. The vortex was gone, and so was Chris. All that remained were two swords. A glimmer of hope settled in my heart. I had to wait and see the end, but now I had hope.

I grinned.

Gil and Frey backed up hesitantly. My grin came across as a baring of my teeth to the two young Hunters. I grinned even more as my understanding grew of what had happened. The two jumped back as the baring of my teeth became even more pronounced. I quickly sat on my haunches and gently shook my head in a quick side-to-side manner. This stopped Gil and Frey's retreat. I then nodded with my lips no longer pulled back. It is very taxing when you have to communicate with body language, especially when you don't have hands; paws just don't cut it.

Time to regroup and decide on our next course of action abruptly ended. Quiet time was over. The Daimonia were becoming active again. Feelings of strife, turmoil, confusion, and rage began to rise.

Frey and Gil were doing a remarkable job of not being swayed. Ms. Cozzi and Flaherty controlled their minds as well. Three of the Daimonia-controlled council members engaged Frey, Gil, and me. Ms. Cozzi and Flaherty found themselves under attack by the remaining two Daimonia-controlled council members. The attacks seemed designed not to defeat us but to distract us... but from what?

The five pulled back and immediately retreated to the far walls of the council chamber. They dispersed themselves evenly among the twelve walls. Each grasped a cylindrical pole and hugged it.

This was their objective? Evenly dispersed and each hugging a pole? Why? To my surprise and dismay, I soon found out. Suddenly, they all disappeared below the floor! These were mini platform elevators. The room had twelve of them, one for each council member.

Gil shouted, "Dogs loosed!"

I swept my head downward and to the side with my eyes looking down. That was my way of saying, "Really?" Calling them dogs was pushing it.

Gil must have seen my gesture. "Okay, I grant you they are mean, nasty, and unruly dogs."

I nodded in a long up-and-down manner, saying a big yes. She smiled. We had communicated.

Frey immediately ran to the council table and started tapping on its surface, with some swipes here and there. After the last swipe, sirens went off, followed by verbal instructions announcing a complete lockdown of the castle. No one in or out. Gil also named the five council members that were to be apprehended.

The table, to all appearances, looked very old, but it had high tech built into it. This castle, to all appearances, seemed to be from the sixteenth century, but Chris and I had found it had all the modern-day necessities. I would even say futuristic tech, but this tech was not built upon electricity; it was centered around hydraulics. Chris would say it was like steampunk from the sci-fi fantasy novels he read. His memories had flowed and intertwined through my mind, becoming my own. It started taking conscious thought to determine if they were his or mine.

I felt all eyes upon me; they were looking at me questioningly. Chris had already become their leader. In the little time that Chris and I had been with them, trust had developed. I was the closest to Chris; therefore, I was now in charge. That was a problem. How could I communicate with humans? Even spirit-filled humans. They were not on the same spiritual frequency as angels. Chris could talk to angels, even the fallen ones, the Daimonia, which were on their own spiritual frequency. How Chris was able to do this we did not know.

I gave a slow nod to the four then looked directly into the eyes of Gil and Frey. I swept my head to one side, turned, and started walking. They followed.

I came to the two swords and pointed my nose at one of them then at Frey. I did the same for Gil with the other sword. They both went over and drew out the swords. They might come in handy. The swords were powerful, but they were nothing on the order of Vyxkry. But that was a moot point, since only Chris could wield that sword.

Over to the platform in the center of the room I trotted, and the others followed. How did this thing work? Without a word, Frey stepped over to the center and pressed firmly with her toe four times. The elevator platform had pressure-sensitive controls, just like the table.

We proceeded downward. As Frey pressed more firmly, the elevator platform sped its descent. We slowed and stopped at the first floor. Putting my nose to the ground, I started sniffing, following a scent trail, only this scent trail came full circle. I sat on my haunches and looked at the floor.

Frey spoke up. "Lost the trail, girl?"

I nodded.

Gil spoke. "Of course she lost the trail. The five were never on this elevator platform. They used the minis."

My behavior was intended to make it blatantly obvious that we needed someone other than me to help track the Daimonia.

Flaherty spoke up. "Why do we even need to track them? The names of the five council members to be detained were announced."

"Many may not know the five by sight, and they might just have the ability to alter their appearance like the fake Barry," Frey answered.

I began sniffing again then sat back on my haunches, shaking my head side to side in futility. I was down to playing charades. Chris's memories didn't help me to actually be good at this game.

Ms. Cozzi interjected, "That leaves tracking them as the best way to catch them. But if she can't"—she pointed at me— "who else can track Daimonia?"

Then it hit the four, and they all shouted together, "The doggie!"

I nodded enthusiastically for a yes. Ms. Cozzi's question had nailed it. Charades over. I hadn't done all that bad for my first time at playing the game. Now, it was not true that I couldn't track. But the doggie was superior in tracking since she was trained for this and knew the scent of Arthoxos and the Daimonia he got rid of.

Frey and Gil stepped back onto the platform. "We'll be back with the doggie. Don't get into any trouble while we're gone!" Frey blurted.

Gil turned and looked at Ms. Cozzi and Flaherty. "You two, go and coordinate the search with those that are familiar with any of the five."

While I waited, I tried out my sniff ability. Could I find Majoriteen's spiritual scent? The mini elevator platforms would be the place to start. Two of the twelve platforms were spiritually stronger and reeked with spiritual vileness, though one was the winner... Majoriteen the Greater. The other was... I decided to call him, call it, Majoriteen the Lesser. It seemed Majoriteen had two hosts now. When Chris had run into him at the age of seven, Majoriteen had five hosts. Sabboth had trimmed him down substantially.

Gil and Frey returned with the doggie in tow. She was much more manageable after having lost a boatload of mean and nasty Daimonia that had been transferred to the five council members. They had her tethered by the wrist with Frey holding the other end, just like parents with rambunctious children did when out in public. The doggie was all hyper, super excited, and ready to track. She started sniffing exuberantly, pulling Frey along as she went from mini platform to mini platform. She was zigging and zagging, going to and fro, but always coming back to the same two that I believed were Majoriteen.

Gil spoke up. "Let her get her fill of those two scents. They're probably the vilest of the Daimonia. Then let her loose." Frey was going to object, but Gil put her hand up. "Frey, do you want to be pulled and jerked all over the place? Where is she going to go? The castle is shut down. How would we ever lose her? She is as big as a sumo wrestler."

Frey shrugged and unleashed her. The doggie bolted down a hallway with us in hot pursuit. We ran right past Jorge and Vic on our way out of the castle keep.

They yelled as they ran to catch up with us, "What's going on? Why the lockdown for council members? Where's Chris?"

Almost out of breath, Frey answered, "The floor swallowed him up!"

"Whaaat?" blurted Jorge and Vic in unison.

Frey continued, "Some shadow thingy!"

"What?" Jorge and Vic cried out again.

"Just follow us," Gil said. "We'll fill you in as we go."

"As we go where and do what?" Jorge shouted breathlessly. "And what about finding Chris?"

Frey responded, rather choked up, "Chris is—is—I don't know if he's coming back! This shadow creature disintegrates then absorbs..." Frey's words just trailed off.

Jorge and Vic both gasped!

Ms. Cozzi and Flaherty had relayed search instructions to the castle residents. These were made up of the Hunters and Castlers—other people that chose to live at the castle among the Hunters.

It had become rather frenzied and chaotic within the castle walls. They had rounded up only one council member but quite a few Castlers. The Hunters were not affected, having far more spiritual training, which enabled them to resist and overcome the Daimonia influences.

The doggie meandered through the people, zigzagging and backtracking. People gave the doggie a wide berth; they shied away from me also. She was on Majoriteen's trail. We must have come to a fork in the Daimonia scent trail, the Greater Majoriteen going in one direction and the Lesser in the opposite.

Just then, we heard shouts of "Breach! Breach! There has been a breach of the castle!"

The rounding up of the loosed dogs abruptly stopped. Everyone was taking time to digest what was occurring. I knew deep down that the Greater and Lesser Majoriteen had escaped. But something else big was brewing. I could sense it.

Suddenly, I felt a heaviness. Now what was happening? Everyone seemed to give me a wider berth than before. Frey, Gil, Jorge, and Vic even backed away. What? Had I become rabid suddenly?

They all seemed to be looking up above me. I hesitantly stretched my neck and looked straight above where I stood. Could things get any worse? Yes, yes, they could! Above me was a dark, ominous shadow...

Sabboth!

RECORD VIII

THE RETURN

G IL AND FREY DREW THEIR swords, and the other Hunters followed suit. The Castlers backed up even farther. I tried moving out from underneath the shadow, but no matter how quickly I moved, it continued to hover above me. I finally stopped trying to ditch Sabboth. No longer did I look upward but now forward. I waited... and waited... and... it seemed like an eternity. I thought to myself, *Sabboth, why are you waiting?* This was getting annoying.

I stood all majestic, threw out my chest, and allowed my back guard hairs to stiffen. Then I let out a long, low, vicious battle snarl. The crowd directly in front of me fell backward and to the sides even more. Yes, I was intimidating. It took a few moments before I figured out the crowd wasn't backing out of the way because of me. The shadow had come forward about a hundred feet in front of me and started descending ever so slowly. At eye level, it stopped.

The crowd continued to part to the side and behind me. They gave Sabboth a wide berth, yet no one ditched. They were all too curious. You've heard the saying "Curiosity killed the cat." Well, curiosity can kill people too. Most didn't want to give up the best seats in the house despite the possibility of imminent death.

Did they honestly think they were going to survive an attack from Sabboth? Had they put that much faith in the Hunters and me? I didn't think they had any inkling that I was a Cherub in the form of a wolf. Even if they did, that would've been a false hope. I wasn't that powerful in the physical realm, not without Chris. Now to be fair, they didn't even know about Sabboth... but you'd think people would be extremely cautious when something ominous was occurring and clear out fast.

They decided to stay—not a wise choice.

The air started to swirl around the blackness, around Sabboth, picking up sand from the ground. It continued to swirl and enlarge to twenty-plus feet in diameter. A vortex was forming. The swirling within was ominous. It looked like dark nimbus storm clouds coalescing, then lightning bolts crackled and flashed within, coming from all directions. They became stronger, and their frequency increased, bathing us in a near-blinding light. The thunderous noise given off by the lightning strikes continued to mount to a deafening roar.

The air became electrically charged. All my hair stood on end. I looked like a giant puffball. Everyone else's hair shot straight out as well. Even their clothes billowed out on some of them.

Something started to take shape within. We were finally going to see Sabboth's form in the physical realm. What developed first was its head. It was monstrous, long, narrow, and with skin like an alligator's: scaly with pronounced ridges and spikes.

My eyesight was keener than a wolf's. Even from a hundred feet, I could see precise detail. No, this wasn't reptilian skin. It was actually plates of armor of gunmetal black, all glistening with silver and blue hues. The armor plates from over its eyes seemed to come alive, shifting and retracting, revealing two bright, piercing pink eyes.

What eventually lumbered out of the vortex went on all fours, about the size of an Asian elephant, not nearly as tall, and longer in body. I had envisioned Sabboth to be more intimidating, disgusting, and loathsomely scary. This creature was imposing because of its size but not really disgusting.

The claws protruding from its feet though were downright wicked, easily eight inches long with a not-so-subtle curve like that of sickles used to reap grain. They were bright white like the sun-bleached bones of a long-dead animal scorched in an arid desert.

Now its tail was long and whip-like. I would have said it was cute if it hadn't been for the deadly two-foot-long needle-like spikes that fanned out from the tip of its tail. I should mention that the entire length of its tail was covered in armor plates.

It was armored to the hilt, fully battle ready. The chest was massively armored, and its sides draped with sheets of flexible armor nearly touching the ground. Slung over its armored back were twelve canvas bags that looked to be body bags! There were six on a side, each over six feet long and a good two feet in diameter, nearly touching the ground. On top of its back, more of these body bags were heaped. All the bags were totally crammed full. If these body bags contained dead bodies, that in itself was disgusting and somewhat loathsome.

The creature waddled off to the side, with the Castlers and even the Hunters giving it plenty of space.

The vortex came alive again. It ramped up with a rapid succession of lightning strikes followed by deafening bursts of thunder, coming to a crescendo. Something else was coming through. What walked out—yes, I said walked out, as in having two legs—was what looked like a man. Now was this Sabboth, coming in the form of a man? This was somewhat disappointing. I was still envisioning something loathsome, something gnarly, something twisted, something ugly, something disgusting, not like a man and his pet.

This figure was buff, over six feet tall, and fully armored. The glistening gunmetal-blue color of the armor was striking. It had iridescent rainbow colors shimmering on its surface like those that danced along the blade of Vyxkry. The armor seemed alive, the colors flowing with motion like a thin film of oil moving on the surface of water.

Whatever was wearing this armor stood and carried itself like a man. It lifted one arm slowly toward its head. I covered the hundred feet between us in mere seconds, ending in a twenty-foot launch.

It touched its temple with its first two fingers. The armor plate receded, folding back on itself, revealing…a man… a boy… Chris!

Impact!

He backpedaled a few steps as he caught me in a full-body hug, then slowly lowered me to the ground. Chris stepped back a few paces.

Thank you, Tassi, for such a friendly and endearing greeting!

I lunged at his chest with my full weight propelled by a blast of spiritual power drawn from Chris himself. He caught me this time, not even budging. He easily absorbed the spirit power I hurled along with the force of my body. Chris's ability to not only give spirit power but also absorb it was continuing to grow.

Tassi, I would have told you my plan, but the full energizing of the vortex nullified our spiritual link.

I actually wasn't mad at Chris. I was mad that he had been taken from me, that he might have been gone forever… like Amemnon. I had to take it out on someone, and Chris was that someone.

I could sense Chris was inwardly smiling somewhat smugly at me not controlling my newfound human emotions very well. Now the releasing of my pent-up grief and anger was like turning on a light switch. All of Chris's memories and experiences when he was MIA were totally downloaded into me virtually instantaneously. Though it did take conscious, concerted effort to bring those memories to mind. It was as if he had never left, that we had experienced everything together. Our link was truly something special.

I was interrupted with a visual from Chris. I saw through his eyes that he was slowly scanning the Aharonites.

Frey, Gil, Jorge, and Vic were the first to crouch on one knee as they recognized Chris had returned. The others followed in complete unison as if they had practiced this, many times. Each lowered their head and brought their right arm across their chest with a lightly curled fist gently touching their heart. They were ready to follow Chris anywhere. Little did they know that they were the only thing standing between the takeover of Aharonite and... the complete subjugation of the human race!

Our fighting force was mainly teenagers, those twelve years old to just under the driving age. Arthoxos when he had posed as Barry had nearly all the seasoned, well-trained Hunters, technicians, and scientists sent on a ruse to Arizona. This was where Chris had made eight hundred people comatose. Camp Aharonite was now basically left defenseless with only a civilian support staff and teens.

Arthoxos thought he was just being Arthoxos, looking out for himself and messing with everyone, even other Daimonia. He was not aware that this idea, the thought of sending out all the able-bodied Aharonites, had not been his but Kakos's! Arthoxos was not only being used by Kakos but controlled by Kakos. Chris had learned much of this from his time within Sabboth. Majoriteen's Daimonia had been a treasure trove of information before they were completely absorbed and integrated into the mind of Sabboth. His mind was in its infancy. But the more Daimonia Sabboth absorbed, the more intelligent and sentient a being he was becoming.

The real kicker to all this was that Sabboth was not the only one of his kind. Chris was not sure how many there were, but for some reason, he kept coming to the number three. Someone or something was masterminding the releasing of them, and it was not for the good. Where were the other two? Were they here in camp? Could this get much worse?

Aharonite, outside the castle walls, was in turmoil, in chaos. The majority of the dogs loosed had escaped the castle walls, and their Daimonia were influencing or inhabiting many of the Aharonites.

Majoriteen was out there.

Sabboth was out there.

Possibly Arthoxos too.

As I was reflecting on all this... my question about whether this could get much worse got answered.

Yes, yes, yes! A scene like a movie trailer came to my mind from Chris. An enemy force was amassing at the portal entry to Aharonite! Kakos, a.k.a. Joshua Smitely, with hundreds of ninjas, thousands of Anarkons, and thousands of animals: bears, cougars, wolves, elk, deer, and yes, even badgers.

Aharonite had basically only teenagers to defend it. Yes, these were mostly Hunters, but they were those with little to no battle experience to stop what was close to the end times—Armageddon. We needed support and reinforcements: seasoned, battle-proven troops and weapons.

Chris was awfully quiet. There was something else going on, and he chose not to think of it... a far greater threat was happening than the forces amassing at the portal. I did not search his thoughts for it. He would reveal it when it was time. I had not noticed till now, but my head had drifted to looking downward at the ground as I was deep in thought. I raised my head to look directly at Chris. He was impressive. Sheer power emanated from him, spirit power. He was bathed in an aurora like a sun's corona. I could see it, but others not so spiritual did not. They did see the effects when he produced lightning and thunder.

Two thoughts kept coming to the forefront of my mind. *Where's Vyxkry? And where is Sabboth?*

Chris, where...?

Later, Tassi...

Chris was focusing on what he was going to do next.

He stretched forth his fingers. The air began to crackle as small flashes of light began to appear. He raised both arms in front of his face, palms and fingers facing each other as if holding a softball. Small, very thin lightning bolts shot forth from his fingertips. They increased in size, power, and frequency, with each bolt of lightning adding to the others as they were contained within a translucent sphere the size of a softball. His hands made spherical motions all around as if polishing its surface. This dazzling sphere of lightning bolts grew in size to that of a basketball. I could feel my body vibrate as well as the ground tremble underneath my feet in sync with the rumbling of unceasing thunder. It was near deafening as the lightning strikes continued to intensify. It seemed he had contained a full-scale lightning storm within that basketball-sized sphere.

Nosi interjected, "*One average lightning strike can generate enough energy to supply the entire city of New York with power for a full year.*"

There were hundreds of lightning strikes within that sphere! He slowly turned around, facing a slowly spinning calm vortex. With a sweeping, fluid motion, he cast the lightning sphere into the vortex. The immensity of the power that was unleashed produced a blinding brilliance like that of a supernova.

The vortex came alive. He had reawakened it, but for what purpose? I didn't even have time to search Chris's thoughts—my thoughts—before the answer came forth out of the vortex.

THE REUNION

T ASSI WATCHED AS THREE ARMOR-CLAD, four-legged creatures were forcefully hurled out of the vortex. No, they leapt out! Two landed on either side of me, while the third propelled itself over the top of me and landed in front, facing forward toward Tassi.

The vortex was not yet done giving up what remained in it. Two human-like figures walked out, both also armor-clad. One was large and well-fed, the other statelier. The armor on the stately man receded from his head… revealing silver-gray hair, thick like a lion's mane.

Barry! Tassi exclaimed. *The other must be…*

The second figure touched his temple with his hand. The armor pulled back, exposing the head of…

Momi!

The armor around the heads of the three four-legged creatures now receded, revealing none other than…

Cami, Kora, and Nila! Tassi exclaimed.

Now, of course, Nila was the one out in front, looking as tankish as ever, except now she had the armor of one.

I had not only survived Sabboth—I had brought reinforcements! I could feel questions racing through Tassi's mind.

You found time to rescue them from the Land of Nod! How much time elapsed during your disappearance? Were you gone for hours, days, or even weeks? I lost out on all the fun!

That made me smile. The fun, if you wanted to call it that, came to her as quickly as snapping one's fingers. All she had to do was think about it. It was just as if she had lived it herself. Our link was truly a great way of keeping each other up to speed on what we did. Not unlike that of syncing computer files from the cloud, but with memories. In an instant, I lived through what Tassi had been through.

Tassi! You were playing around with dogs when I was gone!

Tassi did a mental downward shrug of her shoulders with a prolonged sigh. I walked over to her and placed my hand on her head. The armor receded from my hand and fingers. This armor was so—

Tassi finished my thought. *Koosh.*

Yes, Tassi, it is.

I nestled my fingers in her soft, inviting, and comforting fur. She lifted her head to look directly into my eyes.

Vyxkry is your armor? she quizzically asked.

I smiled while looking directly into her brilliant blue eyes. Tassi and I didn't need to converse, since we did have full sharing, but it helped to bring up thoughts that were pertinent or related that the other may not have known.

Tassi smirked. *Right after you were swallowed up by the vortex, a ray of hope came to me. I noticed only the two other swords remained where we had Sabboth contained. Vyxkry had disappeared! I then knew you called it. How did you know Vyxkry could—*

I responded before she could finish. *Tassi, I had no inkling that Vyxkry could transform into armor. I only had a theory that the sword could protect me. It was a long shot, but I didn't have a choice anyway. I surmised that the swords not only anchored; they also repelled Sabboth. Vyxkry seemed to perform this same function. I figured with my speed, I could swing Vyxkry to shield myself, even move within Sabboth and ultimately escape.*

Tassi blurted, *Quintarium is Sabboth's kryptonite!*

I nodded. *He really dislikes it, not only to the point of it repelling him, it actually weakens him. Now could it kill him? I have no idea.*

Chris, Vyxkry is one hundred percent Quintarium, far more than the other swords. It could be the key to vanquishing Sabboth.

Vyxkry seems to be a key to many things. It is a master key! For now, it allowed me to escape.

Tassi laughed. *It gave him an upset tummy.*

I ruffled her head fur with my fingers then stepped back. I knelt on one knee and proclaimed loudly, "I bring gifts, your Majesty, from a land far away."

Tassi was shaking her head ever so slightly. *Chris, you're such a ham and so melodramatic. You know we're in a battle for all mankind and spirit kind! We don't have time for all this. The enemy is—*

Tassi, it is not yet time to engage the enemy. We need to wait.

A low rumble interrupted us. All of Aharonite felt it! And heard it!

Chris, I don't think that was God chuckling. I think that was the other thing that's happening. Now. Here at Aharonite. That you happened not to mention earlier.

I didn't respond but instead reached behind my back, detaching a group of seven nested metallic rings. Tassi's eyes narrowed on them as I brought them front and center. I selected the second largest of the rings.

It's showtime!

You know, Chris, all eyes are watching you... the Hunters and the Castlers.

That's the point, Tassi.

You want them to believe everything is under control, that you're not concerned at all, that we will overcome. That's why you're giving such a show.

Plus, I just liked to have fun. I was living the moment, enjoying the moment, being the moment.

I said out loud, "I pronounce you Tassi the Great!" and placed the ring on her head.

I grinned and pulled the ring, her crown, down over her ears and snout to rest at the base of her neck.

Tassi berated me. *You put a collar on me!*

I pressed on the side of the ring.

Tassi stiffened then shrieked, *Chris! I can't see! And this... this...* thing *is strangling me!* She started hyperventilating.

Relax, Tassi. Let yourself go.

She took a long, controlled, deep breath and exhaled slowly. She shook her head from side to side. *I still can't see!*

A gruff yet caring voice spoke up. *"You're still not letting go, girl."* Then Nila gave Tassi a firm but loving head bump. *"Now close your eyes and take ten deep breaths,"* Nila said forcefully.

Kora and Cami, in unison, softly spoke, *"Tassi, just do it,"* in a motherly, reassuring tone.

After the tenth breath, the plates receded from over her eyes.

"Okay, that's better. I can see again, but I feel like I am wearing something over my head and neck."

I looked directly at her, and she saw through my eyes. She had armor on. Well, just from the neck up.

She poked me in the chest with her armored nose. *"You did that on purpose!"*

"What?"

"You could have warned me!"

"And miss all the fun? Never!"

Nila spoke up. *"He did the very same thing to us. Chris teaches army style—just throws you to the sharks and sees if you survive!"*

Kora jumped in. *"He's just playful, having fun."*

Cami brushed alongside Tassi and rubbed her neck gently with the side of her head. Cami encouraged by physical touch.

Tassi nudged me again with her nose, harder this time.

"Tassi, it takes a little time for the armor to synergize with your mind and spirit."

Before she could anticipate or read my thoughts, I took the largest ring and quickly swept it under her back feet. She stiffened. It enlarged as I pulled it up her back legs and over her tail to rest around her waist.

"Aren't you going to let me know what to expect?"

"Just don't tighten up your belly."

I then released the ring. She immediately started squirming and wiggling her hips then forcefully sat. Tassi took several deep breaths with long exhalations.

"Don't you say... even think... a—a—word! You knew I would tighten up when you told me not to. Nila, Cami, and Kora! Why didn't you warn me?"

Nila responded, *"And miss the fun?"*

Cami added, *"Nila was first, but she didn't warn Kora or me either."*

"Tassi, I did warn you." I smirked.

"Chris, it nearly cut my midsection in half!"

"You were telling it to!"

"You could've told me to expand my waist and belly."

"Tassi, I was just allowing your mind and spirit to learn how to control the armor by doing it."

"Yeah, like the method some people use to teach others how to swim—by throwing them in the water. They either sink or swim."

"Army-style teaching. And you didn't sink," Cami said softly.

"I floundered, ended up doing the dog paddle."

Nila barked, *"You didn't sink or get eaten by sharks. Your spirit and mind learned what was necessary. You will improve and master the armor in time."*

"Chris, I don't know if I want to don any more armor."

I pretended not to hear her. I quickly proceeded, placing a ring over each ankle, and the last one I stuck at the base of her tail. I touched each of the ankle rings and the final armor ring at the base of her tail and waited...

"I look silly with my butt, tail, and legs bare, unarmored, with just riii..."

She never got to complete her bellyaching before the armor energized and completely encapsulated her.

"Chris, I can't move!"

"*Tassi, here comes the next swimming lesson. You need to learn to float, be one with the water—in this case, one with the armor. Now relax and allow the suit to synergize with your mind and spirit.*"

The girls, in wolf fashion, decided to get Tassi's mind to relax by distracting her with a little physical wolf camaraderie: nuzzling, neck rubs, headbutts, walking in circles around one another, and finally, the nose touch.

It worked.

As Nila was giving her the last neck rub and nose touch, Tassi's armor fully integrated. She moved smoothly and naturally, now joining the others in some playful wolf antics. To all watching, it looked like a battle among four wolves jockeying for dominant position in the pack. The four girls were not really wolves, but their wolf constructs seemed, at times, to take over.

Tassi was not thusly affected; she had more human traits because of our link, but she knew how to respond in wolf kind.

Tassi's head armor retreated, and she trotted over to Barry and Momi. Each stroked her head fur and plunged their fingertips into its softness. They ended with the playful rub and grab of her neck fur.

Barry spoke. "We're glad to see you, too, Tassi."

Momi yawned then laughed. "To much sleep... glad rescued from sleepy land."

Nila, Cami, and Kora had bounded over to the large creature that was sporting lots of luggage. Momi walked up to the creature and touched near the base of its neck. The armor proceeded to draw back from its head and neck. Tassi shook her head in a "I should've known" gesture.

The pink eyes and long claws should have been a dead giveaway!

She trotted over and stood up on her back legs with her front paws resting on the sides of the creature's snout. They were nose to nose.

Roscoe! It's Roscoe! Her excited words echoed in my head. *Wait... wait... that means you were at the cave, Orion's cave!*

I internally mouthed, very softly, *The House of Orion.*

You've been a very busy boy, Chris. Rescuing the team from the Land of Nod and *going to the House of Orion.*

Tassi had a gazillion questions. She started surfing my—our—memories.

I interrupted her search. *I'll tell you what. Since it isn't time yet, I'll give you a spoiler to hold you over. As you know, the sword is a key in the sense that it can open and close the door—to the Great Abyss. But... it can also open the door to Orion's cave from limbo land or wherever I was with Sabboth! Vyxkry is a Master key.*

I walked over to Roscoe and rather briskly rubbed the underside of his snout. He cocked his head toward my hand, enjoying the rub. *Tassi, this guy is no ordinary possum.*

That's an understatement, Chris; he's the size of a small elephant.

I mean he's not a meek, timid, and nonaggressive creature as are possums. He mopped the floor with me when I entered the cave.

Tassi savored a quick snippet of Roscoe's welcoming. She saw his head butt me into the cave wall three times then his tail spiral around me.

Tassi interjected, *I didn't know possums could use their tails like that.*

Neither did I! What's more, his squeeze is like that of an anaconda strangling its prey. The strength of his tail would have crushed the life out of any normal person. Roscoe then proceeded to dash me against the floor from side to side with the massive sweeping of his tail, as if squeezing the life out of someone wasn't enough. I'm glad I am Anarkon durable and have the armor of Vyxkry.

Tassi laughed. *Roscoe seems to have a real savage streak in him. A fighting possum? Go figure!*

That was why I brought him along with us.

For no other reason, Chris? Tassi knowingly asked.

I laughed. *Plus, I needed an armor-bearer to carry all the cool toys we boys found in our wanderings of the cave.*

Tassi sighed. *That's a relief. At least they're not bodies in those body bags.*

I shook my head and smiled. *We found a cache, a full armory of weapons for fighting Daimonia. These weapons will at least help even the odds somewhat.*

We are definitely going to be outnumbered, Tassi added, *but Kakos's troops will not be as well armed. The destruction of those buildings that warehoused Kakos's weapons and the elimination of many of his ninjas was also very fortuitous.*

Tassi, I didn't destroy any buildings or kill any of the ninjas.

That's my point, Chris. Badgee seems to be helping you—us. But what is he really after?

He said he was waiting for me to reach my full potential.

I think there is more to it than just that.

You are probably right. We will need to figure it out before he makes his move; otherwise, we will be in for a world of hurt.

Suddenly, we were hit with a shock wave like that of a sonic boom from a jet that had broken the sound barrier—but there was no jet.

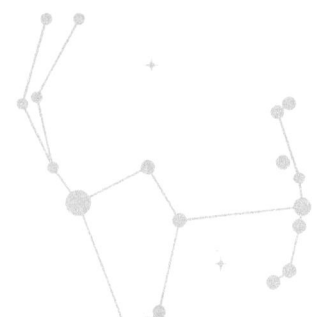

CHRONICLE 35

BOYS WITH TOYS

T HE THING I DIDN'T MENTION earlier... was undeniably happening here at Aharonite!

Tassi inquired, The convergence is not where the Hunters and most of the Aharonites have been sent... is it?

Correctamundo, Tassi, a singularity is sustaining the convergence exactly where the Great Abyss was closed.

Chris, Vyxkry was used to close the Great Abyss. That means the opening is... the large green pillar!

Bingo, Tassi.

It just hit me. Swen and Vwen are not here to guard and protect Aharonite... they're here to guard and protect the Abyss from being opened!

Tassi nodded in agreement.

Did my removing Vyxkry cause all of this to be happening?

No, Chris, the convergence and the singularity were already occurring. Vyxkry is the key, and like any key, it is used to open and close a lock.

Tassi, who leaves a key in a lock?

Chris, no one was able to remove it... till you! And since you possess the key, you will probably be called upon to use it.

Oh, lucky me. Or should I correctly say, fortunate me. I am glad Swen and Vwen are on top of it! I laughed. Tassi stayed somber and just shook her head slowly, in a manner that expressed—like really at a time like this.

I'm being lighthearted; a time for being serious is coming soon enough.

I sprang upon the back of Roscoe, a full eight feet above the ground, with an easy upward spring of my legs. Slowly, I turned full circle, gathering everyone's attention.

"Aharonites!" my voice boomed. I was heard throughout all Aharonite. The armor—Vyxkry—had not only amplified my voice but it had connected to the Wi-Fi and PA systems of camp as well. That was so koosh!

I continued, "We are under attack…"

A collective gasp sounded throughout the castle interior.

"Forces are massing at the portal entrance at this very moment." I paused to let the gravity of the situation sink in.

"The Great Abyss is in jeopardy of being opened." Everyone was deathly quiet. You could've heard a pin drop.

"And we have Daimonia loose within Aharonite."

Chris, aren't you going to mention Sabboth?

Tassi, they have enough to focus on. Besides, they can't fight a shadow. Leave Sabboth to us!

All eyes were focused upon me as I said, "Leaders have been chosen from among you." I gestured toward Gil, Frey, Ms. Cozzi, Flaherty, Jorge, Vic, Barry, and Momi. They each stepped forward as I called out their name.

I paused then continued, "Take your assignments from these leaders with all confidence… and see the mighty hand of God deliver us victory!"

The skies had become dim as twilight, an omen that evil was upon our horizon. As if on cue, mighty cracks of thunder with a vivid array of jagged lightning lit up the skies of Aharonite.

All took a knee, bowed their heads, and brought their right fist to their hearts.

Chris, that was powerfully delivered. Before I responded, Tassi sent a snippet of what she saw: my standing tall in stature, powerfully built, bathed in a bluish aurora with intense pure-white sparks flickering off my armor and bare fingers.

The view shifted to my face. My eyes were brilliant blue with mini lightning storms raging within.

The sky crackled again with another round of lightning followed by a series of mighty thunderclaps.

Chris, how did you do that?

Tassi, that was the convergence… well, converging!

I'm not speaking of the lightning and thundering. Look up!

There up above was the constellation Orion, shining brilliantly; a beacon, God's promise… the enemy to become crushed under the mighty foot of Orion!

All stood, lifted their right arms skyward, and, with fists clenched, shouted in unison, "Orion! Orion! Orion!"

Big Mel is making sure beyond a shadow of a doubt that I am the Orion!

Chris, I don't think it was Big Mel.

Yeah Tassi, you're right. It was the Hand of God.

But it's going to be my foot doing the crushing!

Even with the approval of God himself, what lay before us was daunting.

I took a deep breath then looked out over the Hunters and Castlers, putting to memory the faces of all I gazed upon. Most were teenagers, my age. How many would not return?

Tassi interrupted, *Chris—with Moses and Joshua, when the Israelites obeyed God's leaders, there was no loss of life for God's people.*

I bowed my head, eyes closed, and reserved the moment.

A soft, gentle voice spoke within. It was Dad. *"Chris, life or death is not your burden to bear!"* He let it sink in. Then he gave me a heads-up. *"It is now time, Chris. They are here."*

I raised my head, my eyes radiating blue brilliance that cut the twilight. My voice boomed, "Our Hunters have returned." I paused, letting it sink in. "They have met the enemy that has gathered itself at the portal entrance."

Cheers erupted throughout.

Tassi spoke. *Chris, you were busy when you were gone. You had time to visit even your mom?*

No, Tassi, I sent Mom a text message.

Our phones still work?

No, Tassi, the convergence has even put a kibosh on our spirit-network phones. I paused, and Tassi waited for me to continue. *Ghris was waiting at the Land of Nod. He had already delivered the pink cell phone to Mom with my text message.*

Chris, at least she knew you were okay, that you made it through the sandstorm... Wait... if the network is down now, how did you send another text message to her phone?

I didn't say her phone.

Tassi hesitated. *Chris, you still have your phone. I've been hearing you talk to Nosi.*

I sent it via another... Momi doesn't have his phone.

Tassi laughed. *You got him to part with his new toy?*

I nodded.

The Hunters and Castlers had assembled with their respective leaders. I reached down and, with a quick pull on the drawstrings, released the body bags from Roscoe. I learned my knots when in Boy Scouts. The quick-release trucker's hitch was a favorite of mine.

The bags plopped down on the ground. Tassi spoke up. *Chris, you should be more careful; those aren't toys, they're weapons.*

Tassi, they have their safeties on.

Chris, you really didn't. You did!

Sometimes it wasn't so good having someone able to access your spontaneous thoughts. My current mental focus had gone to Momi and me gathering and testing the weapons at the cave.

Chris, you can't call that testing. You totally trashed much of the Orion cave. Tassi saw vivid images of Momi and me playing with—I mean testing—the capabilities of the weapons.

That's going to take months of cleanup and repairs! Tassi shook her head from side to side as an image of Barry firing one of the weapons appeared. *Not Barry too. You boys!*

In our defense, we didn't have time to read the user manuals.

Chris, you even named them.

Their technical names were too difficult to remember and too hard to pronounce.

But Chris... screamers, tanglers, tinglers, pacifiers, and discombobulaters? Really Chris? Discombobulaters?

I shrugged then jumped down from Roscoe, landing softly among the weapon bags. I looked over at Momi. "You were right. Let's use dizziers instead of discombobulaters."

Momi smiled. Dizzier had been his name for the weapon.

Tassi shook her head. *Boys with toys!*

I walked among our troops with Tassi by my side. Momi and Barry were giving the other leaders their assignments and instructing them all on the use of the weapons. It was a crash course; they were going to learn in the field under battle conditions. These were spiritual weapons, and it took spirit to energize and empower them. The young Hunters would do well. They had been instructed from an early age about the spirit within them and how to manifest that spirit— bring it into physical concretion. The Castlers, on the other hand, might not be able to operate the weapons at all.

Momi was showing off to those he was instructing. I was impressed with his skill and ability in using the weapons.

Momi is quite powerful spiritually, Tassi said. *He is a quick learner and picks up spiritual matters like he does technology, especially computer stuff—fast! It is like he was meant to be in our time.*

Yes, Tassi, he does fit into our time rather easily. That doesn't fully answer the question; why was he taken from some two hundred years ago?

When the need to know arises, Barry and Mel will let us know. Tassi changed the subject. *Chris, your military plan is bold and ambitious. Do you think our unseasoned troops can carry it out?*

They will have to. We'll be overrun if they can't. My mind flashed to one of my strategy video war game missions, where I was overrun by a horde of zombies. I shook my head to clear it of that ghastly memory.

Tassi, they need to bring this fight to the enemy. They must keep the enemy—and there is more than one—unbalanced and in disarray, hitting them on multiple fronts with precision and timing.

Our troops keeping the enemy scrambling will allow us—that's you, me, Momi, and the girls—to find and take out the big guns—Kakos's generals and whatever or whoever is causing havoc with the convergence.

Chris, you left out who is going to take out Kakos.

You know the saying "fight fire with fire"? Well, we need to bring chaos to Kakos himself. I laughed. What a truly poetic way to take down the Lord of Chaos.

Tassi sighed and shook her head. *But, Chris, do you think it wise? Sabboth... allowing him—*

Sabboth will cause much chaos for Kakos!

That's quite the gamble.

Tassi, for all his power and the threat he poses, he is our best way to defeat Kakos and his armies. Sabboth has revealed his habit pattern with Majoriteen; it makes him predictable. He will hunt out the strongest and most powerful Daimonia to feed on... Kakos's generals and... even Kakos himself!

But, Chris, he will become even stronger through consuming, feasting on the Daimonia.

Yes, but the taking out of Kakos's generals will help immensely. They are the ones keeping Kakos's ranks unified, coordinated, and on objective. Allowing Sabboth free rein, will give us our best chance of defeating both. And without putting as many of our troops in harm's way.

Chris how is this going to help defeat Sabboth? Tassi mentally shook her head as she caught on. *Chris, that is quite a devious and ingenious way of taking out Sabboth. But will it work without having Nod?*

Tassi, we still have Vyxkry. She gave a slight growl. *It better work, or we'll be in a hard way.*

Choosing to come to Aharonite before getting Nod's containment vessel was a calculated risk.

We are where we need to be, Tassi.

Shouts and commotion came from the castle gates interrupting us. Our Segways were being lifted!

"This neighborhood is going to the dogs!" I blurted. Tassi inwardly chuckled.

Jorge and Vic were already on it. They hopped onto two Segways parked inside the gates. The chase was on! Jorge and Vic were far more adept with the Segways than the doggies and caught up with the three rather quickly.

Visuals of the chase came up on nearby castle walls. It was like being at the movie theater without the popcorn, soda, and a comfortable chair. The security cams of Aharonite captured everything from multiple angles. Jorge and Vic even had body cams that gave us close and personal views of the action. The Segways weaved in and out among the trees and benches, scattering any Aharonites they came upon. It became quite physical. First came ramming and bumping of the Segways. Then quick jabs, elbow thrusts, and kicks were traded. Jorge and Vic inflicted the majority of the pain and physical mayhem. Jorge even spun donuts while delivering multiple jabs to the upper bodies of all three.

It became obvious that Jorge and Vic were herding the doggies between two buildings. These buildings abruptly ended into a third. Waiting for the three were Aharonites called up by Vic.

Two of the doggies tried to head up the steps to the front of the middle building. This ended in complete failure. The two were flung headfirst to the waiting concrete. They were definitely not experienced Segway riders.

The battle had now turned into a street brawl. We had multiple closeups and views of the battle. Some of the Aharonite reinforcements, though, had turned to the other side. The rounding-up earlier of those infected, those inhabited by Daimonia, had not been entirely successful.

Suddenly, three grayish streaks, one with a reddish hue, flew into the melee. The cavalry had arrived. The reddish streak was none other than Nila. She was battle-born, a Cherub drawn from the depths of a sun's fiery molten core. Nila was intense, fierce, and primal, definitely born for battle. Cami, on the other hand, was controlled, peaceful, and directed by purpose. Kora was just downright playful—childlike, even.

Tassi interjected, *Chris, you are like Kora in this manner... but you also are like Nila: headstrong, brash, impulsive, a risk taker, ready to do battle.*

I smiled inwardly.

The three wolves, Cherubim in wolf form, made short order of the battle. It had become vicious as more aggressive Daimonia inhabiting some of the Aharonites surfaced and took full control of their hosts.

Nila did several body throws, sending groups of attackers to the ground. Cami and Kora did cleanup with quick headbutts and shoulder thrusts to keep them dazed and down momentarily. When Daimonia took full control of their hosts, it was like they were on that street drug...

Nosi cut in, *"PCP, a.k.a. angel dust. It gives the user superior strength, quickness, endurance, and complete obliviousness to pain; the user feels completely disassociated from their body and... remembers nothing afterward."*

Angel dust, yeah, it should have been called *evil* angel dust; it magnified and brought out the evil qualities of the user, not unlike those of the fallen angels... the Daimonia.

Nosi continued, *"There are documented cases back in the 1980s of police riddling angel dust users with twenty and even a few with over thirty bullets, ripping their body apart, yet the users continued to attack until eventually succumbing to death."*

I bet those special cases of angel dust users were those possessed by some very nasty Daimonia, which really exacerbated their evilness and superhuman ability to fight past physical death.

Back to our situation—how some of Aharonites had been taken possession of, we didn't know yet. The physical, mental, and spiritual checks the Aharonites went through each time they entered and exited Aharonite were quite thorough. These fully controlled

Aharonites that Jorge, Vic, and the girls were fighting had become rabid dogs, whipped into a frenzy.

Jorge and Vic had pulled out what looked like small versions of a cattle prod, an electric-shock device that would bring a half-ton animal to its knees.

Nosi interjected, "*Nottlinger: a device that neutralizes or paralyzes Daimonia.*"

Jorge and Vic's devices were mini versions of what Momi and I called pacifiers. They were far less powerful and less destructive than the battle type we had brought from Orion's Cave, which was more on the order of cattle prods on steroids.

Jorge and Vic proceeded to zap the downed Aharonites. They now became *pacified*—submissive—and were easily led away. The mini pacifiers had to be precisely positioned behind the earlobe in that sweet spot between the jaw and the skull and then directed upward. These devices were not meant for battle, but they worked well on the crumpled and dazed humans that had been taken down by the girls.

The mop-up crew came as the last combatant fell. All were gathered up and taken away to makeshift detention areas. They would be detained until they could be purged of their Daimonia. The viewscreens on the castle walls took notice that all was finished and went dark, blending back into their surroundings. This castle had a lot of koosh features.

The groups of our ragtag militia were beginning to head out to their assigned positions in Humvees.

"*Humvee, or HMMWV, stands for high-mobility multipurpose wheeled vehicle. It is made in fifteen configurations ranging in size from a jeep to a semitruck. The Humvee is used for transport of troops, cargo, and even light combat use.*"

I smiled at a spike of annoyance in my thoughts from Tassi. Nosi was showing off her depth of knowledge... again.

Barry's group and mine were the last to leave. I had three transport vehicles for my group, two jeep-like vehicles that carried myself,

Tassi, the girls, and some Hunters. The third was a troop-carrier Humvee, semitruck size. It was reserved for Roscoe and of course Momi, with some more Hunters tagging along.

We passed through the Shroud that hid the wall surrounding Camp Aharonite from the physical senses. The girls, Barry, and even Momi saw the immense wall and five-hundred-foot-tall trees as we passed through; the Aharonites did not.

I heard Momi gasp in awe. He was totally flabbergasted, even at a loss for words. It didn't take too long before he came out of his stupor and started babbling, all excited. The others in our company just looked at him in disbelief and bewilderment.

We continued about two miles out of camp before disembarking from our vehicles about a quarter mile away from Swen and Vwen's location. We formed a perimeter, roughly circular, encompassing the area. The skies grew more overcast, a sign that evil was escalating its ugly head in Aharonite. A series of lightning strikes began, followed by a succession of thunderclaps building to a crescendo, heralding...

"*The thing you didn't want to mention,*" Tassi said.

The convergence had now fully come to Aharonite.

We could see the sky starting to dissolve vertically like a curtain being ripped from top to bottom. It was a thin, jagged tear, black as black could be, running right on through the green pillar.

This was going to be ground zero—just where I wanted to be.

Chris, this is just where you need to be... where we *need to be.*

The air shimmered in waves of distortion that rippled outward from the edges of the tear. The distortions were akin to the surreal heat mirages seen on a hot, dry, sunny day. Though they were not beautiful or appealing like the mirages of a lush oasis or a delicious thirst-quenching blue body of water. These were harbingers of a grotesque world where misshapen and unnatural creatures roamed...

We were looking into the Abyss and what was waiting to enter our world. The Great Abyss was opening!

CHRONICLE 36

LIGHTS OUT

"**N**O, THIS IS NOT ARMAGEDDON, *Chris.*"
Barry answered the question I had not yet vocalized. He had come from behind and placed his hand on my shoulder. There was a great sense of comfort in his presence. I was brought back to the day I had been thrust into all of this. I recalled meeting Barry for the first time in that grocery store and stopping Mr. Anarchy Rules from doing something horrible. I had been exactly where I needed to be.

"Yes Chris, just like that day at the grocery store, we are right where we need to be." Barry just chuckled at my shocked face. "And no, I'm not reading your mind or listening in to you and Tassi. It's just that obvious."

Momi sauntered over with the three girls. "We going to kick butt!" he cheerfully piped.

No matter how bad the situation or how much I might screw up… Momi had a way of making me feel better and ready to take on the world—just like my mom.

Maybe that's why Momi is here… he's your Mom away from Mom. Tassi giggled.

I gave her a mental glare of *yeah right.* Bring someone from two hundred years ago to be a mom substitute.

Barry and Momi stayed behind, getting their people into battle positions. Tassi and I pushed forward to ground zero with the three girls. Nila was just drooling for a good battle, and this battle was probably going to be more than she could chew.

Tassi laughed. *I don't think Nila would take kindly to those references as a drooling and chewing wolf. She's a millennia-old Cherub.*

Yeah, I'm glad she can't hear my thoughts anymore... otherwise there would be payback.

We had just started entering Swen and Vwen's territory, where they had barred Tassi from entering when I'd had my first encounter and epic battle with them. It was like wading through chest-deep water. Then, suddenly, we were on dry ground with no resistance, and we weren't even wet. My armor, Vyxkry, was phenomenal. I could feel it repelling or cutting a path through what seemed to be an invisible barrier—a forcefield of spirit energy.

Swen barked, "You can't just barge in here, breaking through our barrier!"

Vwen quipped, "They just did... and, I'd say, rather effortlessly."

Swen shook his head. "Boy—and I'm still going to call you 'boy'—that spirit barrier should have been impenetrable or, at the minimum, really slowed you down. You continue to amaze."

Vwen looked us over. "Love your new attire. Those battle suits are quite impressive!"

Swen piped up, "They'll stop Tassi, Nila, Cami, and Kora from morphing into their full Cherub forms." He then waved an arm dismissively. "No more time for talk."

Swen walked off toward the pillar. Vwen quickly followed.

The two grew to their Titan size of fifty-plus feet. They started attacking—or should I say shadowboxing—around the green pillar. This escalated into the two Titans ramming and throwing their weight at an invisible foe. It was kind of comical; the two looked like they were pantomiming as giant sumo wrestlers. They grabbed, pushed, heaved, and even belly-bumped their invisible foe.

The struggle was real, and they were losing ground. The two were pushed farther and farther from the pillar. Swen and Vwen intensified their efforts to no avail... the effects of the convergence continued to expand. These effects... aberrations... were now starting to take on subtle but noticeable physical form.

The two were fighting against what looked like a translucent gelatinous fluid. Their grabbing, pushing, and heaving sent shock waves into it that only produced a mild rippling effect and were quickly quashed.

That was what we saw in the physical realm. This was serious; it was no longer comical.

They hunkered down and pressed forward with all their might. This battle was in the spiritual, fought with spirit power. They were undoubtedly releasing massive amounts of spirit power not seen in our realm.

Swen looked over his shoulder and barked, "We could use a little help here."

"We could use a lot of help!" Vwen pleaded.

Swen remarked rather snippily, "Vwen, that was just rhetorical."

"I know this is a dumb question, but what are you two trying to do? Besides looking silly!"

"Boy, are you trying to rile me up? Isn't it obvious? The physical and spiritual worlds have intertwined... converged. We are trying to separate the two. If we are successful, then the singularity should dissipate." Swen grunted as he pressed into his invisible foe.

Vwen added, "The convergence and singularity seem to reinforce each other. We've never had a singularity develop before."

Swen and Vwen continued to intensify their attacks—their sumo wrestling with the two realms.

I spoke up. "Big Mel—"

Swen interrupted. "I don't know how you get away with calling him Big Mel. You have some audacity."

I shrugged. "Anyway, Big Mel told me Daimonia were amassing in the Abyss. Couldn't this amassing be causing the singularity?"

"Chris has a good point," Vwen said as he threw his shoulder into the convergence.

The two Titans stopped. Swen spoke. "Chris, that's an interesting assertion... that the amassing of Daimonia in the Great Abyss is causing the singularity, which in turn, is causing the convergence."

"Swen, you called me by my name!"

"Boy"—he laughed—"I have great respect for you. For being a human, you're not all bad."

Tassi smirked. *Swen has such disdain for any being that's not a Cherub.*

But was I really a human anymore?

Chris, Swen considers you a human even though your body is now an Anarkon archetype. What more confirmation do you need... than Swen? She chuckled then continued, *You'll always be human no matter what your form is.*

I really liked that our internal conversations were private between Tassi and me, but this did lead to us frequently getting interrupted.

Swen unknowingly butted in, "I don't believe the amassing of Daimonia could cause a singularity, but I do agree with you that the singularity is causing this convergence. Question is... how do we take out the singularity?"

Vwen coughed lightly, followed by a few louder, more throaty coughs.

Swen barked, "Speak, Vwen! What's on your mind?"

"Chris can..." Vwen coughed out.

"Chris can do whaa..." Swen trailed off.

There was an uneasy silence. Even the aberrations from the convergence stilled.

Swen broke the silence. "That would border on insanity."

"If we don't, the Abyss is going to erupt," Vwen strongly stated.

"You don't know that for sure."

"Swen, I know you can feel it too. The Abyss is going to open. We can either control its opening or let it erupt."

Tassi, are they saying what I think they are?

Yes, they want you to open it. You have the key.

I shook my head. *It's going to be total carnage. All hell will be loosed!*

Chris, you are the Orion. You not only have the key to the Great Abyss, you are also the Bearer of Light. Light overcomes darkness.

I hope you are right.

Chris, if you open it, you can also close it. If we let it erupt, we may not be able to repair it... to close it again.

Tassi, you know this has all the earmarks of a setup.

Yes, it has the fingerprints of Heylel... Lucifer all over it.

Swen butted in... again. Well, he didn't really know that Tassi and I were conversing—or did he? It was decided I would open the Great Abyss.

And I am coming with you! Tassi strongly asserted.

No. I would like that very much, but it would be better for you to stay behind and cover my flank. When I power up, you can draw power from me to wield against my attackers. Besides, from your vantage point and your keen senses, I can have advance warning of whatever's coming at me.

Tassi knew I was right, that we could protect each other better being separate.

Swen and Vwen took a couple of steps over to where we were standing. The ground shook with each impact of their voluminous footsteps.

I looked up at the two Titans. "How am I going to get through to the pillar? You two were easily rejected by the convergence."

"We were trying to dispel it, not move through it. Vwen and I will part a path through the convergence, which you will go through."

Vwen queried, "Swen, who will propel, guide, and shield Chris?"

"Tassi can with the help of Nila, Cami, and Kora."

"Wait, wait. I need to be shielded?"

Vwen spoke. "Chris, your armor may not be enough to protect you. This has never been attempted before. We are just taking all the precautions we can think of."

"Guys, this isn't really thought through…"

Swen cut me off. "Chris, we don't really know what to expect, but it's probably going to be like trying to travel through an asteroid belt."

"We will clear a path by punching through, and at other times we will open up portals to make minuscule jumps," Vwen added.

A familiar voice spoke. "The aberrations from the convergence are ever-changing. Physical and spiritual laws are twisted, contorted, and even superseded."

We all looked to where the voice was coming from. It was none other than Big Mel. He was in his usual casual attire: a red Angels baseball cap, an overly large Hawaiian shirt, khaki shorts, and, of course, striking, vibrant athletic shoes. This time, the shoes had fluorescent lime-green soles with purple tops interspersed with random zigzag patterns of the lime-green color running throughout.

"Mel, you must tell me where you buy your shoes!"

Mel laughed. "That's one of the things I like about you, Chris. Even in serious times, you never lose your sense of humor."

"Have you come to help us?"

"Yes, yes I have."

"It looks like you're here more to observe than to do battle." I motioned at his casual attire, which made him look like some tourist on vacation.

"I am in full-on battle attire." He combined six of the deadliest martial arts styles into a unified kata with a series of backflips at the end. His hat didn't even fall off.

Swen broke in gruffly, "Are there any other reinforcements coming?"

Big Mel responded, "None are needed. I am here!"

"Hmmpf," Swen replied.

Mel got serious. "Putting all joking aside, the aberrations from the convergence in the spirit realm are far more severe and disruptive than here in the physical realm. I am all they could spare." He didn't wait for a response. "I will help Tassi guide, propel, and shield Chris to the Abyss."

"What about the girls?" I inquired.

Mel shook his head. "Girls? They are age-old spirit beings and some of the most powerful ones to boot. And you refer to them as girls!" He shook his head and smirked. "They will assist and be our first line of defense. Tassi and the... girls should remain in their physical constructs and fully armored. What will be coming out of the Abyss will be best handled by speed, agility, and body armor."

Swen barked, "Suit up, boy."

Mel, with a quick sweep of his hands, lifted me off the ground and propelled me into the convergence—or, should I correctly say, the aberrations caused by the convergence.

"Mel! Guys! I'm not even ready!" My voice trailed off.

I was being tossed around like one of those steel balls in a pinball machine, bouncing, spinning, and being hurled back and forth, side to side, getting nowhere in particular.

I heard Tassi say, *Chris, concentrate! Project your armor!*

I had forgotten that my armor had been pulled back from my head and my hands.

Thanks, Tassi.

Now I was completely encased by Vyxkry; hopefully, it would protect me.

Chris, we have also put a spirit field around you. You should be adequately protected.

I could see through Tassi's eyes that the gang was working feverishly. Swen and Vwen were doing their sumo wrestling thing, and Big Mel looked like he was swatting flies with his hands. In the physical it looked silly, but they were releasing massive amounts of spirit energy.

There was not much for me to do. They were in total control of my journey. I just hunkered down, gritted my teeth, and enjoyed the fun. It did take a lot of mental concentration in controlling my thoughts, so as not to lose my marbles to the extreme sensation of vertigo. This was dizziness and disorientation to the max.

I set my mind on our goal by focusing my thoughts and eyes on the green pillar, just as Mel had taught me during our first encounter. I tried not to let my mind waver, but at times, I did slip up.

How am I going to stop...

...am I going to overshoot?

...what am I supposed to do after opening it?

...am I to take on the singularity?

and where is the singularity? Is it deep within the Abyss?

Extreme nausea and total disorientation quickly set in. I brought my mind back to just focusing on the goal... eyes riveted to the pillar.

The sensations ebbed and became tolerable.

Now, I was taking an extreme amount of abuse. Like I said earlier, it was like being a pinball belted by flippers into forcibly hitting very hard objects just to be bounced unmercifully back and forth, up and down. Even with Vyxkry as my armor and a spirit shield projected around me... it was still almost unbearable.

Suddenly, it all stopped. I was no longer hurtling through an asteroid belt anymore. I was falling—no—rocketing downward, like in my earlier descent after I first met Mel.

Though this was much worse. The g-force was extreme, and the heat. Hotter than hot!

I heard Tassi yelling, *Chris! Put the brakes on!*

Then I felt Tassi spiritually projecting a tether that was anchored to something in the opposite direction of my descent. I added my spirit power to hers, visualizing this tether as a bungee cord, slowing my speed. I hoped it was an unbreakable bungee cord and one not too long!

Boom!

I hit rock bottom.

Yeah, a little too long a tether. My armor, Vyxkry, absorbed most of the impact that the tether failed to. It was still jarring enough to bring tears to my eyes, even with my rugged Anarkon body. A few days ago, I would have needed a full body cast and a year to recover.

I was at my destination, on top of the rock-like green pillar. Carefully, I unfurled from the fetal position I had assumed while being bounced around so unmercifully. Standing up, I surveyed my situation. I was like in the eye of a tornado, where everything was calm and peaceful.

Tassi interjected, *Chris, hurry. The aberration is just momentarily pushed aside; we cannot hold it for long!*

I envisioned Vyxkry in my hand… the armor melted and flowed from my body to form the sword. I quickly grasped it with both hands and brought it, point first, forcefully into the green pillar.

Maybe a touch too forcefully. It went in all the way to the hilt.

I pulled it back while twisting it counterclockwise like I was pulling a cork out of a wine bottle. I figured counterclockwise was the normal way of opening something.

I heard Mel through Tassi. *"Keep twisting."*

Suddenly, the pillar faded away, and I was consumed by blackness.

Lights out.

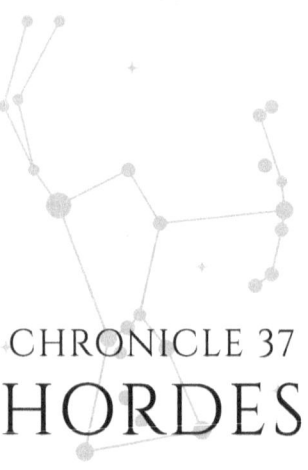

CHRONICLE 37
HORDES

TOTAL AND ABSOLUTE DARKNESS ENCASED me as my head, the last of me, was swallowed by the Abyss. I was free falling into total oblivion. Would I continue to fall forever? Fall... fall... fall... It did seem like a long... long... long... time, even though it was only a matter of minutes until my feet met something. Whatever I landed on was heading upward. It was squishy and very wriggly, though firm enough to hold me up. I was being carried out of the Abyss!

I shot high into the sky. My deliverer abruptly and forcefully moved downward and outward, leaving me treading thin air! I was now falling... again. I extended my body spread eagle to slow my descent and glide myself away from my deliverer and the Abyss. I took a quick glance behind me. My curiosity needed to be appeased, and my eyes had finally stopped tearing up from the drastic change of total absolute darkness to the brightness of daylight. I could clearly see once again. What was coming out... was a swarm of... bat-like creatures. I had been delivered by bat thingies!

Abruptly my descent stopped with a slight bounce like dropping onto a firm mattress... a feathered mattress. I had landed atop Ghris, my feathered friend. He had come to my aid.

Ghris made a slew of clicks and chirps. He was speaking to me... and I understood. The portal to Aharonite had been breached. The battle had commenced! Kakos had entered with his armies: poisoned-stinger-equipped Anarkons, bow-and-arrow-equipped ninjas, and heavily clawed and hooved wild animals.

Ghris had flown in ahead of them. Now there was something mighty different about Ghris though. He had grown up. He was no longer normal size; now he was *supersized*, with a wingspan of thirty-plus feet. He was the size of a Piper Cub airplane!

"Thanks, buddy. Now let's kick some butt."

The words came out of my mouth as a series of clicks and chirps, the sounds that an eagle would make, at least this eagle.

I crawled forward on his back to just before his wings met his body. I sat up and hugged him tightly with my inner thighs. What a sight: a boy atop a giant golden eagle!

He swooped toward the swarm that had carried me out of the Abyss. My deliverers at a cursory glance did look like bats, but upon closer inspection, they were not! They might have had the color, the texture, and the wings, but that was where the similarity ended. Their bodies were actually ribbonlike and ended with circular mouths full of needlelike teeth. They reminded me of very flat lamprey eels with bat wings.

"What are those things?" I exclaimed.

Tassi had to ask Mel for me.

Nosi added her two cents. "Lampreys are not eels; they are actually fish." I just ignored her. They look like eels so close enough.

Now, Tassi and I didn't need to be in close proximity to communicate like other spirit beings. That was quite koosh. And so far, we hadn't found our maximum distance.

"*Those are Langshiers,*" was Mel's response, relayed by Tassi.

That's real helpful. Do they suck your blood like a vampire bat? I quipped.

Tassi relayed Mel's response. "*No, Chris, they suck or drain you of spirit.*"

That doesn't sound any better. But... we... can use... I trailed off.

Tassi hesitantly spoke. *Chris, do you think that's a good idea?*

Tassi, you know one of my battle tactics: using the enemy against itself.

Yes, I am fully aware of your and Amemnon's battle tactics. They aren't orthodox and are quite risky.

I ignored her concern and powered up. *Have Big Mel inform the Hunters to get back into the portal and advise any of our forces in the open to take cover.*

I formed a lightning orb the size of a baseball, which was a much less lightning-packed version of the one I had used to restart the portal. This was going to be a test of how quickly I could produce the lightning orbs and how effective they would be against the Langshiers.

Producing the orbs was easy. The hard part, the part that took a little learning, was being able to have them explode—or, more accurately, release their pent-up energy at the right time. A few times, they released right in front of Ghris, almost causing us to fall out of the sky.

The orbs were immensely effective in taking the Langshiers out—hundreds per orb fizzled out into nonexistence. I even shot out electricity bolts from my fingers. That was so koosh looking, and it felt so tingly. It was nowhere near as effective as the orbs, and it only worked at close range.

Tassi interrupted my thirst for mayhem on the Langshiers. *Chris, I thought you were only going to take out a few.*

Oh. Right. I got a little carried away.

I was able to direct the Langshiers by exploding the orbs at appropriate places and times. This allowed me to herd them like herding sheep, but instead of sheepdogs, I had lightning orbs.

Tassi, in my defense, I did steer most of them toward Kakos's armies... away from us. There are still plenty of them to cause his armies a lot of problems... namely draining the life out of his troops!

She quietly acquiesced with a mental sigh.

The Abyss belched out another great black cloud. This time, a swarm of locusts emerged. These were no ordinary locusts but fierce, six-inch-long, teeth-baring, scorpion-tail-equipped versions. The lightning orbs had very little effect on them. The beasties did not have enough body mass to attract the lightning—that is, not enough water within their bodies to attract electricity. I had to wait till they were in close range and zap them with finer bolts of electricity that fried them. I later found out I was actually emitting microwaves that superheated not only the water in the air but also the little bit of water inside them. It was kind of fun, in a sadistic way, to see them curl up and drop from the sky.

They were just little menaces that were ravenous. The creatures attacked and tried to eat anything in their path, and this included Kakos's army. They were low-flying ground huggers that caused no end of chaos. Kakos should like that: more chaos.

Our sparse troops took cover under and in the Humvees or under tarps they had thrown down. The Langshiers were still having a field day with Kakos's armies, draining them of spirit energy. Our main adult Hunter force kept Kakos's armies from retreating into the portal. His animal army in particular was going berserk with the hordes that had been released from the Abyss. Hadn't Kakos taken this into account? Had he not forced us to open the Great Abyss?

Tassi interjected on my thoughts, *Chris, Kakos is a pawn in all of this. Heylel—Lucifer as you know him—is the one ultimately pulling the strings, whether Kakos will admit it or not.*

The Abyss belched again. This time, it disgorged swarms of beady-eyed black dragonfly-like creatures, again—get this—with scorpion stinger tails.

Tassi, what's up with everything having scorpion tails with stingers?

Heylel always likes to inflict fear and pain. Scorpion-like creatures seem to elicit this well in Earthers.

Oh, we're called Earthers now? I acted offended. *But yeah, you are right, they do make one's skin crawl.* I decided to give it back to her for that "Earther" remark. *I am really glad Ghris came, otherwise I would be a Grounder too.*

Tassi laughed. She and the other Grounders were having to fend off the three waves of creatures—the Hordes, as I called them. To our advantage, most seemed to have been drawn outside of the area, far from the Abyss. Not to say that my campaign of air strikes with Ghris hadn't played a role in this. Plenty of them still plagued the good guys. Our teenage troops had taken cover, but Tassi, the girls, Barry, and Momi were out in the open.

Tassi spoke up. *We have armor on.*

Swen, Vwen, and Big Mel didn't have armor but dispelled them spiritually. They were tapped into spirit power.

The three did look comical. Swen and Vwen still looked like sumo wrestlers, and Big Mel? Still swatting flies.

Chris, you'd be looking comical too. You don't have armor without Vyxkry.

Now you went and done it. Reminding me of my loss!

I'm sorry, Chris.

I decided to change my thoughts and focus not on the loss of Vyxkry—a temporary loss, I hoped—but on my gain. I had Ghris now. Live the moment. Enjoy the moment. Be the moment.

Flight is a beautiful thing—such freedom, exhilaration, and what a view. *Look at those Grounders!*

Tassi coughed at my dig.

It was as if twilight had fallen on Aharonite in the areas surrounding ground zero. Ground zero, as I liked to call it, extended from the opening of the Abyss basically about a mile radius. It was the aberration from the convergence that continued to expand outward in erratic hiccups.

Most of the hordes extended from this radius, where the physical laws were still in effect. Within the one-mile radius, spiritual laws took precedence. Spirit power was now accessible. A gateway had opened to the spirit realm. This was where Ghris and I mainly focused our attacks. Once in a while, we veered off for short little air-to-ground strikes outside this area. We didn't veer off far, as the spirit energy waned outside this area. Without the spirit energy influx, he would start shrinking back to normal size, which was definitely not big enough to support my weight. As he shrank, we continued losing altitude, and this was a sign to get back quickly to ground zero.

Kakos's armies were still in disarray because of the Hordes. These menaces were indiscriminate, attacking everyone and everything. That was buying us time. They kept Kakos and his armies from mounting an all-out attack on us.

I could sense Kakos was getting stronger, though. He was feeding off the chaos—even from his own forces. Soon, he and his generals would get things under control, and then our forces would have to engage his.

Sabboth was out there too, feeding... feeding off Daimonia... growing ever stronger. I hoped Sabboth had taken out many of Kakos's generals.

It was starting to get, or should I say, just getting uglier out there among Kakos's armies. The Langshiers were morphing into even more unholy monstrosities. As they fed off the Daimonia, they morphed into creatures that were much like horny toads... but the size of small kangaroos. What was more, they belched black, foul-smelling ooze that pretty much dissolved anything in its path. The smell was noxious, like burning sulfur.

Who was going to clean up after them?

And guess what: They had scorpion tails with deadly stingers.

We used the Hordes to our advantage; they were a big help. But I knew deep down in my heart that the Abyss was not done.

I wondered, *What else will it cough up?*

I didn't have to wait long. Out arose none other than the winged creatures right out of the book of Revelation!

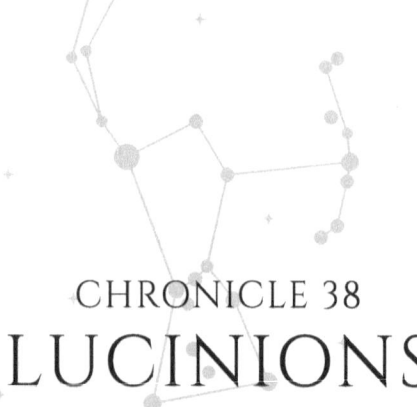

LUCINIONS

ONSTROSITIES WITH A BODY LIKE that of a horse, face like a man, hair like a woman, teeth like a lion, wings like a locust, and, yes, a tail like that of a scorpion. These were the locust horses right out of the Book of Revelation. The Bible refers to them as locusts… with a body like a horse, and yes, they had other gruesome features, but locust horses is an apt name for them.

They just spiraled upward and outward from the Abyss. Many of these scattered to the skies, while the rest took to the ground. I was glad some of these flying monstrosities decided to ground themselves; it was getting rather congested up here.

Ghris and I were circling above the Abyss when suddenly, he went into a dive. I didn't think he could read my thoughts, but that was just what I had been thinking of doing. *Bring it on!* I wasn't one to wait for trouble to come to me, and Ghris wasn't either. He dive-bombed them. We must have sent hundreds spiraling out of control, and these took out hundreds more.

I had my legs tightly wrapped around Ghris's body so I would not be thrown off by his spirals and spins. It took anticipating his maneuvers and a very tight squeezing of my legs. Firm and strong, hugging was necessary since he did not speak or even telegraph by body language when he would do one of these maneuvers. Ghris let out a squawk; he was a bird of few words, or should I say squawks. When translated, he was scolding me for squeezing too hard with my legs. Sorry for not wanting to be thrown off!

Ghris leveled off as the locust horses were regrouping. I powered up and started producing my lightning orbs. It was fun hurling them as Ghris flew in a wide circle, slowly spiraling downward. They reeled backward as they were pelted with the lightning bolts released from the orbs.

I firmly tightened my legs around Ghris but not too tight. We were being barraged by dazed and unconscious locust horses as the lightning strikes connected. Ghris did a good job of dodging these out-of-commission locust horses as they eventually plummeted downward, taking out even more of their own. Many had the unfortunate end of being swallowed up by the Abyss… again.

Now what was also koosh in all this was that my body acted like a lightning rod for any lightning bolts that missed their targets. This spared Ghris from being struck indiscriminately by these strays.

The battle was also on for the Grounders.

Careful, Mr. Red Baron. Tassi chuckled.

Nosi joined in, "*The infamous Red Baron was a ruthless and bloodthirsty German fighter pilot in World War I. He was bold, daring, unrelenting, and showed no mercy.*"

I shook my head and laughed. Well, the bold, daring, and unrelenting part, yeah, that was me. The showing no mercy—no. I was merciful, but not to these monstrosities.

Tassi continued to relay Mel's and my words to each other. It was as if we were talking directly to one another.

"*Chris, this spiritual influx will eventually spread throughout all Aharonite. The Daimonia will then have access to their spiritual abilities too.*" Mel paused. "*We need to close the Abyss before that happens!*"

"*Mel, you were all for having me open it. Now you want it closed!*"

"*Chris, opening it was the only way to keep it from rupturing. It was just a temporary stopgap measure. We need to go in there, take out the singularity or whatever is causing the convergence, and close the Abyss."*

I didn't like the idea of going back, but Vyxkry had to be retrieved anyway. I was hoping Vyxkry would just appear in my hand. Then we could both go back in there together and take out whatever was causing this convergence and shut the Abyss.

Mel intensified his attacks on the locust horses. They were feeling his wrath, his ire—or was it his need for urgency?

"Mel, out with it," I barked.

"Chris, I sense that... it... is... coming."

"Mel, do you mean the six overlords and their minions?"

"No. I feel one single but ominous presence."

I waited, nothing but silence, then Mel blurted... "The BEAST!"

"You mean the one mentioned in the book of Revelation?"

"Yes," was Mel's in-depth response. Tassi gave me a series of images to expound.

The Beast was an unholy atrocity with horns all over. It had multiple heads, tails, and arms, a creature that should only live in one's nightmares. The size of this thing was also frightening to say the least. It looked to be as tall as a forty-story building, that's over four hundred feet high!

I shook my head to clear it of those images. I needed to focus on the *now* and not the *what if.*

A second wave of creatures shot out of the Abyss. These were wingless, two-legged versions of the first—the locust horses. The locust horses swept in and carried many of these second wavers off on their backs. Well, at least most. The ones that missed a horse landed on the ground with a thud. These were now the infantry, the ones on foot. Fortunately for these, they were extremely durable and survived the fall virtually unscathed. Those that got rides made up what I called the air cavalry.

These two-legged creatures were far more heavily built than their winged counterparts. Their lower body was that of the hindquarters of a stout horse, upper body of a muscular man on steroids. And yes, they still had those menacing scorpion tails. Oh, by the way, they had ram horns protruding from the sides of their heads. Now to make this picture even scarier and deadlier, these monstrosities were also completely battle ready. They had chest armor and sported weapons… maces, sickles, mauls, hammers, swords, and spears. At least none had guns!

Mel spoke. *"These are Lucinions. They are well trained, fierce, and ruthless, warriors for Lucifer and—"*

"And what, Mel?"

He did not respond right away.

"Mel…?"

"They precede and fight alongside the BEAST*!"* He blurted.

"This just keeps getting better and better," I muttered.

This second wave—the Lucinions—were more intelligent than the first brute beasts, the locust horses. They were well organized and had a plan. The ones that made up the air cavalry came upward toward me, and the others that were the infantry or ground cavalry guarded the Abyss. Now this Lucinion air cavalry may have had flight, but locust-winged horses were no match for a supersized bird of prey—Ghris.

The only reason these unholy steeds were able to fly and carry their riders in the physical realm was because of the spirit energy influx. Their wingspan was about the length of their body. They were not designed to fly in the physical realm, even without a rider that was half their weight!

A few of the air cavalry were just getting to our altitude. We waited to welcome them as they arrived. Our first engagement was a learning one. The Lucinions worked in groups of three. The strategy was not just to overwhelm an individual fighter. It was smart; it was ingenious…

One of them focused on directing spirit energy at me forcibly and viciously. Spirit darts were hurled at me and exploded within my body. These released painful and crippling spirit venom within, impeding and slowing my ability to energize and wield my spirit power. The second of the triad focused spirit energy to affect my mind. It deceived my mind into not seeing what was actually there and then scrambled my thoughts into incoherent ones, causing overwhelming fear to rise within. The third's focus was on the physical, attacking my physical energy and crippling my movement then coming at me with blinding speed and force, all empowered by spirit energy.

Without Tassi's and Ghris's interventions, I would have been diced to pieces. I was totally unprepared. Tassi worked with me as she had when I'd fought Swen and Vwen.

When we *fought Swen and Vwen*, Tassi interjected.

Anyway, she could see not only from her vantage point but through my eyes what was truly happening. Tassi was able to help me break the Lucinions' spiritual attacks within my mind and body, or at least nullify them to some extent. That was the beauty of our link: we were independent, yet we were one. She was not in the slightest affected by their spiritual attacks on me.

Ghris countered the physical attack by doing a spin maneuver. He took out three groups of triads with his wings and talons while spinning as I hung on for dear life. They were hurled outward, out of control, taking more out in a domino effect.

I quickly refocused my mind with Tassi's support. I knew it wouldn't take them long to regroup and come back at us, and it didn't. They came from every which way. I formed several lightning orbs and let them have it. The orbs released their pent-up energy on target but to no avail. The Lucinions' armor attracted the lightning bolts, diffusing them among many targets. If only I'd had Vyxkry, I could concentrate the energy into a single, extremely powerful bolt that would probably vaporize them completely.

Tassi nudged me mentally. *Chris, picture your meteoric descent within one of them. Keep it small, focused, and not too powerful.*

That moment was still so vivid and real to me. It was why Tassi had suggested it. I pictured that intense meteoric heat the size of a dime within the chest of the closest guinea pig. I decided to call him Gary.

Gary stiffened and became catatonic, then poof! He was vaporized into tiny multicolored bits of light that sparkled oh so brightly and then fizzled out, leaving behind, unscathed, his armor, his weapons, and his steed. That was so koosh. Now whether he was gone for good, or if he would reappear somewhere else, I had no idea. The other two of the triad hesitated at Gary's demise, looked at each other, then attacked.

I hopped off Ghris onto the back of the riderless steed. The creature bolted. It even tried to sting me! Can you believe the audacity? I was glad these creatures didn't have great control of their tails. Well, I wasn't going to put up with that kind of behavior. I leaped up and spun around then forcefully snapped its darting tail with both hands at the first joint before the stinger. My Anarkon strength made it possible; even the strength of the strongest human would probably not have cut it. The steed went into a bucking spree. That must have hurt! The stinger and first segment of his tail just hung limply. I reined him in somewhat by squeezing tightly with my legs. On a normal horse, the force I applied would have crushed its rib cage.

I directed the beast by applying more pressure to the side opposite where I wanted him to go. I used heavy equal pressure on both sides to slow him down and multiple hard kicks in quick succession to his belly to signal him to speed up. The chase was on once again.

I drew some of the Lucinion air cavalry away from Ghris. This made it easier for him to go on the attack. Ghris came from above and dive-bombed the group chasing me. The riders and their steeds collided into one another and took out others in their free fall. I watched as hundreds plummeted to the ground. They even wiped out quite a few of the Lucinion cavalry and infantry that were on the ground.

Mel did his best to thin their ground ranks. Moving at blinding speed, he was just a blur, throwing and shoving infantry and calvary with quite a degree of accuracy toward Swen and Vwen. These two were at Titan size, fifty-plus feet tall. They grabbed, crumpled, and twisted the Lucinions and the locust horses with their large hands. They even stomped on them with their huge feet for good measure. The Lucinions with their armor were like ticks, nearly impossible to squish or mutilate. The locust horses could take quite a foot stomping too.

Our troops in the ground zero arena were few, just Barry, Momi, and the girls. Oh yeah, Roscoe too. They took advantage of those temporarily dazed or incapacitated and dispatched them. Though the Lucinion cavalry and infantry quickly filled in their thinning ranks around the Abyss.

Barry and Momi used the tingler, which was a close-range type of weapon we had brought from the House of Orion. It did far more than just send a tingling sensation; it completely fried the nervous system of the locust horses, causing imminent death… at least they never moved again. Now it took multiple blasts from within several feet. The Lucinions were not so easily done in. They were designed for battle and wore body armor. To take them out, the tingler's tip had to be thrusted into the base of their scorpion tail, where a nerve ganglia complex is located. Focused blasts of spirit power from the tinglers then traveled through their entire nervous system. The Lucinion guards actually vaporized into flashes of multicolored light. It reminded me of the flickering light show from kids waving sparklers on the Fourth of July.

Nila, Cami, and Kora worked with Roscoe. It was fun watching that mammoth of a possum, fully armored, lumbering through the Lucinion ranks. He even rolled over at times, taking out tens of their infantry and cavalry. His tail was a force in itself, with two-foot, needle-sharp spikes jutting out around the tip. He wreaked havoc on them with that lethal tail of his, and lethal it was when it became soaked in stinger venom and impaled a Lucinion or locust horse at the base of its tail. It wasn't fast acting like when Tassi and I had impaled the Anarkons with their own stingers. Far more venom was injected by the stingers as they were still attached to the tail and continued to pump venom which speeded up the outcome... death.

It took around ten minutes after Roscoe had skewered a Lucinion or locust horse at the base of their tail for the pending demise of the unfortunate victim. They would regroup and continue to fight, only to stiffen up without warning and then slowly vaporize into sparkles of light. This was a cool phenomenon to watch. All over the battlefield at different points in time, I could see Lucinions and locust horses vaporize into tiny flashes of flickering light. Now why the Lucinions and their locust horses vaporized into flashes of light while the Anarkons dissolved into puddles of ooze, I don't know. In any case, I definitely didn't want to get stung by a Lucinion or a locust horse.

The girls took out the ones that had been stunned by Roscoe's trampling, body rolling, and tail thrashing. Cami and Kora would bite down into the nerve ganglia complex at the base of their tails. They then focused and projected spirit light through their canine teeth.

Bye, bye, Lucinions and locust horses.

True to her nature, Nila liked to take down her own prey. She was ferocious and unstoppable. She relished wading into larger groupings of the enemy, shrugging off blows like the tank she was, only to crush her foes when they thought they had her. She was only hit when she wanted to be. Her speed and power were supernatural. Normal human perception would only have seen a blur of all that was going on in this battle; the speed of a spirit being, whether evil or good, surpassed normal physical sensory perception. Nila was blindingly fast, even to spirit senses.

Chris, Tassi interjected, *you are equally on par with Nila or any Cherub. Cherubim are the guardians, the protectors of the physical realm. We are the fastest and the most powerful spirit beings when operating spiritually in the physical realm.*

Nila was proving just that. She was tearing into the Lucinions without mercy, without reservation. She twirled, pounced, lunged, and rammed her opponents with unwavering energy. Whether she fought a Lucinion or a locust horse, she took no prisoners. She was pumped, taking down multiple warriors at a crack. Once they were down, she would tackle and bite into their nerve ganglia. At times she would toss a bitten Lucinion at other riders, knocking more off their mounts to become victims. All this happened before the tossed Lucinion fizzled into nonexistence, joining his fellow bitten ones. What a light show!

Tassi stayed out of the battle unless it came to her. She would then promptly dispatch the attackers, quickly and effortlessly, with poise and grace. Her primary responsibility was to provide overall movements of the enemy, projection of possible areas of engagement, and provide spirit power support.

Tassi chimed in, *My top responsibility is keeping you alive. You don't make that easy to do!*

I smiled inwardly.

I turned my attention to our junior Hunter division. They had been positioned outside of the spirit influx perimeter. They stayed a few hundred yards away and moved as it expanded. Kakos's armies were still in disarray and had not yet made it this far into Aharonite. When that time came, our adult Hunter force would attack, then our junior Hunters would engage. We would squeeze Kakos's armies between our two forces.

Sabboth was carrying out his part perfectly. He was absorbing Daimonia at a record pace. Kakos's armies were weakening, and Sabboth was increasing. What little intel I received from our ground troop's surveillance indicated Kakos was starting to engage Sabboth.

That's so koosh. Maybe they will defeat each other!

Chris, I have a bad feeling about using Sabboth against Kakos.

We don't have much choice, Tassi. Our fighting force is not large enough to contend with Kakos or Sabboth, let alone the Hordes, the Lucinions, the Singularity, and possibly the Beast. We have to use them against one another as much as possible and believe we can handle whatever remains.

Without this tactic, we would have been overwhelmed already regardless of the prowess and might of our forces.

As more time passed, even I, our Red Baron of the skies, was reaching my limit. Thousands of Lucinions had come out of the Abyss.

Tassi, I can't fend off the Lucinion air cavalry much longer. It's getting so congested up here.

You'll have to! It's just as congested and more so down here on the ground.

Tassi, I believe it's time to commence plan B.

CHRONICLE 39

ON THE FLY

M Y WARHORSE WASN'T OBEYING; IT was a very stubborn locust horse. I had to yank its mane hard just to get its attention. Now its mane was gross, of course: grimy, long, stringy, foul-smelling hair. The horse wasn't responding well, and I needed for it to start heading toward the ground. Finally, I heaved my entire body onto its neck and wrestled with it. We went into an uncontrolled spin downward.

This got my unruly horse's attention. Its self-preservation kicked in. I backed off with my weight slightly, and the horse leveled off. I adjusted myself back to a normal sitting position. The steed now obeyed, albeit rather reluctantly.

Chris, I like your devious plan.

Thanks, it came to me on the fly.

Funny, Chris. This is no time for puns. You need to get a little more serious.

Tassi, being serious takes away from my peace, and one needs peace at times like this... spiritual peace, that is.

Now Plan B had two parts. The first was to get the air calvary to chase me. Well, they were already doing that, but I needed them to do it en masse. The second part was to get them to chase me recklessly without regard.

My plan was to lead them over a cliff, so to speak... past the outer perimeter. Here they would lose spirit energy and thus their ability to remain airborne. The Lucinion air cavalry would tumble out of the sky. These unholy locust horses were not capable of flight even without a rider in our physical realm; they needed spirit energy to sustain flight. Even gliding was totally out of the question with their short, body-length wingspan. Riders and horses would go splat!

First step was to get more of them involved in the chase. We allowed them to separate us. Now it looked to them like it wouldn't be long and they would have us—well, more me. They wanted me the most and swarmed after me in droves. It didn't take long, and they threw all caution to the wind and chased us without concern. More and more came to get in on the action. Step two had become a reality. They were now completely absorbed in getting us... they would realize too late that they needed to turn back.

Swen and Vwen, along with others, had started moving toward the direction of the fringe where I was leading the Lucinion air cavalry. Tassi had already informed them of my plan: plan B—Bottomside!

Swen and Vwen energized their massive swords, nearly twenty-five feet in length. The swaths these swords cut through the ground calvary and infantry ranks were massive.

Anything in the physical world that housed spirit mirrored the force and momentum of the spirit blows. The swords cut right through the riders and horses without severing them, but spirit energy did transfer to corresponding physical movement. I remembered my initial encounter with Swen and Vwen, how painful it had been when their swords connected with my body. Not only did they cause pain, but they also absorbed spirit energy, thus weakening me spiritually. Since the spirit blows also caused me to be thrown about in the physical realm, I didn't come away unscathed physically. I had been bruised, battered, bloodied, and fatigued.

Now Barry, Momi, and the girls were mopping up after Swen and Vwen. Mel continued with his spirit blows, keeping them from amassing any organized attacks against the others. Some of the Lucinion air calvary decided to ground themselves to help fill in their thinning ranks around the Abyss.

High in the sky above the Grounders, Ghris and I continued our ruse of fleeing as the remaining Lucinion air cavalry recklessly chased us. They smelled blood… my blood, and all of them wanted to be in on the kill. They were oblivious to what was about to happen.

We passed through the fringe with them in hot pursuit.

They did not pick up the fact that they had been losing altitude. Now it was too late for them to turn back; they were past the point of no return. Plan B—Bottomside had succeeded.

It looked like meteor showers as they fell out of the skies. I enjoyed watching the locust horses and their riders nosedive or spiral out of control. They even took out more of their own on their way down. On the ground was a gnarled and twisted mess of Lucinions and locust horses. Very few tucked and rolled or landed on their feet. Their healing abilities were phenomenal, but without the spirit influx many had suffered broken and shattered limbs. There would be no time to heal… we were all over them. Nila, Cami, Kora, Roscoe, Barry, and Momi were greeting the new arrivals from the sky. They were fully armored, so they took the brunt of the battle.

My locust horse started spiraling down, but not as fast as the others. I was much lighter than a Lucinion with all its armor. My horse still had an imminent appointment with the ground. I decided I would be merciful, ha ha, and put my horse out of its upcoming misery. I tore off the loosely connected stinger segment and jammed it into the base of the tail. The stinger pumped venom—death was not far behind. My horse went into violent seizures, heaving me off.

It wasn't difficult reaching another locust horse, since the skies were still very crowded. I overpowered the nearest rider, separating it from its weapons and kicking it off. I stayed on the steed for mere seconds while slicing, dicing, and stabbing other riders and their horses with a sickle-like weapon and a short sword. I continued jumping from horse to horse as we spiraled earthward.

Their weapons were very effective against their own kind. Black blood and carnage flowed. I continued my leapfrogging from horse to horse in an upward manner till there were no more above me. I probably had only a thousand feet before impact with no more to take out. They were descending at a far faster rate than me.

I kicked off of my last steed and released my weapons. I slowed my descent slightly by spreading out my arms and legs. I knew I could survive the 120-mile-per-hour crash into the ground. My body was extremely durable and had quick recuperative abilities, but it would be very painful and would take some time to recover. I should have stayed on my last steed and let it absorb most of the impact with the hard ground. Well, it was too late for that. I decided to go head down with my arms by my sides, increasing my speed, and headed back toward the fringe.

Would I make it there? Probably not! I flipped over onto my back to see where Ghris might be. Could he come to my rescue?

Tassi spoke. *Chris, you should be able to slow your descent spiritually.*

How do I do that? No one ever said I could do that! Tassi, you know that would have been a koosh thing to be taught.

She interrupted my tirade. *Chris, don't you remember the spiritual tether we did together? How we slowed your descent earlier?*

Yeah... I guess... but that was you, mainly. What do I anchor the tether to?

Anything, Chris. It's spiritual.

Oh. How about the moon?

Chris, that actually exists, but if you can believe, it will work. You better hurry, or you're going to be like Humpty Dumpty!

Funny, Tassi. Searching and sifting through my childhood memories, are you?

Tassi mentally shrugged. Being spiritually linked with a Cherub who had access to my memories and thoughts was truly a double-edged sword.

It did work! Maybe not great; I did need practice in this. I only slowed to maybe fifty or sixty miles per hour then leveled off. It was so koosh and quite handy to be capable of accessing spirit energy anywhere. I was not limited to the spirit influx area.

Tassi shrugged and shook her head in a back-and-forth "I don't know about you" manner. *Chris, by now, I would think that you would remember that!*

Tassi, in my defense, I was speeding toward the ground at 120 mph. My mind naturally wasn't all there!

That's par for you, Chris.

Funny... funneee, Tassi.

Just then, I bounced—rather, skipped—like a pebble across the water. I was still facing upward, still on my back. Ghris had come up underneath me. He was substantially smaller now but big enough to glide us into ground zero territory.

I slid—or rather tumbled—off his back onto the ground as he landed, beak up and tail down, wings flapping strongly forward. It was a short, abrupt landing. He didn't have much area to land in. Mel had only been able to clear a short section, but it was Lucinion free.

A thought popped up in my head.

Tassi answered, *No, Chris, you can't access spirit energy and make Ghris grow to supersize. You and I can transfer spirit energy between us; we are spiritually linked.*

Barry came over, laying out a few Lucinions on the way. He patted me on the back. "Nicely done."

"Welcome back," Momi grunted as he engaged three Lucinions.

Roscoe's welcome-back was impaling a Lucinion with his tail and wiping out eight others as he flung off the unlucky one.

The girls were on the front lines, in the heat of the battle. They were taking out a mess of Lucinions and their horses that had fallen from the sky. I wondered how that had happened.

Don't be so smug, Chris.

Tassi, I just like it when a plan comes together so well.

Our young Hunters zapped them with the needlers, sending them to nothingness. Most Castlers, since they were not trained spiritually, were given screamers or netters. These two weapons were battery powered—can you believe that? Spirit batteries!

Tassi interrupted where my thoughts were starting to go. *Chris, don't you dare try to charge those batteries with your lightning. You would probably fry them and the entire weapon.*

Barry has informed me that we have extra battery packs in the Humvees if needed.

These two weapons were designed for longer-range use, thus keeping the non–battle-prepared Castlers at a somewhat safer distance.

The screamers did immobilize Lucinions, but it was only for a short time. The Hunters could then dispatch them using the needlers. Screamers pulsed high-pitched sounds interlaced with spirit power at massive power levels. These were aimed directly at the Lucinions or their locust horses, preferably at their heads. Even though the screamers were directed at targets far from me, the spillover of the spirit-energized sound hit me as a harsh screeching, like scraping of nails on a chalk board. That sound induced sheer discomfort; it made my skin crawl. The effect was extremely nasty and totally disabling on those it was directed at. There was no effect on humans—normal humans—at least none I was aware of.

Chris, the weapons you brought were designed for use against the Daimonia and their constructs.

Oh, that's just peachy. So I am the only one on our side that was affected?

You seem to be spiritually attuned to the Daimonia, and… your body is based off an Anarkon construct.

I'll take that as a yes to my question. Now back to the weapons being used.

The netters were far more humane on the Lucinions. They shot out a lightweight but extremely strong webbing not unlike that of a spider. Then it was energized with spirit that held their captured prey in spirit nets. These two weapons only temporarily incapacitated the Lucinions. These monstrosities were designed for battle; they were extremely powerful and had phenomenal regenerative capability.

Tassi continued to relay info to Mel on the enemy. We were always a step ahead. Tassi and Mel were great at anticipating their moves. They also slowed the enemy's movements by scrambling their minds by overwhelming them with useless random thoughts.

Swen and Vwen continued working on opening a pathway to the Abyss. It was always quickly filled with a resurgence of Lucinions, whether infantry or ground cavalry. The Lucinions weren't going to allow anyone into the Abyss. They kept it stacked at least a hundred rows deep with their infantry and ground cavalry. It would take a lot to punch through, even with a large group of warriors and even if these were assisted by Cherubim. We would have to find another way in.

Ghris had taken to the sky shortly after dumping me off. He was back to supersize and causing the enemy no small problem. We needed more troops to take out the dazed and stunned enemy.

Barry dispatched a few of these on his way toward me. "Chris, gifts should be coming." He smiled then pointed.

Not far off in that direction, I could see a Humvee plowing through the Lucinion ranks. Mel and Tassi were obviously opening a path, but there were still a few stragglers to plow through.

The Humvee did a controlled skid, coming to a stop a few feet in front of us. The doors opened, and none other than the twins, Gil and Frey, stepped out. Gil, the more aggressive and outgoing one, had been behind the wheel. That probably explained why the Humvee had gone out of its way to take out any Lucinions even remotely near. The back opened, and out filed more Hunters.

Gil and Frey saluted, then both grinned. They each withdrew a sword from a scabbard on their back. These were the two swords from the four that had been used to imprison Sabboth.

Kneeling, they presented the swords to me. Gil spoke. "Barry thought you could use these." There was a slight hesitation, then in unison both pleaded, "Please don't destroy the swords."

Barry looked at me. "These swords have enough Quintarium to allow them to absorb spirit energy, but how much or how long they can emit or unleash it—that is unknown. I would error on the side of caution... too much energy flowing out of them at once, and they will probably go poof!"

Gil and Frey both cried out.

Barry reached out and patted me on the shoulder. "Go easy on the swords. They cannot handle anywhere near the power you can wield. They're not made of pure Quintarium like yours."

"Oh, you mean Excalibur."

Barry chuckled. "Really, Chris, how original. You named the sword Excalibur!"

The two swords felt feather light in my hands. I engaged the enemy in some swordplay: dicing, thrusting, and slashing. I could feel the spirit energy being absorbed from their bodies with each successful blow. The swords seemed to be handling the absorption of spirit energy well but nothing even remotely on the order of Vyxkry's.

The two blades were a blur, making beautiful music as they siphoned off spirit... *Shing, shing... shing... shing-a-shing, shing-shing.* Most likely, the music came from engaging the Lucinions' armor or their extremely tough hide, which was basically a form of armor. I didn't think even armor-piercing bullets would penetrate their hide. In ground zero territory, where they had access to the spirit realm, it took a spiritual weapon to have any effect on them.

I didn't know where all the spirit energy went that was drawn off from the Lucinions. I felt the energy flow into my body, but I felt no pent-up energy. That was probably a good thing. I wouldn't want to overload myself with spirit energy and go boom!

Chris, stop playing around with the Lucinions. We need you to do more than just slowly drain their spirit till they are eventually dispatched into sparkling lights. We don't have that much time, Tassi implored.

All right then, let's find out if these swords can handle some real Chris power! I shouted within.

Tassi retorted, *The swords will go poof!*

I'll be gentle, I'll think small... plus, with two swords, the power will be cut in half. I hoped the swords would start to strain before going poof!

Tassi sighed.

I envisioned power. For me, it took thinking of a spring welling up inside, with the waters amassing and filling a dam to near overflowing. Then I imagined two sluice gates I could open to let the power flow like two rivers of water gushing forth.

The Lucinion cavalry and infantry were mounting a full-out assault... then suddenly they started backing away. Tassi sent me a view from her vantage point. I was crackling with blue and white charges like miniature lightning bolts. My eyes radiated blue light like that of a blue dwarf star. This energy superheated the air around me, causing currents of air to flow.

I had a nice breeze blowing. My hair rustled in the gentle wind, and my clothes fluttered. It was awesome, and the breeze was actually cool. At least I wouldn't get overheated.

I opened the sluice gates to let the rivers of power flow through my hands and into the two swords.

Pure, blinding, bright-white beams of light the diameter of a baseball shot forth from the tip of each sword. The two swords started to hum at a low pitch that increased quickly to a single pure high-pitched note like that from a tuning fork. The swords started vibrating uncontrollably.

I quickly released my grasp, and they clattered to the ground.

The Lucinion cavalry facing me had prepared. They had thrown up a spiritual shield. Two beams of light had shot forth: one enveloping the first horse and rider on the left and the other on the right of me.

Snap.

They were gone. Second one behind—snap. Gone. Third—snap. Gone. Fourth— snap. Fifth—snap. Gone. Gone. They each vaporized into nothingness. There was no smell, no sound, no expression from the unlucky targets. The sixth in line for both streams of light was not so fortunate; it was only partially vaporized! The horse's front half was gone, except the two front legs up to its knees were left. The rider did not fare any better; its whole front was gone. What was left of horse and rider crumpled to the ground... not a pretty sight.

I had two white-light lasers! How koosh was that? Even in a fraction of a second, I had released enough power to take out nearly six deep of rider and horse with each sword.

Could I produce other colors like red, green, or purple?

"*The most powerful are white lasers....*" a familiar feminine voice stated.

Nosi, you're still here? I said, surprised.

"*Yes, Chris. My full presence is downloaded on your phone. I have a vast amount of knowledge even without the Internet.*"

Tassi butted in. *I thought Nosi was gone,* she said with an air of annoyance.

Nosi continued, "*Recent scientific and technological advancements have pointed to the possibility that white lasers may indeed be feasible.*"

Yeah, you think so? I said teasingly.

Tassi stated, *You are the Orion, Bearer of Light. If anyone can produce a white laser, you can!*

Nosi continued, "*The white laser is by far the most powerful. It can disintegrate any substance... anything!*"

We were interrupted by the enemy I had momentarily forgotten was there.

The Lucinion cavalry filled in the gap around the two partially dissolved heaps of Lucinion and horse. I quickly bent down, picked up the two swords, and swept one to the right and the other to the left. I sent out short, rapid bursts of light with the swords by quickly alternating between releasing and grasping. The spirit energy force field the Lucinions emitted gave them a fleeting moment to contemplate their nonexistence before being overpowered. Three rows deep of Lucinions and horse evaporated with a slight delay like a snap of my fingers between each row.

The simple act of rapidly releasing and regripping of the swords kept them from being overloaded. It was not an option for me to turn my spirit power on and off quickly. It didn't work that way. It took too long for me to close and reopen my spirit sluice gates.

Now the Lucinions were not going to let me just sit back and take them out. I was annihilating row after row. What a beast I was! They decided to try to overwhelm me with their sheer numbers. I didn't give them a chance by staying in one place for very long. At times, I jumped up into the air twenty or thirty feet and zapped them with my laser swords. More often, I jumped from horse to horse, taking out their riders as I went, and then leapt into the air, spun, and took out the horses I had left behind. Now, the animal rights groups would not have been happy, but in my defense these were not really horses.

The Lucinion air cavalry repopulated the decimated ranks of their ground calvary. Even their infantry came from the sides to fill in any holes. We were still not making much headway in getting to the Abyss, and time was on their side.

Mel interrupted my swashbuckling. "Chris, there is more activity from below."

I popped the question, not that I really wanted to know. "Okay, Mel. Is the Beast ready to spring forth?"

"No, Chris."

"Mel, let's have it."

There was a slight hesitation. What could be worse than the Beast?

Mel obliged. "Two or three more legions of Lucinions are forming down below, with the Beast not far behind!"

Oh, that was bad, really bad… not only the Beast but the Beast plus two or three more legions! We were having a hell of a time with the one legion of Lucinions.

I looked skyward. Now where was Ghris? I waved the swords like an official at the Indy 500 indicating the first-place driver had crossed the finish line.

I was hoping that Ghris would look this way. He must've taken notice, because I saw Lucinions being scattered as something in the sky started heading toward me. Ghris had remarkable eyesight, far greater than any eagle and even better than my Anarkon vision.

Ghris was nearing my position. I took a few more riders out, then when he was about twenty or so feet away, I jumped high into the air. He swooped under me, and I landed, straddling his shoulders. Wow, that was quite an impressive feat, as if we had practiced it hundreds of times before. The only problem… I was facing in the wrong direction. I was looking at his tail!

I quickly flipped around. Time for a different strategy.

Tassi shouted, *Chris, no!*

I released the two swords; Mel guided them safely down. I didn't want the swords where I was going.

Tassi pleaded with me, *Chris, we can find another way…*

SINGULARITY

G HRIS SHOT UPWARD. THE SKY was still cluttered with way too many Lucinions and their locust horses, that even they were having issues. These Lucinions needed an air traffic controller.

Ghris suddenly dived. Lucinions went helter-skelter as we brazenly ploughed through them… toward the opening of the Abyss!

Chris, I don't believe for a minute that you are going in there on just a scouting mission. You know I have access to all of what you are thinking.

Tassi, time is running out for us. We don't want more legions of Lucinions and definitely not the Beast. Besides, something is beckoning me… summoning me from within.

Chris, I sense that too. That's really a good reason for not going in. It could be the Beast!

It's not the Beast. It is already coming. This also is not the end times… that means the Abyss gets closed… and I believe we will close it! That's why I'm going in. I'll take out the singularity or whatever it is, then Mel and the rest of you… will seal the Abyss.

You'll be stuck down there… forever!

No… If I find Vyxkry, I have my way out.

Chris, if you don't find Vyxkry?

Not forever, Tassi. God will have the Abyss opened, as prophesied in the book of Revelation.

That could be a very, very long time, Chris!

Tassi, I have great faith in you and the others getting me out... somehow.

Chris, Chris...!

I tuned her out, focusing on what I needed to do. As I looked out at our forces and my friends, I caught a glimpse of Barry, who seemed to be giving me two thumbs up. The incident in the grocery store seemed like ages ago now, but I strongly felt Barry's words, even now: "I am always where I need to be." That was becoming true for me. This is what I am meant to do... "I am where I need to be." I closed my eyes.

It felt like plunging into water from a very high dive. First the jarring impact with the surface followed by intensifying body pressure diminishing to normal as one buoyed back to the surface. In my case I was not returning to the surface but instead continued deeper into the unfathomable depth of the Abyss. It was like I had a diver's weight belt for a 300lb person strapped around my waist. Ghris and I were going nowhere but down, down, down.

I heard Tassi say faintly, *Chris, all of their ground calvary and infantry guarding the Abyss are following you in!*

That was great! Now our troops only needed to battle the ones outside the fringe. Those air cavalry that got snookered by my plan Bottomside... and fell from the sky. This was at least good news topside.

I didn't sense any of the Lucinions that followed us in. Now that was good news for me. It was absolute darkness in here. Even with my phenomenal night vision, I doubted I would be able to see anything. My guess was that they had gotten lost. Score ten points for Chris and company. The Abyss reminded me of limbo land. There, if you didn't enter at the same time, you were not together.

Now I did sense something ominous, a fleeting darkness that passed through the face of the Abyss at the same time we did. What it was I don't know. It might have been Daimonia. It was so quick that I wasn't sure if it was just my imagination or if something piggybacked a ride with us. Why would anyone or anything want to enter the Abyss? Well, at least it was less for topside to contend with.

As Ghris and I continued deeper into the Abyss, it started to gradually become less dark. I was glad I had superb night vision, even better than that of an owl, or was I seeing spiritually?

The calling or beckoning sensation became physical. I felt a slight tug; it seemed something was pulling us toward it. We had to be getting close. The pull was getting much stronger.

Then it appeared! *What is that?* Whatever it was, it wasn't the Beast. It was immense and radiated a soft, dark, purplish-black glow. There were waves of black, dark purple, and dark blue dancing along its surface and at times being shot outward. It looked much like the sun's corona but all in the dark-blue spectrum. We were jolted by concentric shockwaves as this thing suddenly went through a series of contractions.

It was shrinking! And sending out massive bursts of energy!

Chris, I believe that is what is causing the convergence.

What? Our link had been severed when I entered the Abyss. How could I be hearing Tassi? I now felt her presence. She was very close.

Tassi had hitched a ride. She had merged with Ghris! At the last second, as Ghris and I crossed the face of the Abyss. And no, she was not that ominous presence I thought I felt upon entering the Abyss.

I'm glad you are here, Tassi. I don't know how you did it, but I'm glad you did.

Chris, there was no stopping you, but I wasn't about to let you go alone. You would probably need me to bail you out.

Thanks for that vote of confidence, Tassi.

I felt a weird connection to whatever this thing was… a spiritual one? Maybe that was what drew me here.

Tassi offered her analysis. *Chris, the energy it gives off is much like when you go into Anarkon mode. When you go all dark, where your eyes become black orbs and you release that purple-black energy. The energy from rage, hate, fear, destruction, misery... death.*

But Tassi, what drew me here was light... love, goodness, hope, peace, healing... life ... I think... this thing... was of the light, and now it has been... morphed, somehow transformed into dark... into evil.

As Ghris circled overhead, I threw a few rounds of energy bolts at it. They just fizzled into nothingness. We took a few more strafing runs, and I unloaded several high-powered lightning orbs. They, too, just fizzled out, seemingly having no effect.

Chris, stop! The more you throw at it, the more—

Suddenly, the thing emitted powerful and violent shock waves. In a quick series of contractions, it collapsed from a size that was as far as the eye could see to that... of a few football stadiums. What was happening up on the surface, outside the Abyss, we did not know.

Tassi, this is probably just what the enemy wanted me to do!

Chris, this thing is becoming a singularity on its own. You just sped up the process a bit.

That makes me feel so much better.

Chris, no!

I had just done one of my brash things—I jumped off Ghris. We were approximately a hundred feet above the center of the thing.

Tassi's thoughts inundated mine. *You're brash, impulsive, reckless, overzealous—*

Okay, Tassi. I get your point.

I plummeted downward into the unknown. Lately, for me, most everything I did was into the unknown.

I landed without a thud on a surface that was spongy yet supported my weight. I wasn't even attacked. How koosh was that?

Don't get a big head, she huffed.

Just keep an eye out for the Beast, Tassi.

I truly felt I had a connection with this thing. Then it came to me... it was all so clear. I knew what it was!

It must have been caught up in Amemnon's casting of Lucifer's henchmen into the Abyss.

Chris, check it out before... Tassi implored.

I knelt and reached down with my hand. I touched its surface. It was teeming with power—*dark* power—but that I already knew. The dark energy started to flow up my fingertips through my hand and arm. I couldn't remove my hand! I felt the raw, undiluted, savage, dark power consuming me!

Chris! Chris!

I could hear Tassi shouting. I was being pulled into it... then I was gone!

PREVAILING LIGHT

I WAS GRASPED BY THE SHOULDERS and shaken vigorously. "Jennifer... Jennifer!" Shark shouted.

My eyes fluttered open. Shark was looking directly at me, a concerned expression on his face. He gently guided me around a Humvee and sat me down. We were now somewhat out of harm's way.

"I—I—I... had a vision! It was a place that was black, with an eerie purplish-blue glow emanating from deep within. I—I... heard Chris's voice but couldn't make out what he was saying!"

"Jennifer, I thought you were being spiritually attacked! Now relax, get peaceful... prepare yourself. The vision will return if there is more," Shark gently reassured me.

Shark was short for Sharcosian. I preferred calling him Cosian, pronounced "cozy-an." It didn't bring up images of a predator that was savage, ruthless, and merciless. I grabbed my phone, put it on record, and cupped it in my hands on my lap.

"Cosian, nothing is coming!" That nickname sounded so much more comforting, cozy even... Cozy-an.

I thought of the battle raging on. We were keeping the enemy from retreating back through the portal. We had barricaded the portal with Humvees, and the Hunters held off Kakos's armies. The swarms of nasty little flying creatures were wreaking havoc on Kakos and his armies. For some reason, they preferred the Daimonia inhabited. Even that shadow creature's voracious hunger was drawn to them. From our surveillance equipment on the Humvees, we were able to watch Chris and a huge golden eagle take out many hideous flying horse creatures with riders even more monstrous.

Then we saw the great eagle with Chris suddenly dive. Lucinions went helter-skelter as they brazenly dove through them... toward a black, ominous void. Then they were gone...

Suddenly the vision was back. I was back in the black. I spoke what I saw, heard, and felt out loud for my phone to record. The purplish-bluish light was off in the distance, and the giant gold-colored eagle was flying in circles over it—the same eagle Chris was on. Where was my Chris?

Then I heard Chris's voice. *"I cannot be turned evil. A heart of light prevails. I cannot be turned evil. A heart of light prevails."*

Chris continued repeating those words over and over. A very, very small dot of brilliant-white light appeared from deep within the purplish-bluish light cloud. It started to pulsate, then it began to become methodic, even rhythmic, in time with the words Chris was repeating. Had the dark, ominous cloud thingy swallowed Chris? Had it imprisoned him within it? The white light started to grow more brilliant, pulsating in rhythm to his voice as both escalated to a feverish crescendo in tempo and intensity.

Suddenly, rays of white light shot forth from the brilliant speck of pulsating white light, piercing through the purplish-bluish light cloud. The purplish-blue light gradually began to recede as the white light effervesced from the rays. The purple-blue darkness was being replaced, swallowed up.

Now only a white light cloud remained.

Tassi spoke. *Chris, you have done it! You transformed it back to its original state... of a Light Elemental! We have prevailed. It has been restored.*

Tassi yelled, *Chris, Chris! I cannot moderate your power any longer. Stop... stop! You're going supernova! Chris!* Tassi shouted one last-ditch plea.

Chris could not control the power he had summoned to heal and restore the Light Elemental. He continued to escalate out of control. The brilliant speck of pulsating white light that was Chris rapidly expanded in size and intensity within the light Elemental. The Elemental began to swirl within itself and then enveloped Chris in a blanket of subdued white light. The intensity and brilliance of Chris gradually diminished and shrank in size. The form of a young man became visible...

Chris!

The Light Elemental had absorbed Chris's excessive power; no longer was he in the state of going cataclysmic. He was clothed in a soft white glow, his eyes an intense, brilliant blue. From the center of his chest, a small region of bright white light the size of a tennis ball pulsated in a heartbeat-like fashion.

The Light Elemental shot forth out of the Abyss, carrying Chris with it. Tassi and Ghris were flung to the side to remain prisoners of the Abyss.

Chris's body was now hovering far above the ground as the Light Elemental continued to emanate from the Abyss.

Suddenly, the Light Elemental winked out, leaving Chris momentarily suspended in midair. A beam of white light shot downward out of Chris into the Abyss. The face of the Abyss glowed with a brilliant-white radiance that gradually dissipated, leaving a smooth, translucent, crystalline surface.

Chris's brilliantly blue eyes dimmed and closed. His body went limp and began to fall.

Mel used what little spirit power he had left to slow Chris's descent. Swen and Vwen, still fifty feet tall, ran over. Swen caught Chris and gently lowered him to rest on the smooth face of the now-sealed Abyss.

Mel's voice boomed to the Aharonites not because of spirit energy but because of Camp Aharonite's PA system linked through the Humvees.

"Chris and Tassi have succeeded. The Spirit and Physical realms are restored with the ending of the singularity and the convergence. The Abyss is sealed, the evilness from within is imprisoned once again. The battle still rages on, but we will be victorious for our two fallen… Chris and Tassi!"

Momi solemnly and tenderly picked up Chris's limp and lifeless body in his arms. Vwen picked up Tassi's and followed. Nila, Cami, and Kora went ahead with their heads down. Chris and Tassi were laid in the back of a Humvee, with Tassi's head resting on Chris's chest. Momi stayed by Chris's side.

Roscoe came and stretched his head inside, sniffed the two, then bowed his head.

Shouts and commotion came from the front of the vehicle. Roscoe's head jerked sideways, hitting the side of the vehicle, nearly tipping it over. He withdrew his head and turned his body, barricading the entrance to the vehicle. Six choppers came barreling in, oblivious or unconcerned about their safety. Nila, Cami, and Kora were already on full alert and had stationed a defense perimeter around the Humvee.

The leader hefted himself off the bike. It rose a full foot off the ground, no longer supporting his massive weight. The Hunters that had surrounded the intruders backed up. His seven-foot-four, four-hundred-plus-pound presence was daunting.

Mel, along with Swen and Vwen, added their support. The two Cherubim were now only their normal height, but ten feet was still intimidating. Barry came running up and pushed through the Hunters to embrace the big man.

"Hey, Bubba, what brings—"

Barry was cut off as Lul jumped off a neighboring bike. "I am here to protect Chris and the other."

Gil and Frey coldly stated, "You are a little late!"

Lul continued as if uninterrupted. "Nod foresaw this as the most probable outcome. My Hypnos and I will protect them here till the battle is over. Then we will escort their bodies back to the Land of Nod... no matter the outcome of the battle."

Mel, with disdain and solemness in his voice, broke the tension. "Lul and Nod, with their abilities, will keep anyone or anything from inhabiting Chris and Tassi's lifeless bodies."

Outside the portal, cloaked by the trees, a man stood, draped with a badger pelt over his shoulders. A raven had perched itself on a nearby tree limb. The man grinned approvingly as information of the events within Aharonite were spiritually relayed to him by the very large black raven. He turned and stepped into the encroaching darkness with his form melding into the blackness, becoming one with it.

Chris had spiritually joined Tassi in her abode within Ghris. They were all three now trapped within the Abyss!

Chris, you are needed above more than down here... Tassi said in despair.

The vision ended...

EPILOGUE

IT HAD BEEN A FEW hours since I... we had lost Chris. Cosian glanced over at me and could see on my face where my thoughts had turned... thinking of Chris. He reached over and put his hand on my shoulder. "Jennifer, we will find a way to get Chris back."

My mind wandered to the battle still going on... Kakos's forces were—still out there, the swarms of hideous creatures were—still out there, the Lucinions were—still out there, but the shadow creature—nowhere to be seen. What happened to it? Where did it go? Chris and Tassi were also gone. They were alive but residing within that giant eagle in the Abyss. They had no physical bodies! And what about the fake Barry, where did he go?

Suddenly, I sensed I was going to have a vision. I whipped out my phone and fumbled to put it on record. Cosian quickly pulled the Humvee over and parked.

"Jennifer, wha... aat—"

A vision began. I spoke...

Barry and one of the council members entered through the castle gate. The gate guard looked at the council member suspiciously.

Barry spoke up. "He has been purged of all Daimonia."

The guard waved them through with a flippant gesture of his hand.

The two moved purposefully to the castle keep. The council member was viewed suspiciously again at the entrance to the keep by another guard. Barry explained the situation, and the guard allowed them entry.

They moved quickly to the library, which was void of people. The two tore off wall tapestries and pulled paintings down. They quickly looked over any object that caught their attention and then discarded it roughly.

Beyond any doubt, they were hunting for something. They ransacked the first floor of the library to no avail.

The two stepped on the platform elevator in the center of the room and took it to the second floor, where they proceeded to ransack it like the first. Barry's form started to shimmer and waver. A red-haired youth appeared.

Arthoxos grimaced. He looked at the council member and said, "Maintaining a visage of Barry is very draining... but posing as him gave us carte blanche to go anywhere." He looked down at his host's appearance and shook his head in disappointment. "Fortunately, this ruse, for now, is not needed."

The council member then laughed maniacally. "You do put on a good impersonation of Barry. But you need to find a more impressive host than that boy, Fred!"

"You shouldn't talk, Majoriteen... or what is *left* of Majoriteen. You now reside in a council member's old and *frail* body, with only a small portion of your original self!"

Majoriteen sneered. "Let's just finish what Kakos sent us to do: steal some Facsmeres."

Shouts came from the first floor.

"The impostors are not here!"

"They must have gone up!"

"The jig is up, Majoriteen. We should forget doing Kakos's bidding."

"We can take these Aharonites easily, Arthoxos. But you may have a point. We could just ditch Kakos and the Aharonites for good."

"How do we do that?"

Majoriteen pointed upward. "Our ticket out is in the council chamber."

The decision was made nonverbally, quickly, and unanimously. Both ran to the platform, almost cutting each other off in their haste.

The Aharonites came flying up the spiral staircase just in time to see the platform pass through the third-floor ceiling.

"They're in the council chamber!" shouted one of the Aharonites.

Gil and Frey motioned to the far corners of the room. "Use the single platform elevators."

Jorge and Vic, along with four other Aharonites, each took a platform that was nearest to them.

They were just in time to see the two impostors shimmer and vanish into the dodecagon blue crystal that made the top of the council table.

Gil rushed to follow the two, but Frey blocked her path. "No, Gil, we don't even know where that goes! It would be reckless and dangerous to follow!"

Gil relented. "Oh, all right. We will station men inside and outside the library."

Vic spoke up. "Securrity will vatch council room and library vith vid cams."

"Hey, Frey, what were those two looking for?" Jorge inquired.

Frey's countenance darkened. "I would place a wager they were looking for Facsmeres. Barry has recently brought his latest collection for safekeeping."

Gil motioned everyone to the center platform elevator. "We need to find out if any are missing!"

"The third floor is where the most recent and most crucial Facsmere is hidden," Frey said.

They went down one floor. Gil and Frey led the way to one of the twelve walls of books. Gil partially pulled out and pushed back six books in a rhythmic pattern. They all backed up as a four-foot-wide-by-fifteen-foot-high section of wall slid forward and rotated a hundred and eighty degrees. There, on the back—or now the front—was a Facsmere of Chris and Tassi.

It showed an older Chris, near twenty years old. His brown hair, streaked with blond wisps was just partially covering his eyes and gently blew in the wind. The eyes were not the green eyes he had been born with but shone like brilliant-blue sapphires. He had a wolf pelt draped over his shoulders that added to his formidable appearance. A majestic, metallic-silver-furred wolf with rust-colored highlights stood all of four feet tall by his side. Chris's fingers of his left hand were caressing the head of the wolf by his side. They both looked deep in thought.

"It's still here... safe and untouched," Frey and Gil said in unison.

The vision ended. I was mentally drained, but the vision hadn't been all that bad. Even with the battle still raging and what had happened to Chris and Tassi, the Facsmere hadn't changed from when I had seen it in Barry's apartment. Chris was still going to reach his twentieth birthday with Tassi by his side. Somehow, someway, they would escape the Abyss and reclaim their bodies!

Cosian sat by my side, and we talked over what was revealed to me.

We sat there for quite some time as I reminisced about Chris. Suddenly my eyesight wavered to a haziness, and then it began... another vision commenced!

It showed the Facsmere of Chris and Tassi. But... but... some... something was happening to it.

"No... no... no!" I shouted.

Chris and Tassi were fading. The entire Facsmere wavered then winked out to absolute blackness... only to be replaced by one depicting horrific destruction. A reddish glow cut through the sheer blackness as flames and smoke shot out of fissures in the scorched ground. Bodies of gruesome unearthly creatures littered what was a battlefield with two well-armored, hideous creatures standing in the midst of the carnage. They had a lower body like that of the hindquarters of a stout horse, an upper half like a muscular man on steroids, a head like a man but sporting ram like horns, teeth like a lion, hair like a woman, and they had a tail like a scorpion—the same monstrosities Chris had been fighting!

"Noooo!"

ACKNOWLEDGEMENTS

Thanks to my Heavenly Father who gave me the inspiration, imagination, guidance, strength, and the confidence to fulfill the writing of this book. There are eight more to come in this series!

To Susie, my wife, who made sure I was fed, had clean sheets, took extra care of the kids, making it possible for my endless hours of writing and still have quality time as a husband and father. Along with all that, she kept me on target of keeping the writing family friendly. To Jared, my son, for being the centurion and the muse behind my caffeinated writing sessions and the reason my hair has remained full and youthful in color... no gray! To Samara, my beloved daughter, who was not only a motivation in writing to young readers but also helped me in keeping it G-rated.

ABOUT THE AUTHOR

Jason is a man of great determination, vision, and spiritual wisdom who decided to become a writer to heal and inspire the hearts of others.

A husband and father who enjoys living in the great lakes states, a handy man who finds a way to accomplish any project, with the help of his wife's strong prayer life!

Embarking upon a ten year transformative journey, Jason looked to God to teach his hands to write and always have time to live, enjoy, and be the moment with his family. With each stroke of his pen, Jason used the written word to illuminate the way for all who seek to be bearers of light.

CREDITS

ILLUSTRATION AND FORMATTING:

To Glendon and his team at Streetlight Graphics for their amazing book cover and the personable guidance through the whole process of getting the book out to the readers.

EDITING/PROOFREADING:

To Lynn McNamee and her staff at Red Adept Editing for doing far and above what is the norm in the copy editing and proofreading.